I0727905

New Dragon Soaring

Dragon Shadows, Book 3

By G.S. Carline

This is a work of fiction. All characters, organizations, places, and events portrayed in this novel are either products of the author's imagination or are used fictitiously.

Cover art by Joe Felipe of Market Me (http://www.marketme.us)

 Published in the USA by Dancing Corgi Press

This book is dedicated to my son.

A Brief Note

I love writing fiction because I believe that in fiction is where we find eternal truths. That being said, the Caribbean islands I am about to transport you to, do not exist. I wanted to tell a pirate story and I wanted it to have a Caribbean feel. What I did not want was Caribbean reality. I don't want everyone getting fussy about what year it is and who was ruling Europe and attempting to establish themselves in Jamaica or Tortuga or whatever island that really exists. It means a lot of research on my end just for insignificant details that detract from the story of a young noblewoman who is transformed into a pirate—and more.

So, my story takes place in a small group of make-believe islands, an archipelago if you will, somewhere to the east of Tobago and Trinidad, called Los Peces Pequeña (The Little Fishes). Back in Europe, there are always kings who send nobles to conquer islands because everybody wants to rule the world. And there is magic wherever you look.

New Dragon Soaring

Chosen path,
Forged in flame
New life rises
Dreams to claim.

Dragon Shadows, Book 3

Lisette scooted to the edge of the bed, wrapping her arms around her midsection, and taking small breaths to control the pain. The sun had passed its high point and now angled its beams into her chambers in the castle. She pushed the covers from her body and swiped at the perspiration around her temples.

As she struggled to rise, Pinar held her arms gently, pushing her back toward her pillows.

"Lizzie, I know how upset you are." Her friend and fellow pirate sister hovered in front of Lisette while she attempted to restrain her. "Rocco and the guards are on the trail. They will stop the thief."

"I shall not stay here while my baby has been taken from me," Lisette growled, allowing Pinar to reposition her in the bedcovers. "You say Ruhee is missing? I cannot believe she would do such a thing. Why?"

Captain Begum Derya strode into the room. "Because her love for Rocco has taken a dark turn. I am sorry. I knew he captivated her, but after her disastrous attempt to woo him, I thought she would nurse her wounded heart and find healing."

Lisette shook her head. "I don't blame you. I, too, believed all was well and forgiven."

Pinar adjusted Lisette's bedcoverings, looking out at the balcony, and squinting into the afternoon sun. "It grows late."

"Yes," Begum said. "Pinar, you should go to the kitchen and bring Lisette sustenance."

"I cannot eat—" Lisette frowned.

"The sooner you heal, the sooner you can help Rocco chase after the kidnapper. And without food, you will heal more slowly." Begum gestured to Pinar, who nodded and left. "Oleta is on her way with her bag of herbs."

"I wish Lamya was here," Lisette said. "She'd know what to do. She might even heal me faster."

"Yes, it would be good to have the guidance of an Ancient One."

Lisette looked at Begum. "If Ruhee wanted to kill her, we'd already know. But just taking her…what would she want with our baby?"

"To make you suffer. Knowing your child is dead allows you to grieve. Wondering where she might be, whether she is safe, does not allow you to rend your gown and mourn." Begum walked to the foot of the bed and turned toward the arches to the balcony. "The ache in your heart does not heal."

"Begum…" Lisette reached into the drawer and withdrew a small book. "Since we are alone, I have a question. This is my mother's journal."

The captain of the *Dişi Aslan* turned toward her. Her green eyes were usually stern and commanding, but today they revealed someone Lisette had never seen. Someone softer, more uncertain.

The chamber door opened and a small, wiry woman with a full head of furious curls strode inside. "You called for me?"

"Oleta!" Lisette set the book down on the table. "I need your help. I must regain my strength to join in the search for Alara."

Oleta went to her bedside. "I'll do everything in my power, but you know I am not a god, yes?"

"Do as much as you can," Begum said. "Lizzie, we will speak again. Alara's return is most important at the moment."

Lisette watched the captain leave and slipped her mother's journal back into the drawer for another time. She looked down to see Oleta lifting her gown to look at her injuries. Oleta pressed around her stomach—Lisette squirmed and hissed a few times when she pushed too hard.

"My apologies," Oleta said.

When she ran her fingers across Lisette's ankh-shaped scar, she frowned. Lisette pulled away.

"Sorry, but it burns like fire when you touch it," Lisette told her.

Oleta stood and helped Lisette rearrange her gown. Lisette noticed her grim expression.

"You can help me, yes?" she asked.

"I have herbs to help with most everything," Oleta said.

"Most?"

Oleta sighed. "I am worried about Ruhee's use of the ankh. Do you remember anything about it?"

"I was in much pain and bleeding from a tear in my womb—I had been stabbed on Isla del Lagarto. Ruhee pressed the ankh on my stomach…" Lisette winced at the memory. "It felt like I was being branded, and she was chanting in a language I didn't understand."

"She stopped your bleeding, no doubt, and for that I am grateful. And the ankh is a symbol for eternal life, which should be a blessing. Still, I have an ill feeling about it—when I touched the scar, I saw a darkness I cannot explain." Oleta took Lisette's hand. "But I will do what I can to help. I require one more ingredient—I shall return quickly."

She hurried out the door, and Lisette was left alone with a head full of thoughts, none of them good.

It was a single tiny footprint outside the back gate of the castle, pointing in a different direction from the rest of the trafficked dirt, that got Rocco's attention.

"This path is trampled." Luis Delgado, captain of Duke de Martinmas' guard, studied the ground. "What is so striking about that print?"

"It is alone and headed away, toward the road." Rocco gestured. "There is no matching print for the other foot, which tells me it was an accident—the person wants no prints left behind. The foot is small, which says woman, and deep, which might mean she is hefty, but I think means she is carrying something. Pinar said that Ruhee was missing—she would be the size to make this print."

"How could they have gotten a squalling infant past everyone?"

"She could be sleeping, or drugged." Rocco frowned. "But from what Lizzie says, Alara is calm, unnaturally aware."

"Alara," Luis repeated. "Unusual name."

Rocco shrugged. "According to Lizzie, she chose it herself."

Proceeding down the wall, Rocco looked for more evidence that the thief passed by here. He was halfway around the castle wall when he saw something flutter in a thick frangipani shrub. Running to it, he picked it from the branches.

"Luis," he called. "A ribbon."

"Alara's?" Luis asked.

Rocco held the strip of violet in his fingers. "From Pinar's description, yes."

Two sets of footprints separated from the beaten path, moving toward the road, one large and one small. The small feet pushed hard into the dust, although the right foot seemed heavier.

"You're right," Luis said, pointing. "She carries something in her right arm. A basket?"

Rocco nodded. "And it appears she has a companion. A large one."

Besides the footprints, wagon wheels and hooves traveled along the path. From carriages to buckboards, the road was so well-tracked, it was difficult to know what was recent. Just across from the castle's front gate, the footprints stopped, pointed toward the wagon wheels, and disappeared.

"They've gone to the village," Luis said.

Rocco nodded, scowling. "No doubt to get a ship."

"You think they will leave this island?"

"They must." Rocco turned to him, a deadly glare in his eyes. "Do you think they do not know what will happen to them when I catch them?"

Luis nodded. "Let us get horses. Maybe we can overtake them."

Quince was tightening the girth on the last horse when they arrived. The chestnut mare snaked her neck at him, teeth bared and ears flat. He stepped from her way and completed his task.

"I heard about the baby," he told Luis and Rocco as they entered. "Figured you may need these beasts to chase down them thieves."

"Good man, Quince," Luis told him, and swung into the saddle of a dark gelding.

Quince handed Rocco the reins. "Do take care with 'er, sire. Hope she don't throw ya."

Rocco approached the mare's head, holding his hand out to her. "We met the other day, remember? Now, be a good horse and help me find my child."

He placed his foot in the stirrup and quickly mounted. The mare gave a small prancing step forward, but he kept the reins loose and did not try to discipline her. After getting his other foot in its stirrup, he reached down and rubbed her mane.

"Be swift," he said, and nudged her to go.

She trotted off, behind Luis' mount, slowing at the gate. The two men steered their horses to the road outside, pointed them toward the village, and pitched the reins forward. The mare galloped off, followed by Luis' gelding, who quickly caught up. As if they raced for prize money, the horses vied for the lead, neither being able to get more than a nose ahead.

As he rode, Rocco appreciated the mare's willingness. He could travel faster as a dragon, but he had no idea how to manage whatever dragon he had become. He had transformed during the battle at Mercedes' castle when he saw Lisette being attacked. It would seem his transformation was linked to his anger but why didn't he turn now? Having Alara stolen certainly lit his rage.

His transformation to human also did not follow any particular pattern. After the battle, he heard screams outside Mercedes' castle wall. He arrived in time to see Pinar holding something squirming and crying, and Ruhee pressing something against Lisette's stomach. The girl was uttering words he could not understand, but they sounded like the same words being said over and over. The uttering became louder until nothing else could be heard, and Lisette screamed in agony.

Rocco landed to be with her. He realized, to his horror, he did not know how to return to his human form, so he had to sit by and watch Marisha pick Lisette up, cradling her and walking back toward the Martinmas castle. Pinar held Alara, wrapped in a torn piece of clothing, and Ruhee walked behind, her fingers caressing the ankh in her hand and her eyes on Pinar's bundle, a curious smile on her face.

If only he'd known what that smile meant.

Ruhee stared at the large ship at the end of the pier while Amoy arranged their passage. It was *El Buscador*, a Spanish galleon that transported goods and people between all the islands in their archipelago. It was so much larger than the *Dişi Aslan*, and so much slower.

She was gripped with momentary guilt. *What have I done? My sisters will know by now that I was involved. I can never rejoin my crew.* She shook her head. *I will show Rocco that I am the best mother for this baby, and he will love me. Or at least, he will stay with me as I give him more children.* Ruhee smiled. *This is the last baby Lisette de Lille will ever bear, and she will never see it again.*

Footsteps startled her and she turned to see Amoy and a young man striding toward her. "Yes, those are our bags." Amoy pointed at Ruhee's feet. "Ruhee, come with me."

The boy stuck one valise under his arm and grabbed the other before reaching for Ruhee's basket. She yanked it away from his hand and heard a small mewling in protest from underneath the silks. The young man stopped and looked at the basket quizzically.

"My kitten," Ruhee told him. "I'll carry it."

He led the two women up the plank and across the deck, to stairs that deposited them on the lowest passenger tier before the mast. Their cabin was at the end of the step, a tight affair with bunk beds, a wash basin, and a porthole. Dropping their bags, he bowed and left.

"Ugh!" Amoy looked around the space. "It's so small in here! A cockroach would have trouble turning around."

Ruhee shrugged and set the basket on the floor, kneeling beside it. "No smaller than any other cabins, except maybe the captain's." She opened the silk bedding and looked at the baby inside. "She looks hungry. Where's the wet nurse?"

"The what?" Amoy was digging through her bag and throwing things on the lower bunk.

"The wet nurse," Ruhee repeated. "For the baby."

"It won't need a wet nurse." The large woman continued to root about. "Soon as we get out far enough, we're throwing it overboard."

Ruhee opened and closed her mouth, like a fish flopping on deck. Amoy glanced at her, a warning in her scowl. Ruhee held her breath to keep from arguing, especially when she saw the large knife Amoy placed on the bed.

What am I to do? She looked down at Alara, who still stared at her as if she might also pull out a blade. "It will be some time before we are far enough to dispose of a— anything without being detected. Should we not have milk for the child until then?"

"Why?"

As if on cue, Alara opened her mouth and wailed an

infant's cry so loud it pierced ears and brought an immediate knock on the door.

"Is anything wrong?" A female voice asked through the wood.

Amoy shushed at the baby, but it only screeched louder. Ruhee picked Alara up, which made the baby's face redden and stop long enough to take in a breath and wail with even more volume. Ruhee ran to the door, Alara in her hands, over Amoy's protests.

Standing at the doorway was a small woman, dark-skinned and bent with the years. Her gray hair was knotted atop her head and her hazel eyes sparkled.

"Oh, I knew it was a baby," she said, lighting her face with a smile. "Is she okay?"

"Yes, she's—" Amoy snapped.

Ruhee cut her off, still trying to bounce and cuddle this siren of a child. "Actually, we are in trouble. This child's mother died giving her life. I am—we are—to take her to her mother's sister on Isla de la Soledad, but our wet nurse abandoned us, along with all of the supplies for the child."

The old woman nodded at the story, expressing astonishment. "I am so sorry. Perhaps I can be of some help. I have raised many babies and know their needs well." She held out her arms. "May I?"

Ruhee did not want to relinquish Alara, but her unhappy screams were relentless. She handed the baby to the woman, who cradled her in both arms, nestling her against her shoulder and rocking back and forth. As soon as Alara left Ruhee's arms, the screaming stopped. The baby snuggled the woman, cooing her pleasure.

Amoy scowled at the woman, but Ruhee saw her shoulders relax. "Thank you," Amoy said, biting her words tersely, "but we shall manage, I'm sure."

The old woman smiled at Ruhee, a strange smile. Her eyes penetrated Ruhee's to the point that Ruhee flinched and looked at the ground. She handed Alara back to Ruhee.

"If you need me, I'm down the hall, second door left. My name is Kurta."

Ruhee took Alara into her arms and closed the door. Alara stared up at her, green eyes wide as if sizing her up and finding her lacking. Wrinkling her face, the infant wailed again.

"Shut that baby up!" Amoy snapped.

"She's hungry," Ruhee said. "It will be days before we are far enough away to do what you want. She will not stop crying until then."

Amoy stepped toward Ruhee. "Then maybe we don't throw her overboard *alive*."

The girl stepped back, holding Alara away. "And how do you explain it? The old woman has seen her."

"Whose fault is that? I told you not to open the door. So much for your kitten!"

"I doubt if anyone in the whole ship believes this is a kitten!" Their voices kept rising over the wails of the baby, who seemed to be competing with them for volume.

"Fine!" Amoy screamed at last. "Get the old woman to feed the brat!"

Ruhee opened the door and trotted down the hall, carrying the screaming Alara. Kurta was standing outside her room, smiling.

"I heard you coming," she said, opening her arms. "Let me have her and come inside."

Kurta's room was no larger than Ruhee's, yet it appeared spacious. The two bunk beds had been draped in richly colored silks, the basin was surrounded by a wooden shelf, and a small table and chairs sat in the middle. Kurta also had a porthole but hers brightened the space with light.

"I have milk prepared for the child," Kurta said,

gesturing to the shelf as she sat down. "Could you bring it to me?"

Ruhee turned to the shelf and picked up a bubby-pot to hand to Kurta. She stood for a moment, watching the old woman cradle Alara, bouncing her gently and offering her a gnarled finger to mouth. Anger flashed through her that this old woman was bonding with her child. Handing Kurta the pot, Ruhee took a seat at the table.

The child is just hungry. Once she is full, once I know how to fix her food, we will bond.

Kurta offered the cloth-tipped pot to Alara, who sucked at the milk, her eyes soft, holding the old woman's finger in her tiny hand.

A small jolt rattled the room, followed by a familiar sound. The anchor was being hoisted, the chain's metal clanking against itself as it was wound. *El Buscador* was heading out, on its way ultimately to Isla del Lagarto. Soon they would be asea.

Ruhee wondered how far out the ship would be before Amoy decided they could toss the baby. She looked at Kurta and frowned—this old hag comforted Rocco's daughter when she could not. These women were both interferences in their own way.

But she would have Rocco in the end—no matter what it took.

4

"Help me up." Lisette held an arm toward Oleta.

"Lizzie, you are still not healthy enough—" Oleta was frowning.

"Am I bleeding? No." Each word held her frustration. "Help me or don't. I'm getting out of bed and seeing if I can walk."

"Help her, Oleta." Begum had returned. "She needs to work her body now."

Oleta sighed and offered Lisette her shoulder, wrapping her arm around Lisette's back. "Up you go, take it easy."

As her feet took the weight of her, Lisette grabbed her stomach to keep everything contained. Removing her hand from Oleta's shoulder, she wobbled until she could bear weight on her own.

"It is good that you have been a pirate," Begum said. "Even with your difficulties, you will heal faster than a pampered noble."

Lisette smiled and shuffled one foot forward. Her lack of balance was apparent, and she quickly brought the other foot alongside. Looking at Oleta, she set her jaw and nodded.

"Let me go."

With tiny, shuffling steps, holding her stomach, Lisette made a slow journey to the chamber door. She turned, a triumphant glow on her face.

"You see, I am perfectly fine."

As she stepped back toward her bed, an ache radiated down her leg and up through her hips. She attempted to ignore it and walk it away, but by the third step, she collapsed to her knees. Begum and Oleta rushed to her side and helped her back into the bed.

"I know it is hard," Begum said. "But you cannot help Rocco until you are better. I don't think you realize how close to death you were."

"Closer than that morning on Isla del Lagarto?" Lisette asked with a wan smile.

"M'lady has done things a noblewoman should not and has paid a price each time." Begum patted her arm. "Sometimes that price is time spent healing."

The chamber door opened, and Pinar rushed inside. "Captain, the duke is on his way to visit Lizzie."

Begum nodded. "As I do not trust this duke, I take my leave. I shall help you in any way I can."

"Captain—Begum," Lisette said. "It would help me if you helped Rocco find Alara. The *Dişi Aslan* is fast, faster than *L'Implacable*, and if anyone knows how Ruhee would think, it would be you, or members of your crew who are close to her."

The captain smiled. "It is done."

Oleta reached into her bag and withdrew two small pouches. She handed a tan one to Lisette. "This contains herbs that will help you with pain."

Lisette gestured to the black bag in her other hand. "And that?"

"Why I give this to you I do not know, but my instinct says you will use it. These are leaves called velvet tongue. They are a sort of truth plant. Feed half of a leaf to anyone you suspect of lying. If they are telling the truth, the taste is pleasant—creamy, if you will. If they lie, it will be as if they've bitten into a thistle bush, thousands of needles attacking their tongue."

Lisette put both pouches in the pocket of her robe. "Thank you. I am grateful for all you've done—both of you."

"You are—our *Dişi* sister," Begum said. Her body was stiff, and she appeared to choose her words carefully. "We will always be here for you."

Begum nodded to Oleta, who joined her on the balcony, where they grabbed vines and easily swung to the ground to make their escape undetected.

Lisette pushed back against her pillows at the knock on her door, followed by the click of the latch. The Duke de Martinmas entered, looking cautiously about.

"Lisette, may I enter?"

"Yes, Sire. You will forgive me for not rising to greet you."

"No, no," he said, waving his arms. "It is not expected in your condition. I've come to see how you are faring."

"I am healing, although not as quickly as I'd like." She gestured to a chair by her bedside. "Please. Sit."

"I understand the birth was quite hard on you. And now, to have the baby snatched away by an unscrupulous trollop, why, it's beyond the pale." The duke settled himself uneasily into the small chair.

"Yes, I wish to be out there with my—with Rocco, hunting her down." Lisette fought her tears. "Tell me, Sire, how goes the cleanup of the Medina castle? I heard you were leading the work."

"Yes, I surveyed the grounds, dispatched the dead to an appropriate graveyard." The duke smoothed his vest. "As a matter of fact, that is why I stopped by—in addition to inquiring after your health. As you are here, I've decided to take up residence in the old Medina castle." He looked around the room. "This has always belonged to the French, no matter who El Rey installs in it."

"Thank you." Lisette frowned. "Although I do wonder if it is yours to give. Are you certain El Rey will not send more Spanish nobles to claim this space?"

He nodded. "It is a possibility, but perhaps he and your King Henri can work out an arrangement. I am willing to make this gift to you, at least until our respective rulers tell us otherwise."

Lisette shrugged and smiled. "I humbly accept, Uncle Oscar. Until I am healed, I have very few options for a place of rest anyway."

"Good, I am praying for the safe return of your daughter. It is a pity that our priest gave his life in my service. I would have him say a special mass for—what is her name? Alara? For her health and safety." He looked around as if regarding the room for the first time. "You require sustenance. I shall send staff in with meat and rum to feed your blood."

"I do wonder, Uncle, if you try to solve every problem with food."

"Food is life." He patted his expansive girth. "But you are thin, child, almost painfully so. I was not directly told very much, but I did overhear that you lost a lot of blood. We must remedy your ills so that you may be healthy when Captain Rocco and Alara return to you."

She smiled. "Captain Rocco? So, you would

recognize the rank of a pirate?"

"With some objection, yes. He fought valiantly and saved many of my guard, even if he did strand me in a rowboat."

"He stranded us both, and he usually does not leave survivors."

"Yes, but you can forgive and forget—you are in love with him."

"And admit it—you can respect him."

The duke stood, carefully, as the chair squeaked its relief. "That is what keeps him alive when in my purview. Pinar will return shortly with your food. You will eat and grow strong."

Lisette shook her head as he walked out the door. Worrying over Alara did not induce hunger, but he was correct. She needed her strength back to get to her daughter and deal with her kidnapper.

As she waited, her hand drifted across her stomach, willing the muscles to firm up and the soreness to leave. Through her nightclothes, she ran her fingers over the scar left by Ruhee's ankh and a cold chill rattled her. Oleta had said it concerned her. The night was a blur of fear and pain, recalled in only snippets and flashes. Lisette remembered the burning sensation that grew until she was aflame.

And there was a chant that grew, not just in volume but in intensity. She did not understand any of the words. One word kept repeating—it sounded like "KHA-hill-uh." She repeated it to herself several times to remember. A member of the crew should know what it meant, once she caught up with the *Dişi Aslan.*

Lisette took out her mother's diary again and read it. There seemed no doubt that Begum Derya was her mother, along with the additional evidence of the baby clothes in her cabin and the characters on the note, the same characters as the setting on her emerald. Her father had given her this emerald when she turned 20. Her father the French duke and Begum Derya the Turkish pirate…

What was there to believe in anymore?

Pinar entered, carrying an oversized tray of food and drink. Lisette leaned forward as if to rise.

"No, no, no." Pinar shook her head. "You are not to be out of bed."

Lisette swung her legs around. "Let me at least go to the table. Even Begum said I needed to start walking to regain my strength."

"Very well." Pinar placed the tray on the small table by the chaise. "But let me at least guide your steps."

She rushed to Lisette's side and extended her arm for support. Lisette stood, wavering for a moment, and shuffled forward with her hand lightly touching Pinar's shoulder.

"I am stronger than my first steps this morning," she said.

"Yes, Lizzie." Pinar grinned and eased her down to the chaise, where Lisette collapsed against it.

Lisette frowned. "Tomorrow will be better."

Pinar filled a plate with roasted meat and vegetables. "I had cook prepare this without the sauce for you."

"Thank you. Rich food and a bad stomach are not what I need at the moment." Lisette stabbed at a potato and a slice of pork, reminding herself that this would strengthen her.

Pinar poured a goblet of rum and placed it on the table next to Lisette. As usual, there were two goblets.

"Does the duke still think he might stop by?" Lisette asked.

"As always, he makes plans."

"And I have other ideas." Lisette nodded toward the pitcher. "Pour yourself a splash and fill another plate. I cannot possibly finish this."

Pinar did as Lisette asked, laughing. "If I take care of you for too much longer, I shall need ropes to lift me onto the ship."

"Not you." Lisette grinned. "You may be a quiet woman, but you are strong and always busy. I often see you working, even when others are idle."

"It is my nature to be occupied."

"Pinar, you were there when Ruhee stopped my bleeding and saved me…" Lisette trailed off, uncertain whether she was stating fact or asking a question.

"Yes."

"She was chanting in a language I did not understand. Did you understand it?"

Pinar shook her head. "It was Arabic. I understand a few words, but not all. She was speaking so quickly, and my focus was on the baby. I'm sorry."

"I remember only one word that I kept hearing over and over—" Lisette carefully formed the word. "KHA-hill-uh."

"Yes, I heard that word, too." Pinar paled, shaking her head. "*Qahil.* It means like a desert, dry. *Barren.*"

Rocco and Luis pulled up at the end of the pier, having careened their horses through the main road, nearly running over several villagers. A ship could be seen leaving port, far enough away to be a silhouette.

"She is on that ship, I will bet my life," Luis said.

Rocco nodded. "Let us see what we can discover here."

Dismounting, they led their horses toward the livery stable. As they strode past the inn, Rocco looked over to see Horace unhitching his gray pony. He walked toward him, raising his hand in greeting.

"Good morrow, Horace. How are you out so early?"

The large black man smiled as he unbuckled the last backband and led his pony from between the shafts. "I was asked to give a friend a ride to the port. And you?"

"My friend Luis and I are hunting a thief—or a pair of them." He moved closer and lowered his voice. "I don't suppose you could give me the name of your passengers?"

"Ah, so you know there were two." Horace nodded, his face creased in worry. "One was the girl Ruhee, whom I have known as a faithful member of the *Dişi Aslan* crew. Her companion was a tall, self-important woman, who did all the talking and ordered me as one whips a lazy mule. I assumed Ruhee was playing a role, as the *Dişi* women often do, pretending to be a lady's maid in exchange for information."

Luis had joined the two men and turned to Rocco. "Amoy."

"Yes, she would want to do us harm."

"Might I ask what has been stolen?" Horace asked. "Perhaps it can be replaced."

Rocco shook his head. "I'm afraid not. Amoy and Ruhee have stolen Lisette de Lille's child."

"Terib!" Horace's native tongue blurted. He looked out at the port and saw the ship well out of range. "That is horrible. How could Ruhee have done this thing? And I was an instrument of their escape—no! I am gutted." He leaned against his pony, his face buried in the shaggy mane.

Rocco laid his hand upon Horace's shoulder. "They deceived you, friend. You bear no blame."

"Nonetheless, I must redeem myself for the part I played." The large man stood up, wiping at his forehead with the back of his hand. "How can I help?"

"What ship do they sail upon?" Rocco asked.

"*El Buscador.*"

"Luis and I must hurry to my ship and give chase. We need someone to take our horses back to the Martinmas castle."

Horace regarded his horse. "I cannot keep your

speed, gentlemen, and Ti Gason here could not bear my bulk. However, I can re-hitch and follow behind, if you can leave your horses tied where I may find them."

"It is much appreciated," Luis said, mounting his horse.

"Do you know where to find the windward cove?" Rocco asked.

Horace smiled. "Only when no one is around to follow me."

"Good." Rocco nodded and swung into his saddle. "Thank you for your kindness and do give those at the castle as much information as we have shared here. If there's anything the duke can do to help, we need every hand to pray."

"Why are you so determined to return this baby of the marquise's?" Horace asked.

Rocco's mouth set in a grim frown, his own fear a surprise. "Because I am the father."

7

"Tell me about this baby," Kurta said. "What is her name?"

Ruhee stammered before blurting out, "Zaina."

"Zaina," the old woman repeated. "Yes, she is lovely."

The baby continued to drink as Kurta rocked back and forth. "And you, child? How is it that this baby is so far from its mother?"

"Why, they were…separated. Yes, separated when pirates attacked a ship. The wet nurse escaped in one boat with the baby, the mother in another. The mother ended up on Isla de la Soledad, and the baby here."

"My apologies, I am old and forgetful. I thought you said the mother had died in childbirth and the wet nurse deserted you."

"Yes," Ruhee spurted, before quieting her voice. "What I meant was, I meant the mother died in the attack on our ship. She'd just had the baby and was too weak to walk, so they threw her overboard. I saved the baby, intending to take it to the mother's sister. The wet nurse saw her chance to survive and took it, but it separated us."

"Interesting that a new mother would need a wet nurse." Kurta took the bubby-pot away and handed it to Ruhee. She pressed her fingers to her lips and whispered, "Shh, she's asleep."

Ruhee nodded, her palms sweaty and heart pounding from her lies. "Thank you. Perhaps you can show me how to prepare her food, and I will not trouble you any longer."

"Oh, no, it is no trouble." Kurta kept rocking the baby. "I am alone on this voyage and in need of busywork. There is no work better or more honorable that caring for a baby."

"But I would like to be the one—that is, she is my responsibility." Ruhee's cheeks flushed. "I cannot in good conscience ask you to do more."

"You are not asking. I am a happy volunteer."

Ruhee stood. "I know you mean well, but I cannot keep running over to your cabin to feed or otherwise care for this child. Now, could you please show me how to prepare her milk?"

"I will show you, but if you will forgive me, I worry that your cabin mate might harm this little one—she does not seem to be a patient woman. It might be safer to turn Zaina's care over to me for the voyage, and I can hand her back when we reach port."

"No! She is mine!" Ruhee's anger startled even her.

She reached down and wrenched the sleeping baby from Kurta's arms. Alara's eyes flew open, and she looked up at Ruhee. Ruhee glanced down to see the baby staring at her, forehead wrinkled, and eyebrows knitted in a frown. She opened the cabin door and fled up the stairs to the deck, jostling the wailing baby at every step.

Amoy wanted to kill the baby and Kurta wanted to keep her. She needed to get away from both of these options. But where?

Walking around in the fresh sea air normally calmed her—if only the baby would stop crying. The sun was on its way to the horizon on the starboard side, but the deck was still warm. Other passengers strolled as well, although some were leaning over the rail, unused to the rolling movement. They all gave her the same disapproving glance as she passed.

Alara finally lowered her wails to a fussy whine as Ruhee strode to the stern, where she saw stacks of dinghies. She imagined herself lowering one and rowing away from this madness, but quickly discarded the notion. Even if she could drag a boat to one of the davits and lower it herself, they'd just reached open sea—there would not be an island in sight for perhaps six days—not until they reached Isla de la Soledad. Six days by ship would be more by a little dinghy.

And she did not dare return to Île des Oiseaux.

She glanced down at Alara, who had quieted from full-throated shrieking to disagreeable grumbling noises. For being only a few days old, this baby was strangely aware, and Ruhee could feel her intense dislike. Being this child's new mother might be harder than she imagined.

Maybe Amoy is right. We throw the baby overboard, and I am left to create a new one with Rocco.

"My apologies." A soft, crackling voice startled her, and she whipped about to see Kurta.

Ruhee pulled Alara close. "What do you want?"

Kurta smiled. "Only to say that I am sorry for frightening you. I did not mean to usurp your responsibility for the child, only to lighten your burden. I confess, I miss tending to babies and I leaped at the chance to do so again. I was obviously too excited."

The baby cooed happily, and Ruhee looked down to see her eyes focused on the old woman, a toothless smile on her face. The rejection made Ruhee burst into tears. She thrust Alara at Kurta.

"Take her, she hates me!"

"Now, dear, that is a strong word." Kurta enfolded the baby in her arms. "This baby cannot be old enough to judge you…" She glanced at Ruhee. "Perhaps you judge yourself?"

Ruhee's eyes widened. "Why would I judge myself?"

"It is obvious, girl. This may be—did you say it was your friend's baby? But you are desperate to make her your own."

"I—I merely want to get along with the child. It is a long trip to Isla del Lagarto."

"Isla del Lagarto? I thought the baby's aunt was on Isla de la Soledad."

Caught in another lie, Ruhee took a breath to calm her voice. "She is. The baby's mother was my friend. Her sister is on Soledad, but the baby's father is on Lagarto. That is a large part of the argument between Amoy and me. She wants to be rid of this child quickly. I think her father would want to have her."

Kurta nodded. "Of course. That is reasonable."

Ruhee looked up at the woman's face. Her eyes were warm and kind but there was a slight upturn of her mouth. *She knows I am lying.* "No matter which island is our destination," she said, sighing. "I would like your guidance in taking care of Zaina. What is your destination?"

"Ultimately I am bound for the far islands, but I am old and love the sea life, so I take many trips. I usually leave my destination to fate."

"Can you teach me to take care of her?"

"Yes, child, all you need is to develop some skill and confidence. Little Zaina can feel your discomfort." Kurta turned. "Come with me, back to the cabin and I shall show you how to change her clout and teach you to rock her properly."

Ruhee nodded, wiping the dampness from her cheeks. "Thank you."

"I fear I'm terrible with names, my dear," Kurta said as they walked down the steps. "What was your name again?"

"Ruhee." She sucked in air as she said it, afraid that she had revealed too much.

Kurta nodded and repeated her name a few times before stopping at her cabin door. "Should you let your companion know where you are? I'd hate for her to think you've gone overboard."

Ruhee glanced down the corridor. "No. She'll know where to look for me."

Rocco stood at the helm, shouting orders at the crew to bring *L'Implacable* about to the southeast. They had been chasing *El Buscador* for four days.

It had only been a few months since he'd been on his ship, but it seemed like years. He had missed this feeling, of the bow cutting through the water and the sea air whipping across his face.

It was unfortunate that he was hunting his child's kidnappers. Enjoying his ship while fearing for his baby stirred his anger. When he caught Amoy and Ruhee, there would be no leniency. He would strike them down.

If I but knew how to transform into this new dragon. It is obviously not controlled by the moon anymore. I should like to rend those wenches with teeth and talon.

Luis approached the helm. "Mizzenmasts secured, Captain. Are we certain we are on the right path to capture *El Buscador*?"

"She had a day's start." Rocco kept his eyes glued to the horizon. "We know she's bound for Isla del Largarto, but we don't know if that's her only stop. I confess, I am guessing at her route."

"We'll catch her," Luis said, stepping closer. "Those women cannot hide from you."

Rocco nodded, although frowning. "My ship is fast, but it is not fast enough for my impatience. Wings would be better for a time like this."

"I did not ask, Captain, but I wondered. The night of the battle—I saw you briefly before the heavy attack began. Then I only saw the dragons."

"I was white with red." Rocco patted his friend and smiled. "It takes time to believe."

"I am growing more accustomed with each day. Why are you not flying to find your daughter?"

Rocco scowled. "It is a complicated matter to explain, but I do not know how to transform."

They were silent for a few moments, Rocco scanning the open water and Luis regarding the sails.

"I'll trim again, Rocco. See if we can get more wind."

Poussin's voice rang out. "Ship ahead!"

Rocco brought his spyglass up. He could see the tip of a mast ahead. "Harden up, men! Trim those sails! We chase that ship!"

He turned the wheel to adjust the rudder and get more out of the sheets. The wind was in his favor and quickly filled the canvas, propelling the ship forward. This had to be *El Buscador*, and he was going to run them down.

A familiar voice greeted him from below the helm. "Cap'n," Chunk said. "The crew needs to know if we prepare cannon."

Cannon? Was he going to fire on this ship and risk Alara's life?

9

"Thank you," Lisette said as she allowed Pinar to help her back to bed after the meal. The young woman fluffed the pillows and tucked the covers before taking the tray and heading toward the door.

"Take heart, Lizzie," she said in the doorway. "Rocco is insatiable when he is searching for something he wants—or someone."

Lisette sank back, closing her eyes, but once Pinar left, she pulled off the covers and swung her legs around. She tested her weight on the floor again, standing when it felt safe. Taking one tiny step at a time, she shuffled toward the balcony. She kept her eyes on the archway, progressing until at last her hands found the stone railing.

Resting a few moments, she imagined her mother standing outside, ranting at the heavens about Father's arrogance. *If Rocco had come home with a baby—why the gall!* Of course, she and Rocco had already consummated their love. She didn't feel as abandoned as her mother must have felt.

The view from Mama's balcony was glorious. The sea's different blues were ribbons that followed the coast, from bright as a robin's egg to dark as a storm cloud. Lisette looked at the horizon and wished, with all her heart, that she was in flight again, soaring.

Cautiously, she said, "I am a dragon?"

The feathers that normally hugged her now squeezed her bruised body with no mercy and she sank to her knees. "I am a human! Human!"

Sitting on the stone floor, she waited until her human body was restored. There would be no transformation while she was hurting. In the meantime, her only task was to heal, something that was taking much too long. At least the duke was kind enough to open this castle up to her, so she could recuperate in luxury. Having Pinar to help was a blessing.

The duke said this is my castle now, although who knows for how long? Political intrigue is such a bore.

She pulled herself back to standing and shuffled toward her bed, attempting to stretch taller and pick each foot up more with each step. By the time she returned, she was standing mostly erect, but the mattress looked appealing. Perhaps she could nap.

"No," she told the room. "I can't sleep, so I might as well work."

Lisette continued around her bed and reached into the drawer for her mother's journal. Clutching it in a tight grip, she made her way toward the chaise, picking up more speed with her feet, and hissing less through her gritted teeth.

She arrived at the lounging chair wanting to collapse but put her hand on the arm and lowered her body into the overstuffed fabric. A small squeak of pain escaped her, followed by a few panting breaths.

At last, she found a semi-upright position that felt comfortable and opened the book to the last entry she had read.

May 12th

Is there no end to the indignities I must endure married to this man? I realize that we were not joined by love or even choice, but his behavior is inexcusable. We had but three short weeks after our wedding to consummate our marriage, and yet he was never able to even be in the room with me after sunset. When he was ordered to lead an expedition to the Ottoman Empire, he left with barely a peck of a kiss good-bye.

Lisette reread her mother's words, "…he was never able to even be in the room with me after sunset." Was it possible that her father was a blood dragon? If he had been, he wasn't on the night she was abducted. The moon was in its crescent phase and Rocco the dragon had appeared to her.

Father spent the whole evening as a human.

One more reason to hate that my parents are dead. I love them and miss them, but Father could have told me so much more about the past—his past, and my birth.

She read on through the diary, looking for more clues to herself and her mother. Mama was not thrilled with raising another woman's child and she made that clear in her neat, measured script. Her plan was to have the nanny raise Lisette, but Father doted on the baby. This angered her. It also gave her the idea that if she took more part in Lisette's life, Father would love her for taking such care with his daughter.

A tear crept from her eye. Juliette de Lille had used this bastard baby to get close to her husband. Lisette could not fault her—what wouldn't she do if she believed Rocco did not love her? Still, it stung to know that she was nothing more to her mother than a pawn in a game.

She turned yet another page and found a surprisingly joyous entry, dated two years after being handed a baby to raise.

December 27

He has come to me at last! Last night my husband finally came to my chamber and took what I had been offering for so many years. I confess, it is a brutish act, all shoving and panting like a beast, but I feel now officially wed to him and cannot be tossed aside. My prayer is that I am pregnant soon with a child that is my own.

He gave no reason for his sudden amorous inclining toward me, except to say that after the recent death of the Duke de Laurent, he felt reborn. I know his hatred of the duke ran deep, as the duke was responsible for killing his parents and replacing them in the king's court. Still, it is an odd excuse for amorous congress with the wife he has avoided for years.

I will not offer complaint, as I fervently pray for a child to reward me for my long suffering.

It could not have been clearer to Lisette—her father spent years as a blood dragon, attempting to avenge his parents' death by killing this Duke de Laurent. That he did not feel at liberty to tell Mama did not surprise her. She resisted telling anyone about being a dragon, even those she trusted. How she wished he was still alive, and they could compare their experiences!

The door opened and Lisette looked up to see the day had grown late. It was the duke, being followed by Pinar and several servants, all carrying trays.

"I thought I might sup with you tonight," the duke said. "You are lonely and in need of company."

"Naturally, Uncle Oscar." Lisette smiled and quickly rolled her eyes at Pinar, who was setting a massive tray of food on the table.

"Allow your dear uncle to help you to a proper seat." The duke extended his hand. "And try not to roll your eyes at your relations."

Lisette laughed. "My apologies. I was merely opining because I don't feel I've spent a moment alone since I was brought here. But, yes, I have missed supping with you."

He pointed to the journal. "I see you've had a little time to read."

She closed the book and put it down on the chaise. "I am too restless to nap, wondering if Rocco has caught up with the ship. It occurred to me that reading might calm my anxious nerves."

"Has it?"

She gave him a wan smile as she carefully took her seat. "Calm is not the word."

"Cap'n?" Chunk's voice was questioning but insistent. "Do we prepare cannon?"

Rocco looked down at him. Firing on the ship that held his daughter sounded like a bad idea. Not firing on the ship would be taken as weakness.

"Aye, Chunk. Have the dogs get the guns ready."

Rocco kept his eyes on the course, chasing the ship. *L'Implacable* was swiftly closing the distance between them. He became aware of Luis, standing and staring.

"Haven't you some work to do?" His voice was taut. "Chunk can use a hand with the chase guns."

"Are you really going to fire on the ship with your daughter in it?"

Rocco set his jaw and kept his focus. "Not unless it's necessary. We'll use the chain shot first to knock down their masts and attempt to board. No broadsides." He glared at Luis. "I won't let them escape."

Luis nodded as he ran down the steps. "I'll go help Chunk. We'll get her back."

"Ship on port stern!" Poussin's voice ripped through the air.

Rocco spun around and focused his spyglass on a sleek vessel cutting through the waves. She was still afar back but gaining rapidly. He trained the glass on her flag. It was too far to see yet. Chunk had come up to the helm.

"She's a ways off," Chunk said. "But thar's only one ship it could be."

Rocco nodded. "The *Dişi Aslan*."

"I come to tell ya, we're ready with guns and shot." Chunk raised his brows. "If it comes to that."

"Thanks." Seeing Begum's ship lightened his spirits, and Rocco smiled. "We might be able to do this without killing anyone."

The ship they were chasing had finally come into close enough range to see its colors. The brilliant red and gold identified it as Spanish. Underneath was the standard of the Crown of Castile. And painted across the stern was exactly what Rocco sought—*El Buscador*.

The Seeker.

He stepped back to the wheel and adjusted the rudder, shouting orders at the crew until *L'Implacable* slowed slightly and tacked to port. Chunk joined him at the helm.

"Orders?"

Rocco nodded toward the ship they chased. "We allow *Dişi Aslan* to catch us. She can tack aft and prepare to cut them off if they attempt to turn starboard. We'll hem in *El Buscador* while I make my request to board, with all guns trained on her masts."

"Aye. We'll be standin' by."

The small, sleek vessel behind them wasted no time closing the distance, and Rocco ran up a flag of greeting to Captain Begum Derya. The *Dişi Aslan* responded with a flag of their own. Soon, a dinghy approached, bearing a single occupant. Chunk assisted Captain Derya onto the deck and escorted her to Rocco's cabin.

"Begum." Rocco gestured to the table with the pitcher of rum he held. "I would enjoy pleasantries, but we have a mission and I wish to get to it."

"Understood." Begum sat and held her goblet out for a pour. "I assume you are as loathe to fire on this ship as I am."

"Yes. I have a plan." He joined her at the table. "We'll flank *El Buscador* and your ship comes in aft, prepared to help us battle or to make a swift turn to hem them in. I will make my case for their consent to be boarded and searched. Do you know this captain?"

Begum shook her head. "Not well, but my spies tell me he is new to his command, which will make him either reckless or agreeable."

"I shall board his ship with a fair contingent of my best fighters, search the decks, and find Alara."

"How do we ensure he will not be stupid enough to put up a fight?" Begum frowned.

"We don't. But our ships have guns trained upon them. At the first sign of resistance, we fire—aiming for the masts."

"It is a risk." Begum stared down at her drink. "I only ask one thing. I would like to be part of your contingent."

"Both captains risking their lives? Is that wise?"

"True, it is not. Oleta has requested to go—I can send her in my place. But I very much want to save that baby."

Rocco sipped his rum. "You are fond of Lisette?"

"In my own way, yes." Begum stood, draining her cup, and placing it on the table. "Let us to it then."

Rocco ushered her back to the deck and her boat. "I shall see you next aboard *El Buscador*."

Returning to his spot at the helm, Rocco tacked further to port, yelling at the crew to ease the sails accordingly. Begum's ship mirrored him, tacking starboard. Fortunately, *L'Implacable* had the wind and could pick up speed. Even though the *Dişi Aslan* had the most work to do, they were still the faster ship.

He looked up to see *El Buscador* had opened their sails. It was obvious they'd spotted the two pirate ships and were going to make a run for it. Rocco knew they were too heavy to outrun the advancing brigands. He hoped their captain knew, too.

"Don't worry," he told the heavy galleon, "I'll let you live. All I want is my child."

It took barely an hour to catch up with the ship, Begum circling starboard and Rocco to port. *El Buscador* had opened its gun ports and cannons had been rolled out.

The pirate ships kept with their target but stayed well out of shot range.

"Run up the parlay flag," Rocco instructed.

A blue and gold flag was hoisted, under the *L'Implacable's* skull and crossbones. Rocco kept his place at the helm, waiting. It seemed as if time stopped. The breeze died to a whisper, causing the ships' sails to flap loosely, searching for wind. Rocco gave enough orders to keep the ship in place, while he glanced at *El Buscador's* helm.

If their plan was to ignore him and hope he went away, he was not a patient man. Rocco summoned Chunk.

"Bring me the trumpet and take the helm."

The first mate went on the run and returned quickly with a speaking-trumpet to amplify Rocco's voice.

Rocco stepped to the starboard side and brought the instrument to his mouth. "Ahoy, *El Buscador*! I am Captain Rocco of *L'Implacable*. Your captain can speak with me, or he can speak to my cannons, and those of the *Dişi Aslan* to your starboard."

A few moments passed, enough to make Rocco open his mouth to order an advance and attack. "Chunk—" he saw a white feather round the stern of *El Buscador*. A lithe young man stepped out to the rail, his own speaking-trumpet in his hand.

"I am Julio Suarez, captain of *El Buscador*, and we do not entertain pirates."

"I am not asking for entertainment, Captain Suarez. I seek someone who I believe is on your boat. You can surrender them to me or surrender your entire ship."

Rocco observed a second man wearing a red bandana joining the captain. They held a lively conversation, before Suarez addressed him again.

"We do not surrender paying passengers," Captain Suarez yelled. "Fire to port!"

Four guns on the port side of *El Buscador* belched

smoke and sent cannon shot toward *L'Implacable*. They fell short of their marks, as Rocco had moved his ship out of range of most normal guns, and these were woefully small to be used to attack.

"Chunk!" Rocco's response was immediate. "Over the bow."

Cannon was aimed and lit. Within moments, cannonball blazed across *El Buscador's* bow, skimming the deck and putting a large hole in the fore course sail.

"Reload!" Rocco yelled, loud enough for the other ship to hear him.

He waited for *El Buscador's* response. Men scrambled to their defensive posts and stood, no doubt awaiting orders. The man with the red scarf ran up to the helm and held an animated conversation with Captain Suarez. Rocco did not hear all the words, but distinctly caught, "endanger" and "reckless."

"I suggest you allow me to search for my missing people, Captain Suarez," Rocco shouted as *L'Implacable* was brought about and repositioned. "It is the only way to keep your ship from being scuttled."

"I do not deal with pirates!"

Rocco took a breath. He glanced at Chunk, who wore his worry like an ill-fitting hat. "Chunk—the mast!"

A word from his first mate and a blast from one cannon released a chain-shot that splintered their main mast, crumpling the topsails as it folded in half. The sailor in the crow's nest gave a pitying wail as everything went upside down and he fell onto the deck, followed by the weight of the rigging.

There was a flurry of action on *El Buscador*, men flying to keep from being struck, and the man in red leaping back to the helm, arguing again with the captain. Whatever the captain's response, the man disagreed with his decision, so much so that he called to his crewmates. Rocco did not hear all the words

The entire crew of *L'Implacable* stood at the rail to see the melee that ensued. Captain Suarez had but two defenders. The remainder of the crew clashed swords until one defender lay at the captain's feet and the other bowed on his knees. While four of the men took the captain and his aide below, the man in red picked up the trumpet.

"Ahoy, Captain Rocco. This here's First Mate Roberto Galvan, and we don't want no trouble. What are yer terms that'll keep us alive?"

Rocco smiled, thankful that the first mate had more sense than his captain. "We seek two women and a baby. They are aboard your boat. Allow us to board and search for them and arrive alive at your next port."

The first mate and the rest of the crew huddled together for a few moments. Rocco saw the first mate nod, and the rest of the crew disappear below deck. Roberto picked up the trumpet again.

"Easily done, Captain. We await your boat."

"Captain." Luis had crossed from his post and joined Rocco at the helm. "I do not feel confident having you board the boat, especially alone. Let me go. I know Amoy."

"I'd have ta agree wit'im," Chunk said. "Send someone what knows the women."

Rocco looked out to see a small boat approaching. It was Oleta and another woman from the *Dişi Aslan*. He frowned. "Very well, I will send you, Luis, and take one of the other crew. Chunk, I need you to stay here and aim the guns if they try to trick us."

Luis ran down to the ropes, tapping one of the other men as he did. Chunk returned to the cannons and prepared the next shot.

Rocco picked up the speaking-trumpet. "First Mate Galvan, I send my envoy to help with the search. I warn you—if any harm come to them, your ship will be sunk without mercy."

Standing at the rail Rocco maintained his focus on the small dinghy pulling alongside the galleon and being stabilized. Once his crew were aboard the enemy ship, he realized he had been holding his breath. His left hand fidgeted on the wood, preparing to give the order to attack if he saw the glint of one weapon again Luis, Oleta or the others.

The crew from the dinghy gave small nods to the first mate and his men, and they all disappeared below deck. Rocco paced around the helm, wishing to be aboard *El Buscador*, opening doors and hunting down the two snakes who stole his child.

The minutes stretched out until he wanted to explode. At last, he saw the red bandanna heading to the port side, waving his hands. Luis was next to him, holding the horn.

"Captain," Luis shouted. "They are not here."

"Impossible!" Rocco exploded. "I'm coming over."

The dinghy couldn't be lowered fast enough for him to launch himself down the ladder. He wished he could transform and fly, but knew that would be troublesome on many fronts, even if he could do it. Poussin sat in the boat with the oars, ready to row. Rocco snatched them from his hands.

"No offense, boy, but I need haste," Rocco said and shoved away from the ship, pushing both oars furiously through the sea.

Arriving at *El Buscador*, Rocco handed the oars back to Poussin. "Stay here. I'll return."

Luis and First Mate Galvan awaited Rocco as he climbed up the ladder. Galvan was tall and rail thin with a dark stubble on his scalp that wound its way down to his chin. They both wore the expressions of men who expected to be drawn and quartered.

Rocco glared at them both before asking, "What did you find?"

"We checked all cabins, Captain," Luis said. "Two were unoccupied, although there were still belongings in them. The first pass through the ship did not turn up any wayward passengers, but the crew continues to search."

Rocco turned to Galvan. "What do you know about the passengers in those two rooms?"

"Bertrand!" Galvan called. A young man looking to be Poussin's size and age ran to the first mate. "Tell Captain Rocco here about the women."

"I carried their bags, showed 'em their rooms." Bertrand's voice squeaked and trembled. "Women. Two women shared the cabin what still got clothes in it, a smallish young'un and a big older gal."

"Did either of them carry a basket?" Rocco asked.

Bertrand nodded. "The young'un had a basket—said it was her kitten and wouldn't let me carry it."

"Ruhee and Amoy." Rocco's jaw clenched. "Show me where they bunked."

As Bertrand led them below deck, Luis asked, "Out of curiosity, who was the woman in the other cabin?"

"Ah, she was old. Frail like, but kind." Bertrand reached in his pocket, looking nervously at Galvan. He held out a small gold coin. "She give me this when I helped her."

Rocco took the coin and examined it. "Sandoval's gold. Very few people would have such currency."

"What does it mean?" Luis asked.

"I can only guess," Rocco said. "Someone who has had dealings with Captain Derya's crew, or…"

Bertrand stepped away and let Rocco and Luis enter.

Rocco walked around the room, picking up clothing, holding it out, and tossing it aside. There were small tins on the table. He opened each one, sniffing at the contents.

"Nothing here, but I would bet that these herbs and potions belong to Ruhee, and the clothing looks large enough for Amoy." He strode out the door and turned to Bertrand. "What about the old woman's cabin?"

"This way," Bertrand gestured and opened Kurta's door.

Rocco went to the middle of the room and turned around. The only things in the cabin were the table and chairs, and two bunks covered in colorful silken scarves. Something caught his eye hanging from the edge of the upper mattress. He reached underneath and pulled out a feather, hard-shafted and purple.

"Alara was here," he told Luis. "The old woman has something to do with this."

They ran back up to the deck to talk to Galvan who waited on the port side near the dinghies. As they reached him Oleta strode to the men from the stern of the ship.

"Captain Rocco, we found two dinghies missing."

"One mystery solved," Rocco said.

"Why would three women need two boats?" Luis asked.

"I have my suspicions," Rocco told him. "One of the women was not wanted on the journey."

"But followed anyway," Oleta said.

Rocco turned to Galvan. "I thank you for your patience at helping me search. My apologies for the damage done, but your captain was quite unreasonable, especially when dealing with a pirate who lets so few ships survive his attacks."

"Speaking of my captain," Galvan said. "I'm in need of counsel."

"What kind of counsel does a king's sailor need from

a pirate?"

"The kind that will keep a king's sailor from swinging on a rope." He looked down, his right foot sweeping at imaginary dirt. "In the sudden attack and heat of the moment, I fear I lost my head and overruled our captain. He will surely see me punished."

"I suppose tis true. That your head was cooler than your captain's desire for glory will mean nothing. That you saved all the passengers from death, saved any goods and riches you are carrying from plunder, none of that will matter."

"It certainly will not matter." A voice came from the starboard side. Two of the ship's crew led a familiar figure forward, one wearing a hat with a white feather and a rope binding his wrists. Captain Suarez raised his chin and all the arrogance that came with it. "The king's ship will not barter with pirates for their goods or their passengers' lives, not when the king's pride is at stake."

"I always knew El Rey was unmoved at the deaths of his subjects," Rocco said. "In many cases he is completely unopposed. But sacrifice his bounty? His gold? Have you sworn no oath to deliver the king's riches to him by any means necessary?"

Captain Suarez stretched himself taller and puffed his chest out. "I have not."

Rocco laughed. There was nothing so comical as a small man in an oversized uniform, attempting bravado. "You should have."

"I thought you could talk a bit o' sense into him," Roberto said. "Make him see that savin' folks made him a hero."

Rocco studied the captain from his boots to his feather. "I don't think he can be convinced."

"What can I do?"

Rocco gestured for Roberto to walk with him, away from Suarez. "Of everyone on the ship, who do you think will bear witness against you?"

Roberto frowned and studied his hand. "Why, just the cap'n, I spect. No one laid a hand o' help towards him when we took him below."

"So, you only have your captain to silence then?" Rocco let the question hang in the air.

"Yes," Roberto said, and his eyes widened. "You're not suggesting I…"

Rocco smiled. Such a niño under all that scruff. "No, I gather you haven't the stomach for what must be done to save your neck from the noose. Although perhaps you could be persuaded if you understood—you are saving your crew as well."

"Well, no, I'd not have my men to the gallows. Twas my own fault, after all."

"Might I suggest, then that you and your crew limp your ship to the nearest port, with the story that you were attacked by *L'Implacable,* and the good Captain Suarez lost his life attempting to defend the king's gold and subjects." Rocco looked at the captain, reaching to pluck the hat from his head and handing it to Galvan. "It will be close enough to the truth."

Rocco nodded to Luis, who encouraged Suarez with the point of his blade to descend into one of Rocco's dinghies.

"I suppose…" Galvan's voice drifted off. "I'm unsure what to think."

"Then do not think of it." Rocco made a grand gesture toward his men. "Think of saving your men, your ship, and your passengers. For king and country, yes?"

Rocco, Luis, and the men climbed down the ladder and pushed away in their dinghies, followed closely by Oleta and the crew from the *Dişi Aslan.*

"Godspeed, Galvan!" Rocco waved to him. "You are free to go!"

Rocco looked out at *L'Implacable* as the sounds of

Galvan barking commands could be heard behind him. They were at the ladder to *L'Implacable* before Rocco addressed the still-defiant captain in his boat.

"Power is a fickle thing, Suarez."

"I shall see you hang, pirate." Suarez spat at him.

"I think not." Rocco looked up at the ship. "Chunk, toss the chains down."

Suarez smiled. "So, you believe the rope won't hold me, pirate?"

Rocco picked up the length of heavy chain, along with a padlock. "The problem with rope," he said, winding the chain around Suarez and locking the ends together. "Is that it floats."

Nodding to Poussin, Rocco climbed the ladder. As he reached the top, he heard a single scream, followed by a splash.

In Kurta's cabin, Ruhee watched her undo Alara's gown and clout, and wipe the baby down with a damp cloth before putting her into clean clothes. The old woman kept a steady monologue of instruction, telling Ruhee how to undress and dress a baby without straining their fragile arms and legs, and the proper way to fold a clout to keep it firmly on the baby's bottom.

"You are wondering why I have infant clothes," Kurta said.

"Yes."

"I told you, I have taken care of many babies in my lifetime. In my younger days, I was even a wet nurse for a few. I am on my way to nanny for a noble family and brought supplies with me." She took one look at Ruhee's confused expression and added, "Surprisingly, nobility are not as prepared as a villager who has seen many children being born and growing up around them."

Ruhee stood to the side, watching everything, and wondering if she would be able to steal this woman's baby items before they docked at Isla de la Soledad.

Kurta picked Alara up and nodded toward a chair. "Now, Ruhee, you will sit in the chair, and I will show you how to enchant a baby."

Ruhee did as she was told, executing all of Kurta's instructions to her best ability.

"Sit back. Relax, girl, your tension feeds nervousness to the baby. Open your arms—now embrace the baby as if you were enfolding your lover. No, no, *tenderly*." Kurta busied herself with folding garments and repacking a small satchel. "Yes, that is better. Now, sway your body just a little. Hum a song if you wish."

Ruhee looked down at the baby in her arms, now asleep. Rocco's child. Soon, she would be with Rocco and Alara would have little half-brothers and sisters—as long as Amoy did not toss Alara into the sea.

"Ruhee, slow your rocking," Kurta admonished her. "You keep speeding up. It is too fast and violent."

"Yes, I am sorry." She relaxed again and contained her movements.

"Something worries you." Kurta said it as a statement, not a question.

Ruhee nodded, frowning. "I fear my traveling companion."

"Yes, it looked so." Kurta sat down, pouring herself a cup of tea. "What do you fear?"

Ruhee hesitated. This old woman was quick to find her lies. "This baby…is my sister's. It was…stolen from her, and I am returning her to the rightful place." Technically, Lisette was her *Dişi* sister, and the baby was stolen. *And her rightful place is with me.*

"Uh-hmm." Kurta nodded solemnly as she swirled

her tea with her index finger. "Continue."

"When I first met Amoy, she said she knew my sister and also…wanted the baby to go to the right place." Ruhee's brain was on fire with her imaginings, and she kept her eyes averted from both Kurta and Alara.

"She lied?" Kurta's head was down, her eyes focused on her tea.

"Yes." At last, she could be truthful. "Amoy says when we get to open water, she will throw the baby overboard. She hates my sister and wants her to suffer."

"Hmm." Kurta sat, rocking and nodding. "Then we must prevent that."

"Yes, but how?"

The old woman smiled. "We are in open water now?"

"Yes, just." Ruhee frowned and held Alara tighter, causing the baby to whimper and stir. "And I overheard the crew say we would anchor at Isla de la Soledad in four days. I fear the nighttime when Amoy could carry out her plan unseen."

"Then we shall have to escape before then."

"Escape? Where do we escape on a ship?"

"Do no worrying, Child." Kurta rose and shuffled to a small bag, where she rooted around for some time. At last, she pulled out a snuff box, plain with a tree etched into the tin. "You will take a pinch of what's in this box— just a pinch, no more—and put it into whatever Amoy drinks tonight at dinner. When she sleeps, knock on my door and I will come."

Ruhee stopped rocking the baby, looking at the old woman in alarm. "We are not killing her, are we?"

Kurta pointed to the tattoo Ruhee's wrist. "As a pirate, is that so shocking? No, we are making her sleep well and wake with a sore head."

"How—" Ruhee looked down at her exposed lioness head—much like her lies, it was difficult to keep covered.

"I still do not know how we will escape on a ship in the middle of the ocean."

"Leave all to me." Kurta gestured to Alara. "She will be waking soon and asking for her next meal. If she might stay in my cabin temporarily, you can learn Amoy's mood for the evening and whether she will take dinner with the other passengers. There might also be a way for you to straighten your things and prepare them for a quick departure without Amoy's realization."

Ruhee frowned. This woman was taking far too much control of Alara, even as she admitted to herself, grudgingly, that she had been helpful.

If I get out of the chair and Alara is quiet, I'll take her with me.

Holding the baby gently with one arm, she pushed out of the chair with the other. Alara wiggled in her blankets, opened her eyes, and focused on Ruhee, staring daggers through her, to the point that Ruhee shrank back, holding the bundle out to Kurta.

"Perhaps she is hungry." Ruhee handed the baby off as if it burned her.

Kurta embraced Alara, opening the blankets fully and offering her finger to hold. "Is the little one ready for more milk?"

Alara cooed a response, and Ruhee's shoulders sagged. This baby hated her. Perhaps Amoy was right—toss this one. She and Rocco could make another. But taking care of this child was Rocco's proof that she was a better mother and would continue to be a better mother for all of their children. She picked up the snuff box and stuffed it in her pocket before she moved to the door.

"Knock quietly this evening," Kurta told her. "I'll have everything ready."

Ruhee returned to her cabin. Amoy was not there, so she hurriedly prepared for her getaway. There was not much in her small bag, except a shirt, a pair of breeches, and a dagger in its sheath. She put the sheathed dagger in her pocket, making certain she could withdraw the snuff box easily. There were a few tins of herbs on the shelf that she'd taken out to make herself tea—she chose the ones she needed most. If there was time, she could grab the rest on her way out the door.

She felt heat on her chest and reached down to close her fingers around the ankh on its chain. It was warm to the touch, and it seemed to speak to her: *But are you a healer?*

Of course, I am, she argued, *I healed Rocco, I healed Lisette.*

But did you heal them?

Yes! She frowned. *Rocco would have died of blood illness without me. Lisette would have bled to death. I held their lives in my hands and I made them live.*

You also cursed them.

"No!" She stomped her foot.

"Have you gone mad?" Amoy walked through the door. "Many people talk to themselves but very few shout."

"Sorry." Ruhee felt the blush rise. "I was tidying up. I suppose I let my mind wander too far."

"I was speaking with the crew." Amoy took the shawl from her neck and placed it atop her satchel. "We are four days from Isla de la Soledad, and there is beautiful blue sea everywhere. I've had a slight change of mind. Tonight, we rid ourselves of the baby, and then we disembark at Soledad. I can pick up another ship to Isla del Largarto, which will make me harder to track. You are welcome to come but I won't force you."

"But what about the others, the ones who've seen me carrying a baby?"

"Figured that out, too." Amoy flopped on her bed with a sigh. "You can carry a bundle of empty blankets."

"And Kurta?"

"Well, that is a shame, but if the old woman makes a fuss, she will have to follow little baby Alara to Davy Jones' locker."

Ruhee's eyes widened but she kept her back to Amoy and nodded. "After dinner, I assume?"

"When the noise atop is died down. And don't you get ideas about saving that baby or the old woman."

An object whooshed by Ruhee's shoulder and thwacked into the wall. It was a knife. Ruhee stared at Amoy, who rose slowly and strolled to the dagger, plucking it from the wall and putting it back in the sheath on her belt.

"I hit what I aim for, and I'm only keeping you alive so's you can tell Rocco and the missus what I did to their darling."

Ruhee smiled as she fixed Amoy a cup of tea that evening. When the large woman was asleep and snoring, she picked up her bag and snuck to Kurta's door.

15

"Good, child, enter." Kurta's things were still strewn about the cabin.

"You do not look ready," Ruhee said.

"These things?" The old woman gestured around the room and pointed to a small satchel. "I need only what is in this bag. There will be no sign that I am not still here, somewhere, on the ship."

"Where are we…how are we…I do not understand."

"You do not have to. Stay one moment. I will return."

Kurta disappeared out the door, leaving Ruhee alone with Alara, who was awake and watchful.

"Amoy wishes to do you harm," she told the baby, "But I will save you."

Alara twisted her face into a snarl, one that usually preceded her screams. The cabin door opened, and Kurta walked in, calming the baby immediately. Ruhee sighed.

"Come." Kurta picked up Alara. "You carry the bags. Quickly!"

They shuffled softly up the stairs to the deck, staying in the shadows, although none of the crew were about. The ship seemed eerily silent. Ruhee looked up and could not see anyone in the crow's nest. She opened her mouth to ask Kurta, but the woman put her hand up to stop any attempt at speech.

Kurta hustled to starboard aft with Ruhee on her heels. Ruhee was amazed at how fleet the woman was for being so old. They arrived at the railing, where a dinghy swung on its cradle.

"The two of us can't do this," Ruhee whispered.

"Do no worrying," Kurta said. She reached to the lines and untied them, lowering the small boat over the side and into the water. "Get into the boat. I will hand you the baby."

Ruhee hesitated. "You promise—you will hand her to me?"

"Instead of what, child?"

"Instead of keeping her." Ruhee frowned. "And setting me adrift."

Kurta went to the rail and looked over at the dinghy now hugging the ship's hull. She took her bag and tossed it into the boat.

"There," she said. "Zaina's clouts, clothes, bubby-pot, all of it. Get in the boat and be quick. I shall hand you the baby."

Ruhee climbed over the rail to the ladder. It wasn't a perfect sign of faith to ease her mind, but it would have to do. She scurried down to the boat, glancing up often to ensure that Kurta was still there. Once her feet hit the bottom boards, Ruhee looked up, extending her arms.

No one was at the rail.

Ruhee grabbed the ladder to run back up, and saw Kurta reappear, swinging her legs over and climbing down. Ruhee backed away to give her room, horrified that the baby was not there. Kurta stepped into the boat and turned away from her to detach the dinghy from the ship's lines.

"What did—" Ruhee barked, then quieted her voice to a snappish whisper. "What did you do with Al—the baby?"

Kurta picked up an oar before turning to her. The baby was strapped to Kurta's chest, facing outward and regarding Ruhee with an alarmingly judgmental expression.

"She is here," Kurta said, pushing against the hull of the ship with the oar. "I told you to do no worrying."

The motion of the boat swinging away knocked Ruhee back onto the stern seat. Kurta deftly untied Alara's straps and handed her to Ruhee, who couldn't help but notice the baby's scowl when she looked at her.

Once free of the child, Kurta shoved the dinghy further away and rowed in quick, broad strokes, putting distance between *El Buscador* and their little rowboat.

Ruhee sat in wonderment. How could a woman so old be so…powerful?

"You sit with the baby," Kurta said. "I will row."

"To Isla de la Soledad?" Ruhee asked.

"No." The old woman pulled the oars through the water for a few moments. "There is another island nearer. It is safer."

They were well away from the ship when Ruhee heard a splash and the familiar thunk of a small boat tapping a big ship. She looked behind them to see but the night's darkness hid everything except the dark outline of *El Buscador*.

"Did you hear a splash?" she whispered.

"Yes." Kurta maintained her rowing pace. "But it is

of no importance."

In the darkness, Ruhee watched Kurta gaze at the sky. Saying a prayer for our lives, she decided. *Perhaps I should be praying, too.*

As she closed her eyes to ask for divine guidance, she felt a chill and looked up. A deep fog had rolled in and swallowed them. She added to her prayer, that they would not be forever lost asea.

16

"Enough," Lisette said and threw back the covers.

Marisha set down the tray of food and tea and turned to Lisette, hands on her hips. "It has been a week since you birthed and bled and nearly died. Healing takes time."

"Well, I am alive, and I am not bleeding, and my baby is God-knows-where." She got out of bed and walked to the table, slowly but steadily. "I need to find Alara. And where is Pinar?"

"Pinar is in the village, purchasing food from the ship that arrived today. Duke sent her special because she knows what you like." Marisha sighed. "Sit and eat, then, and I will help you in any way I can."

Lisette looked at the table. More meat, more fruit, and roasted vegetables. The pot of her mother's tea looked appealing. She reached for the pot but as she took the handle, the realization that Juliette de Lille was not her mother hit her. Allowing her hand to remain on the teapot, she took a deep breath and let the feeling pass.

"Here, sit and let me pour that for you." Marisha took the pot from her and filled her cup.

"I'm not hungry."

"I do not doubt it. The duke, he thinks everyone has his appetite." The young woman put small amounts of food on Lisette's plate. "But I am more willing to help you once you eat a little. Your journey to find Alara may be long."

"Bribery of the worst sort, even if you do make a good point."

Marisha sat down. "While you eat, we shall make a plan."

Lisette nodded. Impatience would not do when she was trying to find Alara. "I've no idea where to start looking."

"I can get you started." Marisha looked down at the table. "We have been keeping news back from you, to keep you from attempting to leave before you are healed."

"I'd be very angry with you," Lisette said, frowning. "If I didn't believe you meant well. Where is my baby?"

"Rocco and Luis traced tracks that stopped at the road, across from stopped tracks of a cart." Marisha helped herself to a small, savory roll. "Ruhee is not traveling alone and got into a wagon or carriage in order to go to the village."

"Who could Ruhee be with?" Lisette asked. "Did the men say anything about the footprints?"

"Yes, one small set, one large. Rocco had guessed the small prints were Ruhee's. They joined up with the larger set at the corner wall. They could be man or woman."

"They could be," Lisette said, frowning. "But I have a bad feeling. Amoy is most unhappy that Rocco and I killed her brother."

"Do you think they are hiding in the village?"

Lisette shook her head. "Not for long. If there's a ship, they'll want to get far from here."

"Of course. That's why Rocco and Luis returned for horses—to try to catch them before they sail."

"I wonder why Rocco didn't fly." Lisette looked around at her surprised face. "Did you not see him at the battle? The white dragon tipped in red?"

"That was Rocco? We were happy for the help. Battles are easier with a dragon on your side. But I had no idea."

"I watched him transform." Lisette tapped her finger against her cup of tea. "It's possible he does not know how to do it. It is not like being a blood dragon."

"Lord, don't tell me there are other kinds of dragons." Marisha scowled. "I ain't got the energy to keep up with this."

Lisette shrugged. "I will try to tell you only as much as you require."

The chamber door opened, and Pinar entered, waving a small roll of parchment. "I have news." She unrolled it and read, "Ruhee and Amoy escaped with baby. Chasing their ship. Possibly on Isla de la Soledad. R."

"Amoy—I knew it." Lisette sat up. "If they've got Rocco and Chunk on her trail, they'll not get away."

"And Captain Derya," Pinar said. "The *Dişi Aslan* has been their constant companion, aiding in the hunt."

"I need to be searching with them," Lisette said and scooted her chair back to rise.

Marisha cleared her throat.

"What?" She looked down at her plate. "You're right, it is a meager amount. I shall finish, but then I am off to find my daughter."

"Lizzie, I know this is unimportant at the moment," Pinar said. "But I have more news to tell."

Lisette shoved a bite of potato in her mouth and nodded.

"Since the duke is taking up residence in the old Medina castle, the Mendoza family has written to the king, requesting that your home be occupied by their daughter and her husband."

"You are correct, it is unimportant to me." Lisette tried to eat quickly without choking. "I am no longer enamored of this place and will gladly vacate it."

"I do not judge you for not wanting to live the pampered life," Marisha said, pouring more tea. "But do have consideration for the other people who live here—the villagers and the servants. The duke is kind, in his way, but he only plans to be here until El Rey sends someone more permanent. The Mendozas, though. I have heard from their servants. They are as cruel as Mercedes was, and their plan for this island is to strip it bare—wealth, crops, anything that will make them richer."

Lisette took her forehead in her hands, massaging her temples. "Nobility. Greedy nobility…I'd gladly lead a revolt against all of them, turn these islands back to the people who revere what is here."

"It might be possible," Pinar said. "Look at Isla del Lagarto."

"Yes, but it would take—" Marisha said.

"A few dragons." Lisette smiled. "Let the Mendozas try what they might. When Rocco and I have completed our mission, we shall return to *encourage* them to leave."

"It will take some time for them to get the king's approval," Pinar said. "Especially since their letter was intercepted and destroyed."

"Good." Lisette stood up and held her plate to Marisha. "Empty enough? Help me get ready."

Marisha crossed her arms. "First, show me your body is mended."

"Fine." Lisette stretched tall and walked to the door,

turned, and walked to the bed. Once reached, she turned and strode to the door. Turning, she ran to the bed, wheeled, and ran to the door. Each pass quickened her heart and her breath, but she hid it from the two young women.

"You hide it well," Marisha said, "but I do see the blush of your cheeks."

"I have not had to strain myself for a week—more really, as I was not exactly quick on my feet when I was heavy with child."

Marisha looked at Pinar and nodded. She went to the mantel and pulled a sword from its mounting. Handing it to Lisette, she said, "Show me you can still spar with this."

Lisette took the ornate hilt and swiveled the epee in her wrist. More decorative than useful, it was not well-weighted, but it would have to do. Pinar stood before her, sword drawn and ready.

The two women smiled as they lunged and parried across the bedroom, reading each other's moves to attack when possible. Lisette's breath came hard, so she used spare movements to protect herself, looking for the opportunity to use a larger move to finish the duel. The moment finally came when she feinted and saw Pinar's eyes telegraph her next move. Parrying quickly, she rounded her blade as she stepped back and leaned forward, her point at Pinar's chest. They both saluted and lowered their weapons.

Lisette looked over at Marisha. "I'm ready to join the hunt."

Pinar scurried to Lisette's wardrobe to find a dress.

"Actually, Pinar, do you think you could find something plainer, more in line with a servant? I have the feeling that where I'm going, I need to blend in as a local and not stand out as a noble."

"I shall return." Pinar slipped out the door.

"Now then, where is my dagger and its sheath?"

"They're in your own chambers," Marisha said. "That first night, we put you in there, until we learned there was a cradle in this room. I'll go get them."

Alone, Lisette looked toward the bed and the small stand next to it. She walked over and took her mother's journal from the drawer, running her hand over it. There was no guarantee that she'd entertain Begum Derya in this room again, but her flight could take her to the *Dişi Aslan*. How to carry a book, though…

She tore the pages from the journal of her mother's anguish at having to raise a bastard daughter, folded them carefully, and placed them in her cleavage. When the time came, she and Begum would have a talk.

Pinar returned with Lisette's blue-edged dagger, its sheath, and a bundle of fabric.

"I brought something from the servants' quarters," she said. "They might be a handier outfit for what you must do."

"You are correct, thank you." Lisette quickly shed her robe, stepping into the dark skirt and top. She attached her dagger's sheath to her belt, along with a small pouch to store a few coins. Pulling her mother's journal entry from her camisole, she put the folded pages into the bag as well.

Pinar raised her eyebrows at seeing the pages.

"These solve a riddle," Lisette told her. She turned and walked, in short deliberate steps, toward the balcony. Stopping at the end of the bed, she looked down at the cradle. The small violet feather that Rocco had found was still there. She picked it up and carried it outside with her, turning it around in her fingers. She was amazed at the way it changed color. In the relative shadows of her chambers, it was a dusty-gray violet, nearly silver. As she walked into the sunlight, the color left the plume, until it could only be described as transparent.

What kind of dragon are you? She placed the feather in her bag.

Once on the balcony, Lisette turned to Pinar and Marisha, who had entered the room. "If either of you are squeamish about dragons, you may want to leave. I fly to Isla de la Soledad to find my daughter, but first I need to make a stop at the duke's. I do not know if the Mendozas will attempt to take this place while I am gone, but I shall attempt to leave protection behind to help you."

Pinar nodded and stayed, straightening her spine. Marisha shrugged and took a few steps back.

"We will see you off on your journey," Marisha said. "Godspeed and our prayers are with you to find Alara and bring her home safely."

Lisette smiled. Bring her home—was this where she would live? *We will consider that later. At the moment, I am Lisette de Lille, and I am a dragon.*

The change was quick and painless. With a polite nod to the two young women standing gape-jawed, she opened feathered wings that were each the length of her body and lifted up into the sky, above the clouds, and toward the de Medina castle. She and Uncle Oscar needed a quick talk before she set out for Isla de la Soledad.

She arrived in short time and found the grove where she'd first hidden to land and change. Once in her human form, she headed to the back gate, hoping it was unlocked.

The back gate was not only unlocked, it stood open, broken from its hinges. The battle had been fierce and not everything had been righted. Lisette walked across the courtyard to the kitchen where she hoped to see at least one familiar face. She was rewarded with the young woman Amoy had been berating during the first time they met. As before, the girl was washing dishes, although with a much more relaxed look to her shoulders.

"Good morn," Lisette said.

The girl turned and smiled. "Good morn, m'lady. It is good to see you feeling well again."

"I was wondering if you knew where I could find the duke."

"Oh, yes. He is in the library." The girl dried her hands on her apron. "I will take you to him."

Lisette followed her down the hall, past the great room, to an alcove just left of the formal entrance. Beyond the alcove, an archway led to a large room of dark wood and shelves. The girl gestured with a curtsy.

"Thank you." Lisette entered the space to find a large man taking books from the shelves, leafing through their pages, and tossing them to the stone floor. "Why, Uncle Oscar, what have you against literature?"

The duke looked up and grinned. "Lisette, my almost-daughter, how lovely to see you up and about. These?" He pointed around the room. "I have not found more than five books worthy of reading. They are all drivel, tripe about the superiority of the Spanish and the goal of domination."

She smiled coyly. "Do you not believe in Spanish eminent domain?"

"Well, naturally, I believe myself to be superior to most, but I have lived too long and seen too much of the world to believe that Spain should rule it all. And some of that, I admit, I ascribe to my time knowing you, Frenchwoman. Little known fact, I grow weary of feeling like a placeholder, a bookmark to keep an island for El Rey. What does he do with them? He does not visit, and none of these islands produce enough goods to make reliable export."

Lisette laughed. "I came to discuss a matter with you, sire, and I feel like you've already discussed it with yourself!"

"Come, sit, and tell me all." He walked over to an overstuffed chair and gestured to its twin.

"I have received much news," Lisette said as she sat. "Rocco believes that Ruhee may be on Isla de la Soledad, hiding with Alara, so I am on my way there to help find her, now that I am healed."

"Do you require a ship?"

She stared at him. "I think we know I have a faster method of getting there."

"Yes, of course." He blushed. "I was not certain if you were still—afflicted with that particular malady."

"It is not a malady, uncle. It is a blessing and something well under my control." She poked at his arm, teasingly. "I shall not be lighting anyone on fire anymore."

"Then I wish you a safe journey and luck for finding your baby."

"The other rumor that has reached me has to do with this island, and possibly you." She paused. "I'm told that you remain here only until El Rey sends your replacement, and that the Mendozas plan to take my castle for their daughter and soon-to-be son-in-law."

"Your information is correct as far as my plans." The duke folded his hands atop his chest. "I have also heard the rumor about the Mendozas. I cannot confirm it, but I do trust the servants when it comes to gossip."

"I cannot stay to defend the castle, but I would hate to return and find it occupied, especially by the Mendoza offspring. Rumor also tells me that they plan to strip this island of anything valuable in order to line their coffers and curry favor with the king."

The duke nodded. "Yes, it is unfortunate and true. They have made a name for themselves everywhere they go. Even now, they tried to 'borrow' my guards and the land behind this castle for their own use."

"I will come straight to it, sire. My castle requires protection during my absence." Lisette looked at him, her expression grim. "And when I return, I plan that the Mendozas should leave this island, either by ship or by grave."

"Understood. I am loathe to willingly plan a noble's death, but it is not on my conscience if they are an accidental victim of dragons." He leaned forward. "I cannot publicly refuse the king's commands unless I plan to be a pirate myself—which I do not. The most I can do is to attempt to stall their plans until you return to do what I cannot."

"Of course. I should be happy for any assistance, even if it is benign avoidance."

"I shall do what I can." He frowned. "As far as encouraging the Mendozas to leave…how were you planning to accomplish that?"

"By my particular malady, one that Rocco shares with me. They will leave or they will die. I'll not have them ruin this island. I may not wish to rule it, but I should not like it to be destroyed." She stood. "I must be off now. My daughter is my priority."

The duke escorted her to the door. "Agreed. Do not worry about your home. It will be awaiting your return."

Lisette made her way back through the kitchen, nodding at the young maid who was kneading dough on the large table. She strode through the broken back gate, to the glade, where one quick wish and she was soon airborne again, her sights on the island to her south.

As she flew, she let her mind focus on her daughter, thinking softly, *Alara? Alara, where are you?*

It took a day to reach Isla de la Soledad's northern coastline. As she banked toward the lee side a small familiar voice came to her. *Mama, I miss you. I hate this woman who has taken me. But do no worrying, I am safe in the arms of a friend now.*

A friend? Lisette frowned and increased her speed. She knew where Rocco had originally anchored the last time she visited the island. He had just kidnapped her and presented her to Viscount Barragan. She'd repaid his kindness by killing the viscount and returning to the ship to force him to…what? Return her to her family?

No. She'd returned to the ship because she needed to be near him.

There were two ships anchored in close enough proximity to help the other if one came under attack. She recognized both flags. Begum had joined the hunt for Alara.

I may have that discussion with my mother soon.

18

Rocco stepped out of the dinghy onto an unobserved beach on Isla de la Soledad, along with Chunk and three of his crew. Luis had been left to man the ship, although he gave a slight protest at not being able to help. Begum and Oleta waited for them, the morning clouds obscuring their arrival.

"*El Buscador* will not be arriving for at least a day," Rocco said. "And rowing a dinghy would take twice that, if not more. I do not think we will find them here yet, but we should prepare to search *El Buscador* again when it is in port."

"But no one could find her," Chunk said, "and the dinghies was missin'."

"True enough," Begum said. "But she could have hidden and released the dinghy to deceive anyone chasing her."

"Aye," Rocco pointed to one of his men. "Giorgio, get to the dock and await the ship. Watch the passengers that leave, then make your way below deck. Search all the rooms as you can. If another boat comes in, search them as well. They could have been picked up along the way."

Giorgio nodded and strode toward the village. The others waited until he was significantly ahead before starting off, discussing their ideas for finding Ruhee.

"She will need supplies for the baby," Begum said. "She cannot feed an infant unless she has kidnapped a wet nurse."

"True, one of us will go to the merchant's shop." Rocco nodded. "I suggest a woman. And I will go to the inn. We need to find if she has friends or family on the island who might aid her."

"Agreed," Begum said.

"If I might suggest." Oleta spoke up. "I have friends in this village, healers. They might have information."

"Please." Rocco looked at Chunk. "Know anyone around who could help?"

"Not 'zactly, Cap'n, but I been in this port enough times t'make acquaintances."

"I think we've all made 'acquaintances'." Rocco laughed. "Spread out, talk to people."

They were now at the northern edge of the small village. A few people were out, mostly sweeping porches and strolling toward the surrounding brush, baskets in hand for gathering wild fruits and vegetables. One by one, the group separated, Oleta slipping down an alley, Begum turning down the boardwalk for the general goods store, and Rocco and his men scattering among the people near the inn.

What was usually a place of raucous music, voices, and fighting, the inn stood quiet in the morning light. Rocco walked in, checking the room, and followed closely by Chunk. A rail-thin man was setting mugs on the shelf, bald with a long gray mustache.

"Good morn," Rocco called. "Is there bread and meat to be had here?"

The man smiled at them, showing a significant lack of teeth. "Always, m'lord, always."

Rocco and Chunk sat at a table near the bar and kitchen, their backs to the wall. The innkeeper disappeared into the back and returned with a board of crusty bread and dried meats.

"To drink?" he asked.

"Cider," Rocco said, while Chunk requested rum at the same time.

"Oh. Oh, yes. Cider," Chunk corrected himself.

The man returned with a pitcher and two mugs. "Help yerself, gents. Name's Ernesto if you need anything else."

"Thanks, Ernesto. I'm Julian and this is my friend Miguel." Rocco cut a piece of bread and loaded it with meat, looking at Chunk to do the same.

"Cap'n," Chunk whispered. "Don't we wanna—"

"We will, Chunk." Rocco patted his arm. "Patience."

Ernesto continued his morning chores, glancing at the two every once in awhile. When they were almost finished with their meal, he said, "If you're interested, I do have a fish stew that should be ready."

"Yes," Rocco said. "We are waiting for *El Buscador* to dock, so we have nothing to do except eat."

"You have someone on the ship?" Ernesto dug two bowls out and wiped them with a cloth. "I do not think I've seen you before."

"We came in on an earlier ship last week and are meeting my friend, who has cousins here." Rocco said. "Perhaps you know of someone named Vaishya, or Simone?"

Ernesto leaned down to put the bowls of stew on the table. "Let us be honest men. I know you to be Rocco the pirate, along with your first mate. I do not care, but I will not help you find someone you intend to harm."

"Understood." Rocco smiled. "We wait for the ship because it may carry a young woman and her partner, Ruhee Vaishya and Amoy Simone. They have stolen a baby and were on *El Buscador* but might have escaped the ship in a dinghy. We mean them no harm."

Chunk gave Rocco a sharp look. "No, we jus' want the child back."

"I see. The name Ruhee is not known to me, but I have met Amoy Simone many times, much to my grief. She bullies me into giving her free food and drink, starts fights, and is generally disagreeable. I should not mind if you meant her any harm." He shook his head. "Haven't seen her since monsoon season."

"Thank you, Ernesto." Rocco stacked coin on the table and stood.

"If I see her again, I shall run up my flag," he said, pointing to a yellow and white triangle. "I will try to delay her, or at least watch her departure carefully."

Rocco nodded and motioned to Chunk. "Let's go."

They stepped out of the inn and strode toward the main street.

"Where to next?" Chunk asked.

"It is against my every desire," Rocco said. "But now we wait. We've searched their ship, we cannot possibly find a small boat in a large ocean, so we must trust that sooner or later they will land."

The two men turned toward north, toward their ship. As they passed a narrow side street, Oleta appeared.

"Any news?" Rocco asked.

"There is a girl here," Oleta said, "She thinks she might know Ruhee. The last name wasn't familiar to her, but there is a Ruhee who purchases herbs and powders from her."

"She had plenty o'those last time I saw 'er," Chunk said.

"But I did find someone to help with the search," Oleta said.

Rocco looked past her to see Lisette trotting toward him. As he opened his arms, she broke into a run. He embraced her as if molding her into his own flesh, running his hands down her spine and around her waist. She nestled her face into his neck and sighed.

"Together," she exhaled. Her head tilted upward, and he felt her lips warm on his ear. "We will find her."

He nodded and released her, allowing his hands to drift to hers and hold on. "The innkeeper knows Amoy and will watch for her."

"I suppose she and Amoy could have parted." Lisette frowned.

Rocco looked at Lisette. "Something tells me you don't think Ruhee is coming here."

"This will sound odd," Lisette told them. "Since early

in my pregnancy, visions of Alara have appeared to me. She would speak of things that were to be, and that would happen. I had such a message from her as I traveled here."

Chunk looked confused, but Rocco and Oleta nodded and bade her continue.

"She told me she was safe and in the arms of a friend, but she also said how much she hated Ruhee." Lisette stared at Rocco. "Wherever Ruhee is, there is another person with her, someone Alara knows and likes."

"But who could that be?" Oleta asked. "Who would Alara know and trust? She is but weeks old."

"It would not be Amoy," Rocco said. "The cabin boy of *El Buscador* told us an old woman was also missing from the ship. I found this in her cabin." He held up the purple feather.

"An old woman," Lisette said, looking at Rocco. "It might just be an old woman sailing on the ship, but Alara said she was a friend. Could it be…?"

Heavy footsteps at a run made them all turn. Georgio, the man assigned to search *El Buscador* scurried to them.

"Cap'n, I bring news!" In between panting, he said, "The ship is here. I didn't see Ruhee or Amoy leaving, so I went down to the cabins agin. I was in the old woman's room when one of the crew come in to clear out all the woman's things. Told me he spoke with her often. Her name was Kurta. Kurta Rici."

"Kurta Rici?" Oleta asked, laughing. "Kurtarici is the Turkish word for *rescuer*."

"Rescuer?" Rocco turned to Lisette.

She pointed to the feather and nodded. "Our baby is with Lamya."

"Any news?" Begum had joined them. "I'm afraid I tried at the shops without luck."

"We may have had good fortune," Rocco said, and filled her in on what they discovered. "I admit, it is calming to believe she's in Lamya's hands."

"She is the only one Alara could count as a friend," Lisette agreed. "Still, I am restless without having her back in my arms."

"Of course," Begum said. "What do we propose to do now?"

"We must decide where these women and the baby might be," Rocco told her. "Lamya would not come here, not when Île des Anciens is so close, and according to Lizzie, Alara is with 'a friend.' So are Ruhee and the baby with Lamya on Île des Anciens, and Amoy gives chase? Or do Ruhee and Amoy chase Lamya and Alara?"

Lisette shook her head. "I think the best course of action is for Captain Derya and her crew to continue to wait on this island for Amoy or Ruhee, while Rocco and I head to Île des Anciens."

"Yes," Rocco said. "If Alara's on that island, you and I will know how to find her."

Ruhee sat at the bow of the dinghy staring at Kurta's back. The old woman propelled the small boat through the water with the oars, her humped back now straight and her gnarled hands belying her strength.

They had been asea for hours. Ruhee watched the sunrise, noted the light growing and sun inching higher and higher. The air grew warm as the day progressed, although the steady breeze kept her from being roasted.

"Keep watch on the baby," Kurta told her. "Check her face and feet. She should not be overheating."

Alara lay quiet in Ruhee's arms, something Ruhee should have welcomed, but each time she looked down to smile or coo to the baby, Alara frowned and threatened to wail.

Ruhee shook her head. This baby was but weeks old. She should not have this level of understanding, this awareness. Granted, she had not taken care of many babies, but none cared who held them as long as they were fed and dry.

Rocco's transformation surged across her mind. He was a dragon. She shuddered and opened Alara's blankets, remembering the small feather she'd found inside. Feathers were nothing, a trifle, usually. But this baby had a father who could turn into a feathered beast. Amoy's words came back to her. Perhaps they should have tossed the child.

"You are quiet, child," Kurta said. "But I sense you have questions."

"No," Ruhee blurted, a bit too quickly. "I am…uneasy. My plan was to sail to Isla del Lagarto and meet…my relatives. My choice of traveling companion was a poor one, and now I pay the price. Where are we going, and how shall I get to my destination?"

"Do no worrying." Kurta kept her steady motion with the oars. "Soon we will be in a safe place, on land with plenty to eat and drink. I am positive that within a few days, a ship will stop and give you passage."

The old woman stopped her efforts and turned to look northeastward. She pointed. "That is where we are headed."

Ruhee turned to follow her gesture and saw an island, upright as if only the top of it poked up from the sea. All of the islands were lush and green but this one was remarkable for the depth of its hues.

"Why did we row so far south of it?" Ruhee asked.

"The beach landing is on the other side," Kurta told her. "We cannot land on the side toward Isla de la Soledad."

Ruhee nodded. "How long until we reach shore?"

"By sunset." Kurta rose carefully and drew items from her bag, placing them at the stern. "Here is the bubby-pot with just enough milk to see Alara off to sleep.

And a clout for changing—I am certain she is wet. I will lay down a few silks for you two. The sun is still harsh, but you and the baby should sleep. The bottom of the hull is not as quiet a ride, but there is more room for you to stretch out."

Ruhee held the baby and gingerly made her way from the bow, to the midsection of the boat where Kurta had spread silken sheets. Once seated in their midst, she took the pot and offered it to Alara. The baby made a face but put her lips on the cloth-covered tip and suckled. Ruhee frowned.

Kurta had picked up the oars again. "Is the baby not eating?"

"She is eating. Is it possible for a baby to be—more than a baby?"

"I am afraid I do not understand."

"This child is mere weeks old and should not be mindful of where it is or who it is with, so long as it is comforted. I would swear before God that—Zaina—scowls when she sees me and coos when she is with you." Tears popped from Ruhee's eyes and ran down her cheeks. "When I offered her the pot, her entire face told me she was only taking it because she was hungry, and that she would like to refuse anything offered from my hands."

"You are right, she is a baby and too new to know what she likes or dislikes." Kurta chuckled. "But sometimes God has his little laugh with us."

"Well, I do not think it is funny." Ruhee watched Alara finish her meal and placed her down to change her clout. As she unfolded the blankets, a feather fell out. It caught the wind and lifted into the air. Ruhee reached up to catch it, but it sailed up and over to Kurta's lap, dropping down to land softly in the crease of the old woman's dress.

Ruhee held her breath.

Kurta kept rowing, oars gliding, sinking, pulling, and

gliding again. She glanced down at the feather, grinned, and gazed up at the sky. "What kind of bird flies over us today? It leaves a most unusual feather."

"I…do not know." Ruhee finished changing Alara, rinsing the used clout over the boat's edge. She tried to be vaguely interested in the feather, but Kurta's silence bore into her as if the old woman awaited much more from her. She blurted, "There are parrots on some of these islands, perhaps it is from one of those."

Ruhee's hand drifted to her forehead and wiped at the sweat on her hairline, trembling. Self-conscious, she lowered it quickly and fussed with Alara's blankets. A tiny hand escaped from the swaddling and pushed against Ruhee's efforts. The baby's frown convinced her to stop. In that instant, she knew.

Alara will not learn to love me as her mother—she will actively fight me.

"Lie down, Ruhee," Kurta said. "We have a few hours until we are at the beach, and I would want you rested. I will need help setting up our camp."

"Yes." Ruhee placed the baby on top of the bedding and curled up beside her. Alara whined, stopping only when Ruhee scooted away from her. Ruhee closed her eyes, her tears running onto Kurta's fine silk.

Her dreams were trips into the worst outcomes of her choice. Rocco appeared, beautiful and desirous, reaching out for her and the baby. Instead of embracing them both, he tore Alara from her arms, his rage transforming him again. She backed away, a scream caught in her throat as his talons closed around her and all turned black.

Her next vision was on the *Dişi Aslan*. She had somehow escaped Rocco and now stood on the deck, among her crewmates. They gathered around her, although no one spoke. The group parted and Captain Derya came toward her.

"Ruhee, you stole something of great value to many

people. What is your excuse?"

She lifted her chin. Surely the captain would understand. "My love for Rocco is sincere and unyielding. I believe that Lisette de Lille will not be an adequate mother—she is torn between the world of pirate and nobility and her child will suffer. I offer Rocco a true pirate's wife, raising a pirate child."

"Love has its way of beguiling us. It asks that we sacrifice our reason and submit to its demands." Begum nodded to the crew. Four women stepped forward and held Ruhee by the arms. "But we must say no when it orders us to cause pain. No *Dişi* sister betrays another. That is the rule. You have taken Lisette's child and caused her anguish. You attempt to take her lover, though that would never come to pass. I'm afraid the cost of your actions is steep, Ruhee. You are no longer a *Dişi* sister."

Oleta stepped beside the captain, holding a torch and a large broadsword. She handed the blade to Begum, who walked toward Ruhee as the four women held her left arm down on the rail. Begum touched Ruhee's wrist with the sword before raising the blade high.

"You will no longer wear the sign of the lioness," she said.

A harsh bump of the boat combined with sheer terror jerked Ruhee awake.

"No, captain!" she mumbled as she opened her eyes and realized where she was.

"A bad dream?" Kurta was stepping out of the boat and into the shallows. "It is of no consequence. Come, help me pull the boat ashore."

Ruhee nodded and rose quickly, hopping overboard and steadying her side of the dinghy while tugging it onto the sand and away from the soft waves. Kurta kept pulling and insisting, until the boat was under the thick mangrove that grew everywhere. At last, she appeared satisfied and plucked the baby from the boat.

"Now, you will go up that path," she gestured to Ruhee, handing her a cloth bag. "On the left is a coconut tree. Under the tree are wild yams. Bring me two coconuts and four yams."

"If you know where they are, wouldn't it be faster for you to retrieve them?"

Kurta gave her an icy stare. "Can you light a fire and get the camp ready for sleep tonight?"

Ruhee lowered her eyes. "No." She turned to the path and stepped, hesitating, toward the interior of the island. Dragging one small foot after the other, she trudged up the trail.

"The faster you walk, the sooner your task is finished," Kurta said as she gathered dried wood and leaves. "There are things in the dark that you should not want to meet."

Ruhee's stroll became a stride, and a trot as she scurried away to find food. She'd been running over a kilometer when she saw a tall, curving palm tree. As she approached, there were several brown-husked balls on the ground. Picking one up, she shook it. No, these were too ripe and would not have enough milk. She looked up at the fronds hanging with fruit and sighed.

Sticking her dagger between her teeth, Ruhee wrapped her arms about the tree, finding fingerholds in the rough bark that ringed the trunk. Taking a small leap, her feet dug into the bark, and she worked her way up to the fruit, much like an inchworm moving her arms and her feet and her arms again.

Each reach upward scraped her palms and the insides of her arms. Each thrust of her body and grasp of her feet was like being dragged across a splintered deck. Thankfully the sun was sinking softly behind the grove of trees, but there was no breeze to give her respite. The sweat running down her brow mixed with the tears that flowed down her cheeks until she didn't know whether she was crying or overheating.

I do this for a baby who hates me. That baby is bewitched. No Christian baby would look at me with such evil in its eyes. Born of a dragon-man, what else is there to expect? No, Rocco would be better off without this baby. It will steal his immortal soul.

Ruhee reached the top of the tree and thumped on a nearby fruit. It made the swishing sound of liquid inside, so she cut its stem and let it fall to the ground. Kurta said two, so she thumped a few more until she found a nice full one and cut that down, too. From her vantage point, she took a look around before descending.

This island was unknown to her, its mountains of green that rolled down to the sea. The small beach where Kurta brought them appeared to be the only place to land. To her left, in the distance stood a plateau of reds and oranges, glowing in the setting sun like a torch being lit against the darkness. Ruhee remembered the old stories she had heard about such a mount in an old and dangerous place. What had they called it? She remembered with a gasp—Jazirat Mashur—Bewitched Island!

She half-scrambled, half-fell down the tree, her heart racing. A cursed child on an island of magic, and that old woman—who was she?

I must escape. I shall pretend that all is well and then tonight I shall take the boat and escape. That demon child can stay with her demon nurse.

Hand over her heart, she waited until her breath slowed and calm washed over her. Walking around the base of the palm trees, she quickly discovered the dark, heart-shaped leaves she sought, and pulled several yams from the ground. She placed the two coconuts in her bag, then the yams, and headed back down the trail.

Kurta had built a fire and sat with Alara, rocking her body back and forth, staring at the baby as if in conversation. Ruhee felt a chill run down her neck.

"I have what you requested," she said, holding up the bag.

"Ah, that is good." Kurta smiled. "I have fresh water

to rinse the yams for roasting. Come. I will help.”

Kurta laid the baby down in a nest of silky covers, leaving her unswaddled. Alara stretched her legs up and reached out with unsteady hands, apparently fascinated by her own toes. It was a typical move for an infant, yet it troubled Ruhee.

She shook her head. *Everything about that baby troubles me.*

“Why do you scowl so?” Kurta dunked the yams in a small bowl of water, running her hands across the skins until they were clean. “Do no worrying. Tomorrow we climb to the crest where you can hail the ship that will soon pass.”

"Where *I* can hail the ship? What about you?" Ruhee took Kurta's large straight blade—where had that been hiding? She raised it to cleave open a coconut, was reminded of her dream, and faltered, allowing the blade to glance off the tough hull and slice a small cut on her left wrist. Dropping the sword, she grabbed at her arm in pain and looked at it. Blood bubbled from a scrape across the lioness' mouth.

She tried not to let it have meaning but everything now had meaning and this meaning was clear: she was a liar.

"Let me see your wound." Kurta had come to her side. "You are tired and distracted."

Ruhee held her wrist to the old woman and turned away, tears standing in her eyes. She could not bear to accept this woman's care of her. There was a pressure against her wrist and cold water and a stinging oil, and finally a warm wrap.

"It is well," Kurta said. "Go tend to the yams while I open the coconut. Alara will need her dinner."

Ruhee walked to the fire and put the yams close to the edge, then picked up a forked stick to keep the yams rolling and cooking through. She glanced at the baby again, who was happily cooing at her own feet.

Kurta came to the fire with bowls and two bags, one small and leather and the other larger and cotton. She rolled the yams from the fire and into the bowls, where she mashed them with mangoes and other fruit that Ruhee did not recognize.

"These grow on this island and are very good at filling the growling stomach," she said, handing a bowl to Ruhee. "Eat, please."

Ruhee took the food, picking up the pieces, sniffing them and touching her tongue to them.

"Eat." It was less of a request this time. Kurta took a piece to eat while she warmed the leather pouch over the fire. At last, she picked up the baby and found a comfortable place to sit, leaning against a large hunk of driftwood, her bowl of food next to her and Alara cradled in her arms. She stretched fabric over the pouch's opening and offered it to Alara, who suckled eagerly. "When you and Zaina have finished your dinner, you can sit with her by the fire and get to know one another better."

Ruhee noted Kurta's face becoming more wrinkled as night moved in and the low flames highlighted the skin at the top of the crevasses. Her hazel eyes were dark in the firelight, black and impenetrable, and her mouth in a permanent state of finding something amusing. The baby inclined in the crook of her arm, eyes closed and hands tapping on the leather as she drank whatever potion Kurta had concocted.

What if Kurta was feeding the baby something that

made the baby love the old woman and hate her? Ruhee held her bowl in midair, watching the pair and wondering. Maybe this could be saved.

"I should like to know what you feed the baby," Ruhee said. "It will help me take care of her when our ship comes."

Kurta did not answer, being in deep concentration with the baby, wiggling the bag and smiling at her fingers grasping at the creases. At last, she wiped Alara's face before raising her to her shoulder and patting her back.

"It is easily done," she said at last. "The coconut milk is filling, along with the strained mango and yam for growth and strength. Of course, you will be with the baby's auntie soon, yes? She will have what the baby needs."

"Yes, the baby's auntie…" Ruhee trailed off. "But I thought I saw you put some dried herbs in the milk as well."

"I did." Kurta kept rubbing and patting Alara, until Ruhee heard a small burp. "Turmeric root and caraway seeds, to relieve gas and feed the blood."

"Turmeric and caraway," Ruhee repeated. "Nothing else?"

"Oh, no. Babies are delicate things. Even the herbs I give her are in small amounts—pinches, so that I don't overwhelm her young body." She rose and gestured to where she'd been sitting. "Come, sit here. I will change Zaina and give her to you to hold."

Alara was smiling and chasing the large pendant worn around the old woman's neck. That Kurta wouldn't reveal everything in the baby's milk was no surprise. Who else would have brought them to a bewitched island except a witch? A witch who could easily cast a spell on a helpless baby—it was like having a blank page of paper to write upon.

"If you do not mind, I'm very tired," Ruhee told her.

"I think I would rather sleep."

Kurta smiled. "Of course. Get your rest. I will watch over Zaina."

Ruhee nestled into the silks, drawing them around her until her face was partially hidden. She made a pretense of closing her eyes and slowing her breathing, all while leaving her eyes open enough to watch.

The fire was dancing lower now, crackling at the edges. Kurta knelt on the other side of the flame, fussing with fabric, and humming a quiet song, no doubt to the baby. She leaned down to the baby's face and kissed it before scooting over and settling into her own bed space, still humming.

Ruhee's eyelids grew relaxed. Kurta's song was lulling her to sleep. She took one last deep breath before sinking into her dreams. As she released her mind to slumber, she heard Kurta whisper, "Sweet dreams, my Alara."

Did Kurta call the baby by its real name? Or am I dreaming?

The moon was a high sliver when Ruhee awoke. She sat up, looking at the sleeping forms of the old woman and baby. They appeared sweet in the slender light, not like the demons she suspected them to be. Rocco's child—she had such plans. She would be the perfect mother and Rocco would love her, if only for that, and she would bear him more children, as many as he desired because she would never tire of laying with him and receiving his love.

But this baby was hateful. She would never accept Ruhee and would drive a wedge between her and Rocco. The question was, should the baby and old woman remain here, or should they both perish? Even if they attracted a ship, what lies would Kurta spread?

She might convince them to throw me overboard. Ruhee shook her head. *Better to cut my losses and leave this place. If Captain Derya doesn't know, if she doesn't find out, I can return to the crew.*

Ruhee crept from her bedding and softly made her way down the short beach to the mangrove where the dinghy was hidden. As she moved, she kept looking at the sleeping pair, and listening for Kurta's deep breathing. At last out of their view, she hurried to the grove and reached underneath to ease the boat from its spot.

Their dinghy was gone.

"What does this *Lamb-yah* look like?" Chunk asked.

Lisette laughed, remembering all of Lamya's guises. "She looks like whatever is needed. I suspect at the moment she looks like a harmless old nanny."

"No doubt." Rocco looked at Lisette. "I agree, we should let Begum and her crew remain here. They know Ruhee better and might guess wisely at where they might find her."

"You and I will visit Îles des Anciens." Lisette nodded. "If this old woman is Lamya, I'm certain she could pilot a dinghy home, one way or another."

"We will comb this place," Begum said, gesturing to Oleta. They turned to leave up the path.

"Wait." Lisette stopped them. "I need to speak with Begum, alone."

There were frowns of curiosity among everyone in

the group except Captain Derya. She joined Lisette, walking back down the side street toward the inn. When they were well away from the crew, Lisette reached into her pocket, fingering the pages of the journal entry she'd torn out.

"My thoughts right now are consumed with my daughter and her rescue, but I must ask you a question and I trust you to give me truth." Lisette took the journal pages out and handed them to the captain.

Begum took the papers from her but did not look at them. "What is it you wish to know?"

"Are you my mother?"

Begum looked at the pages, her hand running across the ink as if to absorb the words through her fingertips. She folded the papers and handed them back to Lisette.

"You are correct, we must talk about this, but now is not the time. I was young and had just signed aboard the *Dişi Aslan*." She touched her wrist. "The ink was not yet dry on my tattoo when you were born."

"Why did you not tell me?" Lisette asked. "When I first joined your crew?"

"There was nothing to tell," Begum said. "You were the daughter of a duke. You deserved a better life than at sea, surrounded by pirates who risk their lives for plunder."

Lisette held out her arm and turned it over, displaying the tattoo on her own wrist. "And yet, here I am."

Begum took her hand, closing the other over her tattoo. "Someday I will attempt to explain myself, but at the moment, we must find your daughter—my granddaughter. As you search, always know that I did not give you away out of shame or for lack of love."

Tears gathered in Lisette's eyes and trickled down. She made no move to wipe them away. Nodding, Lisette looked at Begum, noticing the first time how Begum's green eyes had gold flecks, and how large Begum's teeth were and how much she actually resembled Begum Derya and not Juliette de Lille.

Although Begum could be kind, she was not soft nor given to physical affection. Still, Lisette could not hold back and reached out to give her a quick hug. She was surprised to feel the captain's hands pressing her back in response.

"Go now," Begum said, pulling away and taking her by the shoulders. "You and Rocco have a journey to make."

Lisette nodded and turned away to rejoin Rocco and Chunk. She glanced over her shoulder to see Begum's face. There was a light, a sparkle to the captain's visage and her mouth, while open, turned up at the corners. Lisette smiled back and turned to run ahead.

Rocco took her hands. "What secret binds you to Begum?"

"I will tell you soon, but first we must fly to Lamya."

"Fly?"

"It is faster than even your ship could deliver us."

He frowned and shook his head. "True, but I have not changed into a dragon since the night of the battle. I do not know how this dragon works."

"I feared as much." She stared at him. "It took me many lessons with Lamya to learn to transform into a moon dragon."

"A moon dragon? Is that what I've become?"

"I do not know, but I'm certain Lamya can help us sort it all out."

"If'n you'll pardon me," Chunk interrupted. "I may have had my fill of dragon talk."

"Sorry, Chunk." Lisette laughed and turned back to Rocco. "What are our choices? I fly alone to the island and hope you are not far behind? If I fly and wait for you, I might as well sail with you."

Rocco shrugged. "Then sail with me. We will travel to Île des Anciens as quickly as the wind can take us, and along the way, you help me figure out this new power of transformation, if indeed it is a power I am meant to keep."

"It must be," Lisette said. "Our daughter will need two parents with special skills to raise her. Let us hurry to your ship. I will be glad to sail on *L'Implacable* again, even under these circumstances."

They strode down the path toward the sea and the bay near the inn and away from the port, where ships of undeclared country anchored. Lisette remembered this route well, as the path she walked up with Rocco to the dilapidated boarding house. He sold her to Viscount Barragan that night, walking away with a pouch of coin. She killed the viscount soon after and ran away with a bag of both coin and jewels.

Lisette fingered the emerald at her neck, now heavy with the weight of revelation about who she really was. What would Rocco say when she told him that she was Begum's daughter? *When the time is right for that discussion, I'll know it.*

They quickly caught up to Chunk and scrambled over the rocky barricade to the beach. Lisette recalled her own journey, falling on the rocks in the dark, bruising her legs and hands, yet continuing on, determined to get back to Rocco. It was as if she loved him even then.

She felt a hand at her elbow and looked over to see Rocco helping her navigate the uneven boulders.

"You look surprised," he said.

"A year ago, I would have expected aid. Having spent time as a pirate, I do not enlist help outside of battle."

Once over the rocks, they made their way to the dinghy and set off, Chunk's strong back and arms pushing the oars through the water at a rapid pace. *L'Implacable* sat quiet and waiting, and Lisette wished she could fly them to the ship, then fly the ship to Lamya.

"I feel your desire to find Alara," Rocco told her, putting his hand on her shoulder, and running it down her back. "Ruhee cannot hide forever, and if she is with Lamya, we know she has the Ancient One's protection."

"You are right." She sat back, aware of her stiff posture. "I thought danger had passed and that my new adventure—our new adventure would be raising a daughter with special talents." She reached in her bag and withdrew the small feather. "Can our baby already transform?"

"If she can, it will be quite a surprise to Ruhee." Rocco shook his head. "I feel I am at fault in this. I did not make my rejection of her clear, as she is young, and I wanted to spare her. I merely dodged her attempts to beguile me."

"And I believed she had accepted the way things were, even if she was still unhappy about it. The night I had Alara, she saved my life. She could have easily taken the baby and left me to bleed."

"I understand less than you," Rocco told her. "But here, we are at the ship. We will be away soon."

Confused and frightened, Ruhee crept back to the camp and her bedding. It did not appear that Kurta or the baby had stirred. She lay back, attempting sleep while her mind retraced the afternoon. Kurta had directed the placement of the boat, requiring that it be pulled into the mangrove. Ruhee suspected it was to be hidden for a reason. She could not believe it was pirates, and Kurta made no mention of the inhabitants of this island…or did she?

There are things in the dark you should not want to meet.

Ruhee opened her eyes and studied the darkness. The fire had died to embers, just enough to cast fuzzy shadows on the sand around it. She looked up at the sky for solace, but the stars were filtered through silver whisps of clouds, along with a sliver of moon. Kurta's slow, solid breathing was the only noise—even waves did not lap this beach.

As she listened to the rhythmic breaths, Ruhee's conscience lay like an anvil in her gut. *I am not guilty! I am in love, and love is more important than anything. Even death.*

The morning light struck brutally, appearing on the horizon of sea, and glinting off the water. Ruhee's eyes stung as if pierced by flame and she pulled the silks over her head to stop the onslaught. She could hear Kurta stirring. Through the fabric she saw the old woman sit up, stretch, and look down at the infant sleeping next to her.

"Ah, Zaina, do you wake for breakfast?" Kurta asked.

The baby cooed its response.

"Ruhee? Are you awake? Would you like to feed Zaina?"

Ruhee sighed. It would do no good to feign sleep. "I am awake," she said, rising. "The sun blinds on this beach."

"Yes, but we will not tarry here. We eat and then move to a place that provides a lookout for ships, as well as a more hospitable environment."

"On this island?" Ruhee was hoping Kurta would say no, somewhere else, another, nicer, less bewitched island.

"Yes, child." Kurta seemed almost amused. "Please gather more wood for the fire while I prepare the food for cooking."

Ruhee stood, looking around her, wondering where to find wood.

"I'm certain there are dead and dried sticks from the mangrove," Kurta said. "Back where we stored the boat."

"But—" she stopped herself from protesting that the boat was not there, instead turning toward the mangrove to search for firewood. She could feign enough shock to alert Kurta to her discovery.

The grouping of mangrove trees appeared ancient in the light, their exposed roots so tangled among each other that they might as well have belonged to a single trunk.

There was a good amount of discarded pieces that had died and fallen from the mass. Ruhee cupped her skirt as a sack and picked up both large and small sections to feed their fire. She rounded the base of the first set of roots, looking into the space where the boat had been.

It was there.

She was so surprised, she sat on the sand, scraping her arm on one of the roots as she did. Last night she remembered coming this way, climbing over the first group, creeping up the sand, putting her hands out to feel the hull that wasn't there. She even pushed into the space, thinking the boat had eased itself back further. Had she dreamed it all?

Standing up, she shook the sand from her clothes, picked up the wood again, and headed back to camp. This place was evil, and people who willingly visited it had to be demons and witches and worse. She needed to leave.

"Ah, good," Kurta greeted her return. "You have a good eye for what burns. Put them on the embers."

"I don't see much glow from last night's fire."

"It will be well. You will see."

Ruhee placed the wood on the old, blackened site, stacking the pieces methodically.

"Perhaps you can get a few mangos from that tree." Kurta pointed, her suggestion sounding more like a directive.

Ruhee walked to the green, long-leafed trees that rose in a clearing off the trail. She picked three, feeling their ripeness to get the best fruit. Turning around to return to camp, her eyes widened, as the wood she had just stacked was now ablaze.

"The fire didn't take long," she said.

"As I said, you have a good eye for wood." Kurta's response sounded calm, reasonable, but Ruhee sensed an underlying meaning, as if the old woman was having a joke at her expense.

"And you have a way with fire."

Kurta made no answer, but simply said, "Eat."

Ruhee peeled a mango for herself and looked at the bowl Kurta offered. It appeared to be yams and some kind of riced starch. "What is this?"

"Yam and malanga, chopped. I found a few plants in that glade and dug up their roots."

"I recognize the yam, but…malanga?" Ruhee picked up a bite-sized hunk in her fingers, looked at it, smelled it, and put it back in the bowl, preferring to eat her mango.

"You refuse food?" Kurta asked. "Malanga is good for keeping your stomach full, and the yams give you energy. We have a long climb today, and mangos will not sustain your body to accomplish the task."

"I will be fine. I am not hungry."

"At least have some coconut milk." Kurta held out a leather pouch. "It will give you nourishment."

"No!" Ruhee waved her away. "I do not want what you offer."

Kurta sat back with a smile slowly spreading. "You no longer trust the old lady who saved you and the baby from Amoy Simone's plot to kill you."

"You saved me, yes, but for what?" She felt her heart palpate and her hands shake. "I recognize this island, it is cursed! People come here and never leave as people again! It is bewitched, and you have spells that can make that baby love you and hate me. You will take me up that trail and kill me or turn me into something horrid!"

Kurta laughed, a long, hearty, terrifying bellow that startled Alara, who cried. "My apologies, Ruhee—and Zaina—I did not mean to frighten. It is that I am amused by your belief, that I would be this evil witch who desires ill for you." She stopped to comfort the baby. "I saved you and I saved the baby because that is my desire, to help others. This island is just an island. The rumors and legends that accompany it are only because it is so uninhabitable.”

“But how would you know about this island if no one can live on it?”

“Because I am old and have had many adventures, good and bad. I was once shipwrecked and abandoned here, and of necessity had to find a way to live until another ship could rescue me. I found a cliff that looks out on the trade route and was able to flag down a passing vessel. My only plan is to take you to that cliff so that when the next ship sails past you can signal them and leave.”

“With the baby?”

“Of course, with the baby.”

Ruhee frowned. “The baby who hates me.”

“We have discussed the baby’s discomfort with you,” Kurta said softly. “She is unsure of you because you are unsure of her.”

“No.” Ruhee shook her head. “I see the hatred in her eyes when she looks at me.”

“You imagine it.” The old woman rose and walked to Ruhee. “Here. Take her. Hold her. Tell her that you love her.”

Ruhee flinched but held her arms out cautiously as Kurta laid the baby into them. She looked down at Alara, who gazed up at her as if waiting.

“Good…good baby.” Ruhee forced words from her throat. “You…are very…nice.”

“That is not enough. You must tell her ‘I love you.’”

She took an enormous breath and stuttered, “I…love…you.”

Alara stared at her a moment, glanced toward Kurta, and settled into Ruhee’s arms, giving her a small grin. Ruhee looked up at the old woman.

“You see?” Kurta said. “You receive what you give.”

Ruhee nodded and stared back at the baby, holding

out her finger for Alara to grab. She sat this way for a few moments, feeling tiny fingers squeeze and pinch while Alara's smile widened.

"Now that your fear has left, you should eat." Kurta offered her bowl. "We still have a long climb."

Ruhee traded the baby for her breakfast and ate. The food was good, and she was hungry. *Perhaps it was all my imagination after all.*

Lisette stood at the helm, watching Rocco and the crew raise anchor, hoist sails, and come about. She considered joining the men hauling the lines out and tightening the braces, but they were all working together as a unit, and she did not want to impair them. It had been a bit of time since she manned a sail.

"Harden up," Chunk shouted to the men at the mainsail. "It can take more wind than yer givin' it."

Rocco stared ahead, turning the rudder to adjust for the breeze and heeling the ship to get as much speed as possible. *L'Implacable* cut through the water and headed southeast, rounding the point of Isla de la Soledad and aiming toward the opposite shore of Île des Anciens. Once they were underway, he turned his attention to Lisette.

"We should make our plan. It will still be two days to get to Lamya."

"Yes, two days with only the hope she has Alara." She frowned. "I have not been wrong about Alara's messages to me before, but I confess I am worried. If she is not on Île des Anciens, I will take wing back to Soledad."

"Understood." He gestured aft. "Should we discuss—everything—in my cabin?"

She gave him a small nod. "We need to talk."

The cabin was almost as she had remembered, at least before she destroyed it the last time she sailed with him.

"I'm sorry I broke so much when I was here last."

"It was my fault, I suppose. I shouldn't have tried to kill you." He wrapped his arms around her, pressing his body forward to mold against hers. "I've missed you."

She melted into him, kissing his neck, her hands embracing his shoulders. Moving her fingers up to tangle into his hair, she turned her head to find his lips with hers. A fire sparked inside her, like her first kiss ever and yet the kiss of old memories. He returned her passion with his own and she had to pull away in both body and spirit.

"We must think of Alara," she whispered.

He laid his cheek against hers. "Yes. I want our daughter back."

Lisette went to the table and sat, while Rocco fetched mugs and ale.

"I would very much like to fly to the island, find Alara, and deliver my punishment as a dragon," he said. "To be honest, I am loathe to put a sword through a woman, even though I was willing to dispatch Mercedes by my own hand."

"I understand your hesitancy. Prior to this, Ruhee was nothing but a sister to me on the *Dişi Aslan*. She even completed my tattoo." Lisette fingered the lioness head on her wrist as she spoke. "But she must either let go of her love for you or die. To be left to live and obsess over you has led her to rash choices."

He took a long draft from his mug. "Let us first think of what we can do as pirates."

"We can sail to the island, let down the boats and search, but I can transform and cover more territory. If this is truly Lamya keeping Alara safe, she has untold magic at her command and could have fashioned a hideaway in truly any spot on the island."

Rocco leaned forward. "How do you transform, if you are not in the moon's grasp?"

She smiled. "It was difficult to learn and took me a long time, and yet it is a simple process. I tell myself that now I am dragon, or now I am human."

"And your body does your bidding?" He frowned and looked at his own torso, closing his eyes for a few moments. "No. No, it does not work that way for me."

"As I said, it is easy to say and difficult to do." She took a drink from her own mug. "Tell me about the battle and your transformation."

"I recall being on the balcony. You were in your dragon form and had killed Mercedes. Alwan stepped forward to kill you—he cut your foot with his blade. I saw the blood and felt the fire within me. That's when I transformed."

Lisette nodded. "And you transformed back when?"

"When I awoke the next morning and wanted to fly to your castle." He chuckled. "It was almost as if as soon as I'd decided to use my dragon body to my advantage, the body was taken from me."

She laughed. "It is exactly like that at first." Over the rum, Lisette explained her journey as a moon dragon, the times she changed without thinking, and the times she changed back at the worst possible moments. "In many ways, being a blood dragon was easy. The best part of being a moon dragon, once I learned to transform, was that I always have my own mind. My anger doesn't cause my dragon to take control."

"But am I a moon dragon?"
"I do not know. I am hoping Lamya can answer that."

26

A knock at the door made Lisette look up. A slender young man entered with a tray of food, followed by Poussin.

"Here, put the tray on the table," Poussin told the boy. "Then bow and git." He looked at Rocco. "Chunk says ya mighten be hungry."

"Poussin." Lisette smiled. "I have missed you. It sounds as if you have grown quite up to man's status."

He blushed down his arms and up to his ears. "Now, miss, don't you—" He glanced at Rocco and flinched. "Thank you, m'lady."

Pushing at the young man's shoulder, Poussin ushered him from the cabin, slamming the door behind them.

"You tease my sailor too much." Rocco shook his

finger at her. "He still pales when your name is mentioned."

Lisette pulled a leg from the roasted chicken and took a bite. "He needs to meet more women."

Rocco sat next to her on the bench and pulled her close. "Or the right one."

She dropped her food and embraced him again. "Now that we know what we shall do to rescue our daughter," she whispered. "Perhaps the food can wait."

He turned toward her, caressing her face, his lips working their way from her forehead down her neck to her breasts. She arched back, offering her body to him with a purring moan.

Another knock interrupted them, this time insistently loud. They both sat up and Rocco snapped, "What?"

Luis entered quickly. "My apologies for the interruption but Chunk sent me with the message—we have company, Captain. A ship is approaching, starboard aft. It appears Spanish, and fleet. I believe it is a warship."

"Let us see who this devil is, then." Rocco gave one glance to Lisette before rising. "And how they dare impede our journey to find our daughter."

As he left with Luis, Lisette jumped from the table and went to the wall across from the bed. She tested several blades that hung there until she found one that she could wield easily and still had its edge. Between that and the dagger on her belt, she felt equipped for fighting.

She opened the door and remembered the first time she stood at the bottom of these steps, blade in hand and wondering if she should join the fray. This time she didn't hesitate. Gripping the sword, she ran to help.

"What are you doing up here?" Rocco scowled as he kept watch on the approaching vessel.

"You wanted all hands on deck," she said with a shrug.

"And you know I didn't mean you."

"I'm a good hand in battle. And if I am outmanned…" She made a pantomime of a wing on her back with her left hand. "I shall defend those I love."

His scowl deepened into something of anger, frustration, and pain. "Would that I could join you. We'd make short work of El Rey's henchmen."

"Leave yourself open to the possibility." She kissed his cheek. "We yet do not know how your transformation works."

"Oy, there, Poussin!" Rocco hailed the lad, who had now taken up his spot in the crow's nest. "Any insignia?"

Poussin pulled the spyglass away from his face and looked down at the captain. "*El Tiburón de Hierro.*"

"The Iron Shark," Lisette repeated.

"Delgado!" Rocco barked.

"Yes, Captain!" Luis ran up from the deck, where he was rolling out one of the guns. "I know the ship. She is new to these waters but has kept a channel open from Europe to the Jamaican territory that pirates cannot penetrate. Her captain is Anselmo Gonzalez—fearless, ruthless, some might say reckless. He will do anything to sink you, even at the cost of his own ship."

Rocco nodded. "He came up quickly and is now pacing us. Waiting for our first move?"

"I would guess yes," Luis said. "He takes his time, determines his foe's fighting method and looks for weakness."

"Then we shall make him work to discover ours." He raised his spyglass and looked at the enemy vessel. His mouth set in a thin stripe and jaw tightened as he handed the spyglass to Luis.

"Middeck. Who do you see?"

Lisette looked over, trying to see what he saw. Activity on the other ship looked quiet, like any other day under sail and not like a ship preparing to battle. Two figures stood at the rail. They were quite a distance away, but she recognized their outlines, their hair, their stances.

"Amoy Simone," she and Luis said simultaneously.

She added, "And Willem d'Auguste."

"I believe this captain will continue his method of battle," Luis said, "but these two add a wrinkle to all."

"Yes," Lisette added. "Amoy is independent, angry and manipulative, and Willem spent his youth doing mischievous deeds. I'd say he is the smartest member of the d'Auguste family."

"He may be smart, but independent women are the worst kind in battle." Rocco gave her a stern glance.

Lisette frowned. "All in keeping with our survival."

"You two may want to save the argument for later," Luis said. "*El Tiburón de Hierro* is getting impatient and closing the distance."

"Yes, but I think we will stretch away a little." Rocco shouted orders to pick up the speed and move the ship north, just enough to stay out of range of the other ship's guns. He beckoned Lisette close and spoke softly. "I believe you are capable of conjuring cloud cover."

"How much and where would you like it?"

The enemy ship was still astern of *L'Implacable*, so she found a quiet spot on the bow. Most of the crew were busy with the guns and running the sheets to stay out of range. Stepping to the point, she looked around. It was a magnificent view of the sea, open water ahead and the rushing sound of the bow punching through the waves. Lisette stood facing the breeze and let the wind ruffle her curls. Heavy footsteps made her turn to see Chunk coming toward her.

"Ah, Lizzie, I need ta tighten the bowsprit. Did Cap'n send ya for the same?"

"No, Chunk, he sent me on a special mission. You may not want to watch."

His eyes widened. "Ah, not that. Pirates fight their way out. We don' depend on dragons."

"Pirates use whatever is at hand, yes?"

He nodded. "I s'pose."

She smiled. "My cloud cover can help you take the enemy by surprise. It's not as much about teeth and talons as it is advantages."

"Oh, all right." His shoulders sagged a little. "But I ain't lookin'."

Nodding to him, she closed her eyes. *I am the dragon.*

The familiar warmth spread through her midsection, with feathers that wrapped themselves around her like an embrace. Within moments she was unfolding her wings, fanning them to know they still worked.

Lisette nodded to Chunk and opened her mouth, exhaling deeply, and emitting a thick curl of fog that rolled over the port side of the bow and moved up and out as she rose into the sky. She was able to take in breath quickly as soon as her lungs emptied to keep the cloud propagating between the two ships, at last completely obscuring *L'Implacable* from view.

Now high above both ships, she could see Rocco's plan. *L'Implacable* slowed, remaining still starboard of *El Tiburón de Hierro* until they were now at the enemy's stern. The captain of the other ship was bellowing orders at his crew, attempting to follow the pirate ship into the fog.

The cloud thinned to a mist and the wisps pulled apart, revealing the ships to each other. *L'Implacable* had come about, and Lisette heard Rocco give the order.

"Fire!"

Five cannons belched flame from the port side of Rocco's ship, exploding into the enemy's vessel and sending smoke and splinters flying from its stern. It was a full hit to the deck and obliterated half of the dinghies aboard.

Captain Gonzalez stood at the helm, screaming orders for his men to come starboard and meet Rocco's cannons with their own response. In the meantime, Rocco steered away from the enemy, tacking to reverse course and aim his starboard cannons while reloading those to port. Sails and rudder took *L'Implacable* to the other ship's port side, where they blasted her again.

Lisette watched the action from above, breathing a cloud to hide behind, and hovering over the ships. Her cloud had thinned when she spied Amoy and Willem at the helm, pointing at her and chattering like two squirrels in a tree. No doubt, they were giving away her secrets.

That won't do.

Just as she saw *L'Implacable* come about and release a full set of cannons at the enemy ship, she banked down and left, arriving to pluck two annoying passengers from the helm as the deck shook with the explosion.

The resulting chaos was so complete, she wanted to tarry and watch. Sailors who pointed toward her were in the next instant thrown forward, chunks of wood impaling their arms and backs. The captain was caught looking up at her when the shots hit—he turned to see smoke billowing from middeck, accompanied by flying wood and bleeding men.

He grabbed the wheel and shouted for the sails to be let out as he turned the rudder. "Come about, and load cannon!"

Men ran everywhere. A few ran toward the mainsail, but Lisette saw what they did not—an enormous crack halfway up. She flew down to the mast and wrapped her back toes around it, giving it a push. The mast fell, taking its sail and lines to the deck in a grand tangle.

The men stood and looked at the toppled mast, a look of surrender in their eyes. The first mate ran toward them, screaming, "If ya ain't dead, get yerself on a gun!"

Lisette resumed her ascent, holding the two squirming foes trying to ruin her life. She regarded them. Thus far, she had held them within her paws, using her claws on their clothes only to secure them. They wiggled a few more moments, until they looked down.

"If we fall, we shall certainly die," Willem said, and propped himself against Lisette's claw.

"What makes you think we'll live through this?" Amoy shouted, before doing the same.

Lisette could hear more cannon fire below, so she looked down. For all of Captain Gonzalez's reputation, his ship now sat without masts and taking water astern. Rocco and the crew were swinging aboard, blades drawn. *El Tiburón de Hierro* and its crew would soon be no more.

Amoy and Willem were once again squirming in her paws. She held them aloft, looking at them both and thinking about Rocco's motto. No survivors, which should mean death for her captives. Still, it was difficult. Her moon dragon instinct was to defend, not attack. And they might have use for these two alive, either for information or leverage.

She looked down at *L'Implacable*. Poussin was at the helm, holding the ship to its line. There were two other sailors standing by the cannons and watching the action, their blades drawn and ready to defend against all invaders. Poussin would have a fit if she landed, possibly refusing to even look in her direction. As for the two others, she remembered their faces but not their names. One was the large man who had lifted her into the dinghy the evening she was sold to the viscount. She could still feel her own lightness from the encounter—he had tossed her into the boat like a sack of grain.

Maybe she could wait until Rocco returned. He would complete his task soon. She was tired, so she softly lit on the deck, folding her wings, and curving her tail around to form a sort of barrier for her prisoners. They both took turns attempting to escape, which made Lisette tighten her claws against them just to the point of piercing flesh.

Amoy lifted her chin, harrumphing. "They seem like tender claws, dragon, unable to do much harm."

Her boast emboldened Willem to struggle harder. "I cut my meat with a longer blade."

Lisette sat up on her haunches to look down at the pair. Opening her mouth into a wide grin, she showed her spectacularly sharp teeth as she produced a low, menacing growl from the depths of her soul. She ran her paw down Amoy's body, to her thigh, where she grabbed the large woman's flesh, sinking her short but razor-sharp talons into her leg.

Amoy howled a piercing cry, wriggling on the end of Lisette's claws like a fish on a hook. Lisette turned to

Willem, adjusting her paw around his waist, and running one claw down his arm, tearing his shirt, and leaving a large scratch to his wrist. Willem shrunk away from her. Lisette could feel his entire body quaking. Wet streaks on his breeches and a puddle on the deck told the truth of his fear.

Amoy's screams brought Poussin, who rounded the corner, took in the sight of a dragon torturing two humans, and gurgled something that sounded like, "Oh, no-no-no." He turned to escape and ran headfirst into the large sailor, who had also been brought by the noise. Poussin bounced off him, tripped on a coiled line, and fell against a cannon where he slumped, unconscious.

Amoy's screams had become moans of ache, punctuated by hurling invectives at her. Lisette glanced at her, looked back up at the sailor, and handed Willem to him.

"Aye, I'll truss 'im up good," the sailor said, gathering a length of rope and fastening Willem to the yardarm. He returned and pointed to Amoy. "Her, too?"

Lisette held the woman out to him, backing her claws from the woman's thigh.

As he reached for her, Lisette curled her tail around them both, looking him in the eye. The sailor paused, his hands firm around Amoy's forearms. Lisette turned to Amoy, staring intently.

I am a woman. She transformed back to her human form.

"You are a demon!" Amoy cried. "A witch!"

"Sailor, I remember you well," Lisette said, ignoring Amoy's insults. "But I fear I do not know your name."

"LeFarge." He gave a small bow.

"You do not seem surprised by my transformation."

"I am Basque, m'lady, raised in Forêt Irati. I have seen dragons and more."

Lisette smiled. "Well, LeFarge, tie that one high."

She gestured to Amoy. "I'm certain she'd like a good stretch before the captain questions her."

Relieved of her captives, Lisette ran to help Poussin, who was now conscious and holding his head. She checked him over, looking for blood or broken bones. He closed his eyes, wincing, as he attempted to sit up. Lisette held his shoulders and helped him recline against the gun that had knocked him out.

"Oh, no, not you," he said, opening his eyes again. "I tole ya, no more dragons."

"My apologies, Poussin, but I'm afraid this is what I am." She stood, helping him to rise and balance. "How do you feel?"

"Hale. I am hale and hearty and don't need no motherin' from you." He pushed away from her and took a step, only to buckle in pain.

She caught him and put his arm around her shoulder. "You might have sprained that foot. Let me help you to your cabin."

"No. I am on duty, and you are keeping me from my post." He hobbled toward the helm, taking her with him.

"Very well, I will help you to the wheel and make certain you can stand."

The young man scowled but accepted her help. They reached the helm, and he took the rope from the wheel and resumed his task, making certain *L'Implacable* kept pace with *El Tiburón de Hierro*. Lisette stood beside him and watched for any sign that he might fall. He kept his injured foot propped on its toes, leaning all his weight to the good leg.

Looking about, Lisette spied a small wooden crate. She grabbed it and put it under his leg for his knee to rest upon. He resisted at first.

"What are ya doin'—ah, yes, this feels better."

Having secured Poussin, Lisette looked about, trying to find Rocco on the enemy vessel. There were no skirmishes left, no screams of dying men. She assumed the crew was now pillaging whatever useful trinkets they could find.

"Aiding Poussin now?"

Lisette wheeled about to see Rocco standing behind her.

Halfway up the trail, Ruhee realized that carrying a baby was harder than carrying a bag full of supplies. The baby was lighter, but pots and pans didn't wiggle.

"How much further?" she asked, trying not to huff her words.

Kurta's voice was as smooth and low as if she was at rest. "The trail is soft and wide. We shall reach the top before dinner."

Ruhee let out a breathy sigh and adjusted Alara, who she had strapped to her back. The baby cooed and gurgled, flinging her arms and legs in random directions. She was in constant motion, making Ruhee adjust her own weight to keep her balance. Even with steady shade from the forest canopy, the sun used every patch of clear sky to beat Ruhee with its heat. Alara did her part to keep Ruhee sweating from top to toe.

When Kurta held her hand up and stopped walking, Ruhee had to lean against a tree to keep from falling to her knees. The old woman walked a small circle, looking around.

"Yes," Kurta said at last. "This is the good place."

"I don't suppose you could set our supplies down and help me get this baby off my back?"

Kurta had put her bag down and was riffling through it, pulling out bowls, and silks. "Mothers have no problems getting their babies from their backs. Think. Figure it out."

Ruhee scowled. This old woman was not as helpful as she pretended. This was not her baby, why should she have to bear the entire burden? Still leaning against the tree, the young woman reached to the knot tied around her chest that kept the baby's sling attached to her.

"You might want to sit down for that," Kurta said, still fussing with their campsite.

"It is too hard to sit."

"It is also too far down for a baby to fall."

Ruhee gave an exasperated sigh and knelt carefully until she could sit her bottom on the ground. It was less of a sit and more of a thump. She untied the sling and swung it around her shoulder, barely keeping Alara upright and off the sand. Catching the baby by the shoulder and waist, she breathed relief and glanced at Kurta.

The old woman had her back to her. "That could have been very bad."

Like Ruhee's mother long ago, Kurta had eyes everywhere to catch her doing something wrong. Ruhee took Alara out of her sling and held her away, curling her nose. "She needs changing."

Kurta tossed her a clout.

"I don't know how to do this."

The old woman stood up, taking the bend from her

spine, and turned slowly to face her. "Ruhee, it is time to be clear. You either want to mother this child or you don't."

"I thought I did…but this baby has been so difficult, I don't know."

"Oh, and is that how you will mother your own children?"

Ruhee frowned. "It is different when they are your own."

"No, it is not different. Many times, it is worse." Kurta leaned upon a large stick she had found. "Mothers think their children will be like them, will love them, and cooperate with them. When they do none of those things, mothers must still raise them, love them. If you want this child, you love her and raise her."

Ruhee lowered her head. Kurta made her feel small, like a child who was bored with her toys. She looked at Alara, now squirming unhappily about her cold, messy bum. Placing the baby on the sling, Ruhee took the clean clout and examined it until she figured out the front from the back and the inside from the outside. Slowly and with much face-contorting and gagging sounds, she managed to clean up the baby and dress her anew. She held out the used clout toward Kurta.

"What do I do with this? We are not in the boat anymore."

Kurta produced a pot. "The lagoon is there," she gestured. "Fill the pot with water. Rinse the clout. Toss the water over by the largest tree—look toward the sunset to find it. Do not throw the water back in the lagoon. Do you understand?"

"Do not throw the water in the lagoon." Ruhee took the pot from her and placed the clout inside. She walked toward Kurta's pointing finger.

"Stop." Kurta's voice was that of a scolding parent. "You must take the baby with you."

"But she is here with you. You can watch her."

"Did you ask me to?"

Ruhee scowled. "No. I did not think I needed to."

"If this is your baby, you need to ask people to watch her for you."

"Very well." Ruhee shrugged. "Will you please watch—Zaina—for me?"

"No, I am too busy gathering food. You must take her with you. Guard her well, there are wild animals that would love a small morsel."

Ruhee walked back to Alara and picked up the sling, trying to settle the baby into the fabric and wrap her upon her back. Alara punched her way out of the sling with tiny hands and feet, a gleeful expression on her face. Ruhee felt a knot of anger in her gut, wishing this child would cooperate.

She grabbed the baby's shoulders with a firm shake. "Will you stay still!"

"Ruhee." Kurta's voice rang loud and rebuking. "You do not. Ever. Shake that baby."

"I don't know how to do this." Ruhee let Alara go and covered her face with her hands.

"Zaina is too awake and active for the sling," Kurta said gently. "Pick her up, put her on your hip and carry her. This is what her mother would do."

Ruhee caught her breath, nodding, and hefted the baby to her right hip, steadying her with a firm arm. Picking up the pot, she walked toward the lagoon.

Like her mother would do.

Beyond the camp and away from the cliff, Ruhee discovered a small body of water, blue as a sunny day and surrounded by flowers and fruit trees. She carefully placed Alara down on a mossy bed, protected by thorny bushes and well within her sight from the water.

"Stay here and be a good baby," she told her.

Alara looked up with large solemn eyes, as if she would take her suggestion into consideration.

Down at the water's edge, Ruhee scooped water into the pot, found a decent-sized rock, and washed the baby's clout. It was unpleasant work and she realized she wouldn't like it any better if it was her own child's filth. Perhaps Rocco would allow her a nanny to care for their children.

Rocco. It had been some time since she dreamt of his face, his strong arms embracing her and keeping her safe.

That day, when she helped him to the chair outside—his arm around her shoulder had sent chills of excitement through her body. He had held himself as aloft as he could, but he clearly needed her aid. It felt magical.

Her memories ran on, to the evening's sunset and watching him twist and contort into a hideous beast. It was of the devil, obviously—he had been cursed. But she could heal him. Of that she was certain.

She held the clout up. It looked clean, so she wrung out the excess water and draped it over a low branch. Kurta had said not to toss this water back into the lagoon, but to dump it at the large tree. She looked around. The largest tree was on the other side of the lagoon, a good distance from the edge.

Ruhee looked down at Alara. She couldn't leave her here while she emptied the pot. Carrying the pot full of dirty water and the baby was going to be so heavy. She was already tired from the long walk uphill in the heat with this child.

Kurta will never know. Ruhee walked to the lagoon's edge and gave the pot a good swing to toss the water as far into the lagoon as possible. As the water left the pot, an impossibly high wave rose from the lagoon, one as tall as her, and deflected all of the dirty water back onto her, completely soaking her hair, her face, and her clothes.

Ruhee screamed, sputtering and looking down at herself. Behind her, she could hear Alara's high-pitched giggling. She wheeled and stared at the laughing infant.

"You think this is funny?"

The baby smiled at her. "Aaahaaah."

Ruhee stood for a few moments, mopping her face with the scarf around her neck and quieting her rage. She strode to Alara, picked her up, and stormed back to camp.

"Ah, good," Kurta said. "The meal is ready."

Ruhee thrust the baby at the old woman. "Would you mind watching Zaina?" she said, biting each word. "I must rinse myself."

She turned to go back to the lagoon. A bath in that clear blue water was needed—a bath for her and her clothes.

"I would not try to bathe in the lagoon," Kurta said. "It has already rejected the water from the pot, yes?"

"How did you—"

"I told you, I spent much time getting to know this island. You will have to put more water in the pot and use that to cleanse yourself."

Ruhee scowled but nodded and walked away.

"And bring the clout back," Kurta called after her.

At the lagoon, Ruhee considered Kurta's instructions. What did Kurta know? It was just water. She stepped one foot into the edge of the lagoon. Nothing happened. She tried the other foot. The water did not respond. Confident that the old woman was teasing her, she walked into the water until it was deep enough to swim.

Even with her clothes on, the water was cool and delightful. It had been a long time since she bathed fully. She rolled from her stomach to her back, running her fingers through her hair. This was luxurious.

At last satisfied, she rolled again and swept her arms out, reaching and kicking for shore. Although she could feel her limbs propelling her, the shore remained the same distance away, and she slowly became aware of the water holding her in one place. Ruhee pushed herself sideways, to try to find and match the current.

It did not matter which way she moved her body. The water held her where it wanted her. Just as she panicked, she felt a large swell over her head, pushing her to the sandy floor of the lagoon. She fought to return to the surface, feeling her breath leave her. In a very few moments, she could feel the both the water rushing into her lungs and the total blackness of death.

She awoke in a clearing, dry and wearing clothes she did not recognize—rags of a beggar. Kurta sat before her, expressionless. Ruhee opened her mouth to give an excuse, but the old woman held up her hand, palm out, to silence her. Kurta stood up, straightened her spine…and kept straightening.

Ruhee watched in horror as the old woman stretched taller and her frail body grew until it was well muscled and substantial. Her face lengthened and pointed, and a slender, forked tongue darted in and out of her mouth. She glared at Ruhee with two silver orbs that burned into her soul.

"Kuaket!" Ruhee gasped. She had heard of the goddess of darkness from her Egyptian mother, but she had not thought of such beings for many years.

"Who are you to steal what is not yours?" Kurta/Kuaket's rumbling growl shook Ruhee's body.

"I-I-I," Ruhee stumbled before kneeling. "I love Rocco and must make him love me."

"And what is your right to do this?"

"Love is my right." Ruhee stood, her head still bowed but blushing with defiance. "Love is everything. Love is all I have, and I will take what's meant for me."

The goddess bent toward her until its burning eyes were a finger's width from the young girl's face. Ruhee could feel the heat of them and shrank away, but they followed, scorching her forehead.

"You will not take it," Kurta/Kuaket said. "You have many choices in this life. Some are good, some are bad." The snake-headed goddess moved away from her, straightening again. "Look up, girl. Look at me."

Ruhee slowly raised her head and opened her eyes to see the sky darken and stars shoot from the goddess' fingers. Each finger's stars grouped together, forming ribbons, and the ribbons forked and split into smaller ribbons.

"This is your life, Ruhee Vaishya. The rivers of stars are your choices and the streams of consequences. They are ever moving, ever reaching across your lifetime—except this one." The goddess highlighted a thick ribbon that turned downward instead of up with no forks. It ended abruptly as if the darkness swallowed it. "This is your choice to hold onto your love for Rocco instead of facing your grief and letting him go. This is your choice to kidnap his child, a special child that you cannot possibly raise, even if you avoided capture. This choice will end you."

Ruhee felt herself being lifted from the ground into the air and pulled toward the ribbon's end. The darkness sucked her into it, and she screamed.

Fear bolted her upright, waking her. She looked around, blinking, and pressing her hand against her chest. This was the camp they'd set up. Kurta sat across from their fire pit, engaging Alara in a game of peek-a-boo. The baby giggled.

"Ah, you are awake," Kurta said. "I guess washing a baby's clout is exhausting."

Ruhee looked down at her clothes. Her shift and cotton dress were clean and dry. Did she spill the dirty water on herself? Did she bathe in the lagoon? Did any of it happen? She sat for several minutes, rubbing her forehead and her eyes.

This island is bewitched. Kurta is a demon, sent to punish me for loving Rocco. And this baby—this baby may lure Rocco to me, but that is where its usefulness ends.

"I suppose I was tired after our walk here," Ruhee told her.

"Of course," Kurta said. "I made us a good meal to keep us strong for the day ahead."

Ruhee stretched her hand out to take the bowl Kurta offered. It was much the same as the last food, with a few new spices. She picked a bite of vegetable and the starchy malanga in her fingers and put them in her mouth. They tasted good, she begrudgingly admitted. Although she attempted disinterest, her bowl was soon empty.

"Good," Kurta said. "This afternoon we create the signal that will alert the next ship." The old woman took Ruhee's bowl and handed her Alara. "Take care of Zaina and I will wash your bowl. You and the lagoon do not seem to get along."

Kurta strolled away, toward the water, leaving Alara in Ruhee's lap. Why would she say that about the lagoon, Ruhee wondered. She looked down at the baby, who smiled at her as if she knew.

Ruhee could have sworn she saw Alara wink.

"Poussin doesn't want my help," Lisette said. "I believe he has injured his leg."

"It's a long way from his heart," Rocco told her, and yelled to the helm, "Poussin! Are you well?"

"Fine, Cap'n," he replied.

"Well, then, shall we interrogate the prisoners?" Lisette asked.

Rocco pointed to Amoy. "Do you expect to get anything but lies from that one?"

"Not without a little help." Lisette dug into her pocket and produced a black bag. "Oleta gave me a little something for times like this."

She shook the bag in her hand, looking at both Amoy and Willem and wondering how to force them to take these leaves—steep a leaf in water and give it to drink, or hold their noses and make them open their mouths?

"What are you looking at?" Willem sneered. "Trying to figure out which one of us to beat first?"

"They ain't strong enough," Amoy joined in.

Lisette smiled. If they were going to be so unpleasant, they did not deserve a cool drink. "LeFarge," she called out. "Can you help me?"

The large man lumbered over.

She nodded toward Amoy's face. "Hold her nose. Tightly."

He did as he was told, and they watched Amoy attempt to get away from him, hold her breath in, and finally open her mouth, panting. Lisette took one of the leaves and stuffed it between her teeth, rubbing it into her tongue and lips as much as she could without being bitten. She left it in there until Amoy drooled and choked.

"Very well, LeFarge, you can release her."

Lisette turned her attention to Willem as she heard Amoy coughing and spitting the remnants out. Gesturing to the young man, she smiled at LeFarge. "Again, please?"

LeFarge was a man of great efficiency and little emotion. He reached across to Willem's nose and held it. Willem was a stronger adversary than Amoy and fought harder to escape LeFarge's pinch. The big man solved the problem by using his other hand to catch the back of Willem's neck, holding him like a cat being thrown into the street.

Lisette took another leaf and repeated the process, leaving Willem sputtering and spitting much like his co-conspirator.

"And now," Lisette said. "We shall have a little talk."

Amoy sneered at her. "I ain't telling you anything."

"That is entirely your choice." Lisette waved the black bag in front of her, turning to Willem to do the same. "But those leaves I gave you have an interesting side effect if you are not truthful."

"Yer witchcraft don't scare me."

"Tell me now, where is my child?" Lisette asked.

"I dumped her over the side of *El Buscador*." Amoy smirked. Seconds later her mouth opened in horror as her eyes bulged red and teary. She shrieked. "Aarraahh! Fire! Aarraahh! My mouth!"

Rocco stepped forward, studying the howling woman. "How is this done?"

"Velvet tongue." Lisette watched her face turn from blush to blood red to purple. "Fascinating, the way it detects falsehoods."

"I must find me this magic plant," Rocco said, his eyes large and a grin spreading across his face. "This is most useful."

Tears, sweat, and snot ran down Amoy's cheeks and chin, mingling into large drops that splattered on the deck. "Make it stop, please God, or kill me!"

"It is easily stopped." As much as she was enjoying the show, Lisette kept her voice calm and reassuring. "Tell me the truth. Where is my child?"

"Ruhee and the old woman took her," Amoy said between coughs. "They stole a dinghy and rowed away." As she spoke, her tears dried and her choking abated. "I tried to stop them—" The fire rose in her face again. "No, no, I didn't try to stop them!" She caught her breath. "I think Ruhee gimme me a potion, but I awoke and followed them in a dinghy. They was rowin' towards Isla de la Soledad but I lost 'em in the fog."

"That wasn't so difficult, was it?" Rocco smiled and turned to Willem. "We come to you now, Marquess d'Auguste. I shall assume you've paid attention to the price Amoy paid for her deceitfulness?"

Willem nodded, his mouth set in a stern line.

"Good. What causes you to be aboard a ship that is hunting *L'Implacable*?" He glanced at *El Tiburón de*

Hierro, now engulfed in flames. "Or *was* hunting us, I should say."

Willem opened his mouth, rolled his tongue across his lips, and sighed. "I was sent on a mission."

Lisette let the silence linger before speaking. "It's good to begin with the truth. Continue."

"My in-laws—that is, my in-laws to be, do not want you to occupy your family castle." He looked down and sighed.

"And?" Lisette prodded.

"The count wants to take the island for Spain. He would prefer to take the island for himself and is depending upon the duke to be easily encouraged to return to Isla de Pimienta. The countess believes you are a demon from hell and would prefer you were destroyed." Willem sighed, as if thankful to not have a mouthful of thorns.

"What do you want?" Rocco asked.

Willem's eyes went wide. "I dare not say, m'lord. I am bound to the count's daughter and therefore must follow his orders to remain in good stead. My opinion on the matter is a blank page—I have not considered the rightness or wrongness of it."

Lisette nodded. "So, if you offer what you think you want, and midsentence decide you do not want it…"

"How will the leaf know that I am not lying?"

"I always suspected you were the smartest one of your family." Lisette turned to Rocco. "I feel the need to keep Willem with us. He might come in handy when we travel back to Île des Oiseaux."

Rocco cocked his head, frowning. "Why would we return to Île des Oiseaux?"

"To encourage the Mendozas' exit," she said. "The duke will then leave, and we will have yet another island under island rule again."

"Why would we want the islanders to rule?"

Now it was Lisette's turn to frown. "Because Spain and France have no business here, taking coin and resources away and giving nothing back."

"Haughty words for a French noblewoman," he sneered.

"At least I am willing to put my nobility aside and do what is right." She stomped her foot in anger. "Why are you so opposed?"

He leaned down until his nose nearly touched hers. "Because I am a pirate. I make my living stripping Spanish ships of their coin and resources. Why would I want them to leave?"

"Must you pirate forever?" Her voice had risen an octave and several decibels. "Other ships are doing honest business with Isla del Lagarto. Can you not change?"

Rocco opened his mouth and froze, a curious expression on his face. Lisette could sense the reason immediately. He shrank back as his body disappeared and feathers reappeared. It took only a moment for him to transform into a dragon, white feathers with red tips.

Poussin screamed as if his voice had never changed. LeFarge looked up at him and shook his head.

"LeFarge," Lisette said, "please get Chunk for me."

The ruddy-faced first mate strode around the corner, took one look at the dragon, and sighed. "Not agin."

"Chunk, I think it's best if you took the helm until we get this…" Lisette motioned toward Rocco, "sorted out."

"Aye, no doubt." He pointed to the two captives, still strung tightly to yardarms. "What to do with these?"

"Stow the man somewhere." Lisette scowled, thinking of her fight with Rocco. "Be careful with him— he is both clever and mischievous."

"What about the wench?"

Lisette looked at Amoy, dried blood caking on her skirt, snot and drool staining her apron. She was a horrid woman who wanted to see Lisette dead or ruined, and yet Lisette still felt the pull of mercy in her heart.

Amoy regarded Lisette, her eyes narrowed. She said nothing, but Lisette could feel the hatred burning bright, as if it was steam building in a pot. They stood for several moments, their eyes locked and staring. Amoy took in a deep breath, and spit at Lisette as hard and far as she could.

Lisette took one step back to avoid it and turned to Chunk. "Drown her."

Chunk yelled orders to LeFarge and the crew to cut the two down. "Now what, Lizzie?"

She looked over at Rocco. "I think your captain should visit Lamya and figure out his transformation. He doesn't seem dangerous to the crew but changing could be inconvenient while he is at the helm or trying to lead you."

"True enough."

"I will fly with him and keep him safe in case he transforms back too soon. With any luck we will meet you at Île des Anciens." She glanced at Rocco, who stood on deck as if waiting for an idea of what to do. Nodding to him, she closed her eyes and changed.

Rocco turned to her, twitching his tail. *Do you really think I can fly to the island without changing?*

If you cannot, I can carry you the rest of the way. I must find Alara and know that she is safe, and you must learn how this dragon of yours works.

Two feathered beasts lifted from the deck of *L'Implacable*, soaring upward and northwest. They pushed through clouds, heading toward Île des Anciens, their wings stretching and folding in unison.

Lisette glanced at Rocco. *If we were not frantically trying to find our daughter, this would be a delightful way to spend time with my love.*

I can think of a better way, Rocco answered, and she laughed. In her dragon form, it came out as a chuffing sound that echoed across the waves.

"How will we make a banner?" Ruhee asked, standing at the edge of the cliff. "We have no cloth large enough for a ship to see."

"It is not that kind of signal." Kurta bustled in the surrounding brush, pulling at vines and flowers. She disappeared behind a large tree and came out on the opposite side, dragging two long branches. Making two more trips, she soon had six tall, straight poles, each one twice a good man's height. She dropped the last two on the ground and rubbed her hands. "There."

Ruhee looked at the bare branches. "There, what?"

"There are the bones for our signal." Kurta picked up a long vine. "We shall wind these vines between the poles, like so." The old woman bent down and wrapped the vines around one branch, then another, crisscrossing figure eights as she worked her way up the wood.

"I don't understand." Ruhee frowned.

"We shall build three vine-covered, brightly flowered towers to stand upon this cliff. Any ship that comes by will see the three tall stands, stands that have to be built by human hands. At that point, we shall wave and make ourselves known."

"Do you think that will work?"

Kurta shrugged. "It worked for me when I was stranded here. These are the same poles. But this time, I do not have to raise them alone."

"I suppose I shall trust you…" Ruhee glanced at the ground, littered with greenery that Kurta had pulled from the trees.

"Good. Now, take a vine, like so." The old woman kept her poles two hands' width apart, winding a vine around one pole, reaching across to the other and winding it there, returning to the first pole and repeating the process. "Like this," she repeated.

Ruhee picked up a vine. It was rough to her touch. Her hands had been hardened with deck-scrubbing and line-hauling, and whatever else was necessary to maintain the ship. But this greenery was almost bristled. She wound the vine and passed it over to the second pole. It did not bend as easily as Kurta's vine, and she fought to make it wind correctly. Within a few minutes she was sweating in the late sun and wishing she was back in the cool lagoon.

The memory of her dream stopped that wish, and she concentrated on knitting this vine onto the branches. Squatting over the ground made her legs shake and back ache. She stood and stretched, looking over at Kurta, who had been in the same position much longer.

"Isn't this hard on your body?" Ruhee asked.

"Hmm? No. I am used to labor and have trained my body to relax in any position." She smiled and glanced at her as she worked. "You must be like the tree that bends but does not break."

Ruhee frowned and bent over to work on her vine again, buckling down to her knees to take the pressure off her back. Eventually one long vine was wound around the two sticks. She sat back on her haunches.

"Do you want to be rescued or not?" Kurta asked. "We must get these wound and raised for all to see."

"Yes, Kurta." Ruhee breathed a long sigh and rose with a groan. Another bristly vine, another fight to wind it around. They seemed so long, but each one barely covered two to three hands' width. *This will take forever.*

"It will not take forever," Kurta said. "Sooner or later, it must be done because it is getting done."

"How did you know what I was thinking? Can you read my mind?"

Kurta laughed. "No, but I am not surprised. The words were all over your face."

Ruhee frowned. She was still uncertain whether to trust this woman. A restless cry made her look up. Alara was stirring in her silks by the fire. She had kept a steady sound of contentment all afternoon, cooing and giggling. Now her tone had changed to something less happy.

"Your little girl needs food and another change," Kurta said.

Looking down at her work, Ruhee nodded. She did not want to continue this, but she was not as excited to take care of the child. In her heart, she admitted she would never want to care for this child.

"I know you are anxious to complete this task." Kurta sat back on her heels. "I am nearly done with my tower. If you'd like to continue, I can care for Zaina."

"Yes, thank you. I am most impatient to get these raised."

Kurta stood and strolled to Alara, softly calling to her. "Do no fussing, your mamha comes."

Mamha. Ruhee listened intently. *Where have I heard that term?*

Soon the restless whimpers were soothed, and Kurta could be heard humming a song Ruhee did not recognize. It was a calming melody and might lull the entire world to sleep. Ruhee glanced over from her work. Kurta held Alara up, her hands supporting her head and bottom. She was touching her forehead to the baby's—the two remained that way for a long time.

Ruhee frowned as she stared at the pair, her attention taken from her own hands. Her fingers slipped and slid across the vine where a leaf had been—the bare nub sliced through her left thumb, down to her palm. She dropped the vine with a cry.

Holding her hand out, she examined it in the late sunlight. So much blood, she grabbed the scarf from her neck to wrap around the cut and held her hand up, squeezing at the wrist to stop the flow. She needed to clean the wound and dress it. Abandoning her task, she ran to the camp, toward the lagoon on the other side.

"I've cut myself badly," she huffed as she passed Kurta.

"Do not put your wound in the lagoon," Kurta yelled after her. "Wet the rag and wash the cut."

Ruhee winced as she scrambled for the water, her face aflush with anger at an old woman always telling her what to do. Stupid lagoon. Stupid old woman.

At the shore, she threw herself to her knees and held her hands out, using one to push the other under the water. The coolness hit her open flesh like grasping the flame of a torch. She wanted to scream out but hissed her pain instead. Kurta knew it would hurt—there was no use in giving her the satisfaction of being right. In slow, small increments, Ruhee unwound the scarf, stopping as more water hit the wound and the stinging returned. By the time she removed the scarf, the pain had been replaced by a cold numbness, and the water was not being tinted red.

She looked down at her hand. The gash ran from the

first knuckle of her thumb to the meaty pad of her palm. It curled open and she could see red tissue inside. She was relieved that at least she could not see bone. The skin was white on the edges, signifying it had been in the water long enough. With her fingertips wrinkling, she decided the wound was clean enough and could come out of the water.

Sitting back on her heels, she pulled her right hand from the water and dried it on her skirt. Her left hand stayed, as if someone held it, gently. She frowned.

"No, water." She scolded it as if it held intelligence in its droplets. "Let go."

The lagoon held her hand there, wrapping the water softly around her palm like a lover entreating her to stay. Ruhee felt her pulse rise in panic. The water swirled and enticed her focus to the middle of the lagoon, where it spun and sprayed, up toward the heavens. As she watched, the middle of the spray reddened and became a fire spout that exploded into the darkening sky.

Ruhee's body sagged, her shoulders folding, and a well of sadness bubbled up from inside. Tears rained down her face as she sobbed, shaking her body with grief.

"Please, oh please," she wailed. "You must let go of me. I know I have done wrong. I cannot bear to live with it."

Ruhee closed her eyes, feeling the river of tears running from her and the spasms in her chest. At last, she could hear only her own breath. When she opened her eyes, the spray in the lagoon had receded, taking the fire with it. The water had stilled until not even a ripple moved across.

Both of her hands were in her lap.

She held her left one up and looked at her wound. The gash was red but appeared drier and less angry. She wrapped it back in her scarf and went back to camp, trying to think of what to tell Kurta.

"Why, yes, I disobeyed you," she mumbled as she

walked, "and the lagoon did another magic trick that frightened me down to my very soul, but it was all a dream and I'm better now."

"What was that about magic tricks?" Kurta asked.

"Nothing," Ruhee said quickly and walked to the fire. "I was—I was hoping for a magic trick to heal my hand."

"Here," Kurta gestured. "Let me see."

Ruhee hesitated. What might this witch allow in her body if she allowed her to touch her wound?

"Come, child. Perhaps there is a salve that could heal you."

The young girl's eyes widened, but she held her hand out. Kurta took the scarf off and studied the wound, touching it only twice, gently.

"Hmm, yes, it is quite a gash. You must be careful when working with the vines. They can be dangerous." A small gurgle from Alara made her turn. She picked the baby up and engaged in some animated faces, causing them both to laugh.

Ruhee shrugged, rewrapped her hand, and sat on her silks by the fire. "When shall we eat?"

"I do not know." Kurta kept her attention on the baby. "What are you going to prepare for us?"

"Me? I do not know how to cook! You have been cooking all this time."

Kurta put Alara onto her lap and looked at Ruhee. "Yes, and each time, you look at my food as if it is poison, and I must convince you that I am not trying to kill you or seize your soul or turn you into a banshee. If I am that untrustworthy, I shall stop worrying you."

Ruhee blushed and lowered her head. "My apologies, Kurta. Our escape, this island, there is much to confuse and excite my mind. I am having dreams while I wake."

"Dreams while you are awake? Such as?" Kurta smiled.

"They are of no importance. They merely unsettle me." Ruhee frowned and rose. "Where are our supplies? I shall cook."

Kurta instructed her in each step, from getting pans from the bag to lowering the sack of food from the tree branch. Ruhee set the various roots on the fire to roast and heated the coconut milk. It took longer than when Kurta fixed the meal, but eventually they sat around the low flames with bowls of food.

"I suppose it tastes acceptable," Ruhee said. "It is not as good as yours."

"Next time you should try sprinkling a few spices."

Ruhee squinted at the old woman, her mouth pursed. "What kind of—spices—do you use?"

"Please, child," Kurta laughed. "My spices are no more magical than yours are."

"Mine?" Her eyes widened. "I have no spices."

"Do no lying to me. I am an old woman and I see much of what is hidden. I saw the little tins and bags in your cabin, and when we left, I saw that they were gone." She nodded toward the leather pouch on Ruhee's belt. "I am assuming they are in there."

Ruhee wrapped her fingers around the leather at her waist. "These are just my teas. Herbs to settle my stomach and help me to sleep."

"You must be feeling well, then. I have not seen you brew one cup."

"Yes." The girl pouted. "Yes, I am fine."

Kurta turned her attention back to Alara, playing with her hands and feet. "Baby feet. Look how precious. Tiny yet strong."

Ruhee watched them together and felt the sourness of jealousy in her stomach again. She wanted to be that woman, the one that Alara found enchanting. She wanted to be loved by Rocco's child.

Taking the bowls to the lagoon, she rinsed them, carefully avoiding dunking her hands in the water, and hating herself for being so superstitious. When she returned, Kurta was sitting alone, drinking something from a mug. Alara lay in her silken nest, quietly breathing.

"Your teas sounded good," Kurta said, "so I brewed a little hibiscus tea. Tart, but soothing. You should have some."

"No, thank you." Ruhee put away the bowls and spread out her bedclothes.

"Suspicious still? Come, here are the blossoms. Brew your own and relax into slumber and sweet dreams."

Ruhee picked up the bag and studied the contents. Nothing but dried flowers. No seeds nor stems. Perhaps a cup of tea would stave off the nightmares. She crushed the petals into her mug and poured hot water over them. The aroma was delicious.

She and Kurta sat together, silently watching the flames and sipping their evening drink. A sense of serenity washed over her, a pleasant sleepiness.

It is safe here.

Ruhee smiled at Kurta and eased herself into the silks, where soon her eyes closed, and her breath evened to a slow, rhythmic pace.

Lisette soared over the clouds, pushing her wings up and out to catch the most air. Rocco flew underneath and around her. She kept him in her view at all times in case he accidentally transformed back into a human.

I know you must be a mother now, he told her. *You check on me worse than an old hen.*

Fine, fly where you will, but don't cry to me when you fall into the ocean.

Lisette recalled all of the other times they flew together and wondered at how different it was this time. No slashing of claws or snapping of teeth. No fire raining down. Just a little light arguing. Would this be their relationship—sniping at each other, then making furious love?

That would be acceptable.

More than acceptable, Rocco told her.

Can I not have one thought to myself?

He reared against the night sky and shot a stream of fire from his jaws. *Not when we are in this form, apparently.*

She growled at him and looked toward the horizon. The clouds parted to reveal a small island, bushy and dark. Île des Anciens.

Look ahead, she told Rocco. *We'll be there by nightfall.*

Pity. I am enjoying this new dragon and would like to—

No, don't say it!

As if pressing a lever, Lisette saw a brief flash of light, and Rocco the man hurtling toward the open water. She folded her wings and dove toward him, catching him in her front paws before skimming the sea and pumping her wings to ascend.

Rocco looked up at her. "Thank you."

The island looked a lot further away now that she was carrying weight. She sought out wind currents to help carry them to their destination. It was going to be a long trip.

While she flew, she wondered about their fight on the ship. Would Rocco really oppose her plan to drive the European nobility from Île des Oiseaux and give it back to the people who belong there? They had fought before about much more personal things, like whether she would learn to crew the ship, or not be a slave or prostitute, or even live.

It was not an ideal way to begin their lives together, but she'd fought harder battles with him and won. She glanced down at him. He had repositioned himself to look out at the approaching land, and she was happy that he couldn't hear her thoughts at the moment.

The island was finally below them, and Lisette flew lower to look for any landmark. Rocco pointed, and she saw Dragon's Breath, the tall plateau where she was first taught to transform into a blood dragon. She headed for the top where she descended happily, exhausted from her travails. Recognizing a familiar clearing by a lagoon, she deposited Rocco on the sand and landed a few feet away. Rocco stood where she placed him, stretching. Lisette told herself who she wanted to be and changed into her human form.

"I admit, I am amazed," he said. "How is it you transform so easily and at will?"

"It is easy when you learn it, and difficult until then." She walked around the clearing. "We merely need to find Lamya."

"In the meantime, let us build a fire and find something to eat."

She nodded and they set to their tasks. Yams were simple for her to find, even in the darkness, and she returned quickly with her skirt cradling several. Rocco had gathered the dried sticks and brush together but was having a difficult time finding a rock to spark his dagger on.

"I don't know if it will work," Lisette said, "but let me attempt what Lamya taught me."

She looked at the fire and asked it to light. Nothing happened, so she asked it again. Still nothing. Annoyed, she yelled, "Light!"

The kindling burst into flames as if shot by cannon, throwing Rocco backward.

"What kind of magic is that?" he asked.

"I don't have it quite right yet. Lamya told me not to yell but asking did not work."

"Because you ask as if you know you will not receive," a low voice purred behind them.

They looked around to see Lamya walking from the direction of the lagoon. At least, Lisette assumed it was the Ancient One. As usual, she had taken on a different form, this time that of an older lady, bent and soft as pillows. She carried a bundle in her arms.

"Lamya," Lisette called.

"Come see your baby." Lamya held the bundle out to them.

Lisette rushed to her, scooping her child in her arms, and holding her tightly. "Oh, my Alara, are you well? I got your message. There was only one person I knew you would call friend."

Rocco strode to them and looked into the silk wrappings, his hand on Lisette's shoulder. She turned to him, raising Alara up.

"Would you like to hold your daughter?"

"I—" He stared at her. "Yes. I suppose so."

Lisette smiled and placed the baby into his arms, making certain he felt the weight of her before letting go. A smile spread across his lips as he looked down at his child's face. He was rewarded with a gurgling coo as Alara waved her hands and feet about.

"She is happy to see you," Lamya said.

"How did you get her?" Lisette asked. "I mean, how did you even know what had happened?"

"I am an Ancient One. It does afford me a little knowledge of what is happening in the world, especially what is happening in the world of magic."

"We have so much to ask, so much to learn," Lisette told her. "Is Rocco a moon dragon? And Alara—do you know anything more about her?"

Lamya looked around the clearing. "Hmm, all in good time. First, I believe the yams are cooked, and I have brought a little more food. You will need nourishment and strength for your journeys."

"Journeys?" Rocco asked.

As usual, Lamya ignored the question. "Come and sit. Eat. Then we talk."

Lisette attempted to eat quickly, but it proved impossible. With each bite, Alara took her attention, so that Lisette's blazing hot meal was close to cold by the time she had eaten the final bite. She glanced up to see Rocco had finished his meal as well.

At last, when everything was washed and rinsed and tucked away, and Alara was fed, clean, and in soft sleep, the trio sat at the fire, Lisette and Rocco leaning forward in anticipation.

"To begin," Lamya said. "Yes, Rocco, you are a moon dragon. You have different skills than Lisette, partially because your transformation was born of rage."

"Did Lisette's feather play any part?" He asked.

"What about my feather?" Lisette frowned.

"Rocco did not trust that he would turn into a blood

dragon to defeat Mercedes." Lamya gave him a stern glare. "He used one of your feathers to—hasten his magic."

Lisette laughed. "I could have warned you not to do that."

"Lisette's feather is what gives you both the ability to communicate in your dragon forms. But Rocco, you would have become a moon dragon either way."

"How do I control the transformation?"

"Much as Lisette has told you, it is easy, and it is difficult. I will teach you."

Lisette nodded. "And Alara?"

"Alara." Lamya sat back on her haunches, grinning. "We have not seen her like for hundreds of years. We thought that line of dragons had died out. She is magnificent."

"But what is she?" Lisette asked.

"The name is long and forgotten. To the world, she is the New Dragon. She is a nurturer and a destroyer, both in equal and large amount. She can heal our entire world, or she can ruin it."

"Oh, my." Lisette ran her hand across her forehead. "How do we raise that?"

"With equal parts love and discipline. She must know that people are good, usually, mostly, ordinarily so. She must also be allowed to mete out punishment where it is warranted."

Rocco and Lisette looked at one another. Rocco shrugged. "I am a pirate, Lamya. My life is one of plunder and killing. How do I teach my daughter that people are good when I myself am not?"

"You are not a pirate," Lamya said. "You are a good man driven to vengeance."

Rocco opened his mouth to speak, but she held her palm up to silence him.

"A single count took your wife and killed her. You sought my help in becoming a blood dragon and chased revenge up and down these waters until the count and his family and his household were dead. Your vengeance is complete." Lamya gestured toward Alara. "You have rediscovered love and have proof of that love asleep in those silks. What remains in your heart that still demands the blood of Spaniards?"

"I don't know!" he snapped and leapt to his feet, stomping away into the night.

Lisette watched him go. "It is a fight we need to finish." She told Lamya of her desire regarding the island, and Rocco's opposition to it.

Lamya nodded. "Yes, I know. That is also what we need to discuss."

"Why should you get involved in such matters? This island will never be under anyone's rule."

"Because lives are important, no matter which island. The Europeans have been too long involved in this part of the world. They do not understand it and expect it to bend to their whims. Isla del Lagarto has rid itself of nobility. If Île des Oiseaux falls, the other islands cannot help but tumble."

"I agree, although I am not certain where that leaves me." Lisette sighed. "I do not recall much about life in France. I do not want to rule, but I would like to live here, simply, with my love and my child." She almost added, and future children, but held her tongue.

"It is well, I know of Ruhee's curse. She used the ankh to wish you eternal barrenness. But she is young and does not realize what she has done. The ankh does not appreciate being used as a curse. At the first opportunity, its power will desert her."

"But will I be barren forever then?"

"I will not say yes or no." Lamya smiled. "I will say that Alara will take much of your time and other children may not be feasible. And that Rocco, and your life together, may only have room for one child."

Lisette nodded. "I suppose I am a little sad, and yet it is freeing to know I can focus on my little dragon."

Rocco strolled back to the fire and sat down. Lisette reached over and rubbed his arm, laying her head on his shoulder.

"Now that you have returned," Lamya said. "There are plans to discuss."

"Plans?" Rocco asked.

"You must remain with me to learn how to control your dragon."

"But my ship…"

"Your ship will wait. If you do not know how to transform, you will be changing every time you are angered, and changing back when it is least convenient."

"I can testify to the inconvenience," Lisette said.

Lamya looked at her. "And you must trust me."

"Of course, I trust you."

"By leaving Alara with me—temporarily."

"No!" Lisette's eyes widened. "I mean—I just got her back."

"Yes, and she will be safe with me. You have a job to do, and I believe you know what that job is."

A vision of her castle on the island flitted across her mind. "How involved must I be?"

"Very. Too occupied to worry about your little one. It is better to have her tucked away with her mamha."

Lisette nodded, even though her eyes glistened with pain. "At least her papa will be with her."

Lamya pursed her lips. "Hmm, how to say—yes but no. I must return to camp and Ruhee before morning, with the baby. She still believes I am Kurta Rici, an old woman helping her to be rescued from this island."

"Ruhee? With our baby?" Rocco scowled. "Where

am I supposed to be? I do not want to see that woman again, unless it's to run her through with my blade."

"No, you will not have that blood on your hands." Lamya was firm. "You will be here, resting. Ruhee will write the end to her own story."

"When will you work with Rocco if you're with her?" Lisette asked.

"At night. I have given her something in her tea. She sleeps soundly and awakens pleasantly."

"And you will protect Alara?" Rocco gazed at the baby.

"Alara and I are getting to know one another," Lamya said. "I am explaining much of her world to her. And I will bring her with me each night so that you might see her, even if she sleeps."

Lisette considered her words. "Very well. I suppose my first act is to return to Isla de la Soledad and find Begum. I will need reinforcements to return to Île des Oiseaux."

"You're not going to—" Rocco said.

"Rescue my island from the Mendozas and give it to the villagers? Yes." She smiled. "The faster you learn to transform, the sooner you can come and argue the point with me."

Lamya laughed. "Sleep well, both of you. Rest, Lizzie. You have a long trip in the morning. Rocco, I will see you tomorrow when the moon is cresting over Dragon's Breath. Be ready for work."

"Must you take her?" Lisette ran to Lamya and buried her face in the silks, reveling in the smell and touch of her daughter. She felt Lamya's strong bony hand caress her hair.

"You will be with her soon, and forever." Lamya's voice was soothing. "For a little while, she and her father will get acquainted."

Lisette nodded, still staring into Alara's eyes, and

kissing her cheeks. Alara stared up at her, green eyes flecked with gold. She loosened one chubby arm from her swaddling and held her tiny hand to Lisette's face. Lisette kissed the palm and fought her tears.

"Do no worrying," Lamya whispered. "We must go. Spend the night in the arms of your baby's father. You both have a long journey before you can be a family."

The Ancient One pulled slowly from Lisette's grasp and turned toward the lagoon. Rocco wrapped his arms around Lisette as they watched Lamya and Alara disappear into the trees. There was a white flash of light, and they were gone. Lisette turned her head into Rocco's shoulder.

"How can I miss her already?" Lisette mumbled into Rocco's shirt.

He tightened his embrace and kissed her hair, her cheek, her forehead, down her nose. "Because she is your little wonder, and you will never have enough time for her."

She raised her mouth to his and kissed him, feeling the passion swell, even as it was tempered with melancholy.

"Lamya told us to rest." She looked into his eyes, bright blue against the night. "But I would feel more relaxed if—" She combed her hand through his hair, running her fingers down his beard and across his mouth.

He picked her up and carried her to his bedding by the fire. They lay entwined, kissing lips and necks and tenderly exploring with their tongues. Rocco sat up and removed his shirt, then unfastened his belt and kicked off his breeches.

"It will not do, to be so close to you and not feel the warmth of your body."

Lisette stood and stepped away from the silks. Keeping her eyes on him, she unfastened her robe and let it fall, then untied her skirt and stepped out of it. Rocco was watching her intently as she released the bow from her shift and brushed it from her shoulders, pushing it from her breasts and down her hips until it was a pool of cotton at her feet.

Naked, she walked back to him.

Still kneeling, he encircled her waist, running his hands down to her haunches, where he held her tightly and buried his face between her legs, letting his tongue explore the delicacy there. Lisette caressed his hair, her knees weakening, as her back arched and her head fell back in ecstasy.

He raised his head long enough to guide her down beside him, where he continued to kiss and lick and suck on her body, up her hips to her ribs, her breasts. By the time he reached her mouth, her hunger for him was unbearable. She wrapped herself around him and took him into her, pushing her hips forward for more. Raising up, she rolled over until she was atop him and could sit back to receive him entirely. He groaned as she swiveled against his hips, finding the movements that gave them both pleasure. At last, she felt the pressure building. He arched his back and shuddered—seconds later she felt her own body convulse. Trembling, she collapsed against his chest.

He stroked her hair, panting. "Did we just create another little dragon?"

She caught her breath, feeling the ankh scar on her stomach burning—or was she just imagining? "Must we think about that now?"

His hand rubbed her back, and she could feel the rumble of his chest as he chuckled. "I suppose not. You've just had one baby."

Sliding down to his side, Lisette tucked her head into his shoulder. "I love you, Tristan de Rocco."

"I love you, too, Lisette de Lille." He yawned and enclosed his arms around her. "Is it proper for a noblewoman to marry a commoner?"

I'm not quite as noble as you believe. She sighed. There were many conversations they needed to have. "I don't believe anyone will object."

It was midmorning before Lisette forced her eyes to open. She was on her side, Rocco wrapped around her back, his face nuzzled into her neck. Yawning and stretching, she rolled away from him. He reached out and brought her back.

"Stay."

"It is my deepest desire," she whispered, "but we both have labors ahead of us. I must find Begum and return to my old home to set things right. You must learn how to be a moon dragon."

"I still say, let Spain have Île des Oiseaux," he growled.

Lisette stood and retrieved her clothes. "It is a discussion we shall have later," she said, slipping into her chemise. "Can you at least understand that, while the Duke de Martinmas has been a great help to me, I fear the Mendoza family will always remain a threat to both of us."

"True." He rose and dressed. "All the same, I am loathe to abandon life as a pirate."

She walked to him and embraced his waist. "To be honest, although I know my wishes for my island interfere with your life of piracy, I do not imagine you as anything else."

A shrieking caw startled them, and they looked up to see a large red parrot in flight above. It landed on a low branch and screeched at them again.

"I have a feeling that Lamya sent us a messenger," Rocco said.

"Of course." Lisette looked up at him, fighting her tears. He kissed her and she tried to put every imprint of his lips, every touch of his fingers, the sound of his breath, the smell of his skin, all of him into her memory.

The parrot screeched louder.

"Yes!" Lisette snapped. "I'm going."

Moving away from Rocco but keeping her eyes on him, she sighed and nodded. *I am a dragon.* With great reluctance, she extended her wings and flew.

36

Ruhee rubbed her eyes and sat up, her head clear and heart light. She felt a happiness that had eluded her in months, perhaps years. The aroma of roasting root vegetables and caramelized mango drew her to the fire. Kurta sat with Alara, holding her as if in conversation.

"Good morning," Kurta said. "The breakfast is ready. I heated water if you would like to prepare your own tea."

"Yes, that is good." Ruhee dug her bag of herbs out and crushed a few in her mug. She filled a bowl with the cooked food and took a seat on the sand. "What do we do today?"

"We complete the vine banners to signal a ship."

"But my hand—" Ruhee looked down at the rag wrapped around her thumb and palm.

"It will be well." Kurta stood, still holding Alara. "I

must bathe the baby. You must eat."

Ruhee watched the old woman stroll toward the lagoon, a giggling infant flailing and kicking in her arms. The sourness of jealousy was brewing in her anew, turning into anger.

I shall never measure up.

The happiness of the night's sleep vanished, and each bite of food burned her stomach. She pushed the bowl away, picked it up and nibbled at it, pushed it away again, until she had finished it all. Her stomach calmed somewhat after it was full.

She unwrapped her hand to see what her wound looked like today. Oddly, she felt no pain—she expected it to at least have to peel it away from the scarf. When it was fully unveiled, she marveled. There was a scar, white and jagged, from her thumb down her pad. It looked at least a week old, certainly not a day old. She pressed on the scar. There was a slight ache, but nothing like the pain of last night.

This was a mystery that required an answer. Ruhee rose and strapped her dagger to her belt. She strode to the lagoon, determined to make Kurta tell her the truth. The white sand path wound in and around tall, slender trees, wrapped in vines and sprouting flowers from every leaf. Ruhee had never noticed how beautiful this part of the island was, as if it had been blessed by the gods.

A strange voice addressed her: *How can this be so beautiful and blessed when you are convinced it is bewitched?*

She stopped and turned around, looking everywhere for the source of the question. The only sounds were birds calling and the trees rustling in the breeze. Far off, she could hear a parrot squawking.

"Was it all in my mind?" she asked, startled by her own voice.

Bewitched, blessed, or otherwise enchanted, she had

no desire to remain on this island. She would find Kurta, demand answers, and get their signal trees built. *If a ship has not sailed by this island in two days,* she decided, *I shall set off in the dinghy. I would rather perish at sea than be here longer.*

The path wound further than she remembered, but at last she could hear splashing and Kurta's voice. Her soft, velvet tone was like mother's milk to the child, and Ruhee felt a small pang of loss remembering her own mother. She had not been so coddled as this baby—her mother had demanded her silence and obedience. Her teachings, about herbs and magic and how to use the ankh, were taught for her survival and not shared out of the love of the generations.

When Ruhee had rounded the last curve of the trail, she could see the lagoon through the trees. Kurta was in the water with Alara, but something did not seem right. Kurta's back was to her, and she had let her gray hair out of its bun. It was long and wet and not so much gray as it was silver, a silver that glimmered in the sunlight. Her hands were lifting the baby from the water, and they were decidedly not the gnarled fingers of the old woman.

This was Kurta, but it was not Kurta.

Alara, smiling, looked away from Kurta and toward Ruhee. The baby frowned and flapped her chubby arm in Ruhee's direction. Kurta lowered Alara into the water and turned to Ruhee. The wrinkles in her face revealed the same old woman who had knocked on Ruhee's cabin door those many nights ago.

"Come and refresh yourself," Kurta called to her. "We are finished with our bath and ready for the day."

Ruhee walked forward, dragging her feet like a child who was caught hiding. "I would also enjoy a brief swim." She rubbed her left hand against her right arm, reminding her of why she'd really come.

Kurta was already on the shore, slipping into her

cotton dress before drying the baby. "Do you have a question?"

"No, I—" Ruhee stopped walking, planted her feet, and raised her chin, despite the shaking in her legs. "Yes. I did not come to bathe. I came to ask you about this." She held her trembling hand out.

"You do not remember slitting your hand open last night? It was a nasty cut."

"I remember it well! What I do not understand is how it was an open, gaping wound last night and it is a healed scar this morning!"

Kurta picked up Alara, turned slowly to the young woman, and shrugged. "Sometimes the island helps the weary traveler."

"I don't understand."

"You wish to leave. You must wrap the vines to signal to a ship, a task that is difficult when you have been injured. Sometimes the island helps." Kurta walked to Ruhee. "Take your bath. We have much to do." The old woman shuffled back toward the camp.

"No!" Ruhee turned and shouted at her. "You will tell me—is this island bewitched?"

Kurta waved her hand as she kept walking. "Cool yourself, return to camp."

Ruhee took a few stomping steps after the old woman and stopped. She wanted to follow, but Kurta's instruction—*cool yourself, return to camp*—had the effect of making her return to the lagoon, remove her clothes, and walk into the water.

It was cool, she had to admit, and felt wonderfully peaceful. Her previous anger melted away in the blue rings that drifted out from the center. An underground spring fed this pool, keeping the water fresh.

She lay on her back, feeling the sun's warmth from above and the coolness below. *I can surely stay a while before going back. Kurta and I have an entire day to discuss everything.* Closing her eyes, she waved her arms to propel herself slowly across the lagoon.

A dream came to visit her, of being a small child in her family home. She was in the courtyard with her mother. Mama held up her necklace, a gold chain with the ankh charm dangling from it. Ruhee watched it spin in the sunlight, so shiny and desirable.

"This is our secret," her mother said. "Beyond the herbs and potions, this is where the magic lies. It is powerful and will do as we wish."

Ruhee reached up to hold it in her tiny hand. "Anything we wish?"

"Anything. But beware, my girl—if it is used out of anger, or jealousy, or pride…there is a price to pay."

A price to pay.

Ruhee opened her eyes. The sun was directly in her sight, searing her vision and making her turn away and swim for shore. Mama had warned her. For many years, she listened. She was a good girl, quiet, taken on by the *Dişi Aslan* when she was a child and her mother died. Her father went off to fight a war and left her with relatives who put her out with the dogs and made her work for her daily meals. She hated them, hated living with them, and often dreamed of using the ankh to punish them for mistreating her. But she always remembered her mother's words.

Until Rocco. *No, I used the ankh out of love. Love for Rocco.*

She emerged from the water and dressed. Dropping to her knees, she clutched at her ankh, lifting her face to the sky.

"Oh, please, gods in the heavens and on the earth and of the underworld, help me! I am told by all that this man is not mine and will never be mine and yet I cannot let him go!"

The rustle of trees in the wind was her only reply. She

returned to camp to see Kurta placing bright red flowers into the vines she'd woven onto the poles. Alara was in her sling, riding on Kurta's back, sucking on her fist.

"The first one is finished," Kurta said. "Come help me plant it."

Ruhee went over and grabbed one long, straight post while Kurta held the other. Together, they hoisted the brightly colored beacon upright, pushing the ends into deep holes Kurta had dug into the earth.

"Hold it there." Kurta handed her half to Ruhee and knelt, filling the mixture of sand and dirt into the holes and tamping it all down. "Don't let go," she said, and retrieved a bucket of water, which she poured into the holes, then stuffed more dirt and sand atop it. When she had secured the bottom of the posts, she stood up and motioned Ruhee to move away.

Ruhee took a few steps back and admired their handiwork. It was a fine signal, tall and so fiery red, it was certain to attract a ship.

"We need at least one more," Kurta said. "But it works best in threes. Let us finish yours today and get it mounted."

Nodding happily, Ruhee ran to the edge of the clearing and pulled more vines to complete her poles. She didn't mind the roughness of the stalks and leaves as much now that she saw what they could look like. Squatting, she laced the end of a new vine with the last one she wound and worked this one in and out, back and forth, down the last third of the poles. As she did, Kurta brought more bright flowers, laceleaf and hibiscus, to weave into the vines. By the time the sun hit mid-sky, they had finished and lifted the second signal.

"We shall eat now," Kurta said.

Returning to camp, Kurta added enough dried wood to the fire to bring the flames up again, then set the bubby-pot on the heat in order to warm Alara's milk. She untied the sling and brought the baby into her arms.

"Yes, I would say you need a new clout," she said as she rubbed the infant's nose with her own. "Ruhee, please gather more food for us. I will change the baby."

Ruhee opened her mouth to say that she would change the clout but stopped. She did not want to change the baby and trek to the lagoon and wash the soiled cotton. The more the old woman took care of the baby, the less she wanted to. Perhaps this is why nobles had nurses for all their children.

"Yes, Kurta." She walked up the path and gathered ripe fruits and a few small yams.

As she turned to walk back, she heard an unfamiliar sound. It was a snuffling, grunting noise that crashed through the brush. It was getting louder. Ruhee turned to see a wild boar emerge from the jungle and head toward the lagoon. In her surprise, she screamed.

The boar stopped and wheeled in her direction, its nose in the air and wiggling up and down. With a solitary grunt, it trotted toward her. Ruhee screamed again, dropped her harvest, and ran down the trail. She could hear the pig's feet increase their speed and she cried out as she dashed forward, her feet driving into the sand and propelling her with each step. The path took a turn downhill to the camp and her legs could not maintain her speed, sending her tumbling.

She scrambled upright, hearing the huffing breaths of the boar growing closer. Knowing she should run, panic overwhelmed her—she turned to see the boar launch itself at her.

"Help!" It was less of a scream and more of a high-pitched prayer. She closed her eyes and crumpled to the ground.

The whoosh of an object flew by her ear and ended in a thunk and a squeal. Ruhee looked up to see the animal on its side, a spear through its chest and blood draining into the sand. She sat up slowly and peered behind her.

Kurta strolled up, her expression placid and unconcerned. She stood over the dead pig and nodded. "A small one. Good. His meat is tender."

Ruhee still sat, her legs unable to push their way to standing.

Kurta glanced at her. "I will take this to the camp for slaughter. You—go back up the trail and pick up the food."

"Yes." The young girl used her arms to steady herself as she rose. She felt numb and shaky as she skittered around the dead beast. It gave one last twitch as she was almost past, causing her to squeal and run a few steps up the path.

"Do no worrying," Kurta said in her calm purring voice. "It is dead."

Ruhee looked back at the old woman, who had pulled the stake from the pig's chest and picked up its hind feet, dragging it back toward camp. The young girl shook the shudder from her bones and shuffled back toward the trail, hoping the boar worked alone.

When she returned with her skirt full of fruit and vegetables, Kurta had the carcass hanging from a tree branch and had almost stripped it to its bones. The baby was once again on her back in the sling. Ruhee could smell the roasting meat on the fire and flinched. Eating pork—just one more way she could disappoint her mother.

"I have a bit of work left here," Kurta said, "The meat must be stripped thin and lay in the sun to dry. I will not ask this work of you, so you may continue to work on the last of our signals."

"Do we know when a ship may stop by?" Ruhee asked.

"The last time I was here, needing a ship was many years ago. At that time, it took a full two weeks. But we have more people now, more trade ships, and more pirates. I should expect to see sails within the week."

"Then I shall not tarry." Ruhee turned to the glade to gather more vines.

"One more thing." Kurta stopped her. "I am old and somedays my bones ache. You need to carry Zaina. She grows larger and my back is straining."

The dread of being alone with Alara washed over Ruhee and settled in her gut. She kept her expression pleasant. "Of course."

Kurta rinsed and wiped her hands before untying the sling and helping to fasten it to Ruhee's back and around her chest. Ruhee could feel the baby's constant, wiggling movements, as if trying to escape.

"I am putting her back to yours," Kurta said. "She is more interested in the world and facing outward makes her a more willing passenger. Keep her with you. This morning I found she had rolled over. It is early for a baby, but she is very special. If you put her down, she may roll away."

Ruhee nodded. *It was good, at least the baby will not drool down my neck—or worse.* With Alara snuggly attached, Kurta returned to her carving and Ruhee slowly wandered toward the lagoon, where there were more vines to pull.

She was well into the brush when she finally saw a grouping of ribbons long enough to cover the last poles. Following them to their source, she found they had buried their roots in sand, making it easy to pull. As she leant over to grab a vine, she could feel Alara's weight coming toward her head, the baby's arms and legs flailing, her tiny hands grasping at Ruhee's hair and pulling. Ruhee stood quickly and adjusted the sling.

"Let go of my hair," she scolded, and reached back to extricate the little fingers. "Ugh, why are your fingers so wet?"

Alara giggled as if in answer.

"This is too inconvenient." Ruhee untied the sling and took it off, pulling Alara away and out of her braid as she did. "I must pull and gather these vines. You can sit over here until I'm done."

Carefully propping the baby in the sand against a log, Ruhee nodded. "You should be fine there. I'll be right back."

Gathering the vines took a little longer and a little more effort than she had planned. The vines were long and had wound themselves through the dense underbrush, making her stop and untangle them every few feet. Eventually she had three beautiful green vines of perfect length. She could finish the signal poles and spend her days at leisure, waiting for a ship.

The day had quickly heated to a tropical scorch, and she was drenched in sweat by the time she had dragged the last vine onto the trail. She was anxious to return and complete this task, but the heat felt brutal on her skin and her salty perspiration drew every insect in the area.

A quick dip in the lagoon to rinse a layer of sweat from my body would not be bad. The baby has waited so far—she is quiet and must be asleep.

Ruhee strode to the edge of the water and jumped into it. She swam to the middle, where the spring arose from underground, and let the bubbles surround and scrub her. Her skin tingled with the cold, clean water. She submerged herself and felt the water invade her hair, to her scalp, refreshing her mind.

Satisfied, she swam back to the beach and walked onto the sand. Her clothes were drenched, so she removed them, wrung the water out, and put them back on. They would dry quickly in the heat. Even if they got filthy again carrying the vines, she did not care. At the moment they were deliciously cool against her skin.

She returned to the log to pick up Alara and re-attach the sling to her. Apart from her flapping about, she had not been a bad companion. At least she had not cried or spit up on her or somehow made her feel incompetent and hated. Maybe she and Alara could get along. Maybe Alara would accept her as mother.

As Ruhee came down the trail, she could see the log and the ends of the sling, but she couldn't see the baby. She stepped a little faster, hoping the jungle was obscuring her view. The closer she got, the emptier the sand looked. She ran to the log, as if that would reveal Alara. It didn't, and she stood, looking around the sand, around the brush, around at the sky as if the baby had flown away.

Alara was gone.

It was not a long way from Île des Anciens to Isla de la Soledad, and yet Lisette could not remember a more grueling flight. Even the time she was engulfed in a squall did not leave her this exhausted. All she wanted was her baby and her love, but a strange sense of duty called her. She could not leave Île des Oiseaux to Spain, and certainly not to the Mendozas.

Coming around the southern point to the windward side, she spotted the *Dişi Aslan*, still anchored. She was not surprised—the captain would not leave until she was certain that Alara was not on the island. After all, this was Begum's granddaughter.

Lisette considered her choices, to land on the ship or go straightaway to the island. She did not know where to find anyone on the island, but she also did not know how the rest of the crew would accept a dragon landing on their deck and transforming. The safest thing to do might waste the most time, although the crew might not have an idea of where the captain was, or how to contact her.

Sighing, she headed toward the island, to a clearing just beyond the village. She transformed quickly and strode toward the inn. Begum would not be there, no doubt, but on any island, the inn is the first place of gossip and rumors.

The sun was almost to the horizon, darkness chasing it. Candles and lanterns were already lighted in the inn and Lisette could hear voices that promised to get louder as the night wore on. She smoothed her skirt and adjusted her robe before slipping inside and surveying the space. About half of the tables were already occupied, mostly by men having a meal and some ale. Two women sat at a table, exchanging good-natured jeers with the rest of the room.

Lisette spotted a table in the corner to her left. A tall, reed-thin man with a long mustache scurried toward her with a rag and took a swipe across the table. "Name's Ernesto, m'lady. What may I bring you?" His voice was high and nasally, even as his demeanor was friendly.

"Bread and cheese if you have them. Cider, although I'll take ale." She lowered her voice. "And perhaps information."

He ran his thumb and index finger down his mustache, briefly pinning the ends together under his chin. "M'lady I am an open book."

She smiled and winked. "As are we all."

He disappeared and Lisette regarded the room, studying the people. The men wore the clothes of dock workers, simple cotton breeches and shirts. Most had caps hanging on their chairs, but a few had scarves tied on their heads. Crude dark tattoos ran up their arms.

The women dressed in the wear of servants in her castle, layers of shifts, and blouses and skirts topped with aprons. White bonnets covered their hair, although dark curls escaped from around their temples.

"Here you are." Ernesto sat a tray and a mug on the table. "Do you need the information now, or is it better after a full stomach?"

Lisette smiled. "Now is as good as any if you are not inconvenienced."

He bowed. "At your service."

"There is a hunt on for missing people—two women and a baby. I believe inquiry was made here?"

"Yes." His eyes narrowed for a moment. "Two men came here days ago. Might you know them?"

"If one was tall, broad and dark-haired, with a beard and blue eyes, and the other even taller with a shock of red hair that stood where it wanted, then yes, I know them."

He nodded and drew closer, lowering his voice. "I am an innkeep and care not that you know Rocco the pirate. His coin spends as good as any. But beware the women at that table—they are in constant need of silver. Tonight, they come in with the idea that Rocco might know who killed Count Barragan's older brother—the count's offered a reward for information."

Lisette let her face feign mild interest, even though the tale of the viscount's brother disturbed her. At least no one knew she was his executioner. She suppressed a shudder, realizing how dangerous this trip was.

"I understand," she said. "There might also be a ship nearby of undeclared country…a ship of unusual sailors."

He nodded. "The *Dişi Aslan*? Yes, I've seen them here."

Lisette asked, "Are any of the crew still in the village? I should like to secure passage home if I can."

"The last time I saw them, they were heading up the road by the inlet, where the old boarding house stands." He gestured back and left. "That's where the viscount was murdered."

"Is it?" Lisette nodded as if she found it interesting.

"Ernesto!" A husky, heavily bearded man called out. "How about more ale? I'm dry!"

The innkeeper darted to his customer to fill his empty mug. Lisette turned her attention to food. The bread was stale and the cheese waxy, but she needed sustenance and it would have to do. Frequent gulps of cider aided her digestion. Soon her desire to catch up with the crew overruled her hunger, and she pushed away from the table.

"Could I have a word, m'lady?" One of the women from the far end of the room stood before her.

"Of course." Lisette glanced around. The other woman was no longer there, and Lisette felt a chill of danger ripple up her neck. "Please, sit."

The woman pulled out a chair and plopped her body into it like someone unloading sacks of grain. From far away, she had looked fairly young and girlish, in a clean frock. Upon closer inspection, her clothes were streaked with sweat and dirt, and her face, although young, wore the scars of pox. There was a hard, scheming quality to her eyes that Lisette did not like.

"I hear'd ya talkin' to Ernesto," the woman said. "When ya came in, I thoughts I recognized ya, but couldn't remember. Innkeep can whisper all he wants, but I hear'd the name Rocco. I got a friend says you was walkin' with the pirate that night when the viscount was kill't. Walked right up the street, right towards the boarding house." She sat back, a smile on her face, waiting.

Lisette kept her expression blank, and her mouth shut.

More people had straggled into the inn by now. It was getting dark, and the lanterns had all been lit. Voices rang louder, as well as the scrape of mugs on the table. Someone had a mandolin and was strumming it.

Nothing was as loud as the silence between Lisette

and the woman.

"The count is givin' quite a bit o' coin fer whoever finds his brother's killer." The woman was still smiling.

Lisette let her stew a few minutes more before opening her mouth to speak. "Ernesto," she called. "More cider, please?"

She watched the woman's face fall in disappointment, and again waited without giving her any response.

The woman sat back into the chair, her face softening. "Course'n I only wants ta help ya. Us gals gotta stick together, right?"

Ernesto brought a jug over and sat it on the table. "Help yourself, m'lady." He scowled at the woman as he left.

Lisette poured more cider into her mug, took a long drink, and stared at the woman. "What's your name?"

"Uh, um, uh," she stumbled. "Cleo."

Lisette raised an eyebrow, frowning. "All right, *Cleo*. If you are so certain that your friend saw me with Rocco and if you are so certain that we walked in the direction of the boarding house and if you are so certain that it was the night the viscount was killed..."

Cleo leaned forward.

"Why does your friend not go to the count and collect the reward?" Lisette took another swig of cider.

"Like I says, I wanna help ya."

Lisette stared at her, her words slow and deliberate. "I believe you want to help yourself to my purse. After you've taken my valuables, you'll then turn me over to the count."

"Why, m'lady—"

"But you haven't thought this quite through." Lisette pushed the mug aside and rested her forearms on the table, pushing her upper body toward Cleo. "A woman who walks with a pirate is no piece of fluffery. She might even be a pirate herself, one with a weapon at the ready and friends to come to her aid."

Cleo flinched and moved away.

Lisette felt her body grow warm and worried that her old blood dragon instincts had not completely died. It would not do to transform in this small space. Still, she could not stop herself from a small warning.

"Or she could be something more dangerous."

Cleo sat without reply, staring at Lisette. Her face attempted an angry scowl but there was fear behind her eyes. The silence again surrounded them, Lisette being content to let her words be her last.

"You'll wish y'accepted my help," Cleo told her and pushed away from the table.

Cleo stomped out the door and Lisette noted which direction she went. The white bonnet reflected the moon as the woman strode down the boardwalk and toward the dimly lit corner, where she stopped and spoke with a woman dressed for attracting men and their money. The prostitute stood taller than Cleo. Lisette watched as she backhanded Cleo across the face.

Obviously, Cleo did not work for the count, but for the prostitute. Lisette wondered about the other woman who had been here—was she a confederate or merely a friend sharing a meal and a laugh?

She looked around for Ernesto and found him buried in business, attempting to serve food and drink to five raucous tables. They were all yelling insults at him that he was too slow and too old, and where was their rum? Lisette smiled and rose, meeting him at the bar.

"Allow me to offer my help, before these dogs tear your place apart."

The man looked confused at first but quickly recovered. "Stew's in the back. Just keep ladling and I'll keep serving."

Lisette did as he'd instructed, placing a chunk of bread with each bowl and sending them out as fast as Ernesto could deliver. When the stew was served, she poured ale into pitchers and rum into mugs. Ernesto proved to be a good boss, calling orders without questioning her work ethic.

Soon they had a measure of peace in the inn and the innkeeper could stay ahead of the tables. The mandolin was being banged and strummed and a bawdy song was being brayed. Lisette leaned on the bar and waited to be put to work again.

"I think our dogs have been tamed," Ernesto said. "Thank you for your help. How do I repay you?"

"I've helped other innkeeps in other villages." Lisette recalled Trina on Isla del Lagarto. "I want nothing in return, except perhaps advice."

"Which costs me nothing." He smiled.

"The woman who was speaking to me…"

"You mean threatening you? Yes, I heard. Yes, I know her. Katerina Oliveras. She works for the putain Manuela."

"The other woman with her tonight?"

"Isabel Lopez, servant for Count Barragan. They are close, from childhood. Isabel's parents secured her a position in the castle. Katerina's father sold her to the brothel."

Lisette nodded. "How safe am I to leave this place tonight?"

"Safer if you leave with protection. Do not be deceived, Katerina is desperate for money to buy her life from Manuela. She will be prepared to fight to take all that you have."

She reached into the folds of her skirt, to her thigh and withdrew her dagger. As she did, her left hand drifted to her bodice where her emerald hung, hidden by fabric.

"Have any volunteers to escort me?" she asked.

"Depends," he said as his eyes swept the room. "Where are you going?"

She looked at the darkness outside. Where was she going? She would not find Begum or the crew tonight unless they wandered into the village. Where would they stay?

"Where does someone lodge in this village?"

"Two places, m'lady, depending upon your coin. The old boarding house up the road has rooms for a single piece of silver, although you have to sleep with one eye open. At the corner from there is a nicer place for a bag of silver, one with a bath." He shrugged. "The place you're in now has a few rooms. No bath, but a lock on the door and maybe half the bag."

She stared at him, one eyebrow cocked.

"Quarter of the bag?" he offered.

"Show me the room," she whispered. "We will conclude our business away from prying eyes and ears."

"Behind the bar and through the curtains." Ernesto also kept his voice low. "I will meet you there with the key."

Lisette kept watch of the customers in the inn, looking for the small gestures and head nods that might mean someone was paying attention to her. Ernesto poured more ale in a pitcher and joined the men, enticing them to buy another round. The night was still new, so he had a willing audience.

She took several minutes, stopping to clean the bar, to gather dishes, to look busy as she inched toward the curtain. At last certain that no one cared what the bar girl did, she disappeared into the kitchen.

A stone fireplace lit the room, although two oil lanterns chased shadows from the corners. A large table took up the entire middle, with two large loaves of bread stacked on top. In all ways, it looked like the kitchen in any inn.

She turned to face the curtain when a hard blow hit the back of her head. There was just enough time for it to hurt before everything went black.

39

"Alara? Alara!" Ruhee called out as she searched the sand and brush around the lagoon. "Stupid baby, where are you?"

She picked up the sling and shook it as if hoping the baby was hiding in the folds. Cold, shaking fear crawled up her body and into her stomach. She tried to stop it—if it reached her heart, it would likely kill her.

If I return to Kurta without the baby, she will kill me.

The young woman looked around at the sand where she found the sling. Surely there would be footprints, or the smooth print of a baby rolling somewhere. All she could find were her own feet, trampling on whatever happened here.

Did something carry Alara off? She had not encountered predators, beyond being chased by a wild boar. Would a pig carry off a baby?

Ruhee stumbled back to the vines she had pulled, tears blurring her view of the path. Grabbing them in a sloppy handful, she sighed heavily and trudged back to camp. The meat being cooked made her stomach growl, yet she did not feel hunger. She felt her legs shaking and her throat tightening.

Kurta was not in camp. Ruhee looked around, hoping the old woman had been eaten by something. She could not face Kurta and tell her. Unless…was it possible that Kurta took Alara to prove to Ruhee what a poor mother she would make?

Ruhee scowled. *I put her by the log—I knew where she was! Kurta told me she rolled over once. Once. How was I to know she could travel?* She threw the vines down and walked to the cliff's edge to look out. *Where are the ships? I need to get off this island.*

"Where is the baby?"

Ruhee snapped around to see Kurta standing at the fire, hands on her hips. She was not scowling—yet. Ruhee walked back to the camp, feeling the rivulets of sweat running down her back, her temples, soaking her in fear.

Kurta repeated her question. "Where is the baby?"

"I took her with me to collect vines." Ruhee's voice was breathy and small. "But the vines were hard to pull with the baby on my back."

"So? You have never done anything hard before?"

"No—yes—I have. But…she kept sliding forward on my back and we were hitting our heads and…and I was worried. Worried for her safety." Ruhee's voice found its confidence as she convinced herself of her innocence.

Kurta crossed her arms. "What did you do?"

"I untied the sling and sat Al—I mean—Zaina against a log. I could see her *the entire time* that I was gathering vines."

"Then my question remains. Where is she?"

"Well, the thing is…the problem was…it was just for

a moment…I took a swim in the lagoon."

Kurta's eyes narrowed as her arms returned to her sides, hands clenching into fists. "Where you could not see her—at any time."

"It wasn't very long!" Ruhee broke down. "You only said she could roll over, not roll away! She shouldn't have been able to travel so far!"

"No. You will take responsibility for what you did. You left a baby alone, with no one to watch. You know nothing about this island or the beasts who live here."

Ruhee fell to her knees, shaking her head, the tears flowing. "Help me, Kurta. Help me find her."

"Where do you suggest I look?" The old woman picked up a bowl and filled it with roasted pork, vegetables, and fruit. "I hear no cries from her. You claim you looked everywhere. Did you listen everywhere? And she is a baby—how far could she have rolled?"

"I looked all around the log, into the brush, around the edges of the lagoon, and even gazed into the blue water to see if she had fallen in." Ruhee wiped her forehead with the back of her hand. "All I found was the sling. There were no footprints of man or animal, and no flattened sand of a baby rolling. There was only the sound of birds."

Kurta took a bite of food and chewed slowly. "I suppose she could have flown away."

"What do you mean? Babies don't fly."

"Of course, they do not." She smiled. "Sit, child. Eat. She is either safe and we can find her, or she is not safe, and we may not find her. Either way, we need our strength to find little *Zaina*."

Ruhee picked up a bowl, keeping her eyes on Kurta. She filled it, slowly, and lowered herself onto her silks. The old woman seemed lost in her food, but Ruhee watched her anyway, wondering why she was not more frantic about a missing baby. And why the emphasis on her name?

"Speaking of the baby," Kurta said, still studying each morsel she picked up. "I heard you calling out from the lagoon. Who is Alara?"

Ruhee breathed in so sharply, she choked on the yam she'd just bitten into. Standing, sputtering, coughing, she reached for the nearest skin of coconut milk and swallowed a few gulps. A few red-faced moments later, she could breathe again.

She wished she could think again.

"I'm so sorry to startle you," Kurta said. "But I am curious. Who is Alara?"

"Alara." Ruhee cleared her throat and sat. "I was calling…I mean, it's a nickname my mother called babies. Alara means 'gift of god' in many tongues. I guess…I was crazy afraid, not thinking. If I called for God's gift, he might give it to me."

"Hmm-mmm." The old woman continued to eat. "Yes, losing the baby is distressing. You were only away for only a moment, and old Kurta's warning was unimportant. A baby cannot just disappear."

"I'm sorry, Kurta, you were right."

"I am right about much." She stood. "For example, I am right that you have hidden much about that baby, including her name, and why you have her."

"No, I—"

"Do no arguing, or worrying, for now. We are fed and ready to search." She reached out her hand. "Give me your bowl. I will rinse them today so you will not have to visit the lagoon. It seems to be unlucky for you."

Ruhee watched her turn up the path, bowls in hand. She felt an internal shaking, like a bird trying to escape a cage, and yet her limbs were heavy and numb.

"Ruhee, come along," Kurta called. "We will start our hunt on the trail."

She ran to catch up, not because she was anxious to find Alara, but because her nerves wouldn't let her stand still. Arriving at the clearing, she returned to the place she had last seen Alara, hoping the baby had magically reappeared. The empty space made her weep again.

Kurta was at the lagoon, placing the rinsed bowls in her sack. She rose and turned to the young woman. "Stop your blubbering and show me where you placed the baby."

Ruhee pointed. "In her sling, propped there."

Kurta nodded and examined the area for such a long time, Ruhee wanted to cry out that there was nothing to look at. At the point she wanted to slip away and leave Kurta to look, the old woman stood and looked in the opposite direction, an odd look of surprise on her face.

Ruhee turned to see what she was staring at, but Kurta returned to the log and pointed into the brush.

"You can start by looking through the jungle there. I will search around the lagoon." Kurta wrapped the sack across her shoulder. "Do not return to camp until you have found her—or it is too dark to see."

Ruhee watched Kurta's back as the old woman strode to the water and headed right, along the edge, combing the vines and brush as she went. Sighing, Ruhee turned back to her task. She found a large stick to move leaves about on the ground, looking for a baby. The birds and small animals in this jungle chattered above her, increasing their noise as she moved below them. They made it impossible to listen for a tiny human's cry.

"This is a fool's errand," she told the birds. "There is not a way for that little infant to get this far into the brush."

She pushed her way past the last grove of trees and saw an expanse of low flowing greenery, ground cover of vines and orchids and ferns, surrounded by tall island trees with drooping limbs of long leaves. The sun was well high, making the field sparkle.

As she looked out, movement caught her eye. A small head of dark hair rose from the ground cover and vanished as quickly. Ruhee ran to the spot, but the vines hindered her feet and tripped her. She got to the spot only to hear a baby's mewl to her left. Looking, she saw the head rise up toward the middle of the field. Taking better care of her feet and the plants, she moved toward the sound.

Thus began the game of cat and mouse that lasted beyond sunset. Ruhee chased the sound and sight of Alara until it was dark and all she could chase was an occasional coo. She remembered what Kurta said about coming back to camp if it was too dark to see.

Picking her way out of the field, she started back toward the lagoon and the trail to camp. The moon gave half-light tonight and clouds rolled across the sky. It was not much but better than the new moon. She walked through the trees, always heading dead west. There was no trail, so any attempt at hurrying resulted in tangled feet in tangled vines.

Birdsong had quieted to a few random trills and each step Ruhee took through the brush sounded amplified. Her stomach gurgled and that gurgle turned into an eventual growl. She didn't remember the lagoon being this far away. She looked up through the canopy. The moon had shifted from the eastern sky to the west, which meant she'd been walking this way for several hours.

She was lost.

Leaning against a tree, she covered her face with her hand and cried. "This is horrible. I could be in a castle now, sleeping in a bed and eating at a table, instead of in this jungle, eating with sand in my food and looking for this baby that I never should have taken!"

She walked a few more paces and found a small patch of moss, big enough for a deer to hide under the elephant fern leaves and get some rest. Curling into the space, she laid her head on her arm and closed her eyes. Tomorrow when the sun rose, she'd be able to find her way back.

Her sleep was uneasy and filled with disturbing

dreams. At one point, she could feel breath on her legs and something sniffing her. Was this dream or real? She tucked her legs up tightly and squeezed her eyes. If it was real, it did not matter. She had no place to go.

Once sleep settled into a comfortable darkness, sunlight stabbed her eyes and made her fight against waking. Scrunching her face against the day, Ruhee blinked herself awake, awareness slowly dawning. Her body was warm and covered in silks. The campfire was before her, and the aroma of roasting food made her mouth water. She sat up, wondering how she got back to camp if last night she was lost in the jungle.

"Ah, you are up already."

Ruhee looked left to see Kurta walking down from the trail, carrying the pot and a washed clout. The sling was tied at her chest. She didn't have to guess—Alara giggled happily on Kurta's back, swinging her legs up to catch her toes. Ruhee pinched her eyes shut.

Am I going mad?

Lisette woke quickly from the blow to her head as the two women were tying her hands behind her back. Katerina fished out the small bag of coin from Lisette's pocket. She nodded at Isabel.

"Get the wagon."

Soon a buckboard pulled beside the inn, driven by Isabel. Lisette felt sorry for the little red horse doing all the work. She could count all his ribs, and his entire body screamed that he was old and tired and longed for death. Katerina grabbed Lisette under her arms and lifted.

"Oof, get out here and help me," she snapped at Isabel.

Isabel jumped down and picked up Lisette's legs. "You are so weak."

Lisette relaxed as much as she could and let the two

women pick up dead, limp weight. The two women huffed and groaned as they struggled, maneuvering her into the cart. After some moments, Lisette braced her body against the rough boards of the cart as the women climbed onto the seat. She heard the crack of a whip and a jumping start to the wagon. The loss of her coin did not concern her. These two were going to pay for beating that horse.

The cart rumbled down the village portside to the brothel and right. At the boarding house, the road became steeper, and she realized they had to be going to the castle.

Lisette chuckled quietly, scooting over until she could prop herself up against the side of the buckboard. She could now look up and see the backs of her captors. "Taking me to the count for your reward?"

"Yes—" Isabel said before Katerina shoved an elbow into her side. "Oof. What was that for?"

"Don't bother talkin' to 'er. She's one o' them noble-types 'erself. Twist yer words 'til ya turn 'er loose."

"She's right, Isabel, I am one of those noble-types. It was important to the viscount, you know, that he have a virgin of noble blood to rape and kill."

"Wha—oof!" Isabel received another blow.

Lisette continued. "Have you had much dealing with Count Barragan?"

The women did not reply, although Lisette could feel the tension between them as her question hung in the air.

"I only ask because I have not met him and do not know how deep his affections run for his poor, late brother. My father knew him. We might have much to talk about," she said. "I do recall my father doing business with him. He used to jest that every time he shook the count's hand, he had to count his fingers, to be certain he still had five."

Isabel let out a small whine.

"I do hope, for your sakes, that he actually gives you the reward," Lisette said.

Now Katerina spoke. "And why wouldn't he?"

"Why would he?" Lisette smiled. "He can easily take claim to me and lock you both in his dungeon—or have you executed as my accomplices."

The carriage stopped.

"Executed as what?" Isabel asked.

"Accomplices," Lisette said. "It means that whatever I did, evil wench that I am, you helped me."

"But we didn't!" Isabel cried.

"Shut your mouth!" Katerina hissed at her. "She makes a point. Do we trust the count to deliver the money? Or will he betray us?"

"What do we do?" Isabel's voice rose.

"Let me think," Katerina said, and fell silent.

Lisette needed to find Begum and get to Île des Oiseaux. She took a deep breath, intending to transform but movement further down the trail caught her attention.

"I believe your thinking time has run dry, Katerina," Lisette said as she stared at the approaching shadows. "It looks like the count's guard is coming."

Lisette could feel the breeze as Katerina and Isabel whipped around to see four horsemen approaching the wagon. The road was small and uphill. There was no place to hide, and their pitiful horse could not outrun the guards. Still, Katerina raised the whip to lash the poor beast hitched before them. Her arm was midair when a deep voice rang out.

"Put that whip down!" Four uniformed men on fine black horses surged forward until they surrounded the wagon, swords drawn.

Lisette managed to scoot to a full sitting position. She smiled at the guards and cocked her head towards Katrina and Isabel. "I suspect it's not going to end well for you," she whispered.

Isabel burst into sobs. Katerina dropped the whip and

slapped her. "Stop listening to that witch."

A sword pushed against Katerina's chest and an angry guardsman told her, "Strike anyone again and I shall run you through."

"Good evening, fine sires," Lisette said. "How may we be of service to you today?"

The young man with his blade pointed at Katerina spoke. "We may ask the same of you. How is it you wenches come to the castle, and why is one of you bound?"

Katerina's mouth opened and shut, much like a fish gasping on shore. A small voice squeaked from her, growing into a firm whisper finally. "We have business to transact with Count Barragan, if you please."

"We don't please," the guard said, his voice testy. "And you have not answered me about the woman bound."

"Oh, I can explain," Lisette said, watching the two women's faces pale. Katerina opened her mouth, but the guard held his hand to her face and nodded to Lisette.

"These two women suspect me of murdering Viscount Barragan," Lisette continued. "They've robbed me of my coin and are now going to collect the count's reward…unless he discovers they are lying to him."

"I'm not lying—" Katerina yelped before the point of the guard's sword kept her temper from flaring. "I mean, my friend here is a witness what can tell the count what happened."

"In exchange for reward," Lisette added, glancing at the guards. "What truth has ever been said in exchange for gold?"

"Stop talking!" Katerina screamed and screamed again when the hilt of the guard's sword struck her across the cheek.

The leader of the guards gestured, and they gathered in front of the wagon, their horses close. Leaning in, they spoke in low tones and nodded a few times, looking at the three women before turning inward to speak again. At last, they reined their mounts out and back to the buckboard.

"We shall escort you to the count," the leader said, and looked toward Lisette. "But we will untie this one. There is no reason for her to be the only prisoner bound."

Isabel had not stopped tearing up and now she opened the floodgates, wailing and collapsing against Katrina's shoulder. Katrina pushed her away.

"You are useless."

The guard untying Lisette's hands was quite gentle and took care not to scrape her wrists. He put his mouth to her ear and whispered, "I will help all I can, m'lady Lisette."

She turned to look at him. He was one of the guards at her old castle. She restrained herself from throwing her arms around him.

"Thank you." She stretched her shoulders, sore from being tied behind her back.

A body thudded into the buckboard and Lisette saw Isabel lying next to her, pushing herself up with groans and tears. The leader was now sitting next to Katerina, the reins in his hand. Two of his men had unhitched the poor cart horse and put the leader's horse in the harness instead. Remounting, they started up the hill again, the cart horse now tied to the back and walking with a lighter step.

Lisette smiled at Isabel, who sat white-faced and saucer-eyed across from her. "I guess the guards don't like it when horses are misused. I'm afraid their report to the count will be harsh. We may end up neighbors in his gaol cells."

The girl spouted a new fountain of tears. "I never asked fer this! I only needed a bit o' coin and Katerina—that witch! She says it's an easy job—I jes tell 'em what I saw and it's easy money."

"Witches can be as naïve as simple village maids,"

the guard leader said over his shoulder.

The wagon suddenly shook as Katerina threw herself from the seat. She ran a few steps from the path, but one of the guards quickly caught up with her. Leaning over in his saddle, he grabbed her by the hair and walked her back to the cart, pulling her along by her braid as his horse pranced beside her. Katerina screamed the entire way, loud enough to echo across the island. Most of it was unintelligible, although Lisette discerned a few words that sounded like she was willing to kill everyone.

The leader stopped the wagon and let them catch up.

"Throw her in the back with the others," he told the guard. "Actually, tie her to the buckboard. She's the kind to cause trouble."

The guard walked his horse over to the end of the wagon, where he encouraged Katerina to get in by yanking her hair upwards. Still screaming that he was hurting her, the girl climbed into the back. He let her go as soon as the guard from Lisette's castle dismounted and clasped Katerina's hands behind her, securing her to the slats in the side of the wagon's back end.

The group started toward the castle again.

"This is taking all day," the leader grumbled.

"You could always release us," Lisette said. "I hate to cut into your daily schedule."

"Ah, but this is part of our daily schedule," he said. "We are not without our spies in the village. As soon as these two wenches nabbed you, we knew of the deed. The count sent us to intercept you."

Lisette looked at Katerina. "That doesn't sound good for you."

"Silence," she spat, and adjusted her body as much as possible to sit upright, her chin tilted up. "Isabel and I have done a good deed to deliver you. We are merely getting the count's escort to the castle."

A harrumphing sound from the leader made Lisette

grin and Katerina's chin lower.

"Well, what do these soldiers know, anyway," Katerina said. "They are lackeys and only do what they are told."

Lisette looked across to the guard who rode beside the wagon. He smiled and gave a quick wink.

"We shall see," Lisette said, and turned her attention to the road ahead.

The castle was just coming into view—at least she assumed it was the castle. High stone walls surrounded the front, just as she expected, but no tall stone building could be seen behind them. Where was the edifice with its rooftop sentries and rounded turrets on the corners?

"I see the walls but not the castle," she said.

"Yes, m'lady." Her old guard spoke. "Count Barragan had a different…vision…in mind when he built this fortress."

She sat back, nodding, keeping a focused eye on their destination. All she could do now was wait.

Rocco stirred the embers, adding wood until the fire was reborn. Lamya had left skins of her magic broth, so he heated one and drank it, sitting on his silk bedding and thinking of Lisette.

He was not quite certain why she had to save her home island. She didn't even want to live there but wanted to turn it over to the villagers and the native peoples. There would be no Spanish ships to sail these waters, and he had no stomach for pillaging the local merchants.

Still, Lamya's question bothered him. *What remains in your heart that still demands the blood of Spaniards?*

What did remain? The day Tempest died was beyond painful. In the days that followed he attempted to attain justice. The other Spanish nobles on the island were sympathetic but weak against the Count de Medina. A letter to the king resulted in a tepid response, that "someone would see about the matter" as though it was a dispute between landowners and not a woman's murder.

His fellow sailors, the men he counted on to help him, abandoned him. They felt badly, but what could they do? The count was a powerful man, they had their orders, his grief would end, and he would find another woman. Excuses, all excuses for why they would not risk their skins to aid his search for justice.

When he rose up to face the count, he rose up alone, where he was captured, tortured, and escaped. His friends now fled from him, fearing that they would be held accountable.

Rocco ran his fingers along his dagger. There was no forgetting what the Spaniards had done to him, merely by their abandonment. And he did not forgive them for leaving him alone.

A bird screeched in the tree above him, flying down to light a few feet away. It was large and crimson. It sat, eyeing Rocco with a cock of its head, one way then the other.

He laughed. "All right, bird. Lamya told me to get some rest. I shall not get any if I keep stirring old memories."

Putting the now-empty skin down, he spread his bedding out and laid in it. He did not feel sleepy, but he would do his best. When Lamya ordered something, it was best to do it with no argument. He crumpled some of the silks and used them as a pillow for his head. Clamping his eyes closed, he struggled but eventually drifted away in a sea of darkness and dreams.

The sun was on the west side and heading toward the horizon when he opened his eyes and stretched. The fire had died again, and his hunger awakened, so he rose to put more wood on the embers and toss a yam at the edge of the flames. He had just walked to the pile of driftwood he'd collected when he heard a soft cooing. It was like a dove and yet not a dove, like a kitten yet different. He turned around to see where the sound was coming from.

There was a small lump in his bedding, wriggling with life. Rocco pulled the silks aside and found Alara looking up at him, her face aglow and hands reaching toward him.

"What are you doing here?" He picked her up and held her at arms' length, but she found a way to wriggle until he pulled her close. "Did Lamya bring you to me early? What happened to that wench who stole you? I wish you could talk. I have many questions."

Something sharp poked his wrist and he pulled away, looking for the briar or thorn stuck in Alara's clothing. He discovered a purple feather sticking out from her gown. Holding it aloft, his gaze shifted from daughter to feather and back again.

"Or perhaps my questions have an answer—and new questions arise."

The baby giggled and reached for his face. Rocco watched her hands, allowing them to wander across his nose and swipe at his eyes, only objecting when she took a firm hold of his beard and yanked.

"Ow, no, let us not do that," he implored as he disengaged her fingers. "Papa likes his beard."

Papa. Was that what she would call him? He shuddered. His own father had died before he was born. Would he have called him Papa, or Father? Even among his friends, he could see that their fathers were not their playmates. Their relationships were formal, and most were called Father.

"I suppose Papa is acceptable," he told the baby, and held her up, away from him where he could study her. "Will you fly with Mama through the night skies?"

"Perhaps," a deep purr said. Lamya strode up from the far side of the plateau, in the guise of the old woman. "There you are, Alara. I thought you might have come looking for your papa."

Rocco raised his eyebrows and held out the purple feather to her. "You didn't bring her, did you?"

Lamya chuckled. "She is a special child."

"Does she…talk? I mean, she is a baby, barely two months' old. How…?"

"She is a baby." Lamya smiled at Alara, scrunching her nose, and eliciting a giggle. "But she has powers. Like all babies, she has basic wants—food, sleep, comfort. She did not think, 'I want my papa.' She simply wanted to be with you. Her body did the rest."

"I do not envy Lisette the task of raising our child."

Lamya stared at him. "Or her papa."

"Don't be silly." Rocco laughed. "Men don't raise the children."

"Do not fool yourself. You are an important part of this child's upbringing. You are as much dragon as Lisette. Lisette will encourage the nourishing, protective side of her. You must balance the destructive, angry side."

"Which reminds me, I am here to learn about this new dragon inside me." Rocco bounced the baby in his arms. "What do we do with the little one in the meantime?"

"We take her with us." Lamya gestured away from camp, toward a glade of trees. She reached for Alara. "I will carry her. Come."

Rocco followed the Ancient One into the jungle. Alara sat in the sling on Lamya's back, smiling and reaching out to him. He studied her, frowning, which caused her to giggle. His foot caught in a vine, and he stumbled forward, catching himself at the last. Alara giggled louder. They moved further into the brush, Rocco being distracted by his daughter and getting more tangled in the ground cover.

They had just reached a clearing and he took a large step to get out of the brush. A large green rope of vine wrapped around his ankle and pulled him back. He fell onto his hands and knees. His frustration boiled over.

"Gods dammit!" Rocco pushed himself upright and felt a familiar burning in his bones. Within a heartbeat, he had transformed into a white dragon, feathers tipped in red. He stood in the clearing, looking at Lamya.

Alara giggled again, clapping her hands.

At least my child is unafraid of me.

Lamya kept walking down a small path. "Come, Rocco dragon. We are not at our destination yet."

He walked behind her, turning his head this way and that to look at himself. Apart from his color, he was no different from when he flew as a blood dragon. He held up a front paw to examine it. His talons were still long and deadly.

I hope we are headed toward a lagoon. I'd like to see what I am.

"You will know what you are soon enough," Lamya called back to him as she marched on.

He opened his mouth to shout back and heard several growls and a low chuff come from him. *It's not fair that I can't answer you.*

"You can. I hear you very well."

Alara giggled again, as if in delight at their conversation.

Rocco stared at his daughter. *Alara, can you hear me?*

She cooed and blew bubbles at him, and he shook his head. *No, you're a baby and I'm being a fool.* Alara looked him in the eye and smacked her lips silently.

Rocco heard her sweet high voice in his head. *Papa, you got mad.*

Yes, I got mad. He wondered at their silent conversation.

You turned into a dragon. Her words sounded so accusatory, he wanted to apologize. But apologize for what? He was here with Lamya to learn this exact skill, to transform into a dragon.

"Do not apologize to her," Lamya said. "She is not scolding you. She is merely reporting the fact."

"Then why do I feel scolded?"

"Because you scold yourself." Lamya stopped walking. "Here. This is where we work tonight."

Rocco the dragon looked at the view before him. A small lagoon, growing inky in the night's shadows, lapped water to his right. To his left, the clearing stretched, broadening to an expansive field that rolled gently downward. He sat, watching Lamya prepare camp. Most of her tasks were for dexterous hands, like retrieving bowls and laying down silks. She untied the sling and pulled Alara around to her arms.

"A little food and a change of clout," she told the baby, "And you may sleep while Papa works."

After piling dead branches and leaves in a small pit, she turned to Rocco and stepped away. "Light this, please."

Happy to use his skills, Rocco built the fire down in his chest and breathed it only the kindling. Flames shot everywhere before settling into a pleasant blaze.

"Thank you," Lamya said and placed a bubby pot near the heat to warm. "Perhaps while you are a dragon, you could work on tempering your fire? You could have lit all the campfires on the island with that one burst."

Rocco laughed, but his dragon form made it sound like a chuffing snort. He nodded so she would understand, remembered that she could read his thoughts, and chuffed again.

Soon Alara was fed, clean, and ready for sleep. She insisted on being rocked by Papa, so Rocco sat up, holding her in one paw while his tail acted as a rocker to push him to and fro. Her tiny hand reached up to grab a chunk of feathers, relaxing only when she had finally drifted into full slumber. Lamya gently took the baby and laid her in a silken nest.

"She will sleep soundly while we work," she told him, and pointed to the wide, rolling path. "This is where we start."

He looked ahead. *This feels different than learning to transform and control my blood dragon curse.*

"It is different. So much so. First, this is not a curse, and you must clear your heart of that belief. This will be a blessing, although you might not see it now."

Rocco growled. *In the meantime, how do I get back to human form so I can actually use my voice again?*

Lamya tsked. "So much impatience, so much anger. Go. Sit by that altar, facing it and the moon."

He looked up and saw the waning gibbous moon. It still gave good light across the field, showing the outline of a stone altar, ringed by what appeared to be glass eggs. As he grew closer, he saw that they were also stones that had been smoothed and polished to a uniform shape. He looked back at Lamya, who stood quietly expectant, her hands on her hips and head cocked.

Who's impatient now?

"Go. Sit. The moon hastens."

Rocco sauntered into position and sat, curling his tail around him. He regarded Lamya, awaiting her orders.

"And it does no good to roll your eyes at me," she said. "Look at the altar. Focus on it. Breathe slowly—into your body, hold, out of your body."

Rocco did as he was told. *This feels distinctly foolish.*

"You are only a fool if you disobey me." She waited, silent, until she could see him breathing as she instructed. "Picture yourself in your human body. Tell yourself, 'I am a man.' Keep picturing, keep telling yourself. Do not rush or push it."

Rocco kept his breath slow and rhythmic, until his breathing was all he focused upon. The movement of air in and out of his throat easily quieted his body until he sat in perfect stillness.

"Rocco." Lamya's sharp call interrupted him. "Picture your human body. Tell yourself 'I am a man.' Listen to my words."

He closed his eyes and saw his human body, his face and hair, the sword in his hand. The deck of *L'Implacable* was at his feet and the wind whipped across his clothes and into the sails.

I am a man.

It was a slow, low burn, like the early morning sun's crawl across the ship. His arms and legs were first, followed by his torso. Within a few seconds, he was Rocco the pirate again.

"Ah, very good." Lamya smiled. "Your first lesson, you do very well."

"So that's it? That's how I become human again?" He laughed. "Seems too easy."

She shrugged. "For you, it may be. Transforming to dragon may not be so simple."

"I'm still unsure. Why should I transform? And what kind of dragon am I?"

"Like Lisette, you are a moon dragon. Unlike Lisette, your power lies in your anger." She sat in the soft green moss and grasses. "You must harness this feeling in order to transform and be the kind of dragon your daughter needs."

"I know you keep saying I must help Lizzie raise Alara, but I just don't see how that will be possible—I'll be at sea for months at a time. Why can't Lisette handle those duties?"

Lamya stood, her eyes full of fire, pointing back at the campsite, her voice loud and words biting. "Because that is your daughter, and you are the edge of the blade on which she walks. Lisette will bring her goodness, kindness, but make no mistake—a child born of two blood dragons is born into righteous anger. Your control of your own rage is what will teach her to do the same."

"And if she doesn't learn it from me?" He stood, both hands on his hips, daring her to convince him.

The Ancient One straightened her spine and stood taller, taller than he had ever seen. She kept growing and changing before his eyes, lifting gnarled arms and hands to the heavens, and staring down at him with eyes like the ocean he sailed. His jaw fell open to see her.

"Is this your true form?"

"I take the form that is needed," she said. "My true form would blind you. This is as much as I dare reveal."

"Lamya, I—"

She stretched a long, gray branch of an arm to his lips. "It is not enough that I tell you why. You must feel the reason in your heart, know it in your head. Regard."

With broad sweeps of her arms, the sky opened to display a vista of bubbling, red turbulence. Rocco had been seated but the scene exploded before him so violently he fell backward, catching himself at the last moment with his hands.

"This is your life, Tristan de Rocco." Lamya gestured

to a small lava stream. "Your childhood was filled with much anger. Your father dead, your mother's family disdainful, your only solace was in her love for you. Pain made you hate."

Rocco looked up, the memories of being taunted and beaten by his cousins, ignored by grandparents, returned and stung his heart as if new.

"The Spanish fleet and Tempest served as your salvation," she continued, pointing out a section of blue. "Your life's river is calm, blue, but underneath..." The azure scene turned purple. "Underneath was fire."

Her branching fingers swept over her head, over the scenes. "Underneath is always fire. You will not escape it, but you can tame it."

"But what has that to do with me turning into a dragon? Or raising my daughter?"

Lamya's eyes flashed like a summer squall, lightning, and thunder within them as she glared down at him. "Alara's life will be different than most, and sometimes harder. She will inherit your rage, even if only by watching how you respond to life. This is not a bad thing. Sometimes she will need anger. But she will need to know how to control it. You must teach her."

"Why can't—"

"No." She stopped him. "Lisette's anger is not fueled by the past. Alara will not witness rage in her, only the fierceness that comes with protecting her loved ones." The Ancient One shrank, keeping her eyes on him, until she was back to a human form. "You are the only one. And I shall teach you."

Rocco sighed a deep breath of resignation. He didn't want to be a dragon anymore, didn't know how to be a father, and what exactly was Lisette off doing? He could not have more islands freed from European rule or his pirating days would be over.

Lamya smiled. "Ah, my Rocco. It is difficult to fight

so much against the unknown. Better that we get started and do no wasting of time." She raised her hand, indicating that he should stand up. "I thought this was the best place to transform, but I am now changing of my mind. Come with me."

He followed her, leaving the mossy clearing, and heading back toward the lagoon and the sleeping baby.

"Sit," Lamya said. "By the water, facing your baby."

43

Rocco did as he was told. *I suppose the good part of this dragon is that I can choose when to transform.*

"You can choose, but sometimes it will be your only choice." Lamya pointed to the sleeping child. "Look at her face. Let it be the only thing you see. Let her grow in your mind. She is your future."

It was not difficult to focus on the sweet face, for all his discomfort with her. He could see Lisette's eyes and her full lips, mingled with his nose and dark curls. *I do love you, child, but I have no idea what to do with you.*

Do not be afraid, Alara's high, child's voice told him. *You will learn how to tell if I am wet or cold or hungry by my cry. I will learn how to sail a ship by your words. It is unknown to both of us, and we will have wonderful lessons.*

Rocco saw in her face the young woman she would

become. As if startling awake, he was overcome with the urge to help her grow into that young woman. He became aware of Lamya's low purring voice, chanting.

"Chosen path,
Forged in flame
New life rises
Dreams to claim."

The rumble of her voice, and the hypnotic focus on Alara made his body lighten, as if he might fly without wings. He felt the slow warm of bones lengthening and feathers growing, taking his body and stretching it out until he was a dragon. Four legs now supported him, along with a tail balancing in the back. Alara still slept, for which he was glad.

"Very good," Lamya told him. "Now, change back."

His eyes widened. *I just got into this form,* he protested.

"Yes, and you shall leave this form. You must change more quickly, and I have only the nighttime to teach you."

Rocco nodded his head. As much as he wanted to explore this dragon body, she was correct. If he was going to do this and return to *L'Implacable*, he could not tarry. He pictured himself at the helm, guiding the ship and his men. *I am a man.*

The change was quicker into human and not as sharp in terms of discomfort. He sat back into the sand, looking at Lamya.

"Very good. Now, you gaze at that tree. Picture your daughter's face, hear my words, change when you can."

It took longer to turn into dragon, and he struggled to see Alara's face in a tree trunk. Lamya's chant helped, until an image popped into his head of white feathers with red tips. Proud of himself, he wished to remain and admire his handiwork, but Lamya was relentless.

"You are human now."

"You are dragon."

"You are human."

On they progressed, until the sun's rays lightened the sky from below the horizon. Lamya put up her hand as Rocco transformed into human one last time.

"That is enough." She walked back toward the camp. "Come. You will have a meal. Alara and I must leave."

They strolled back, Lamya leading with Alara in her sling. The baby was on the edge of sleep now, her blinking eyes fighting to stay closed and a tiny fist rubbing across her face, finding her mouth, and suckling in contentment.

Once at camp, Lamya turned to him. "I believe you are now capable of becoming what you need to be in a situation, although beware the heat of your anger—it can trigger you to transform when perhaps it is not a good time. You should rest before you return to your ship, but this is your choice."

"I will at least eat." Rocco stared at her, studying the old woman she appeared to be and comparing that to the creature he saw last night. "You will not look for me here when the sun is set?"

"Let us say it is not my plan. Only indecision can keep you here, and you are a pirate captain. I think it not likely." She packed a few things in the tote she carried. "A meal, a quick rinse in the lagoon, and you can be off. You have much to do and will be impatient to do it."

She strolled away into the jungle, Alara on her back and staring at Rocco with wide, solemn eyes. He waved to her, and she raised both hands, flopping them excitedly. At the edge of the brush, Lamya looked over her shoulder.

"I have faith in you." She smiled. "As a dragon, or a father."

Rocco laughed and realized he had not laughed aloud in many days, perhaps months. The lightness of it felt like cleansing his soul. He returned to the ashes of their campfire and added small sticks and leaves, stirring the embers until the dried fuel caught before adding a larger piece of driftwood to the mix. Soon he had enough of a fire to roast a yam or two.

While his food was cooking, he headed back to the lagoon. The vines that had tripped him earlier had been tamped down by their footsteps, and he felt much calmer as he approached the water. Early rays of sunlight sparkled on the water, making ripples out of the smallest motion.

Rocco walked in until the water was at his waist before diving forward into the crystalline blue. It was cool on his skin. He swam to the middle and turned on his back. The morning sky had few clouds and showed the bright blues as the sun rose and chased the ink of night. He closed his eyes and basked.

Lamya said he needed to control his anger, but how could she ask this? The only love he'd been taught was from his mother. She was the eye at the center of his storm, taken too soon from him. He reached up to the silken thread around his neck. A small hand of gold, its fingers folded with a ruby heart in the palm hung on the dark silk. It was his mother's amulet, a protection against the Evil Eye. The ruby was so small it was worth little, but it was all he wanted when she died.

His grandfather took it from her as she lay in the casket, took it and threw it over the rocks toward the sea. Tears in his eyes, he shouted, "There's your protection!"

Rocco saw his grandfather's pain then and knew it was the source of the anger he displayed to his grandson. It should have made him understand, but it made him hate the old man even more. He slipped away from the family and the funeral, down to the beach and searched, sifting through the sand and the tide pools, until he found his mother's necklace. Tying it to his own neck, he followed the beach to the pier and waited.

The next morning, he spied a ship coming into the harbor. Talking his way to a cabin boy position, the twelve-year-old left his home and never returned.

Now, he closed his hand around the golden charm. *I shouldn't be angry? These people treated their dogs better than me. Grandfather would rather hate me than let his grandson soothe the pain of losing his mother.*

A wave came from nowhere and washed over him, pushing him to the bottom of the lagoon and holding him there. Rocco kicked and paddled, attempting to get to the surface. The surprise had caught him with little air in his lungs. He desperately twisted and pushed against the water, looking for whatever had trapped him.

His lungs could neither expel nor inhale more air, and all faded to darkness.

44

Lisette had to admit her admiration for Count Barragan as they entered the courtyard of his "castle." It reminded her much of Madame Adelinde's compound on Isla de la Ballena. Long low buildings of whitewashed adobe and brick, with a smaller open structure across the square of pavestones. Behind it, Lisette could spy a larger building that she guessed was the actual living quarters for the count.

The buckboard and its companions stopped in front of the smaller structure, where the guards handed their horses off to the stable boy.

"Time to meet m'lord," the leader said, untying Katerina's bonds and turning her out of the wagon.

Isabel was next, followed by Lisette. Each woman received her own escort into the castle, Katerina having two to keep her from escaping again.

Lisette ambled toward the door, walking next to her guard, who had his left hand lightly gripping her right arm. They hung back, Lisette slowing her movement to have a private conversation.

"Your name is Charles, isn't it?" she asked.

"Oui, m'lady. I must say, I am thrilled to see you. I had been told the de Lille family did not survive after your kidnapping."

She bowed her head. "It is true, I met my brother on Isla de la Ballena shortly after our parents were killed. He was murdered by a greedy woman."

"You had your revenge?"

"Oui." She looked at him. "It surprises me that you ask."

"We could not guard the family without knowing them. You were kind, generous, but protective of loved ones, and exacting if crossed."

She smiled and shrugged before studying the space around her. The first small building they entered contained weaponry and shields, hung on all walls. The only furniture was a small table and chairs in the corner.

Waving her hand across the room, she asked, "Preparation for battle?"

Charles nodded. "The count feels our armory is too far from where we might be under attack."

The group passed through to another, smaller courtyard with a fountain in the middle, creating a circular stone path to allow carriages to stop at the large house, and move around to the small armory before heading out of the gates.

The large house, aka "castle" was anything but. There were no turrets, no grand stories, or arches, no statues. The only thing to indicate this was the home of nobility were the two large doors with the family crest carved into them.

"Any hints on how to handle this count?" Lisette

whispered to Charles.

The guard kept his focus forward as they walked. "He can be a fair man. He can also be unpredictable. If it's any help, I don't think he was close to his brother. And he seems always in need of finances. I believe El Rey grows weary."

Posted guards moved in tandem to open the carved doors and Charles stepped back to let Lisette go through.

"Time to be your prisoner, yes?" she teased. Taking a breath, she followed the others inside.

Although the outside was unusual, the inside of Count Barragan's house screamed wealth and privilege. Every wall held a painting or tapestry. The doorways were tall arches, inviting grand entrances across the marbled floors. Heavy dark furniture was carved in the Spanish style and covered in burnished leather. Lisette made note of it all, along with every exit as they walked toward the great hall.

At the double doors that opened into the room, the leader of the guards stopped, putting his arm out to signal everyone to halt. Charles and the other two guards took their posts, keeping the three women from escaping. The leader stepped into the great hall.

"Katerina," Lisette said, "you must be excited to meet the count at last."

Katerina lifted her chin, though her skin paled. "Yes. I am looking forward to my reward."

Lisette smiled. "Oh, you'll get your reward." She winked at Charles. "Won't she, sire?"

"The count is unpredictable," Charles said.

Isabel shook with sobs. "I should not have listened to you."

"Stop!" Katerina slapped Isabel's face again. "The wench is trying to frighten us. Do not be swayed."

Lisette crept forward and peered through the crack in the doors. At the end of the hall, a tall, angular man sat in a tall chair on a dais. Count Barragan, receiving visitors, no doubt. She could not see his details, but from afar, he looked more pleasant than his oily brother.

The quick clip of footsteps made her pull away in time for the doors to swing open. The guard leader stopped, looked at the others, and nodded.

"M'ladies." He stepped aside with a grand gesture outward.

Lisette was closest to the door by now. Isabel had shrunk behind her, and Katerina hesitated, weaving indecisively. Lisette straightened her spine and strode forward, only to feel her left shoulder being pushed aside as Katerina barged ahead. She happily assumed the second position and followed her captor.

The women arrived before the count, surrounded by guards. Lisette studied Count Barragan. There was a definite likeness between him and his viscount brother in their dark, sharp features. But where Antonio was old and skinny with a pot belly, this man clearly received the best of his parents' lineage. Broad-shouldered and long-legged with the face of an archangel, Lisette wondered if she would have had the same response if she'd met him instead of his brother in that boarding house.

She certainly would have regretted killing him.

Barragan stood, so Lisette curtsied. She heard the rustle of skirts behind her, indicating Isabel had at least followed her, if not fallen down. Only Katerina remained standing. Lisette peeked up from her bow at the still-upright woman, raising her eyebrows in judgment.

The count gave a slight bow of dismissal to the two women before setting his attention on Katerina.

"State your name and business before this house." He remained standing, and Lisette observed how he towered over the girl, emphasizing his power.

Katerina backed a step before planting herself firmly and looking up. "I come to give witness—that is, I come wit' my friend who can give witness against this wench as the one what killt yer brother."

"You did?" He smiled and walked to the end of the chair's platform, turned, and walked back. "No doubt, you heard of the reward?"

"Yes, sire."

"And certainly, you could use a sack of coin, if only to buy yourself proper manners." He spun to Katerina, his eyes glowing like lit coals, his voice growling with menace. "When you come before a count, girl, you show the proper respect. I am addressed, always, as m'lord and always greeted with a curtsy."

Katerina recoiled, her body getting smaller until it appeared to shrink into itself. Lisette watched her skin blanche and her skirts rustling with her trembling legs. The count sank into his chair, running his fingers down his mustache and grinning.

"You, there." He pointed to Lisette. "What was your name? She called you…Wench?"

"M'lord, I've been called many things." Lisette stepped forward, adding a small bow. "But my name is Lisette de Lille. I am the daughter of the Duke and Duchess de Lille, of Île des Oiseaux, originally of Giverny, France."

"You see?" He looked at Katerina. "That is how you address a count. Deference, yet full disclosure. What did you say your name was?" He turned to Lisette. "What is she called?"

"She may also have many names, m'lord, but her accomplice calls her Katerina."

"Katerina? Not that wench from town who stirs up gossip?" He frowned. "I believe you spread a rumor or two about my brother, may he rest in peace."

"M'lord." Katerina fairly shouted the word. Blushing, she quieted. "I am not a genteel woman, tis true, but I come here today because my friend seen this lady goin' up ta see yer sainted brother, and then she seen her leavin' wit' blood all down 'er skirt."

"Your friend?" Barragan looked past Lisette, cocking his head sideways to see Isabel who stood as far back as the guards would allow, hunching down to appear as small as possible. "You, girl!" He gestured for the guards to bring her forward.

Lisette stood aside and let Charles pull Isabel forward by the arm. Isabel took one brief glance at the count and threw herself on the ground, her face obscured by her hands.

"M'lord, I know nothin' this wench is sayin' she told me we was to make money I got no parents, sire, and must make my livin' however I kin please don't send me ta dungeon it was her idea!" Isabel stopped long enough to take a breath and point to Katerina before wailing anew.

"You liar!" Katerina lunged for the weeping girl, but two of the guards caught her and kept her at bay. "Tell the truth! Tell what you saw that night!"

Lisette watched the scene, keeping her expression placid. She glanced at the count, who sat forward in his chair, stroking his beard thoughtfully. The way he self-groomed, his full sensual lips, made her think of another noble.

"What reward do you offer for your brother's killer?" Lisette asked.

He blinked and sat up. "Pardon? Oh, thirty doubloons."

"Thirty? My apologies, but you have much wealth, m'lord. Thirty seems like a pittance, especially for a loved one."

"Yes, my *sainted* brother." He threw his head back in wicked laughter. "Never was there a more conniving, manipulative, worm of a man as Antonio Barragan. Thirty is overpayment by twenty-nine, but Mama insisted I offer something to keep the family reputation untarnished."

"Then may I turn myself in and reap the reward?" Lisette asked. "I am the wench who killed Viscount Barragan."

"You, a lady of high nobility?" he asked, grinning.

"I was stolen from my family and sold to your brother." Lisette stepped away from the group, toward the count. "You may have heard of his eccentricities."

"Virgins, I believe, of noble birth?"

Lisette nodded. "I tried to extend our evening, at least become acquainted. He disagreed rather forcefully. M'lord, when it is my life or another's, can you blame me for my choice?"

"An excellent point."

Katerina pulled her arms away from her captors. "M'lord, I cannot believe you would give her my reward! I brought her here. I told you what she done. That coin is mine by rights."

"You came with a magnificent story," Barragan said. "One that neither you nor your 'friend' could verify. This young woman was there and can tell me exactly what happened." He turned to the leader of the guard. "The lump of girl crying—when she's all done, show her to the gate. This one—" he pointed to Katerina. "I believe requires a few lessons in manners, in presentation, in honesty—of truth, in everything. Give her a lovely space in the dungeon until I figure out where she goes next."

"M'LORD!" Katerina shrieked. "Not the gaol, please not the gaol!"

"See? She's already saying please. A couple of days cooling off in the cave, and she'll say thank you as well." He motioned toward the dungeon and Charles grabbed her arm.

45

Katerina shuffled in front of him, making him push her along the way. Halfway to the closed doors, she put her hand down beside him, turning toward him as she did. He grabbed his side and crumpled to the floor, a red gash spreading across his uniform from his own dagger, which the girl slipped from him. She still held the blade as she dashed for the door.

The remaining two guards ran toward Katerina, but Lisette was faster. She pulled her own dagger from her thigh, silent and quick. Within two long steps, she'd caught up with Katerina and grabbed her long, dark braid. Sitting back on her heels, she yanked with all her force.

Katerina flew backward and landed on her hips with a yowl. Lisette did not stop, but turned and strode back to the count, dagger in one hand and dragging the howling Katerina with the other. The captured girl tried to turn her body and regain her footing, but Lisette walked too fast, and the marble floor was slick. Lisette slid Katerina to the count's feet and stopped, standing on the girl's arm to take the dagger from her hand.

A dagger in each fist, Lisette stood back to allow Katerina to rise. She shook her head as the girl pushed to her feet and rubbed the back of her head.

"Witch, you nearly pulled my hair out."

"A night in Barragan's dungeon," Lisette said. "Maybe two for your insolence. Instead, you will now swing for this."

"It weren't my fault. I meant ta scratch 'im but he turned. He ran into the knife." Katerina's voice climbed higher and louder. "I didn't do this!"

The guards grabbed her arms and strode forward, pulling her off her feet and jerking her away from the count.

"Take her to the dungeon," Barragan instructed. "She dies at dawn."

Lisette looked at Charles on the floor, holding his hand against his side to stop the blood. She scurried to attend him. Pushing his hand off, she tore open his shirt to see the injury. It was wide, but not deep. Katerina had swiped the dagger at him, instead of pushing the point forward.

"Good thing she doesn't know how to wield a blade," Lisette told him and smiled.

"Hurts all the same," he said.

She nodded and tore a large section of his shirt off. Stuffing it into the wound, she removed his belt and tied it around to keep the bandage tight and the blood staunched. The leader of the guard was just returning from ejecting Isabel.

"What happened here?" he demanded.

"Charles can tell you," Lisette said. "While you escort him to the infirmary. I believe he will require stitches."

She helped the leader ease Charles into a standing position, after which the leader draped his comrade's arm across his shoulder and bore the wounded man's weight to carry him away.

Charles held on to Lisette for a moment, until she turned to face him.

"Thank you, m'lady."

She smiled. "It would be a pity for you to die the very day I see you again."

The men limped out together and she returned to the count's dais. "My apologies for the outburst."

"You know him?" Barragan asked.

She nodded. "Charles. He was a guard at my parents' castle, before the Medina family swept through like locusts."

"Yes, I've heard much about the Medinas. One of my friends visits on occasion. He was at a most frightening wedding involving the family and a pair of dragons if you can believe it."

Lisette looked at him. "This friend of yours—would it be Constantine de Martinmas?"

"Yes." Barragan straightened and blanched. "I am acquainted with the marquess."

"So am I." Lisette smiled and patted his arm. "Perhaps we could sit somewhere and talk, perhaps with a light repast?"

He gave her a small grin, though worry still creased his brow. "Ale or tea?"

"Whatever m'lord offers, I shall partake."

The count rose and pulled a silken cord. A servant appeared in the door. Lisette recognized her as one of the *Dişi Aslan* crew. She longed to talk to her, but the count was on edge and had his own agenda.

"Ale please, for both of us, and a plate of something

to take our hunger. We'll have it in the library." He turned and offered his arm, which she took.

They strolled into a smaller room filled with bookshelves and books, plush leather chairs and a table between. A long desk sat against one wall. Barragan lit the candelabra on the desk and moved the light to the center of the room.

"What a charming library," Lisette said. "It reminds me of the Martinmas castle on Isla de Pimienta."

"Does it?"

The serving girl brought a large tray into the room and disappeared, but not before giving Lisette a pointed look. Barragan poured two goblets of ale and handed one to Lisette. She lifted hers to him and gave a small nod.

"To your health, m'lord."

"And yours," he returned and gestured for her to sit. "I cannot help but wonder, if you indeed killed my brother, why would you return to this place?"

"I did not know I had a price on my head, or I should have thought twice."

"A pittance of a sum for a pittance of a brother."

Lisette frowned. "I am sorry for his death. I would have much preferred to leave him injured but intact."

"I can easily see it was my brother's fault. His low status chafed him, that I was a count and he a mere viscount. He was never content to push when he could shove." He took a sip of ale and chose a piece of dried meat to nibble. "So why are you here?"

"To hopefully stop a terrible plan. Two servant women have stolen something very valuable to me, and I am hunting them. A group of my…friends are aiding me, and I search for them, to see what news they have, if any."

"I see. What exactly was stolen?"

Lisette sipped her ale and sipped again. She looked into his eyes, which were black marbles set into lashes and brows of the same darkness. His expression was neutral.

She took a big breath, paused, and slowly uttered, "A baby."

His eyes widened and chin dropped. "A what? Whose baby?"

"My baby. Servants with a grudge against me kidnapped my baby and sailed on *El Buscador*. It came into port, and we traced them to the village, then lost the trail. I am trying to find my friends to see what they have discovered."

"Might I ask who is the father?"

"You might." Lisette stared at him. "I do not think you have made his acquaintance. Speaking of which, how often do you see Connie?"

He stiffened. "No more often than any of the other nobles."

"He has not told you of me?" Lisette smiled. "More importantly, do you not know of his father's efforts to get him to produce an heir?"

"I am aware." He stared at her. "Your baby—it's not his, is it?"

Lisette laughed. "By the gods, no, although dear Uncle Oscar did everything he could to attempt it. He even tried to marry us, much to our dismay."

"That was you? I heard the story but did not hear the name of the maiden."

She leaned forward. "Then you may ask Connie if he trusts me with his life—and his secret. You have nothing to fear from me. If you feel you must exact revenge for your brother, we shall have another discussion."

Barragan rose and walked to the desk. He took a key from around his neck and unlocked the top drawer, withdrawing a leather pouch that jingled with coin. Returning to his chair, he handed the bag to Lisette.

"A reward to the informant and vengeance is

complete."

She smiled. "Then I shall thank you and take my leave."

Barragan offered his hand to help her from the chair. She took it and strolled toward the door. He leaned forward to open it for her. Two guards stood on either side.

"Take her to the dungeon," the count ordered.

"What?" Lisette turned to him, her mouth agape as the guards grabbed her by the arms. "You said your vengeance was complete."

"It is." He took the pouch from her hand. "But you are not merely Lisette de Lille. You are the consort of Tristan de Rocco, and there is a lovely price on his head if I can but lure him here."

"Why do you need to gather coin at his expense?"

"Because he has cost me in coin, and more. His attacks on Spanish ships have drained my coffers, and I intend to stop him—and recoup a bit of silver."

"Wait until I tell the marquess what you've done," she growled.

"I don't think I shall worry about you ever seeing him again. Once I have Rocco, you are—what is the word? Dispensable?"

The guards dragged her through the hallway and into the great hall, toward the doors to the courtyard. She sat back, making them pull her along, twisting to try to break their grip. Count Barragan followed them.

"Stop." He walked in front of the trio and pointed. "She has a dagger hidden in her skirt, there."

The guard on her right tried to find the dagger in her skirt, but she reached for his every time he loosened his grip. Waving him away, the count ran his hand down the folds until he found the pocket, the gap, and the scabbard at her thigh. He pulled the blade out, holding it cautiously as if it might bite.

Looking back at Lisette, he glanced at her neck.

"What is this bauble?" He grabbed at the emerald on its chain.

"Oh, no." Lisette glared at him. "You shall not have that."

He laughed. "And you should stop me?"

"If she doesn't, I shall." Constantine de Martinmas, son of the Duke de Martinmas, had thrown open the doors and strode into the room.

46

"The food is ready." Kurta filled a bowl and handed it to Ruhee. "Eat. We must finish the last pole today. The ship will be here soon."

"What ship? How do you know?" Ruhee sat up, frowning.

Kurta stretched her hand again, offering the bowl. "Take. Eat. We will talk."

Ruhee reached slowly, as if the food might bite her. She took hold of the warm bowl and drew it to her lap, looking down at it. Roasted and chopped malanga, sweet mango and dried boar meat. Scooping two fingers in, she pinched together a little of each and held them, staring at Kurta and waiting for her answer.

The old woman busied herself with her own bowl, holding it in one hand while she cradled the baby in her arm. She took a piece of mango and held it to Alara's lips.

Alara sucked on the juice and made smacking noises. Kurta laughed.

"Yes, my girl, soon you will have teeth and you will chew good food," she told the baby.

Ruhee's impatience grew. "The ship, Kurta. What ship is coming?"

"Ship?" Kurta took a bite of her food and chewed it, watching Ruhee with a languid expression. "The ship that will come soon. That ship."

"How do you know?" The girl could not hold the exasperation from her voice.

"Hmm, I know because I know. Because it has been enough days that we have been here and have not seen a ship. *El Buscador* passed this way three weeks ago. At least one ship passes every month."

"So you do not know the ship that will sail past."

"Hmm…" Kurta was again lost in eating and playing with Alara.

Ruhee glared at her, muttering to herself, "Old woman, answer me."

"No, *you* answer *me*." Kurta raised her head and caught Ruhee's attention. Her elderly eyes pierced her soul with their ferocity. "You have been lying from the start. Layers of lie upon lie upon lie. You shall never leave this island, never find happiness until you cut the lies from your tongue."

Ruhee shrank away from the fire, dropping her food back into the bowl. "I don't understand…I'm taking Zaina to her…auntie—"

"Her name is not Zaina."

"It…it is." Ruhee paled.

Kurta's eyes narrowed. "Tell me her name."

"Zaina," Ruhee whimpered, before shouting, "Alara! It's Alara!"

"Yes." Kurta smiled. "It is. And whose baby is she?"

"My cousin's?"

The fearsome expression on Kurta's face made Ruhee feel as if her entire body was flattened against the sand and the air pushed out of it.

"She is the child of Lisette de Lille," Ruhee choked out, "and Tristan de Rocco."

"Yes." Kurta smiled. "And why do you have her?"

"They entrusted me with her safekeeping." Ruhee picked up a handful of food and shoved it into her mouth to avoid saying more. She immediately stood, spitting and reaching for water. "The meat is so spicy. Ah, my tongue—it is on fire!"

"It is only spicy for liars. Tell the truth and your tongue will be soothed."

"All right, all right, I shall tell!" The girl was crying. "I stole their baby. I took her to prove to Rocco that I am a better mother for his children. I love him and want him for myself."

Kurta sat back, rocking Alara in her arms. "An honest life is a life well lived."

The stinging in Ruhee's tongue lessened, and the swelling began to ease. She collapsed onto the sand, panting, wiping tears and snot and drool from her face and neck. "What evil magic is this, to make such a torturous potion?"

"It is only an herb, torturous to those who are deceitful, and I sprinkled the smallest amount into our food." Kurta continued to rock Alara, humming to her. "Is it any worse than, perhaps, a forgetfulness potion?"

"Wha—I don't know. How should I know?"

"Beware your tongue, my girl, before you give me answer. Did you not give Rocco a potion to make him forget Lisette?"

Ruhee opened her mouth to deny it and felt the warmth creep up her throat. "Yes," she said, defeated.

Kurta stopped rocking and placed Alara into her sling. "This is not your baby. She has known this from the first day you took her. It is time for you to know this, too." She rose and gathered the bowls. "I shall clean the camp. You can begin making the last signal for the ship that comes."

Ruhee stood but did not follow. "Who are you?"

"I am Kurta. Kurta Rici." She continued to walk toward the lagoon.

"Yes, you're Kurta—" Ruhee stopped, frowning. "Kurta Rici. Kurtarici. The *rescuer*."

"You work now," Kurta said, and disappeared into the trees.

"The rescuer," Ruhee repeated. "How could I have been such an ignorant girl? She was sent to undo all my work, to take the baby from me."

The last two poles lay on the ground by the cliff, surrounded by vines awaiting her hands. Ruhee grabbed the end of one vine and knelt, wrapping it fast about one pole before weaving across the second. As she worked, she recalled her journey with Amoy and this woman.

Amoy was a bad choice to help her. She had misgivings about the woman when they were discussing the kidnapping and escape, but she had ignored her intuition because she wanted Rocco so badly.

That plan was doomed from the start. She would not make that mistake again.

Who was this Kurta Rici and how did she track them down so quickly? Kurta was on *El Buscador* as soon as they were. If Rocco or Lisette had been the ones tracking her, they would have stopped her from even boarding. Kurta encouraged her to take care of the baby, even helped her escape…

To come to this island. Ruhee shook her head. This was the old woman's plan all along, to get her and the baby to this cursed island. *Kurta laid her trap and I stepped into it.*

Ruhee looked down at her hands, watched them braiding the vine, back and forth. The sooner she got these signals done, the sooner she could flag down the ship that would come.

But would it?

Kurta said these poles would attract a ship's attention. Kurta said a ship would be passing very soon. Kurta, the woman who had disguised herself, manipulated their circumstances, held back her knowledge about Alara and Rocco. Why would she tell the truth about this island or the ships that would pass close enough to see poles with vines and flowers?

"Vines on poles—" Ruhee stood and threw the vine away from her. "What a stupid idea. What sailor would look over at this island and see these?"

Nothing that woman said was true. But she has made a mistake by revealing herself. Now I know what she is. Now I can take action against her. But what should I do?

She turned toward the cliff and gazed out to the sea. Life was easier when she was just a sailor on a ship and her crush on Rocco was a mere dream, distant and unattainable. She could return to that…except she couldn't. She had held him in her arms, had nursed him back to health. Sometimes the thing you wanted exacted a price. She was willing to pay it.

First, she reasoned, *Kurta must think I am agreeable. The witch must not know my plans—when I have them.*

She stepped back to the poles and continued the work. These were useless. Kurta set her to this task to waste her time. She would not let Kurta know that she knew.

"Is your work complete?" Kurta was walking up from their camp, carrying an armful of red and orange flowers. Alara rode in her sling, and Ruhee could hear her chattering in her nonsensical baby sounds.

"Not quite," Ruhee said. "I fear I was daydreaming, looking out to sea and wondering which ship would be coming."

"Hmm, that I do not know. It may be a passenger ship on the way to Île des Oiseaux." She grinned. "But that is where you are running from, yes?"

Ruhee frowned. Returning to that island would be a problem. She pulled the vine tighter in frustration.

"Perhaps it is a warship, patrolling the waters for pirates," Kurta continued. "I'm afraid they would not welcome you aboard."

The vine caught across Ruhee's palm and burned her. She dropped it and studied her injury. The witch was raising an interesting point—it couldn't be just any ship. It had to be the right ship, heading the right direction. She was bound for Isla del Lagarto.

"Kurta…" Ruhee tore a piece of cotton from her shirt and wrapped it around her hand. "Is that your real name?"

"I am called by many names. Kurta is no better or worse than any others."

Ruhee wanted to ask what she was but feared the answer. "When a ship comes—when we flag the ship, and they send a boat—are you also going with me?"

"Hmm…" The old woman sat and combed through the flowers she'd picked. "We shall make that decision when it is before us."

And the baby, Ruhee wanted to ask, but knew the answer. *Do not ask. Tell.* She looked Kurta in the eyes, a cold expression on her face. "The baby comes with me."

Kurta laughed, hard and from her belly. Ruhee frowned, confused. After some time, the old woman's laughter slowed and she took deep breaths, wiping tears from her face.

"Whither Alara goes is for her to decide."

"Mobb-ba-bobb-mobb," gurgled Alara.

"That makes no sense," Ruhee said. "She is a baby."

"Yes, she is a baby." Kurta looked away, toward the cliff and the sea, tilting her head until the sun washed over her face. "And she will decide."

Ruhee shrugged and picked up the vine again. Weaving kept her from arguing with the old woman. What good would it do? She had to beware now, not to let her temper heat and say what she might regret. Better to let Kurta think she was following her instructions without complaint.

The last of the signal poles was finished and Ruhee helped Kurta erect them in the dirt, pushing them firmly into the ground and packing the soil around them. Kurta had put many red flowers at the top of the poles, and now completed the task, adding color in a winding pattern down the woven vine.

"The flowers atop get the sailors' attention," she told Ruhee. "But the pattern down the vine is what tells them this was made by human hands."

"Of course," Ruhee said, thinking it was at best a foolish joke. "Now what do we do?"

"Now…" Kurta looked up at the sky. "Now we watch. You will sit here and wait for a ship. I shall sleep. When the sun sets, I will sit and watch, and you will sleep. We take turns in this way."

"Why do I watch first? I am hungry and dirty, and would rather go to camp and eat, and rinse off in the lagoon."

"You are also the one who wishes most for a ship."

Ruhee scowled and turned her back on Kurta. She walked to the cliff's edge, where she could see the flag of any ship as soon as it popped over the horizon. Grumbling, she sat.

"I shall be very happy to be off this island and away from this selfish woman," she muttered.

A flash above her interrupted her complaint—she

looked up to see a streak of pink clouds arching overhead. They looked like a dragon's tail. She rubbed her eyes and looked again. There was nothing to see.

One more evil thing about this evil island. She looked back toward the sea.

47

Rocco opened his eyes to see his boyhood home. He stood in the courtyard, gazing at the arched doorway and aware of pain in his body and his face. Wiping the back of his hand across his mouth, he felt the sting of a cut, and saw the trail of blood on his knuckles.

He was twelve years old again, and he'd been beaten up by his half-brothers. Though younger and smaller, they were adept at teamwork, and frequently ambushed him on his way home from the market. He stumbled into the house, crying, not from the physical pain, but from the cruelty.

Maman was in the kitchen, standing over a pot and stirring. She stopped, tasted, added a pinch of something, and stirred again. Her swollen belly made her lean her shoulders over the stove while the rest of her leaned back. Another child, another half-sibling to torment him. He plucked a hard roll from the plate on the table and nibbled at it, watching her.

She mumbled to herself, "Yes, that is better." Turning, she saw him and cried out. "Mijo, what has happened?"

"Nothing," Rocco said, and burst into tears. Maman opened her arms to him, and he folded himself into her embrace, wanting to stay there forever.

"Tell me," she said, and led him to a chair. She sat and took him onto what little lap there existed. "Who did this to you?"

He never told. It was not the first beating and wouldn't be the last, but he would not tell her that her other children, her other darlings, were ruthless and cruel in ways he didn't understand.

She picked his chin up with her fingers and wiped his face with her apron. "Tristan, I think I know. You will not talk against your family, but I know. I protect you when I can." Her words faltered as tears pooled in her eyes. "I should have sent you away, someplace safe. I loved you too much. When I see you, I am reminded of your father, whom I loved so." She reached up to the amulet around her neck and closed it in her fist. "Mijo, I tell you something now that I do not tell anyone. This baby troubles me. I feel there is something wrong. Promise me if the worst happens—"

"No, Maman." He looked at her face, his fingers gripping her shoulder.

She put her finger to his lips. "Promise me. This amulet I wear is yours. It goes only to you. It is the only thing your papa gave me, apart from the beautiful boy I see now."

He hugged her even harder, and she hugged back, stroking his hair and singing to him. She usually saved Arrorró Mi Niño for bedtime, but the words were needed now. *Hush-a-bye, my son, my sun, my heart.* In her arms he was strong. In her arms the pain was far away.

Heat and a mouthful of sand woke him. He was on the beach, face down in the blazing sunlight. Pushing up to his knees, he looked around, his mind searching for where he was. A lagoon was to his right. He crawled to it and put his hands in to rinse his face.

The memory of being held under water roared back.

He scowled at the lagoon. "What was that for?"

The lagoon shimmered and rippled in the light. It gave no answer.

Rocco rose and walked back to camp, hoping his breakfast had not burned to cinders, as he did not know how long he'd been unconscious and dreaming. It felt more real than a dream, it was an event that really occurred.

Could I have had a vision?

The yam and malanga were nicely soft and roasted when he returned. He mashed them together, adding a few strips of boar meat that Lamya had provided. When he was properly sated, he put out the campfire and rinsed his bowl, leaving it by the ashes. Then he returned to the lagoon.

Sitting on the sand, looking out on the water, he told himself to relax. *I am a dragon.*

For a moment, he believed it didn't work. He was getting ready to try again when he felt the slow burn of transformation. It was much less painful than turning into a blood dragon. He spread his wings and walked to the lagoon to see his reflection.

He was expecting to see something more like Lisette, in that she was fearsome but had a softness about her features. Her teeth were not as large, nor her talons, and her paws looked round and fluffy. He had none of those and could honestly say the only difference between him and his blood dragon was the color.

Lamya had warned him of his temper, and he realized

this accounted for his look. *I look fierce because I feel that way.* He shook his head. *I have no time to consider my past. I need to get to my ship, and…*

And what? Join Lisette in liberating Île des Oiseaux from Spain? What nonsense. There were six islands in this chain. Spain ruled four—Isla del Lagarto had been freed and Île des Anciens had resisted any attempt at conquest. If Île des Oiseaux was also out of Spain's purview, there would be very few Spanish ships for him to loot, very few Spaniards to kill.

This would be a discussion for his trusted crew.

He fanned his wings and lifted into the sky, heading straight up and across to a bank of clouds. As he approached them, they broke apart, causing him to rush to the next formation, a thick, rounded cloud. He headed straight up, hiding above the puff, his tail dragging down like a rudder. After following the drift, he was finally well over the sea and too high to make a significant shadow.

It was time to search for *L'Implacable*.

He pushed forward, scanning the water for signs of his ship, and scolding himself for not having a better plan to meet them. His transformation to dragon had been so unexpected. Lisette had been the one to tell them where he would go and where to meet him. "Île des Anciens" sounded fairly vague, especially when there was no port, and it was not an island they normally did business with.

As he circled the island, he saw an odd grouping of bright flowers on a cliff and realized it was meant as a signal to someone. A familiar form sat at the end of the precipice, focusing outward. Ruhee.

The fire of revenge burned deep in him, along with the desire to reach down and kill her. As he flew lower, Lamya's words came back to caution him. He needed to tame and control this anger, not let it rage wildly. *Alara is safe,* he told himself, *and Lamya will deal with Ruhee. As angry as I am, she is but a young, impetuous girl. She cannot truly hurt me or my family.*

He lifted himself into the clouds again and continued his hunt, enlarging his circle with each pass. It was many passes later when he had almost decided to fly back to Lamya that he saw the familiar flag. *L'Implacable* was several leagues out from the island, on course to pass by within the next day and traveling north, toward Île des Oiseaux.

Lowering himself, he followed the ship, trying to decide whether to land now and startle the crew, or wait until dark, when he would not be so noticeable. Darkness seemed best. Only a few of the men had seen him transform, and he wasn't certain how they all would respond to a captain who was also a dragon. There were many superstitious sailors aboard. They might see him as a powerful ally in battle. Or they might want to burn him at the stake.

That would be unfortunate.

He held his position, too high to be spotted yet over the stern. Darkness would come soon.

They were within sight of Île des Anciens by the time the last of the sun had been tamped below the horizon. Rocco waited as patiently as he could manage, watching the changing of the crew. Poussin was taking the crow's nest position—that might be a problem. His ears still rang from the young man's scream at his transformation.

The night darkened, allowing only stars and a strip of the waning crescent to light the land. Poussin swept his attention from port to starboard using his spyglass. Rocco looked down at the helm. At least Chunk was there, navigating. He could land astern safely and transform quickly. With any luck, Poussin wouldn't see, and Chunk wouldn't mind—as much.

A pinpoint of light distracted him. He looked up and saw it was fairly far away, high and to port of their ship. Poussin was pointing and shouting. Rocco knew at once what it was—a fire on the cliff of Île des Anciens. Ruhee was trying to signal a ship and leave the island.

He smiled and shook his head. *She would not like it on this ship.*

Rocco sailed back to the island and saw a small campfire in front of the poles with flowers, but it wasn't Ruhee on the cliff. It was Lamya. As he grew closer, he heard her calling Ruhee's name.

"Come, girl, there is a ship."

A short distance away, he saw another, smaller fire. Ruhee was standing, then running toward Lamya. She got to the cliff, and Lamya pointed to *L'Implacable*. Even from afar, Rocco could see the girl's body language. She strained to see the flag on the ship before taking a quick step backward. Her entire torso braced, turning rigid.

Lamya pushed her to the cliff, urging her, Rocco supposed, to wave and get the ship's attention. Ruhee backed another step, shaking her head, turned, and ran toward camp. Rocco wished he was a human so he could have a laugh at her fear.

She wants to be with me, does she? Perhaps she should consider what I will do to her if I got my hands on her.

Lamya did not look back to see where Ruhee ran. She waved a hand and doused the fire. As she turned, Rocco saw the bundle on her back. Alara was sleeping in her sling. Satisfied that his child would be safe, no matter what Ruhee did, he turned back to the ship.

Poussin had still not seen him, so he banked around to the helm, landing softly as far astern as the deck permitted. *I am a man.* Four small words allowed his bones to warm, and his muscles shrink. Four legs became two and he strolled quietly to the burly man at the wheel.

"Evening, Chunk."

Chunk leapt away from him, falling against the rail. "Cap'n!"

"Sorry for the scare." Rocco smiled and held his hand out. "I didn't know whether it was better to scare you as a man or terrify you as a beast."

"Thank ye, I much prefer the man," Chunk said and let the captain help him to his feet. "Sure am glad to see ya."

"As am I, and glad to be back aboard. What is our state?"

"Ship is taut and yar, Cap'n. Crew is willing. Supplies are stocked."

"Have we still prisoners?" Rocco asked.

"One," Chunk said. "The young Marquess d'Auguste."

"And I trust we drowned Amoy to our satisfaction."

Chunk looked at the ground and shook his head. "Mebbe, but mebbe not. As we readied the wench with weights, she loosened from the mate's grip and hurled herself overboard. We tried to fish 'er out so's we could kill 'er proper, but she evaded us. If it's any help, I did see fins above water and heading toward her."

"She is a crafty woman and determined to live." Rocco frowned. "If we are lucky, the sharks will take her."

"Now that yer back, where shall we be bound?" Chunk asked.

Rocco looked out at the horizon's thin line lit by the stars. Lisette was on her way to drive out the Mendozas. He had not agreed to that and was not certain he wanted to. Lisette would have to understand. He wouldn't interfere, but he wouldn't help. Still...

Willem d'Auguste was betrothed to the Mendoza marquise, and he was currently in the brig below deck. How much ransom would the Mendozas pay for their son-in-law's return?

"We sail for Île des Oiseaux," he told Chunk. "To ransom Willem d'Auguste. Get some sleep now, Chunk, I'll take the helm. In the morning, I'll want to talk to the crew."

"Aye, Cap'n." Chunk walked down the stairs, his heft making the boards creak with each step.

Rocco took his compass and pointed it at the bow. They were heading north, passing Île des Anciens and soon could steer west to Île des Oiseaux. Once there, he'd send an envoy with the ransom demand. How much silver was their dear Willem worth?

He thought again about Lisette and her plan. Having islanders rule their own island was the end of his piracy. He could not attack merchant ships going to such a place. They needed the supplies, and he did not wish to deny them. For a brief moment, he pictured his crew doing honest business—unloading sacks of grain onto a dock, and he laughed.

He adjusted the rudder to bank to port, calling to the crew to adjust the sails to capture the wind and push them out. He could hear the growl of the wood and the howl of the wind as *L'Implacable* made the turn.

Isla del Lagarto was doing well without the Spanish. Begum was even trading with them. Rocco felt himself turn a corner. Maybe he and his crew could try something different.

Maybe it was time for a change.

48

"Connie!" Lisette smiled and pulled away from the guards.

"Lisette, my darling, what are these ruffians doing with you?" He opened his arms to her.

The guards loosened their grip on Lisette as she ran to hug her rescuer. He was as handsome as every other time she saw him, tall and dark, with the chiseled features of a god.

"I am delighted to see you," she said. "It has been too long."

She turned to Count Barragan, who stood like a guilty schoolboy, his face flushed, and the leather coin pouch hidden behind his back. Connie stared at him, shot a look at Lisette, and strolled toward the count. Lisette could not help but notice how close he stood, and how deeply he looked into the count's eyes.

"Xavier, what exactly have you been up to?" he asked.

"This woman—Lisette—was brought to me earlier." The count's face shone deeper and brighter, and Lisette thought she could hear his heart pounding from where she stood. "A witness told me she was the one last seen going to my brother's room before his death, and afterward, she was seen running away with blood on her dress."

Connie raised an eyebrow. "I had no idea you cared about who killed your brother."

"True, I am not wedded to avenging his death. But Mother insisted, Antonio being the oldest, you know." The count coughed a little, as if to clear his throat. "She is still quite influential in the Spanish court."

"I hope she didn't expect you to fund the reward."

"Oh, yes, she sent a substantial chest of gold." He ran his finger along the collar of his shirt, his neck glistening with perspiration. "Of course, it was left to my judgment just how much of that chest to offer. Two village wenches brought this one—"

"The marquise," Connie said. "She is the marquise de Lille."

"Of course, of course." His hands came forward to appease, the leather pouch jingling. He looked at the pouch, blanched, and said, "I had decided to offer the marquise a reward. She told me what happened. Antonio's death was justified. I consider the matter finished."

"And now?"

"Let him off the hook, Connie," Lisette said, smiling. "He thought he might use me to catch a bigger fish. Not to worry, though. When you arrived, I was preparing to take the entire matter under my wing, so to speak."

Connie grinned in response. "Come, Xavier. Hand Lizzie the coin and say your farewells." He walked to her and lowered his voice. "Beware of returning to Île des Oiseaux. The Mendozas are convinced that you are a sorceress and a heretic. They are laying the whip to the entire island, increasing taxes, and stripping the jungle of anything they can sell—I am certain this will soon include the people who live there. As soon as Willem d'Auguste returns from Isla de la Ballena, they plan to take your castle by whatever force they can."

Lisette nodded and held her hand to the count. "Sire, if the two wenches had not stolen my coin, I would not ask for this. At least you have what you took from them." She glanced at her friend. "Perhaps Connie could help you study your finances. He has a very fine head for figures and could find a way to keep you in luxury without hunting down pirates."

Count Barragan bowed slightly and gave her the pouch. "Thank you, m'lady. Perhaps the marquess can help me."

She smiled and curtsied. "Thank you, good sirs. I must be off now, to salvage my home."

Turning, she strode through the great room to the interior of the island-castle. The corridor went both ways, but she followed the smell of food being prepared. Although not as grand, the kitchen was much like any castle's, full of pots and pans and a fireplace with a kettle on the hearth and meat roasting on the spit. Lisette scanned the room, searching for a familiar face. She found her just outside one of the windows, scraping the skin from potatoes and throwing them in a pot.

Lisette rounded the corner and headed toward her *Dişi Aslan* sister.

"Clarita," she said. "How goes it on the island?"

Clarita looked up, surprised, and stood. "Lisette, I wanted to warn you, but the count is a suspicious man. You need to be away from here."

"It is well, he set me free. I need to know where to find Captain Derya."

The woman leaned close. "They have been looking

for our wayward children. Most of the crew have returned to the ship, but Oleta and the captain are taking one more pass through the village to see if Amoy and Ruhee might find another ship to board."

Lisette nodded. "Good, thank you. We've found our baby and the wenches, who shall come to their reward soon. I am going to find Oleta and the captain—should you see them first, please tell them I need to meet them back on the ship. We've rescued Alara, and now we need to rescue Île des Oiseaux."

"If I could forsake this post, I should like to battle those snakes on the island." Clarita smiled. "Godspeed to you and I shall see you again."

Lisette gave her a quick hug and sprinted around the castle to the front doors. A beautiful cabriolet sat in the shade on the far side of the fountain, its sleek chestnut horse munching quietly on a feedbag. She thought about looking for the buckboard but remembered the switch of steeds. No soldier would allow his horse to be permanently reassigned to pulling a cart.

She found the driver sitting under a tree, finishing his meal.

"Excuse me, sire, but I require transportation into the village, and the Marquess de Martinmas said I could use his carriage." She reached into the pouch and took two small coins from it. "I was told this would be a fair price for a trip there and return."

The man looked at the coin as if hypnotized. "Yes," he said slowly. "That is most…generous."

She smiled. "Then shall we be off?"

The ride back into town was much more pleasant than the ride to the castle. She had briefly toyed with the idea of transforming so she could fly to the village. It was faster than any other form of travel, and she had been about to transform anyway when the count attempted to take her emerald.

"No, I can't just transform for my own convenience."

"What was that, m'lady?" the driver asked.

"Oh, my apologies." Lisette blushed. "I was deep in thought and my tongue was suddenly loosened."

The driver chuckled. "Hope you don't talk in yer sleep, 'specially if there's secrets to be kept."

"Let us pray not, then." Lisette leaned forward. "Count Barragan—he has lived on this island for many years?"

"A few, yes."

"Does he do well by the village?"

"As well as any, I s'pose, and better'n most." He clucked at the horse to quicken the pace. "We was just as happy to lose his brother the viscount, meanin' no disrespect. A thief in the name o' the crown, and too randy fer my liking."

She nodded. "But the count…?"

"Oh, yeah, he lets us earn our wages, leaves the young girls alone." He stuttered for a moment and Lisette could see the blush work up his neck. "Guess he just ain't that type of nobleman."

"Guess not." She looked ahead to see the outskirts of the coastal village. "Looks like we are here. If you could drop me off at the inn, I would appreciate it."

At her destination, she gave him one more coin as he helped her from the carriage to cement their relationship. "If the marquess complains that I kept you too long on the road, just tell him, 'She didn't want to startle anyone by taking the quick way there'."

He grinned, showing a crooked row of white teeth. "Aye, m'lady, and Godspeed."

Lisette wasted no time in striding into the inn and finding the keeper Ernesto. He was bent over a table with a questionably clean rag, wiping. There were only four others in the place, sailors from the look of them and too involved in their reminiscences of the last good battle.

"Good afternoon, Ernesto. Might I have a word?" She touched his shoulder, making certain that the coins in her bag rattled enough to give him hope.

He turned to her at once and shuttled her to a far table, speaking low. "Ah, m'lady I apologize, deeply and humbly, that them greedy wenches used my buckboard to turn you in. It was bad form, and I had no idea."

"Well, then I won't have to kill you," Lisette said with a smile.

He paled and dropped the rag. "I swear, m'lady—"

"It is well, Ernesto, I was but jesting." She pulled a coin from her bag, keeping careful watch of the sailors, none of whom notice the jingling. "I am looking for some of my friends. Women. Strangers in this port. Tall, dark-haired, dressed for…action."

"I know of a few women who fit the description. Would one happen to be the captain of a ship?"

Lisette nodded.

"They were here earlier today. I heard them say they would check the harbormaster to see when the next ship is due. If they ain't there, I s'pose they's either at the boarding house or to their own ship."

"Thank you." She handed him the silver. "I hope you get your buckboard back, but you need to treat your horse with more care."

"That weren't my horse. They stole my buckboard using their own nag."

"Then they should rot in the count's dungeon." Lisette turned to leave, but Ernesto stopped her.

"One moment," he said, and disappeared behind the bar. He scurried back with a clean cloth in his hand and held it out to her. "A bit o' bread and dried meat. Keep yer strength."

She took it, smiling. "Thank you again, Ernesto."

49

Walking out into the midday sun, Lisette stopped at the doorway to look for the small hut near the pier. It did not look occupied, but she walked there anyway. It was a simple building, of two rooms, one for recording the ships arriving and leaving, and one with a cot for sleeping.

"Hail, there," she called out.

No one answered, so she checked each room. Empty. The logbook was on the counter, so she skimmed it until she found *El Buscador*. It was the last entry. Amoy might have been aboard, but Begum would have found her.

Lisette scurried down the boardwalk to search the boarding house next. It was a two-story building, much like a plantation house, with a porch on two sides. It was also at the opposite end of the village.

The doors were open, as were all the windows, to try to offset the building's heat. It was obvious that this was built with European sensibilities, which lacked any Caribbean intelligence. Island buildings were low, whitewashed, with large open windows that were only shuttered in the event of a storm.

Lisette walked into the lobby and glanced at the space as she approached the counter. The small foyer was decorated in soft gold walls, with chairs of heavy and intricately carved dark wood and stuffed leather seats. A long rectangular table sat against the wall, its legs and sides carved in scrolling vines and flowers.

A young man stood at the counter—Spanish by the look of him. Small, fastidious in his dress, with shiny black hair lying sleek on his head, and a precisely groomed pencil moustache. His only defect was a faded red line across his right cheek.

"Good afternoon," she greeted him. "I am looking for my friends and wondering if they stopped by here."

He took a long, slow study of Lisette, from head to hem and back again, his dour expression unchanging.

"I very much doubt it. We do not typically cater to…working women." These last two words were spoken with a disdain that clung to the ears after the last syllable.

Lisette was no stranger to haughtiness, even from a mere clerk. She pulled herself to a most upright stance and angled her chin upward so that she could cast a downward glance at him from her short stature. As she did so, she slipped her hand into her pocket and withdrew her bag of gold coin, which she laid upon the counter.

"I am the Marquise de Lille. I inquire about young women who are serving me on my voyage back to Île des Oiseaux."

His expression remained unaltered, but his complexion went white and red and white again in such a rapid fashion, she wondered that he did not faint.

"Of course, m'lady, I meant no ill will. Perhaps I could have their names or a description?"

"Perhaps. One would be tall, of solid build, with curled hair. The other is smaller, lean with dark-hair and green eyes."

He shook his head, but she saw his eyes flash wide. "I'm afraid no one of that description has inquired at the desk."

She grinned. "Yes, I believe you are afraid. They may not have inquired at the desk, but I detect that you have seen them."

He stood silent, his breathing quick and deep. "They were here," he said at last. "They spoke with one of the servants and left."

"And why does that cause you such fear?"

"The woman they asked after—let us say she left a lasting impression when she was here a month ago." His hand drifted to his cheek, along the scar.

"So, Amoy Simone was here."

"Not exactly. This woman was called Simona Alwan."

"Large woman with her hair in a high, tight bun?" Lisette asked.

He nodded.

"Simona Alwan, of course." She pursed her lips. "Might I speak with the servant who talked with my friends?"

"I suppose," he told her. "Just do not involve me." He patted his scar. "I do not need more of these."

Lisette took a step closer and studied the healing gash. "I do not believe it will be permanent. Rub a good salve on the skin to help dissolve the scar. What remains will add character to your face. And if you make up a dangerous and heroic tale to accompany it, I should say you will never run short of maidens."

He smiled, his first that Lisette saw. "I will bring Adrianne to the foyer. Please be seated."

Within moments, a short, curvy woman in an apron scurried from a downstairs door and approached Lisette. "I am Adrienne. You have questions?"

Lisette looked down to see the edge of a tattoo on Adrienne's left wrist. She stepped closer to the servant and rolled her forearm to show the edge of her own tattoo. Adrienne pulled her sleeve up to show the lioness. Lisette followed. They nodded and sat, speaking in low tones.

"You are not familiar to me," Adrienne said.

"I sailed briefly with the *Dişi Aslan* and have made lifelong sisters." Lisette glanced around the room. More people had drifted in, more than she was comfortable seeing in such a small room. She stood up and motioned for Adrienne to follow her outside, to the large porch. "It is important that I find Captain Derya."

"She was here perhaps an hour ago, looking for Amoy and Ruhee. I heard what that girl did— disgraceful!"

Lisette winced and nodded. Disgraceful didn't cover it. "Did she return to the ship?"

Adrienne nodded. "They are no doubt getting under sail. The only way for you to reach them in time is on a swift horse, unless you can fly."

"Thank you." Lisette patted Adrienne's shoulder. "I will try to intercept them before they lift anchor."

She watched the servant girl hurry back into the boarding house and turned her attention to the village. Begum had an hour's head start, but that was easily remedied if she could find a quiet corner.

50

Across the street from the boarding house stood another public establishment—a church. It was a small clapboard building, white with a steeple, cross, and bell. Rushing around to the back, Lisette found what she wanted—an empty garden behind a building with no prying windows. Taking a breath, she prayed for speed.

I am a dragon.

The warmth spread quickly and soon a moon dragon stood in the churchyard. She turned about and extended her wings—just as the priest emerged from the back door of the sanctuary. His eyes went wide as coconuts as he backed himself against the building.

Lisette had no reason to fight him and no desire to try to explain anything. Bringing one paw to her mouth, she hissed a "shushing" sound and shook her head at him. He shook his head in return, his body still trembling. Within two flaps, she was airborne and headed toward the pirate's harbor and *Dişi Aslan*.

The ship was pulling up anchor by the time she spied it, the deck awhirl with action as lines were adjusted and sails unfurled. From her height the crew seemed miniscule, but she could still hear the booming instructions of Captain Derya.

Knowing Begum was her real mother changed everything about her—even the exacting way she delivered orders felt maternal to Lisette now. Their discussion of the truth was too short, and Lisette longed to fly directly to the helm and engage her in a long talk but she knew this scene must be saved for another time. The captain had a ship to maneuver out to sea. This harbor was like every other pirate's port in that it was difficult to navigate into and out of. If it was an easy place to land, the villagers would have taken it.

She waited until they were into open water. They were heading south, heading round the point before turning north, past Île des Anciens and toward Île des Oiseaux.

Four bells sounded, and most of the crew headed below for the meal. The captain stayed at the helm, no doubt enjoying the sea breeze. Lisette hesitated, not wanting to intrude on her solitary moment.

At last, Lisette dropped out of the clouds, lowering her body gently on the aft deck. There were no hands to witness her arrival. She transformed quickly, stood, and strode to the helm.

"Captain," she hailed as she climbed the steps. "I come bearing news."

"Lisette!"

The two women hugged, Lisette absorbing the affection in Begum's arms. "I have much to tell and a favor to ask," Lisette said. "Where are you bound?"

"We had no luck finding Amoy or Ruhee on

Soledad," Begum said. "We were on our way to the next stop on *El Buscador*'s route, Isla del Lagarto."

"I am delighted to report that Rocco and I have found our daughter and she is safe." Lisette smiled. "Ruhee and Amoy have yet to pay for their crime, but they will have their day."

"Thank the gods. Where is she?"

"With Lamya de Sang, who is, I'm certain, teaching her all bad manner of good magic—or the other way round."

"At least she will keep your child from Ruhee's clutches." Begum grinned. "Now, what can we do to help?"

"I need to drive the Mendoza family from Île des Oiseaux." She relayed what Connie had told her. "We can discuss my own plans at a later date, but I am no longer pining to rule an island and would much rather see it run by the islanders—and pirates—than ruthless nobility who do not want to care for the island and its people."

The captain looked at her, nodding thoughtfully. "Yes. Of course, we will help you. It would be better." She looked out over the wheel and shouted, "We sail for Île des Oiseaux. Set a course when we round the point."

Oleta appeared at the stairs. "Île des Oiseaux, Captain? Why the change in plan?" She leapt to the helm, where she saw Lisette. Her eyes widened and lips opened into a welcoming smile. "Lizzie!"

"Oleta!" Lisette gave her a quick explanation of where they were going, and why.

"When I get my hands on that Ruhee—" She mimicked strangulation. "Such a sweet, quiet girl, a soft, whispering child. Quiet because she was plotting to steal what could never be hers."

Lisette placed her hand on Oleta's back, stroking her calmly. "Don't worry. Ruhee is also with Lamya. I cannot imagine the Ancient One is going to let her off the hook."

Begum shivered. "I would never wish to experience Lamya's version of justice."

"I come to relieve you at the helm," Oleta said. "Time for captains to eat a meal."

"Come," Begum told Lisette. "You should dine as well."

Lisette followed Begum down the steps to the cabin aft. She could already smell the roasted meat and the spices. Her stomach rumbled, reminding her of how little she had eaten over the past few days.

The cozy silks and pillows adorning dark, carved furniture called to her now. What had once merely put her at ease had a reason behind it. She curled into a chair and watched Begum get out the tiny cups for the urn of dark, bitter liquid on the table.

"Coffee?" Begum asked, offering her the tiny cup on the tiny saucer before pouring her own. They sat, sipping and staring at one another.

"How did it happen?" Lisette asked. "Why did you...?"

"Give you away?" Begum gazed across the room, settling her cup into the saucer. "You must try to understand...it is not an easy thing I do. My family had been driven from our village, and I was, in turn, driven from my family. I loved you and would have raised you well, but I would have raised you alone, as a woman cast out.

"Your father is a good man. Do not ever question. He marries your mother because it is good for his king and his family. He is a noble and has much that I have not."

"Riches?"

Begum shook her head. "Yes, but that is not important. He has...how you say...solid ground. He has a wife to raise children, and parents and king who have expectations, and servants to attend to his needs. You would have a tree with strong roots to grow from."

"I understand, but why not find a way to keep in touch?"

"Because once I let you go, I had to let go of you. If I knew they had renamed you, knew of their plans and hopes for you, I would want to scoop you up and take you back. A ship is no place to raise a child." She paused as the cabin girl brought in the meal. Handing Lisette a plate, she continued. "Only when Mercedes de Medina and Eric d'Auguste sent out their ill-advised notice, to kidnap a marquise and earn gold, only then did I know."

"Then why didn't you step forward and offer?" Lisette tore a piece of warm bread and dragged it through the hummus before wrapping it around a slice of meat.

"I tried, but I was too late. Rocco leapt at the chance, he wanted you so badly. I suspected he wanted you for a malicious reason but could not convince him to let me have you." She shook her head. "I even went to Lamya to see if she could intervene."

"Let me guess," Lisette said. "She drew pictures in the sand and said, 'do no worrying'."

"She did." Begum smiled. "According to her, she has no clairvoyance, but I believe she has a certain insight into the way things play out, that the shadows of the future show trouble or triumph."

Lisette nodded and took another sip of black brew. "And when I first joined the *Dişi Aslan*…why did we not have this conversation then?"

"How would that have started? 'Lisette, I am your real mother.' Would you have believed me? You were already torn from your home, at odds with who and what you were. Would knowing have helped or hindered you?"

Lisette sat silent with her memories for a moment. At last, she answered. "You are right. It would have been too much to bear."

Begum helped herself to more food. "So now we are here, and we know what we know. What is our plan for Île des Oiseaux?"

Lisette told her as much as Connie had revealed in their short interaction. "While the Count de Mendoza was not working with Mercedes de Medina, he was willing to let her lead the way toward subjugating the people and taking as much in wealth and resources as they could extract."

"How does the Duke de Martinmas feel about that plan?"

"I do not know for certain." Lisette shrugged. "I can only approach him with the question to see where his loyalties lie. Although I will say, he sent his troops against Mercedes, and he willingly moved from my family castle to the Medina home. I might have some sway."

"Then our first move is for you to contact him and see whether he will fight with us or against us."

"Or step aside and wait for the victor to arise," Lisette said. "I confess, I am uneasy."

Begum reached over and touched Lisette's cheek lightly with her fingers. "The answer is always no until you've asked, Daughter."

Lisette smiled, her eyes glossy with tears. "My apologies." She swiped her eyes to remove any moisture. "To be honest, that was more than my mother—my other mother—ever did."

"No, it is I who apologize. I had hoped your father would invent a more believable story and attract more sympathy from his wife." She studied Lisette's face. "I suppose it was difficult, as you resemble him so closely."

They turned to their food and fell silent, satisfying their hunger.

"Is my old bunk still available?" Lisette asked. "I know the newbie usually gets the one at the bow, but I actually prefer it. Oh…and are we letting anyone know of our kinship?"

"I am proud to call you daughter, although I think it

can be revealed as needed. Mother, daughter, or strangers, all pull their weight on this ship." Begum raised an eyebrow, as if considering an idea. "I do not ask this lightly, but I am thinking…if you arrived ahead of the *Dişi Aslan*, you could scout ahead, talk to the duke, give us information to help us plan our battle."

Lisette nodded. "I agree, it would be most helpful. If I could leave early tomorrow, before sunup, we would at least be past Isla de la Soledad. My trip would be shorter."

"Yes, this would be good," Begum said. "The sun is sinking now. A little sleep and then a quiet launch behind the helm, yes?"

The sky was still dark, with light at the eastern horizon, begging to grow, when a blue-white form extended feathered wings and lifted into the clouds.

51

Rocco stood at the helm, looking down on the crew that had assembled. Good men, all, hard-working and willing to fight for their treasure. He had given many orders, and all had been obeyed, but this time he required their approval.

But did he even approve?

"Men, I have been proud to be your captain on these waters and am relieved to have finally returned to you. It has been too long to not feel the roll of the sea under my feet and the spray across my face. I now come to you with a question that I alone cannot answer." He stopped to gauge their interest. Faces that had been distracted by the lapping waves turned toward him.

"Île des Oiseaux was for a long time held by the French and Spanish equally. We took as many Spanish ships as we could, letting the French get by and knowing they would gouge prices for the Spaniards. The news is that Spain now controls Île des Oiseaux. While I am happy to strip more Spanish ships of their silver, it would seem that Spain is interested in stripping the island of anything worth value."

This caused a reaction in the crew, mumblings of protest, so he continued. "We have been asked to drive out the Spanish. While these Spaniards are hideous and greedy, island rule will most certainly stop any Spanish ships from doing business. We will have less ships to attack. Either we move to larger islands to plunder Spanish ships or adjust to a life of trading goods."

"Or keep the Spaniards where they are?" asked one of the crew.

"That is the question," Rocco said. "Are we pirates or merchants?"

"Pirates!" several shouted, accompanied by loud affirmations from others.

"Hold on, there," a booming voice rose from the rest. Chunk climbed halfway up the stairs, although he was tall enough to be seen standing flat-footed on the deck. "Aye, we're pirates, but think o' bein' merchants fer one minute. Nobody says all our goods is legal—we kin make more silver on goods that ain't. An' bein' a merchant let us visit our families, those that got 'em. No more prices on our heads."

Rocco nodded. "Chunk has a sound point."

"Cap'n," Luis called out. "Could not some of those goods be stolen…from Spanish ships?"

Rocco could feel the energy of the crew turn. Where there was once dissent, a wave of agreement moved across their faces.

"Our treasure's hidden in the caves of Île des Oiseaux," LeFarge spoke up. "It does us no good because we cannot eat it, we cannot send it to our families, and we cannot trade it for coin."

"True." Rocco looked at the big man. "But if we could…what say you men? Can we be pirates and traders as well?"

The majority of the men nodded and shouted their affirmation. Only a few stood silent.

"Luis," Rocco called out. "You do not agree?"

Luis shrugged. "It's not a life I've ever tried, Captain, this buying and selling. But I've never been a pirate before. I am not opposed to the idea—I merely want to try it before I decide."

"Very well," Rocco told him, and addressed the crew. "We have Willem d'Auguste in the hold and plan to fetch a pretty ransom for him from the Mendozas on Île des Oiseaux. What say we also laden our ship with a few of our treasures and head next to Isla del Lagarto to see what prices we may obtain? That will tell us what we are capable of doing. And if we pass a Spanish ship on the way—"

Nodding heads and shouts of "Aye," confirmed the crew's choice. Rocco gestured to Chunk to take the wheel and headed below. Behind him, Chunk bellowed orders.

"Harden up, ya dogs! We sail away from the sun!"

Rocco closed the door to his cabin and filled a mug with rum. It was a risk, turning the island native. There would be no exchange of jewels and gold from nobility on the island back to Europe. Would his crew adjust to that? A knock at the door distracted him. It was Poussin, who carried in a tray of bread, meat, and fresh papaya.

"Poussin, I thought the new boy was now serving the cabin."

"He is, Cap'n, but I wanted t'bring it today." He set the tray on the heavy wooden table, a flush to his cheeks that brightened his sun-kissed face. "It's been a long time since I was able to serve ya."

"Yes, but you're growing in your job as part of the deck. You don't want to go back to this menial task, do you?"

The young man straightened. "No, Cap'n, I like workin' the lines. Only—" He hesitated.

"Speak up!" Rocco glared at him. "You'll know by now I'm not a man for boot licking or toadying."

Poussin cleared his throat, his blush growing stronger. His voice rang, as if he pushed the words out at full volume. "Cap'n, I am a pirate and make no mistake." He softened, as if embarrassed by the outburst. "I have no beef wif what we be doin', either ransomin' that piece o'fluff in the hold, or sinkin' Spanish ships…But you got a child now, and the child of nobility. She be special."

Rocco chuckled. "You can't imagine how special."

Poussin blanched. "No offence, but not as special as you…were…"

"Let us not discuss it." Rocco waved his hand to dismiss the topic. "I have a child. What is your point?"

"My point bein' that it'll not just be yer head the Spanish seek. They'll be huntin' anything that draws you in, hurts you. Anything…like yer family. And what's yer daughter to say of dear papa? 'I'm a noblewoman but me dad kills Spaniards fer their treasure'."

Rocco scowled. "It's who I am."

"Aye, Cap'n." Poussin looked at the floor, kicking one shoe against the other. "An' she'll be who she is. Tis a pity she'll fer-ever be hounded by who you are."

The young man left the room and shut the door behind him. Rocco poured more rum into his mug and sat down. He pulled the leg from the roasted chicken—no doubt stolen from some farmer on Soledad. Would they be actually purchasing their food now? He could not imagine sinking that low.

What would Alara think of all this?

"She'll think what I tell her to think," he said to the room, and laughed.

The emptiness of the room mocked him. The child loved him—now. Of course, so did her mother, regardless of his profession. He tore a roll apart and took a bite, looking at the hard crust and soft insides. It was much like himself.

"I am a pirate," he told the roll. "For now."

It would be two more days before *L'Implacable* reached the hidden harbor at Île des Oiseaux. He needed to make plans with his most trusted men as to how to deliver the ransom demand and how to collect the reward.

Another set of knuckles knocked on his door, followed by Luis bursting into the space. "Captain, a ship approaches from the starboard aft. She's coming fast."

Rocco pushed back from the table and rushed out the door, followed by Luis. He sprinted to the helm and looked out over the stern. A familiar shape cut through the water like a blade through soft flesh.

"It's the *Dişi Aslan*." Rocco frowned. They were on their way to depose the Mendozas. Would they ask him for help? Or would Begum expect it?

Soon, the ships were close enough to communicate. Rocco usually rowed over to Captain Derya for any negotiations, but this time he asked her to come to him.

"Poussin," he called out. "Help the new cabin boy serve. Captain Derya and I will confer in my quarters."

Poussin nodded and gestured to a younger boy of perhaps thirteen. "Cue, come. I shall lead."

Rocco returned to his cabin to clear his desk of papers, in case they required room to plan. He was still uneasy about driving the Spaniards from Île des Oiseaux and hoped this was not the topic of Begum's visit. But he knew it was.

Lisette wasted no time in her flight to Île des Oiseaux. She was glad that the monsoon season was abating—she did not relish trying to fly during any of those blinding downpours. The days were hot and sunny, and the nights were warm and cloudy, and she had no problem reaching her destination.

As she flew, she made her plan. Without the Duke de Martinmas' approval, the Mendozas would be more difficult to extract. But if El Rey caught wind of his betrayal, the consequences would be severe. She had to know that he could at least look the other way and escape any charges.

In the meantime, Pinar and the rest of her household must know that help is on the way. She was heartened to see the familiar island and headed first for her own castle. It was the closest, and her body was nearing exhaustion.

There was no one on the western balcony, so she landed there and transformed, before entering through the door to the lover's cupboard. She paused behind the tapestry, listening. There were voices in the great room beyond. A woman's voice, high-pitched, was making demands. Lisette recognized the second voice as Pinar's, as calm and firm as always.

"Countess, you may make all the fuss you desire, but my orders do not change. I attend to the Duke de Martinmas, and until he has told me to relinquish the castle, he still occupies it."

Lisette finally recognized the first voice as being the Countess de Mendoza.

"But he is moving into the Medina castle," she said at high volume. "He cannot occupy two castles at once! Where are my daughter and her husband to live?"

"That is not my place to say." Pinar pushed back. Lisette could hear the frustration in her voice, and perhaps a little desire to make the countess stop talking forever. "It was El Rey who signed the official proclamation giving this castle to the duke. Would you want him to disobey our king?"

"Absolutely not! We are loyal first and always to El Rey!"

Lisette could hear the deflation in the woman. The Mendozas wanted much in life, much power, much gold, much social standing, but they would not go against the king to obtain it. That is, unless the king never knew.

"Then you shall have to wait for the official decree, I suppose," Pinar said, her voice dripping with reason. "Perhaps it will come on the next ship from Spain."

"Yes, of course." The countess did not sound convinced. "The next ship."

"If there is nothing else, I do have a full household to run, m'lady. The castle must be kept in proper order for when the duke returns."

The shuffling of feet and click of fashionable heels, moving further away, told Lisette that Pinar was escorting the countess to the door. Lisette withheld a chuckle, imagining the scene. She waited until she heard no more sound and pushed the heavy tapestry out enough to peer around the room. It was empty.

She padded quickly to the kitchen, where she thought there would be the most bustling activity and the highest probability of gossip. The aromas radiating from it reminded her that perhaps she could nab a bite of something.

The room was as busy as she hoped, with one woman stirring a pot on the fire, another kneading dough for bread, and two younger girls running back and forth as the cook and baker barked orders. As Lisette stood in the doorway, a shadow appeared at the back entrance, quickly scurrying into the space. Ghreta, the servant from Mercedes' castle, hustled into the room with a basket full of island fruit.

"Duke won't get no bayberries today for his elixir." Ghreta placed the basket on the table. "None are ripe enough. Too waxy. Plenty of mangoes and a few papayas."

Lisette moved further into the kitchen. "Ghreta, so nice to see you."

"M'lady! I was told you was out, searching for the child. We all wanted to go with you, to hunt down those wenches. Amoy was always a cursed strumpet, but Ruhee? So quiet, so eager to please—I barely believe what she has become."

"Nor do I," Lisette said. "But she is in love with Rocco and that love has become an obsession. It is well, though. My baby is safe and with…someone who loves her very much. Ruhee's whereabouts are also known, and she is being watched."

The rest of the kitchen staff turned to look at her and

listen. Lisette shook her head. "Please don't interrupt your work for me. Do you prepare the meal for the servants?"

"No, for the duke," the baker, a small round woman, said. "He spends half his days here and the other half in the old Medina castle."

"I thought he had taken the Medina castle for his new home," Lisette said.

"Begging your pardon," the baker replied, "but when you left on your mission, he feared the Mendoza family would move their daughter and her betrothed into this place. He did not want to give it to them unless you agreed to the arrangement."

Lisette smiled. "Perfect. Is the duke here now?"

"No but we expect him at any moment," Ghreta told her.

"Then we have time for a chat." Lisette felt a rumble in her midsection. "If I could have a mango to calm my noisy stomach."

"No mangoes," the cook said, gesturing sternly. "Girl, get a bowl. The marquise will have stew."

One young woman grabbed crockery from the shelf while another cleared a space at the servants' table and pulled out a chair. Cook ladled something dark and heavenly from the large pot that hung on the rack over the fire, and gently ordered Lisette to sit.

While the stew cooled, Lisette spoke.

"I have heard rumors that life with the Mendozas is no more pleasant than with Mercedes de Medina."

"True, m'lady," the baker said. "Except Mercedes confined her cruelty to her household. The Mendozas are intent on ruling this island by increasing taxes and tributes and stripping the forests of anything useful."

Lisette nodded. "I suspected that was their nature when I met them. I have come to encourage them to leave. That is to say, myself and the captain and crew of the *Dişi Aslan*."

"Are they here?" Ghreta asked.

"No, but they follow me by no more than two days." Lisette hoped no one wanted to know how she arrived without them. "I need to understand what you want, what the islanders want—to be left under Spain with the duke ruling, or to be freed entirely of European rule and become like Isla del Lagarto?"

The women all looked at each other for several minutes. The cook was first to whisper a few words, followed by the rest, speaking over one another and offering points and counterpoints. Lisette ate her stew and watched them debate. At last, they nodded, one by one, until it appeared they were agreed.

"It's a hard thing to decide," Ghreta said. "The rumors about Isla del Lagarto make it sound like life is better for everyone, but they are ruled by a group of people from the island. Could we find such people on Île des Oiseaux? The duke is, for all his bluff, a kind man and rules us with a gentle touch. However, we are at the mercy of Spain and cannot control it if they send the Mendozas, or equally vile nobility to take possession."

"Good points, all," Lisette told them. "And I cannot cast a vote in either direction. All I can do as a member of the *Dişi Aslan*, is drive out the Mendozas, and if you ask, we can ask the duke to return to Isla de Pimienta. I hope you understand, I do not have the heart to be as ruthless with him as with the other family."

"Oh, no, m'lady." Ghreta put her hands up and shook her head, looking around to see the others indicating their agreement with her. "Perhaps…if you concentrated on the Mendozas while we discuss this with others in the castles and the village. We might find our island rule if we look for it."

"An excellent plan." Lisette smiled. "And please, I am not m'lady. I am Lizzie, of the *Dişi Aslan* crew."

"M'lady." A small voice peeped from the group. It

belonged to one of the young girls, petite with dark eyes and curls around her face that escaped from her bonnet. "I mean…Lizzie. You are French nobility. Why do you not take back the island for your family? I was so small when your parents died, but I remember how lovely it was to live on this island. My parents did not complain about money or having enough food."

Lisette smiled. "I would hope to rule as benevolently as my father, but I cannot assure you that France wouldn't send someone of a less generous spirit. I, too, remember the kindness of my house—I also remember the arguments of my parents, when they received letters from Le Roi that we were not sending enough back to France in terms of tributes." She shook her head. "At any rate, I am not as noble as I used to be. I am a pirate, soon to be wedded to a pirate, and we have a child of that union. Le Roi may not even recognize me as a marquise, let alone confer a higher title."

The women murmured their opinions, until the cook spoke up. "But perhaps a once noble, now pirate would be a good member of the group to rule the island."

This was truly nothing Lisette wanted, but she could see how her presence, ruling with others might keep the island stable. But remaining on the island meant not sailing with Rocco. Why couldn't choices be simple?

"Let us say I am not opposed. I am also not volunteering."

The women smiled and nodded, then went back to their tasks, leaving Lisette to rise from the table and take a walk. Perhaps she could speak with others on the grounds, to get their opinions on who should rule. Mostly she was hoping to find someone who wanted to take a position in a governing group.

If I find enough good people, I won't have to do it.

53

The sun was getting lower, but heat still rose from the ground to meet the air, enveloping everything in a sultry dampness that seeped into her bones. Lisette had lived on this island since childhood and yet her French blood never adjusted to the tropics.

My half-French blood. The Turkish side of me should think this is normal.

She strolled to the livery to see if Quince might be at work. If he wasn't around, she could at least rub the velvet muzzles of the horses there. As she grew closer, she could hear the clanging of his hammer on metal. It had a harsh sound, followed by the clarity of a bell.

She spied him at the forge, pushing the heat up with the bellows as a pair of tongs lay against the opening. He stopped and pulled the tongs out. They gripped a yellow-orange-hot horseshoe, which he held against the anvil and hammered. Behind him, a large gray horse stood, its back foot cocked and head down, eyes closed.

Lisette held up her hand. "Good morrow, Quince."

Quince glanced up, smiled and nodded, before proceeding with his work. He submerged the shoe in a pail of water, which bubbled and steamed at the entry. Wiping his hands on his apron, he walked toward Lisette.

"Good morrow, m'lady. It's surely good to see you here."

"I've missed being here, around so many friendly faces." She gestured to the horse. "Is that one of ours?"

"No, it belongs to the duke—at least he does now." He lowered his voice. "Seems that one o' the Mendoza guards rode it here one day and tried to storm the castle, as it were. Duke spooked his horse, then had the guard tossed over the wall. I hear the horse is ours til he gets a proper apology."

Lisette laughed. "Oh, Uncle Oscar!"

"Uncle?"

"Sorry, no, he's not my official uncle. While I was away, we found ourselves being 'uncle and niece' in order to escape certain situations."

"Aye," he chuckled. "What brings you to the stables?"

"I am waiting for the duke's return and thought a walk would do me well. I also have a question for you if you are willing to answer it." Lisette posed her question of island rule to this large, swarthy man.

"Tell ya true, m'lady, I don't like to think o' things that can't be," he said. "But if things could be, I'd like to think I've a hand in my own fate. A gov'ment ruled by plain folk like myself might understand better."

Lisette nodded. "I believe you are right. To be frank, I did not imagine you to have an opinion either way, as you appear so easy to take life as it happens. I am happy that you could share with me."

"You know, meanin' no disrespect, I would not mind it if you governed us. You never acted like I was beneath ya."

"I never felt that way." She smiled, wondering if some part of her always knew that she wasn't as noble as she seemed. "If you know of anyone who might serve with others as peaceful and generous rulers, it might be done."

"What might be done?" A familiar, blustering voice approached.

Lisette spun to face him. "Uncle Oscar, how lovely to see you."

The Duke de Martinmas smiled and nodded. "What was being discussed about generous rulers?"

"Nothing of importance." Lisette could see the pale, wary look on Quince's face. "We were making pleasantries while I awaited your arrival. Why are you here at the stables?"

"To check on our lovely gray. Quince, has there been any word from the Mendozas?"

"None, m'lord." Quince grinned as he answered.

"Uncle Oscar," Lisette interrupted. "Might I dine with you this evening?"

The tall, rotund man stepped forward and took her hand, leading her away from the stables. "My dear almost-daughter, I would be crushed if you didn't."

She allowed him to lead her back to the castle, onto the balcony and into the great room. As they strolled toward the library, he bellowed, "Mari-sara!"

One of the young girls from the kitchen rushed into the room. "Yes, sire?"

"Tea and biscuits for myself and my…niece. In the library!"

"Yes, sire." The girl scampered away.

"Still barking orders, I see," Lisette said. "And I don't think that girl's name is 'Mari-sara'."

"She answered my call, did she not?"

"Or cook just shoved one of the servants out of the kitchen and into your gaping jaws." Lisette moved ahead of the duke into the library and sank into one of the overstuffed leather chairs. "But it is nice to see you again, sire."

"What news of the child?" The duke lowered himself onto a small settee. "You seem relaxed for a mother missing her baby."

She smiled. "You are correct, I do miss my baby, but I know where she is. A good friend is keeping steady watch over her while I attend to an important piece of business."

"Ah, excellent news! I have yet to spend time with your enchanting daughter."

The servant entered with the tray of tea and biscuits as he requested. He whisked her away with a sweep of his hand.

"Uncle…" Lisette admonished.

The duke frowned. "Thank you, Mari—what is your name?"

"Louisa, sire," the young girl whispered.

"Louisa then." He looked to Lisette, who nodded him on. "Thank you."

The girl left and Lisette reached across to tap his shoulder. "Good job, Uncle. Doesn't that make you happy?"

He gave her a sideways, narrowed glance. "I suppose. Now tell me, what is this important business to which you must attend?"

"It has come to my attention that the Mendoza family is attempting to take—firmer—control of this island," she said, and waited for his reaction.

His face registered no expression, although he raised his hands to his chest and clasped his fingers. He opened his mouth and took a breath, stopped and looked at her, and reached for a sweet.

"I realize that things were rocky between your house and theirs, especially given my manner of abrupt departure." She took her tea and sipped, leaning well back in the chair. *Very well. That is the last of my monologue, cher oncle.*

He chewed the biscuit slowly, making certain to not leave a crumb on his pale, high-collared shirt, his cravat tied round so thickly, Lisette marveled that it did not strangle him. She took a sweet for herself and nibbled at the edge, her eyes never leaving his, and her eyebrow cocked, daring him to try to out-wait her.

The more she stared and pecked at her food, the more uncomfortable he looked. His ears reddened—and was that sweat at his brow? She kept staring, emotionless. He finished the biscuit and reached for his tea. His first sip caused a fit of hacking and choking sounds. Slowly his breathing returned, and the spluttering noises waned.

"Quite all right, Sire?" Lisette asked.

"Yes, thank you." He took a few more sips of tea, clearing his throat after each one. "I must hope that you would not have left me to die."

"Of course not." She reached for another biscuit. "You seemed to prefer the silence, and I thought I should only intervene if it became dire."

He gave her a sideways scowl. "Little known fact, certain conversations call for discretion. You are aware that El Rey himself ordered this couple to Île des Oiseaux."

Lisette shrugged. "Were their orders to strip the island to nothing?"

"I am not privy to the king's plans." He took a long, slow breath. "But he has never asked for that of any island."

"I realize that you must remain loyal to your king,

and that action against the Mendozas could be seen as action against the Crown. You are a duke, however, and I would hope, higher in the king's estimation than Fausto de Mendoza or his silly wife."

"Let us hope so," the duke said.

"I am no ruler—I would happily sail to another island and live a simple life. But to abandon my home to these cutthroats—how can I?"

"What do you expect of me?" the duke scowled. "My hands are held."

Lisette rose and paced in front of the unlit fireplace. She stopped and turned to him. "I plan to drive the Mendozas from here. I do not ask you to betray Spain, only to do what is right. Step aside and do not look my way when the battle begins."

"As fond as I am of you, I fear repercussion among the nobility if the other islands discover my inaction." He frowned. "These are troubling times, dear Lizzie. The Medinas were not good people, it is true, but their absence left a hole in Isla del Lagarto that was filled by islanders because Spain could not send anyone quickly enough. What if it happens to Île des Oiseaux?"

"Well, you are here." She patted his arm. "From what I gather, my servants find you a benevolent man who does not ask for more than they can give. Perhaps if Spain sent more like you and less like Juan de Medina or Fausto de Mendoza—neither of them do El Rey any favors with their boorishness."

"It is true, they are not proper Spaniards."

"I have one idea that might help you." She sat beside him on the small divan. "A letter to El Rey, expressing your concerns about the Mendozas. Be effusive, charming, worried only about El Rey, his reputation, and Spain's holdings in the Caribbean. Send it quickly, before I begin my task. By the time it reaches Spain, and anyone can react to it, they will be gone, and your suspicions will have been correct."

"Yes, the king can hardly hold me accountable if I have asked him for guidance." He nodded. "And I remain here, awaiting further orders."

"Of course." Lisette kept her expression pleasant. She had won the first battle, to get the duke to agree to oust the Mendozas. Now, how to get him to leave the island to the islanders?

One step at a time.

54

"Captain Derya, it is a pleasure." Rocco greeted her as she stepped from the dinghy onto the deck. LeFarge had been there to offer his hand for balance. Her fingers barely brushed his palm as she leapt onto the ship.

"Thank you for receiving me." She grabbed Rocco by the shoulders, then gave his arm a rough pat with her right hand.

"Let us go to my cabin," he said. "And discuss matters."

They strode down the steps. Rocco's meal still sat at the table, and he bellowed for Cue the new cabin boy. The young man scurried into the room, shoulders curved, and knees bent in fear.

"Clean this up," Rocco demanded.

"Aye, Cap'n, aye," Cue groveled and gathered all on

a tray. He opened the door to see Poussin standing with a new tray of food and drink, and nearly ran into him.

"Mind where y'are, Boy," Poussin growled.

"Aye, sir, aye," Cue stammered and pushed his way out the door.

"My apologies, Cap'n," Poussin said. "I tole the new boy to come git the noonday meal, but he's takin' a bit o'trainin' to be seaworthy."

"If anyone can train him, you can," Rocco said. "Put the tray down and leave us."

The door closed and Rocco turned to pour the ale. Begum had already cut chunks of bread for each plate and was helping herself to the slices of dried meat.

"My apologies," Rocco said. "I do not have dark coffee or warm pocket bread for us."

"I did not expect it," she replied. "Any bread broken by friends is good bread."

They sat at the table and touched mugs before taking a drink.

"I would be lying if I claimed to not know why you are here." Rocco lit the lamp on the table. The sun was still hanging over the sea, but it was getting lower with each breath.

"Lisette and Île des Oiseaux," Begum said. "And by the way, I am so happy that Alara is safe."

He nodded. "Now we have to keep the world safe from Alara."

She gave him a quizzical look. "What have you learned?"

"I have learned nothing, but I suspect much." He told her of waking to find Alara next to him. "Lamya says she has inherited my temper, and that I must teach her how to control it. I don't know that I can control my own feelings—how can I teach a child?"

"Sometimes those who can't do a thing are better at

teaching others to do it."

He scowled. "I don't believe that."

"According to Lamya, you must. Either that or teach yourself first." She bit into the thick slice of bread and chewed, washing it down with ale. "But let us discuss Île des Oiseaux."

"Lisette wants to drive all the nobles off and let it be under island rule."

"Yes." Begum studied his face. "And what do you want?"

"I want to be a pirate as I've always been. I want to attack Spanish ships and steal their treasures and scuttle them and leave no prisoners." He frowned. "I do not see a way of remaining a pirate if the islands are all turned native. The Spanish will never sail here."

Begum laughed. "Forgive me, but that is the most naïve opinion I have ever heard."

"You mock me?" Rocco slammed his mug on the table, causing ale to spurt upward.

"Yes," she nodded and laughed again. "And don't be such an old crab about it."

He stood and paced about the cabin. Every time he paused to glare at Begum, she giggled again.

"Why are you laughing so?" he asked.

"I do not know. It is not funny, except that you are having a fit about it, which makes me laugh. Come to the table and sit. We will discuss this like two pirate captains, instead of a giggling schoolgirl and a child having a tantrum."

Still scowling, he walked to the table and plopped down, picking up a piece of dried meat and chewing on it.

"Now then." Begum's expression had settled into something more serious, although the gleam in her eye remained. "Spanish ships will always exist for our plunder. Not all islands will want self-rule. Isla de

Pimienta enjoys their rule by the duke and his son, who ask little of the islanders. And driving out the Mendozas does not drive out the duke."

"I suppose you are right." His body relaxed and his face softened. "Does the duke plan to stay on Île des Oiseaux?"

"That I do not know. Lisette has flown ahead to speak with him."

"Yes, I suppose Lisette could always rule the island." He took a swig of ale. "She is nobility."

Begum looked away. "Yes, but I do not think she wishes to do more than raise Alara and sail with you."

"Sail with me? Oh, no, that's too dangerous."

"She did not sail with you before? When it was dangerous?"

"She did, but she wasn't a mother then."

Begum frowned. "What does that matter? You will be a father."

"That's different and you know it is."

"Maybe I do. And maybe it is so for most families. But I have no magic in me and even I know this baby will not be like most babies. She will need both of you."

Rocco waved her words away and tore another chunk of bread. "Lizzie can stay at the castle and have servants. I will visit when I am in port. She can't sail with me at her whim."

"Hmm…" Begum studied his face. "Would it be difficult for you to have only one child?"

"No." He shrugged. "That night, when Alara came—there was so much blood, and after, Lizzie was in bed for many days. It wasn't good on her body, was it?"

"You could say such a thing." Begum took a sip of ale and a big breath. "I must tell you the truth, not because Lizzie won't but perhaps she cannot. The night you stabbed Lisette, your blade nicked her womb. That is why all the blood."

"What?" Rocco paled.

"It is unimportant now," Begum said, holding her palms out in placation. "What is important is that when Ruhee healed her and kept her from bleeding to death, she used an ankh and a spell. *Qahil*. Arabic for 'barren.' Ruhee believes that you will not stay with Lizzie if she cannot bear more children. She sealed Lizzie's womb to make certain of that."

"I will always stay with Lisette," he said. "No matter how many children."

Begum smiled. "Good. Now, why are you bound for Île des Oiseaux if you are not going to help us drive out the Mendozas?"

"To ransom Willem d'Auguste. Should I collect before you begin your attack, or gather my gold on their way off the island?"

"I hate to risk your reward by making you wait," she said, "but turning him loose before we battle gives the Mendozas one more sword. I suspect Willem is no coward."

"He put up a respectable fight before capture." He shook his head. "I know what Lizzie wants of me—you want it, too. Suppose the duke does not agree and joins in the Mendozas' fight? I'll not chase all the Spanish away."

"You may be as hard-headed as your beloved, although I blame hers on being raised as a noble." Begum finished her ale and stood. "Meet us at the pirate's harbor in two days. Lisette will give us the report and we will make our plan for attack."

She strode from the cabin and up the steps. Rocco could hear her boots across the deck, moving toward the dinghies. Knowing he could not make a decision until he heard Lisette's report did not calm his mind.

Whatever the duke agreed to, he was nobility and not to be trusted. They needed a firm count of how many guards were at each castle to know how many potential men they might battle. Would Lizzie know to find that out? She'd been in battle before but had been thrust into it. Even her battle with Eric d'Auguste and Mercedes de Medina had not shown any signs of planning on her part. Just get to the castle, transform, and kill them.

He poured himself more ale and downed it. His dagger clinked against his side, and he put his hand on the hilt to steady it. His fingers closed around it as he remembered the golden dress Lisette had worn and how he heard it rip as he thrust the dagger into her. He had been deliberate about the motion—the blade had to work up her ribcage, away from her heart, her lungs. She needed to live but be unable to kill Mercedes.

He'd been wrong about that, too.

She'd nearly died in childbirth. That was all his fault. Ruhee's intervention came with a curse. Not quite his fault, except that Lizzie would not have needed help if he hadn't stabbed her.

One little string unravels the cloth.

Rocco shook the thoughts from his head and strode from the cabin, up to the helm. The ship had slowed during its rendezvous with the *Dişi Aslan*. Now that Captain Derya was aboard her own ship, Chunk had ordered the sails be filled, to make haste to Île des Oiseaux.

"Cap'n." Chunk stepped aside to let Rocco take the wheel. "Any orders?"

"Yes. After discussing it with Captain Derya, the *Dişi Aslan* plan to attack the Mendoza castle. They will either drive the Mendozas from the islands or fight them to the death."

"And *L'Implacable?*"

"We will ransom our hostage but will not release him until the Mendozas are dealt with."

Chunk raised an eyebrow. "What if the Mendozas are dead?"

"We will give him his choice—return to France alive or die in the Caribbean."

"Aye. Let's hope we get the gold before the Mendozas meet their maker."

Rocco glanced at him. "Why do you think they won't gladly get on a boat?"

"Because them Mendozas ain't from Spain, they're from Portugal. I know. They ruled my village for a time, but the people didn't like their heavy hand, and someone tipped off the king that they was takin' more'n their share of the taxes. They snuck into Spain ahead of the choppin' block and changed their name from Mendes to Mendoza."

"If they ran once, why won't they run now?"

Chunk smiled. "Oleta was made an orphan cuz of them. She won't let 'em run, at least not far."

"Then open up the sails and fly this ship to the island," he told Chunk. "We need to be at the *Dişi Aslan*'s heels to keep them from killing our golden goose."

Lisette returned to the kitchen. "Where do I find Pinar?"

One of the young girls pointed at the back door. "I seen her on her way to back gate. She was travelling fast."

"Thank you." Lisette rushed out after her.

She was almost at the gate when she heard a rustling noise in the yard to her left. The castle grounds held a few crops and animals, especially birds. Quail and partridge were delicacies at the table, but there were plenty of chickens scratching in the dirt. A glimpse of skirt made Lisette turn.

Pinar emerged from the chicken coop holding a pigeon in both hands. She saw Lisette and smiled before releasing the bird into the sky. Lisette noticed the white band around the bird's leg.

"What is your message to Captain Begum?" Lisette

asked.

"Lizzie!" Pinar threw her arms around her. "Did you find the baby? Where's Rocco?"

Lisette gave her all the news, suddenly weary of updating everyone about Alara, Ruhee, and the entire saga. Omitting Lamya's involvement made it especially difficult.

"But tell me," Lisette said at last, "What news do you send?"

"A plea for help—the Mendozas are becoming more insistent every day that they take this castle. We do not dare ask the duke for help, as he will not risk offending them, but we do not know how much longer he can stall before letting them move in."

"Help is almost here," Lisette told her. "The *Dişi Aslan* is no more than two days out. I have come early to determine the best plan of attack—and to make certain the duke will not step in to help the Mendozas out of loyalty to Spain."

"Easily done, I hope?"

Lisette shrugged. "He worries about his status with the king, but when we last spoke he said he was willing to step aside and let us handle them."

"And how are we handling them?"

"That I do not know, but I shall attempt to determine the number of their guard, their weak spots, and their general temperament for fighting."

Pinar smiled. "And afterward, do we oust the duke as well?"

"That remains to be decided." Lisette looked back at the castle, shaking her head. "It is more complicated than I thought it would be."

"It always is." Pinar wiped her hands on her apron. "I must get back and attend to the duke. I'm certain he must be needing something."

"And I must check out the Mendoza castle to find the weak spot in their defense." Lisette turned back to the gate and jiggled the latch, the same way she did as a girl. The gate fell open and she passed through. On the outer wall, away from prying eyes, she took a breath.

I am a dragon.

Sailing upward, she flew into the sun and behind a cloudbank to hide herself from the casual observer. She noticed that most people never looked upwards, which kept her movements unseen, but she took no chances. The layers of clouds allowed her to circle the castle and head inland, past the old Medina stronghold and south, to the Mendozas.

She had been to this castle a few times, as Eric's nearly-betrothed. Her family usually entertained the d'Auguste family, as her father outranked the count, but there were a few parties held at the d'Auguste castle. The architecture mimicked her own home, in a slightly smaller form. Lisette wondered that the Mendozas would let their daughter have the larger estate.

From her vantage point above the clouds, she peered down into the courtyard, the gate, and surroundings. The last time she had encountered the Mendoza guards, they had been sent to help Mercedes de Medina—most had run home, unwilling to lay down their lives for a stranger, nobility or not.

She could tell these were not the same guards. Not nearly as slight of build nor casual of dress or movement, these looked like men of action. She counted ten, which meant there might be as many as fifteen, since there would be a few in the barracks sleeping. Had they received this new crew from El Rey?

A figure stepped out on the balcony, and Lisette lifted higher to stay out of his view. It looked like Count de Mendoza. He stared west, toward Lisette's castle, whose turrets could barely be seen above the hills and foliage. A second figure, in guard uniform, appeared at the arched doorway to the balcony. He spoke to the count, but Lisette could not hear.

She lowered herself slowly to the roof, taking care to settle onto her pads and not let her claws click on the wood. Flattening her body as much as possible, she leaned forward to watch and listen.

"…received from a messenger moments ago," the guard was saying as he handed a folded piece of paper to the count.

The count opened the waxed seal and read, his face turning white as he did.

"Where is the messenger?" he yelled. "Find him!"

"Yes, m'lord." The guard raced off.

The count continued to stare at the letter. A high, grating voice closed in on the balcony. Catalina de Mendoza fluttered out to the count, sputtering complaints.

"Fausto, you must send a contingent to the Lille estate. I was thrown out today by a servant! A servant! I've never been so insulted. She wouldn't even announce me to the duke, and I know he was there. He cannot have two castles—it isn't fair! Our daughter and her husband need that castle."

"Maybe they will and maybe they won't." He held the letter toward her. "According to this, Willem has been kidnapped and is being held for ransom. Two thousand gold ducats, or he dies."

Catalina grasped at her chest and sank down, nearly to the floor. The count gave her a dismissive wave. "Stop that. Willem is not the perfect match for our daughter anyway. He is a Frenchman, turning traitor to serve Spain. El Rey will never trust him with a position of importance."

"But what do we tell Renata? She is fond of the boy. Are two thousand ducats so much? We have that much and more."

"And why should we give it to thieving pirates?"

She stomped about the balcony. "Oh, this does ruin so many plans. We were planning to sail to Isla de la Soledad to meet with Count Barragan and invite him to the wedding. We can hardly ask for gifts if there is no groom for the wedding."

The count put his finger to his chin, tapping. "You know, dearest, there is an advantage to be taken here. If I can convince the duke of my poverty, he has the two thousand ducats, I'm sure, to pay the ransom. Willem goes unclaimed, so the pirates kill him, and we are all the richer."

"Pity, he is a nice young man." Catalina turned to the door. "But it occurs to me that Count Barragan is single…I shall let Renata know we sail for Soledad at the end of the week. She will need someone to comfort her after her betrothed is gone."

Lisette grinned. *Good luck interesting Count Barragan in marriage. I doubt if you have anything he wants, except money. Although truly, I hope he does marry into your family and rob you blind.*

She heard someone call for "Father" within the castle—the voice sounded female and angry. The count looked up from the letter to see Renata barreling onto the balcony, her hands in tight fists.

Lisette's grin widened to a dragon's smile, opening her mouth to reveal a row of pointed teeth. *Let us see what daughter has to say about this.*

"Father, what is this about Willem being kidnapped? And you won't pay his ransom?" She stomped a fashionably shod foot.

"Dear daughter," he said in a soothing voice, although Lisette could see the tension in his backbone. "I treasure your betrothed, but they are asking a large amount of coin and my coffers are not as full as when we arrived. These new guards have cost us twice as much as the old ones, and then there is the decorating that must be done on your new home."

"When am I taking possession? I cannot believe it has not been arranged yet."

"There has been a bit of a snag," the count said and looked at Renata's angry face. "But it should be cleared soon, my dear. Very soon."

"I should hope so. I fear I am so much older than the other marquises who already have their homes established. Willem and I are supposed to be married and ruling—or helping you to rule this horrid place." She crossed her arms, scowling.

"And you will." He patted her arm and lifted her chin. "The Duke de Martinmas will vacate any day now and turn the castle over to you. And we will do our best to get Willem back from the brigands who hold him now." He walked toward the balcony's edge, tapping the letter against the opposite hand. "And if that is not possible, we are visiting Isla de la Soledad soon. I understand that Count Barragan is very handsome and quite single."

Renata's face lightened. "A count?"

Her father turned to her, smiling. "You see, my dear. One way or another, it will work out."

56

Lisette had heard enough. She stretched up quietly and extended her wings, breathing a soft haze to keep her movements unnoticed. Her eyes stayed on the count and his daughter, but they were looking outward toward her castle. They had no reason to glance up. She was able to push off the roof and catch a lovely draft to carry her up and westward toward the pirate's harbor.

She had just cleared the Mendoza castle, making straight for the cove, when she saw figures on the road ahead. Two bodies struggled with a third. As she closed in on the scene, she realized that two men in uniform were attempting to detain someone she knew—Poussin. He had apparently been the messenger to deliver Rocco's ransom demand, and the count's guards had caught up with him.

Although he was a young man, he was still small and wiry, capable of quick movement and athleticism. Lisette enjoyed watching him squirm his way out of the grasp, run a few feet, and be captured, just to wiggle away again. It was great fun, until one of the guards withdrew his blade. The other guard grabbed his arm to stop him.

"Count wants him alive," he said.

"He can still be mostly alive." The guard with the sword drew back as he reached for Poussin's shoulder.

Lisette was directly overhead, so she shot a thick cloud at the guards and Poussin, adding a bolt of lightning which hit the metal blade of the sword and sent the guard flying back. Poussin stood for a moment, his mouth open and eyes wide.

Poussin, you do not have time. Lisette grabbed him in her paws and flew away. His shriek pierced the countryside. Whether the guards saw her, she did not know. Getting Poussin to safety was her only thought.

His shriek died to a whimper as they flew toward the harbor. Lisette cradled his torso in her paws, facing him down so that he could see the land underneath and where they were going. She could feel his body trembling and her heart ached for his fear. At one point, she thought of turning him around to see her but decided against it. He was already terrified of being grabbed by a dragon—did he want to come face to face with it as well?

Soon she saw the cliff that led down to the cove. A narrow path zigzagged through the brush on the other side to allow access, but few people knew of it. To most, it looked like a straight drop down to the beach below.

Lisette landed in a clearing short of the cliff, setting Poussin down gently. His legs shook and knees wobbled, until he sat down, holding his head, and trying to catch his breath. While he composed himself, Lisette transformed back.

"My apologies for the surprise," she said.

The young man whipped about, falling onto his rear end, and scooting away from her. "Surprise? M'lady ya don't know what it's like, to be grabbed by a beast and carried off. I never wanted to hear about no dragons, see no dragons, and especially be carried off by no dragons."

"On the contrary, Poussin. I have been grabbed by a dragon, one who wanted to kill me. Be happy I wanted to save you."

"Happy." He spat the word as he rose to his feet, dusting off his clothes. "Do I look happy?"

"No, but you look alive." Lisette glared at him. "Next time I shall let the guards run you through."

He scowled at her before dropping his gaze to the ground. "I s'pose I am grateful fer that. It ain't that I weren't scared of them killin' me, it's jest…m'lady, I was raised a good Catholic and dragons was of the devil. Mebbe yer good. I jest ain't used to it."

"Understood." She gestured toward the cliff. "While you're getting used to it, we need to get back to the ship."

They hurried up the ridge and took the switchbacks as quickly as they could without pitching forward and falling into the bristled foliage that hemmed them in. *L'Implacable* sat at the entrance to the small beach, anchored, while her dinghies came and left. Lisette could hear orders being barked out, although she could not make out the words.

Another ship was anchored, further toward the shore than Rocco's. The *Dişi Aslan* had also arrived. Activity on her deck was much quieter, even though her boats were cast off and brought in at a similar frequency. Captain Derya gave orders the way she fought—with calm clarity.

The first to greet Lisette and Poussin was Chunk, who threw his large arms about Lisette.

"Lizzie, I'm so happy yer here!" He turned to Poussin. "Did ya deliver the message? I din't expect ya to be back so soon."

Poussin looked at Lisette, a worried frown crossing his brow. "Aye, Sir, I delivered it."

"I can vouch for him," Lisette spoke up. "He's back so quickly because…I offered him a quick passage back. Guards were on his tail and were on the verge of capturing him."

The young man's eyes widened as he shook his head, but Chunk slapped him on the back. "Well done, and thank ye, Lizzie, fer helpin' our little chicken back ta ship."

"It was good to be of service," she said. "But now I must see Rocco. I saw the count open the message and heard his planned response."

Chunk motioned to the ship. "He's aboard, directin' the crew. There's a boat about t'return, there by the caves."

Lizzie ran toward the dinghy, almost filled with sacks. LeFarge was loading the boat.

"Supplies?" she asked.

He shook his head. "Jewels. Chains and gold, all but coin. We're pullin' out some of our treasure to sell."

"That's surprising."

"Cap'n decided—us, too—if they wasn't coin, they needed to be."

She nodded. "Can the boat hold one more body?"

"Sure, m'lady." He leaned in, a sly smile playing on his face. "Prob'ly too bright out t'be flyin' there."

She laughed and leaned closer to him. "How do you think Poussin got back here so quickly?"

He gestured to the boat. "Have yerself a seat and I'll be shovin' off." He turned to the man who was still dragging bags out. "Take the next boat. I got a passenger to deliver."

Their ride to *L'Implacable* was quiet but enjoyable. Lisette was relieved to sit with someone else who knew about her transformations and did not have an opinion about them.

Once aboard ship, she rushed to find Rocco. She had

information to deliver and a battle to plan with Begum Derya, but when she found him, she had to fold her arms around him and turn her face upward for a kiss. He obliged, and from the fire in his embrace, he was just as helpless when it came to expressing his own feelings.

"I have news," she whispered as soon as she could breathe again. "I think Willem should hear it."

"Well, then let us go tell him." He turned her toward the steps, and they descended into the underbelly of the ship. In the lower level, mid-ship, a locked door with a small, barred window held the prisoner.

"Willem." Rocco called him forward.

It was a few moments before his face appeared at the window.

"I have news," she said. "For both of you."

Willem smirked. "Unless it is about my release, I am not interested."

"It may well be," she said. "I was at the Mendoza castle when the messenger delivered the ransom letter to the count. I saw him read it and heard the resulting conversation with his family." She glanced from one man to the other. "The news is not good."

"Don't tell me you asked too much coin for me?" Willem laughed. "Or was it too little?"

"It hardly matters," Lisette told him. "He plans to not pay it, and he is counting on Rocco to kill you instead."

The marquess' already-pale face took an ashen tone. "But…I am his daughter's fiancé. I am the son of a count. I am…I am…"

"You are not his ideal son-in-law."

"How do I know you are telling the truth?" Willem asked. "You could be lying to turn me against them."

"Why should I do that? This information benefits Rocco, and I have no desire to lie to him."

"Or perhaps you told him the truth and you are

working together in this charade."

Rocco scowled. "You are one man, hardly enough to turn a battle, and I do not plan to release you until after the *Dişi Aslan* has accomplished its mission. There is no reason to deceive you."

Willem glared at Lisette. "You must be enjoying this."

"I truly take no joy here." She frowned. "My battle with your brother had nothing to do with you or even your parents, who tried to stop me. Of truth, I often felt you got the worst hand, being treated as less important than Eric. You were by far the smartest in your family."

"I still am." His expression relaxed and Lisette could see the cloud of sadness that settled on his features.

"Did you discuss anything with the duke about the Mendoza problem?" Rocco asked.

"Yes. He was hesitant but agreed to stay neutral as much as possible." She shrugged. "When I tell him that the count is going to ask him for the ransom money, claiming poverty and depending upon his basically kind heart to give it to him, he may change his mind."

"So my ransom will be paid?" Willem asked.

"No. The count will line his coffers with the duke's gold ducats and let you swing from a yardarm."

"That changes the plan." Rocco spoke at last, his expression stern. "You have not told the duke this?"

"No, I believed you were the first in line to receive the information."

Rocco nodded. "I assume you were at the Mendoza castle to obtain information to help Captain Derya."

"The castle has new guards," Lisette said. "Stronger, more trained, unified in their duties. I counted ten but would guess the night crew was asleep."

"At least five more," Rocco said.

"Seven," Willem told them. They both looked at him,

so he added, "If he's going to be a bastard, I can be a bigger one. Would you like to know their schedule and where they are posted around the grounds?"

Lisette pulled Rocco away and whispered, "Can we trust him?"

"I don't know. But we should listen and proceed cautiously. We will know quickly if he is lying."

Lisette grinned. "Does this mean you are joining us in our fight?"

Rocco's eyes narrowed as he glared at her. "Perhaps. After I collect the duke's gold."

"What?" Lisette raised her voice. "How could you take his coin? If anything, you should be looting the count's coffers."

"Oh, I'll get round to them, too." He grinned. "When you've subdued the household."

"When I've—ugh!" Lisette turned and stomped upstairs, shouting, "I'm going to see Captain Derya. We've got a battle to plan."

Her cheeks blazed as she strode to the boats. *Rocco, why are you such a mercenary? Such a brigand, such a— pirate. This is who I am to marry and raise children with. Is this what I want?*

She climbed down the ladder into a dinghy amid four crewmen and watched the water come up to the boat as the boat pushed away from the ship. The wood met the sea and floated. The sea carried the boat to the shore. Rocco was like the boat—rigid, propelled toward its goal. She was the moveable, flexible one, capable of changing course.

It would all be less complicated if she didn't love him.

Once ashore, she rushed to find Captain Derya. Begum was at the entrance to the caves to the left, waiting for her.

"Lisette, what news?" she asked.

"The count has ten guards on duty, and seven additional to cover the evening hours." She told Begum all she had heard from the roof of the castle, plus the conversation with Willem. "We should be cautious, but I believe the guards can be overcome."

"What did Willem say about their posts? Where will we find them?"

Lisette's eyes widened. "Gads, I didn't stay to hear that part!"

"Were you so intent on finding me?"

"Yes, but—no. Not exactly." She lowered her head, her face flushing with red bloom. "My apologies, I let my heart overrule the situation. Rocco and I had an argument and I left, angry."

Begum nodded. "Not the best way to prepare for battle."

"I should not have let my pride get in the way. I have a job to do."

"Yes," Begum told her. "But let us put it aside and discuss what we can." She motioned to a circle of boulders. "Come, sit. We will plan."

Oleta joined the two women and they sat together, drawing diagrams in the sand, and exchanging ideas about the attack. Lisette quickly realized they needed the information that Willem had volunteered about the positioning of the guards.

"Oleta," Begum said. "Find Rocco and ask him about the guards."

The short, dark woman nodded and rose to leave.

"Wait," Lisette said, and dug into her bag. "Here, take the velvet tongue with you. This should ensure we'll get good information."

Begum turned to Lisette. "Could you use your…special skill in this battle?"

"I'd like to say yes." She thought of the few people

she had killed as a dragon. "But the truth is, I do not know. Being a moon dragon is so different than being a blood dragon. My killing is directly related to someone I love being in danger. I could chase and corral the guards, but as long as they are not trying to hurt my loved ones, I'm not certain I could find the strength to kill them."

"Understood."

"Although…" Lisette gazed softly at Begum. "If my mother was in jeopardy as I fought beside her…"

"We have much time to account for," Begum told her, smiling. "It would have been lovely to have you aboard my ship, now that you know. But you belong with your daughter and your—husband? Do you plan to marry?"

"I cannot tell the future." She shrugged. "I know I love him and always will. At the moment, our lives seem to be at odds. I wish to free this island from Spanish tyranny. He wishes to extort as much gold as he can from them and leave them to rule. Is love enough to unite us?"

Begum said nothing for a long time, until the only sounds were the chatter of the crew, the waves breaking, and the boats scraping along the sand. Lisette wondered where Oleta was. To finalize their plans, they needed more information.

"He loved me." Begum's voice was a low purr that cut through the silence. "Your father loved me, of that I have no doubts. He could not marry me, of course, nor even install me in his castle, but he offered to find me a fine home and let me raise you without worry for anything. I turned him down."

Lisette's mouth parted in surprise.

"I am not meant to stay in one place," Begum continued. "I could have been, once, but when I was forced from my village I began a life of roaming, a pilgrimage, looking for a place of peace. I knew, even with his love and even with you, that peace is something I will never find." She touched Lisette's cheek with her fingertips. "I wish I could tell you that love is unity. All I can tell you is that love is something you carry in your heart, no matter where you go. You and Rocco may not be together, but you will love that way, and Alara will help you."

Lisette opened her mouth to say thank you, to call her *mother* and say she understood. A huffing noise interrupted her. Oleta ran to them and hurled herself onto the sand, holding her chest and letting her breath return to normal.

"I have the information," she said between wheezes. After taking a large breath, she reached into her pocket and withdrew a paper. "Willem marked the drawing himself."

"Do we trust this Willem?" Begum asked.

"I fed him the leaf," Oleta told her. "He was more than happy to be truthful."

"The only problem will be if the count has changed things since Willem was last in the castle," Lisette said. "I feel we should study what he has provided and proceed cautiously. If the guards are not at these positions, we shall have to do as we always have done—fight our way in."

Begum nodded. "And the Mendozas? Kill them or capture them?"

"Kill them, of course," Oleta said.

They both looked at Lisette, who sighed.

"I would like to give them the opportunity to sail back to Spain and stay there," she said at last. "I do not relish killing them, if only because they have not, to my knowledge done anyone physical harm. However…"

"Yes, I know the however," Begum said. "Spanish nobility tends toward grudges and revenge. They will not simply sail back to España. They will return to take their anger out on you, or they will send someone to do it."

"I hate to say it, but I wish Rocco would join us in

this fight, if only because he relishes killing Spaniards." Lisette frowned. "It's his special skill, no matter if he's dragon or human."

Oleta's eyes widened. Lisette realized her mistake and reddened.

"Oh my, I've said too much. Oleta—oh, well, what is done is done. Rocco is a dragon, much like me. There, I've said it all. Now if I have to transform, you will not be surprised."

"Surprised, no. But I shall yelp in shock all the same."

Lisette laughed. "And I will not stop you."

"So, the question remains," Begum said. "Death to the Mendozas?"

Lisette rubbed her forehead. "Yes," she whispered. "Death to the Mendozas."

"Very well." Begum's expression was somber. "Oleta will assemble the crew while I meet with Captain Rocco and relay our intent. Lizzie—I assume you also have a task to perform?"

"I should like to visit the duke and warn him of the count's intentions." Lisette looked up at the cliff. "Begging your pardon, but speed will be of the essence. The afternoon shadows are long, and I presume we shall attack at nightfall."

Begum confirmed her suspicions and Lisette sprinted up the winding path to the top of the cliff. Behind the heavy brush that disguised the path was the perfect place to transform, away from the crew.

Soon she had opened her wings, fanned them down and lifted into the sky, away from the setting sun and toward her castle—the duke's castle. Uncle Oscar deserved to know what Count de Mendoza had in mind.

Lisette found Ghreta on the balcony outside the great hall, a large watering can tipped toward one of the stone planters. "You're going to flatten all those blooms if you dump water on them like that."

The servant turned, spilling the water on herself, and spraying the balcony floor.

"M'lady, you surprised me!"

"I am sorry, Ghreta, but I thought it better to surprise you as a human than have you find a dragon staring at you."

"Much."

"Is the duke here? I must speak with him. And please call me Lizzie. 'M'lady' doesn't seem to suit me anymore."

"Yes, Lizzie. I believe he is receiving a visitor at the

moment. Count de Mendoza."

"Hmm." Lisette tapped her chin with her finger. "Do I interrupt, or do I let the count try to deceive the duke?"

"Deceive?"

Lisette relayed what she had overheard to Ghreta, who shook her head.

"Never much cared for them, even when we first met."

"Agreed." Lisette thought of their first meeting at this castle, when the duke tried to strongarm her and Connie into marriage. "It turns out, they are wantonly greedy and seek to gather as much gold as possible—maybe more than possible."

"Whatever you decide, Lizzie, I'll have your back."

"As will I." Pinar strolled out of the arching doorways to join them on the patio. "Have we a plan to remove the Mendozas?"

"Yes, we attack tonight. The moon will be a sliver, making the land dark with few shadows." Lisette looked at both women. "It is possible you will have winged help in battle, but you might just have a noblewoman and her sword."

"And Rocco?"

"Rocco is not—enthusiastic—about the plan. He prefers to keep the Mendozas here and rob their ships. Given enough time, they might move anyway. However, his focus now is on collecting the ransom money for Willem d'Auguste."

"So, we cannot count on him," Ghreta said.

Lisette shook her head and could not prevent a small sigh from escaping. "No."

"He will come around," Pinar said. "It will be after the attack is begun, but he will join us."

"How can you be sure?" Lisette frowned.

Pinar smiled. "Because he loves you."

"That may be true," Lisette said, "but he is a pirate. In the meantime, where is the duke entertaining his visitor?"

"The library," Ghreta said.

"Then I shall be off. I should like the help of the duke's guards tonight, but at the very least, I need him to remain neutral." Lisette strode through the door and into the great hall, turning right to the hall and stopping at a large and partially opened door of dark, carved wood.

This was her library, where she had stood on the ladder, on tiptoes, to pull a volume down for reading. It suddenly struck her as the one and only reason to raise Alara within these walls. The information in the books about history and geography were invaluable to her as a child, as were the flights of fancy.

Knowledge could only help Alara grow in her role as a dragon.

Lisette could hear the voices through the narrow gap in the doorway. The duke's calm baritone sounded deeper than usual—she guessed that he was attempting to establish his dominance as the more masculine man in the room.

"I understand, Fausto, it is a pity that your son-in-law is in the hands of that ruffian. But I fail to see how I can help you."

"Under ordinary circumstances, I would not ask such a favor." The count's voice was soft and pleading. "Two thousand gold ducats is a hefty price to pay for a marquess. I confess, I haven't that kind of available coin to throw at a pirate."

The room fell silent and remained that way for a long, awkward time. Lisette wondered if both men had fallen asleep—or killed each other.

"Little known fact," the duke said. "I accidentally intercepted a letter intended for you when you first arrived. My abject apologies, it came to me, and I opened it before reading to whom it was addressed. I read that you have the extreme honor of receiving five thousand gold ducats every month from El Rey. What remarkable deed resulted in such a luxury of riches?" The duke paused, before raising his voice. "And with what audacity do you think you can ask me for a loan when you have a room in the castle dedicated to your treasures from the king?"

Lisette heard a crashing thud and could only assume the count had fallen into the tea service—or he was pushed.

"Thank you, Oscar," the count said in a shaky tone, "I shall take my leave."

"Do so. And in the future…" The duke opened the door toward Lisette, who hid further into its hinges. "Do not address me as Oscar. I am the Duke de Martinmas."

The count shuffled backward out of the door before turning and striding toward the main entrance, attempting to look important. The stains of tea and cream on his fine jacket and velvety breeches told a different story. Lisette chuckled quietly and slid around the library door, into the room.

"My, my, Uncle Oscar," she teased. "I can't believe you suspected the count of lying just because he wanted to squeeze money from you."

"Lisette, it is so good to see you." He took her hand and kissed it, before ringing for a servant. "But I'm afraid that fiancé of yours is going to cause me trouble. Kidnapping Willem d'Auguste—was that a wise thing to do?"

She shrugged. "I know not, although it has certainly enlightened me on the count's greed. I believe you'll find it interesting that the count plans to scrap Willem, with or without your help, and court Count Barragan as a husband for his dear daughter."

"Barragan." The duke shuddered. "There is no worse match in the islands."

"I don't know…there are many marriages in which love is not important. A few that don't require heirs or will overlook the fact that the marriage hasn't been consummated as long as the baby looks like the father."

"But…Barragan…"

"I have a feeling that the Mendozas will be disappointed. He seems to have his eyes set on someone else."

"Lizzie, please." He sat down as a servant arrived and cleaned up the spilled service. Tapping his finger on his lips, he maintained silence until the tray and its contents were removed, along with the servant. "I have faced the situation and know it to be true, but I cannot have this conversation yet. Perhaps not ever."

"We needn't speak of it, Sire." She walked to the door and closed it. "I'm actually here to warn you of the count's duplicity—of which you are already aware, and to see if your position has changed on the Mendozas being encouraged to leave this place."

"Leave? At the moment, I am content if they are executed."

"Harsh words, but it may come to that." She patted him lightly on the arm and sat in the chair next to him. "My bloodthirsty days are at an end, so I prefer that they leave. I worry, however, that they will not remain gone. My experience with the Medinas, and Mercedes' revenge, has left me suspicious of nobility."

"What I cannot imagine is why the king is sending him that much in gold each month. What task is he supposed to be performing for that price?"

"Securing this island for Spain?"

"Pfft." The duke waved his hand. "I am here, in two castles. I have not seen any uprisings against the monarchy."

"Nor have I." She ran her hand down her neck to her emerald and held the stone in her palm. "Unless…it is not what the count can do for Spain, but what he can do for El Rey."

"Like what?"

"Think of it, Uncle—the king sends de Mendoza halfway round the world and pays him—to stay here. Why does the king want to keep this man away from him? Or this family?"

"Yes, under normal circumstances, if you anger El Rey, you are executed. This man is not executed, but he is not welcomed." The duke gazed at her

"He…has…something…" Lisette said the words as the duke nodded in agreement.

"Something that would ruin the king."

"Something we need to find." Lisette stood. "I predict the Mendozas will happily be encouraged to leave this place—but the count will take his insurance with him."

"And we need someone there when he retrieves it, so we know what it is." The duke smiled.

"I think I can find it, Uncle Oscar." She curtsied and rushed to the door.

Racing through the great room, she stopped at the kitchen and found Ghreta stirring a pot that smelled like curried stew.

"Ghreta, I need you to get a message to Captain Derya."

Ghreta put her ladle in a curved dish and turned to Lisette. "Of course."

"Tell her, I must run an errand, one that will let us win the battle easily, and rid the island of the Mendozas forever."

Lisette ran back to the large patio outside the great hall. This would work if she could act quickly.

I am a dragon.

"All's loaded, Cap'n," Chunk called out.

Rocco stood at the bow, looking at the island, aware of the last dinghy being hauled from the sea. He nodded, though no one was around. They could sail now. There'd be no ransom for Willem d'Auguste, so there was no need to wait. They could dump the Frenchman on an island or into the drink, it didn't matter.

It only mattered to Lisette.

Fighting seventeen guards did not sound difficult. Begum and her crew had fought that many and won easily. Of course, they were fighting from the vantage of their ship and had cannons to back up their swords.

"Captain, are we to sail?" Luis Delgado asked.

"Yes…" Rocco trailed off.

"Pardon me, sir, but you seem uncertain."

Rocco looked over at him. "We came to ransom Willem d'Auguste but the count is uninterested in getting his son-in-law back. We were also asked to help the *Dişi Aslan* uproot the Mendoza family, but I am torn. Why should we involve ourselves with island politics?"

"True enough. What do we do with d'Auguste?"

Rocco shrugged. "We ditch him."

"Overboard? On an island? Here?"

"Not here. Anywhere else is fine." Rocco returned his gaze to the island. "I'm not an unreasonable man, Luis, but I am a pirate, and I like the life. Am I wrong to refuse to help exile the Mendozas?"

"Right or wrong is not for me to say," Luis said. "Although I do not think of the task itself—I only think that my friends have asked me for a favor, and I should say yes."

Rocco frowned. "Yes, my loyalty to my friends means something to me. And it is not Captain Derya who requests this—it is Lisette."

"Pardon my saying, Captain, but does your desire for piracy come before your love?"

Rocco nodded, silent for some time. At last, he sighed. "You are right, Luis. She has sacrificed her title to be with me, and I have sacrificed nothing."

He strode from the bow toward the boats. "I shall see Captain Derya at once and join in their battle."

A flash of white at the helm caught his attention, followed by a familiar voice calling his name. He looked up to see Lisette coming down the steps from the wheel, toward him.

"Lisette," he called. "I've decided that we will help you drive out the Mendozas."

She scampered to him, giving him a quick hug. "Rocco, I need to speak to Willem."

"Of course, but what about?"

"Something that will intrigue you." She pulled him toward the ladder to the lower deck. "Come with me."

They found Willem napping, using his cloak as a pillow. He looked childlike, even though he was one-and-twenty.

"Willem," Lisette called, and again when he did not rouse. "Willem."

He rolled over and opened an eye toward the pair. "Who awakens me now, and why?"

"I have a question." Lisette stood close to the door, her hand on the bars. "Why does El Rey send the Count de Mendoza five thousand gold coins every month?"

"Five thousand?" Rocco asked, incredulous.

Willem stretched, smiled, and sat up. "Because he cannot kill him and be done with it."

"What insurance does the count have?" She asked.

"I do not know the particulars, except that it is a single paper, a trifle of a document, that the count keeps in such a secret location, not even the king's spies have been able to ferret it out." Willem stood. "But if anything should happen to the count, its contents would be revealed to all."

Rocco stepped forward. "I don't suppose you have an idea where it is hidden?"

"Not precisely. But I can take a reasonable guess at the general area."

"Let me guess," Lisette said. "The carriage house."

Willem nodded. "He visits twice a day. How did you know?"

"Because when I was…on my perch and eavesdropping, I noticed how his focus was on that corner of the courtyard." She ran her hand along her fat, dark braid. "But where? A piece of paper will be impossible to find."

"Unless we encourage him to find it for us," Rocco

said.

"How?" Willem asked.

"If we are driving him from his castle, what is the one thing he must take with him?" Rocco grinned. "As long as we can avoid killing him in the battle, he will run to collect his insurance—and we will be waiting."

"Let us tell Begum—I mean, Captain Derya," Lisette said. She turned back to Willem, looking at him and at the padlock on his door. "Willem, I—"

"Think nothing of it. You are right not to trust me— I was until recently betrothed to the count's daughter. Although, technically I still am. I wonder, should I write a note releasing her?"

"So she can pursue Count Barragan?" Lisette laughed. "If he said yes, it would be everything the Mendozas deserve and more."

Rocco frowned. "Why?"

"First of all, I believe Barragan is in a long-term relationship, one that is forbidden yet persists. Second, Barragan is a count, but poor as used dirt, and looking to gather any wealth he can."

Willem laughed. "That would be perfect! A woman who requires constant amorous attention and a full treasury just awaiting someone to gut it."

"We shall attempt to make it a short battle," Rocco said. "If all is as you say, my ship will gladly drop you at any port you desire."

"Godspeed, then, and may you prevail," Willem replied.

Rocco followed Lisette to the upper deck and the small boats. She was fleet of foot and scurried to LeFarge, who was tending the departures and arrivals. Rocco smiled at the sight of her running, her skirts billowing behind her and her braid bouncing against the middle of her back. It suddenly made no sense that he would have hesitated to help her with the Mendozas.

What wouldn't he do for this woman?

Rocco did the rowing, pulling the oars through the water and catching the waves to hasten the dinghy to shore. Lisette leapt out past the breakers and pulled the boat forward, until it was firmly in the sand.

They found Begum and most of her crew assembled at the mouth of a large cave, staying out of sight of the most casual observer. Rocco and Lisette approached the group.

"Captain Derya," Lisette said. "We bring news."

They told her of the letter and their plan for finding it. She nodded. "Let us hope we can avoid killing him—otherwise we must tear the carriage house apart, stone by stone."

"Also, Captain Derya," Rocco said. "My crew is happy to join you in battle. If the Mendozas must go, then I shall not abandon a friend."

Captain Derya smiled. "Thank you." She turned to Lisette. "I know your reluctance to do battle as, well, your other self. But we could use your eyes from the air, to tell us where to strike."

"Yes, I could do that. I shall set out at dusk. Look for my signals." Lisette turned to Rocco. "And you—will we be seeing your other form in battle?"

"I must first lead my men," he said. "But if another dragon can speed our victory, I shall transform."

Begum held Lisette's arms briefly, looking deep into her eyes before embracing her. She gave her a small kiss on the cheek. "Be safe, my Lizzie."

"I will. Let me walk Rocco back to his boat, and I will return." Lisette hugged her and walked back.

They were about halfway to the boat when Rocco said, "That was a rather emotional good-bye between you."

"Yes." Lisette nodded. "We've grown close."

"Begum has always been a good mentor."

"Yes." Lisette was quiet for the rest of their short journey.

Rocco watched her. *She is usually not this silent. I can almost feel her tension.*

They arrived at the dinghy, and she helped him push the boat out. He jumped in and picked up the oars while she continued to help the boat maneuver through the surf.

"I shall see you at the castle," he said.

"Rocco?" She raised her hand in a wave to him. "Begum Derya is my mother."

59

Ruhee sat by the fire, picking at the dinner Kurta had prepared. Across from her, the old woman fed Alara, who wrapped tiny fingers around the bubby pot and suckled heartily. Kurta smiled at the infant, wrinkling her nose, and kissing her forehead. In between her gulps, the baby smiled back, making a gurgling noise. The two looked hopelessly devoted to each other.

Watching them made Ruhee's stomach sour.

I have been too nice. I wanted to take him without force, but it will not be possible. She studied Kurta. Kurta Rici—the rescuer. *How could I have been such a stupid girl? People have always called me simple, and I suppose they have been correct. But that ends now.*

This baby was not her answer to getting Rocco at all. In the wild, animals killed the offspring of their rivals so that they might mate and bear young of their own. If this child was dead, and if Lisette was dead, Rocco would finally be alone.

"The baby is fed," Kurta said. "Would you like to sing her to sleep?"

"No." The answer came out a little more abruptly than she wanted. "I mean, no thank you. I have not finished my dinner and I do not want it to be cold. You took so much time to prepare it, I want to enjoy every bite."

"Very well." Kurta grinned at her, but Ruhee wasn't certain if it was a smile of gratitude or if she was being teased.

Kurta put the baby across her shoulder and patted, rocking and humming. The baby sounded like she was humming, too.

Ruhee ate another bite of her food and gazed at the sky. As she lifted her head, her necklace fell onto her breastbone, the heaviness of the ankh thumping coldly against her skin. She placed her hand on the charm, pressing its coolness into her. The ankh given to her by her mother was a balm to her soul. A soothing talisman, connecting her to her ancestors, magical in its charms—

Her fingers stopped in midair, clutching a chunk of yam. Magical. The ankh had tasted Lisette's flesh once when she used it to close the wound that allowed Alara to be born. She could use the memory within the charm to reach out to Lisette—this time to harm instead of heal.

The moon was new tonight, dark and mysterious. It was the perfect time for a ritual of shadows. Ruhee ate a few more handfuls of malanga and yam, her eyes on Kurta. The old one's eyelids were lowering with each rock of the baby. Taking one more bite of dinner, Ruhee stood, her bowl in hand.

"I shall wash the bowls," she said, reaching down for Kurta's dish.

"It is well, thank you," Kurta told her. "I shall put the

little one to bed."

Ruhee walked up the path toward the lagoon with the bowls.

"Do you not want a torch?" Kurta asked. "The night is dark."

"I am fine. The dark does not hinder me." Ruhee kept walking. "Get your rest. I shall return."

The path was difficult in the dark, and she tripped over roots, and wandered into the brush more than once. Her eyes slowly discerned shapes, so by the time she arrived at the lagoon she could detect the outline of the water.

She knelt at the shore and scraped the bowls out, then rinsed them. Filling one with water, she poured it slowly into the ground, working with her hands to keep it on the surface and moisten the sand. More bowls of water and more work soon resulted in a small, round hill, which she then flattened.

She retrieved the ankh from her neck and laid it on top of the mound, pressing it into the wet sand. The cross of the icon pointed north. She sat, cross-legged, on the south side. The moon was working its way westward, low to the north, and only visible by a faint ring around it. Ruhee placed her fingertips on the ankh and stared at the shadowed orb.

"Goddess Sekhmet, I appeal to you. Grant my prayer. The woman Lisette has stolen from me. She must feel the pain I feel. She must relinquish Rocco to me. She must relinquish him or die." Ruhee picked up the icon and held it skyward. "Alkhasu bi. Mine. Mine. Mine," she repeated, her chin upward and eyes closed, until the ankh fell from her hands into the sand.

She collapsed onto the beach.

Sunlight was peering across the far horizon when Ruhee woke, shivering in the cool morning. Standing, she grabbed the bowls and ran back to camp, brushing the sand from her arms and face as she hurried. As she reached the top of the path, she could see Kurta and Alara in their silks below. They still appeared to be sleeping.

Ruhee carefully slipped into her bedding, placing the bowls near the embers of the evening fire. She closed her eyes and smiled. It was a good ritual. The gods would surely honor her.

Sighing into her silk covers, Ruhee opened one eye to see Alara. Her next target—once the baby was gone, Rocco would be free of all responsibilities again, and free for her to love.

It would be perfect.

60

I hope that wasn't as awkward for him as it was for me. Lisette watched his dinghy approach *L'Implacable*. *I needed to tell him, after all and there was never going to be a good time.*

She walked back to the cave, where Begum sat alone, staring at a circle she'd drawn in the sand. Several small, polished stones sat within it.

"Is that a battle plan, or are you predicting the future?" Lisette sat beside her.

"Perhaps a little of both." Begum passed her hand over the stones. "It is the way I was taught to pray. The focus on the stones helps to focus on the goal."

"Why use many stones to focus on one goal?"

"We never have one goal." She glanced up at Lisette. "Our goals are a tapestry, woven together. Goals for who we are, what we want, the big and the little. These stones help me make the connection."

Lisette nodded. "I was raised more simply, in the Church. Prayers, songs, genuflecting and lighting candles."

"The liturgy is also beautiful." Begum took Lisette's hand. "Ah, Lizzie, sometimes I regret being absent and not teaching you of my traditions. I thought I was doing the right thing, the best thing..."

Lisette squeezed her hand. "It is well. The woman who raised me was dutiful, if not loving. I was an independent, unruly child, which vexed her. Now I see the fear and hurt in her, raising another's child and having that child be difficult. I also wonder about my father, from the journal entry I read—is it possible he was a blood dragon?"

"It is possible, although I cannot confirm. The first few times I saw him, it was never after sundown."

Lisette sighed. "These poor people, locked into their secrets. Papa could not tell Ma—his wife—why he could not spend the night in their bed. She could not ask him."

"Do not be so dainty, Lizzie. You may call her 'Mama' without hurting me."

"It is not that, as much as...it feels...odd in my mouth to form the word now."

"Perhaps you should not have discovered this."

Lisette turned to her. "Oh, no, I am glad! It is good to know my mother's attitude was not all my doing."

"Here." Begum offered her a cup and a skin full of liquid. "It is the spiced broth Lamya taught me to make. It is good to drink it now."

Lisette filled the cup with the contents of the skin. "It's amazing how filling it is, and it somehow renews my courage."

"It brings her close to us."

"Yes." Lisette closed her eyes as she savored the broth. "How did you learn to make this?"

Begum smiled. "It was hard, but I kept asking until she could no longer deny me."

Lisette laughed. The two women sat, drinking their meal and regarding the sky. At last, Begum put her cup down.

"Night is coming. It is time."

The women rose and walked toward the beach, where members of the crew awaited them. Beyond the women, a group of men stood. Rocco strode from among them and met Begum and Lisette.

"Where do you need us?" he asked.

Begum pulled the diagram out that Willem had drawn. "We will attack here, and here." She pointed to different areas of the castle grounds. "That leaves these areas open—if the young marquess has told us true."

"And if not?" Rocco asked.

"That is my job," Lisette told him. "I will be your eyes from the sky. Look to the western tower of the Mendoza castle. If all is as Willem told us, I shall wrap a cloud around it. If there is no cloud, expect more trouble, not less."

"Godspeed to all of us," Begum said. "And pray it goes swiftly."

Lisette nodded and watched the two crews traverse up the cliff. Night was well settled and the moon but a sliver. Their secretive tactics should work well. She waited until everyone was at the top of the ridge, and no one was looking in her direction. There were still those who did not accept her gift as being anything but satanic.

My gift. It was the first time she called it that. Not a curse, nor even a talent. She spread her long wings and felt their strength. They had taken her across the sea, across islands, and now would take her to the Mendoza castle, where she would discover how much truth was in

Willem's statements.

Take care of this island, and then claim my daughter.

The night air was warm but not heavy and the breeze went through her feathers like a comb. She lifted high above the trees, speeding toward her destination. If the guards were not where Willem said, she needed to alert Rocco and Begum.

The first thing she noticed about the castle was that it was strangely well-lit. It looked like torches had been placed so close to one another, they fed off each other's flame. The entire perimeter was ablaze, and guards were stationed at every corner, plus four along each wall. Something was very wrong here.

She counted. Sixteen guards along the outer wall, four at the front gate, and another ten in the courtyard, close to the castle. Lisette banked, turned, and flew straight for the crews. She had to warn them.

They had spread out, once they passed the turn for the de Lille castle, making it difficult for Lisette to find either Begum or Rocco. She at last spotted a lanky young man maneuvering through a grove of trees, pushing the vines from his face. There was no time for delicacy. She landed in front of him, transforming as she touched the ground.

"Poussin, where is Rocco?" she asked. "Or Begum?"

"Aw, ya know howz I feel bout the dragon," he whined. "Cap'n went ahead o' me, huggin' the jungle."

Lisette stepped back and turned to survey the landscape. There was no sign of him—or anyone. She turned to Poussin. "I've got to find him. The Mendozas seem to be ready for us, somehow. We need to stop, re-think our plans."

The sound of a hiss and thud blended together in her ears. She looked outward then turned to Poussin. He was sinking to the vine-tangled floor. She knelt down to where he fell, an arrow in his chest. His eyes were wide, staring up at her, as his mouth labored to draw breath.

"M'lady," he stammered, blood and foam at the corners of his mouth.

"Shh," Lisette whispered, then stopped. There was nothing she could do for him, except let him talk.

He tugged weakly at her sleeve, so she put her ear close to his mouth. "I forgive ye fer bein' a dragon."

His body relaxed and the blood flow from around the arrow slowed. Lisette ran her hand across his eyes to close them. She could not bear to see them stare at the heavens and cloud over.

Another arrow hissed by, missing her head, and hitting the tree behind her. She did not know who was taking aim, but she would not be pinned down like this, not when she had important work to do.

She had never transformed in this position before, but she flattened herself down in the brush next to Poussin and took a deep breath, her anger fueling her change. Another arrow whizzed past. The next one bounced off Lisette's feathers as she rose up and opened her wings, taking flight toward the source of the arrows.

A scream got her attention, and she looked over to see a short, wiry man fall from a tree, his bow flinging out of his hands. He landed on his quiver, the arrows piercing him, and arched his back with a groan. Lisette landed beside him. She opened her mouth to ask him who sent him here and how did they know about the attack?

Nothing but dragon growls emerged from her throat. *Damned be, it is awkward to transform here and back again.* She glared down at him, holding him down with her paw while he writhed. His face was contorted with fear, but his body wore the marks of intense pain.

It doesn't matter who sent you, you killed my little chick. She grabbed his head and twisted. One firm snap, and the archer lie still.

Taking flight, she stayed lower, combing through the

vegetation, and looking for Rocco or Begum. They would know that Willem had been lying when they saw the lights, but would it be soon enough to save them? Were there more archers in the trees?

A shiny object caught her eye to the left. Perched on the limb of a tall tree, a figure in a dark uniform reached behind his back, to a quiver. The trees were too entwined with vines for her to slip in and grab him. Opening her mouth, she exhaled a storm cloud, gray and restless, with strands of angry lightning within. The longer bolt hit him at the base of his neck, knocking him soundlessly to the ground. He was dead before he knew he was falling.

A rustling through the brush made her look up from her victim, to see Rocco run to the guard's body and kneel. She landed a few feet from him and became human. This transformation pinched at her chest and tingled her hands and feet. She could only guess that the constant back-and-forth of her changes was taking a toll on her body.

"Lizzie, did you—?"

"Of course, he was preparing to kill someone." She went to him and took his hand. "Poussin is dead. I had no idea about the archers in the trees until then."

Rocco hung his head, staring at the ground, his hands on his hips. "Such a young pup and killed in such a cowardly way."

"Battles are rarely fair." She squeezed his hand and hugged him close. "In the meantime, the count has somehow gotten news about the attack. The castle is lit up as if daylight is upon it. We need another plan."

He gestured up and left. "Begum has taken her crew there. They were going around to the back gate, while we approached from the front."

"I must find them and stop them."

Rocco nodded. "We will not catch them by surprise if they can see us coming."

"True…although…I wonder…" Lisette looked at the

night sky. "A dragon that shoots clouds and mist might extinguish those torches."

"You'd have to get very close." He frowned. "Too close."

She smiled and shrugged. "As long as I keep my paws curled, I should be safe."

"I'm serious, Lizzie."

"I know you are, but what choice have we? The count knows we are coming—it doesn't matter how he found out. He will be on guard from now on until he is somehow convinced we have given up." She put her hand to his face, running her palm against the scruff of his beard. "I want my baby."

His shoulders relaxed as he sighed. "Yes. You have to do it. But I shall fly with you."

"You spew fire, which would light the torches I'm putting out."

"No, my plan is to light the guards."

"Then let us be off, before our crews arrive." She stepped back to the clearing where she landed, winked at Rocco, and took a breath. Her transformation stuttered for a brief moment—not long enough to be noticeable by others, but she knew. *I cannot transform back tonight.*

She lifted herself above the canopy and watched Rocco below. He stood, hands crossed in front of him, and head bowed. Lisette thought it was a lot of pomp to just tell himself he was a dragon, but she had been that earnest once. He took a deep breath, and she watched a swirl of color envelope him, red and white, sculpting him into a moon dragon.

Even as a dragon, he was magnificent.

He joined her in the sky and together they flew to the castle, remaining in the clouds to avoid detection. The castle made itself known before they arrived—the lights around it were so severe, they could be seen from afar.

Lisette flew past the castle, banking left to loop

around by the back wall. Five large guards stood under ten brilliant torches. She took a large in-breath, arching against the dark sky, before stretching her body out and down, and pointing her muzzle toward the fires. Opening her mouth, she exhaled.

Dense fog rolled in with a deep mist that engulfed the first torch. It snuffed the fire from its wicking, permeating it with so much moisture, it would not re-light. She glided down the line, soaking each torch until the back gate was completely dark.

Something dull hit her side. She looked over and saw archers aiming for her. Their arrows knocked against her puffed feathers and dropped to the ground. Lisette tucked her paws so that a stray point couldn't pierce her pads, took another breath and turned the corner, extinguishing the torches on the western side. She wondered where Rocco was but didn't want to waste time looking for him.

He was where he was needed, no doubt.

She had just thrust the front gate into darkness when she saw a beam of light coming behind her. Whipping about, it wasn't the torch being re-ignited, it was a body lying on the ground, aflame. The other guards scattered, some running toward the village, others heading toward the jungle. She looked up and saw Rocco above her.

The guards are getting bolder, Rocco told her. *They need to be reminded of our power.*

Lisette nodded. *Thank you. I'll finish the east side. Begum and the rest should be here by the time I'm done.*

Will you stay a dragon for the fight?

Lisette looked down at her body. *I may have to. My transformations are becoming painful, no doubt because I have been changing so often.*

A quiet groan made her look down. Oleta had one of the guards by the throat and had run her blade through him. He sank to the ground, and she moved to the next.

I must change back and direct my men, Rocco said. *I*

shall see you on the other side.

He flew back to the front gate, and she saw him descend. Lisette took a position on the castle's roof, watching Begum's crew stalk and kill the guards at the back gate. The courtyard was still well-lit, so she made a few passes across the yard, putting out the flames.

With the grounds sufficiently darkened, the pirates moved in and took on the rest of the guards. The men from the walls ran to the gates to help their fellow guards. Lisette watched below, wishing to be of more help.

A guard ran below her, his sword drawn. She flew down, picking him up by his head, but found she could not kill him, no matter how much he writhed and attempted to stab her. Shaking him vigorously until he dropped his blade, she tossed him into a planter.

I am useless in this form, at least for fighting.

Landing quickly, she closed her eyes and took several long breaths before envisioning herself in her human form. The pain burned through her gut, worse than when she was turning into a blood dragon. She bent over in agony, panting, as a woman. Picking up the guard's sword, she staggered forward to help her *Dişi* sisters.

The guard she had just thrown into the bushes stirred, struggled, and rose to rejoin the fray, drawing his dagger. He surveyed the courtyard, his eyes stopping at her, and charged.

Lisette stretched up from her pain and gripped the sword with both hands, her legs and arms still shaking. As the man rushed forward, she met his dagger with her broader blade, giving her enough time to sidestep his momentum. He stumbled, still moving forward but twisting his body to her, attempting to pivot. She threw her body behind his, forcing her feet to keep up with her.

As she moved, she thrust the sword at his left side, sinking it in and across. Her forward momentum pushed her into his back and shoved the sword to its hilt until it emerged under his right ribs. The pair tumbled to the ground, the guard emitting a growl of pain before twitching into stillness.

Lisette pushed herself from his body and withdrew the sword, which had by now also become embedded in the ground underneath him. She crumpled again, deep breaths to attempt to soothe the pain shooting through her midsection. It was several minutes, several breaths, to calm the burning into a manageable ache.

I am of no use as a dragon, but this seems not much better. She straightened, whispering, "No matter. I have a job to do."

She leaned against a tree, looking about the yard and up at the castle. If she could find the count and his family, she could find out if they could be convinced to leave, or if they could only be convinced from the grave. She thought of the Medina family and the years of hostility and vengeance and sighed.

I cannot go through that again.

The sound of footsteps froze her to her spot behind the tree. The steps were heavy and furtive—they stopped, started, stopped again. Someone was afraid of being seen. She waited until she heard them pass before peeking around.

It was Count de Mendoza, making his way toward one of the outbuildings—the carriage house. She waited until he was well on the path before following him from a safe distance in the dark.

Although technically part of the livery, the carriage house sat adjacent to the stables. Count d'Auguste had it built specifically to hold his pride and joy, a magnificent four-horse carriage he'd shipped from France. The passenger compartment was completely enclosed with velvet seating, and the outside was ornately painted with the fleur de lis, and gilt accents.

It had proved to be an impossible vehicle for the island, being too large and delicate to handle the rough-hewn roads, and horribly stifling for the passengers in the tropical heat. Lisette could still picture the count demanding that it be washed, and his beautiful team of grays brought around to be hitched. He and the countess would dress in their court finery, step into the carriage, and be driven once around the village. They refused to acknowledge the perspiration that poured from them as they stepped out.

"Good job, driver," the count would say. "We shall require it next month as well."

Lisette peeked in the open door, watching Count de Mendoza scurrying to his carriage, a rather plain cabriolet that took half the space of d'Auguste's masterpiece. He reached inside, under the left passenger's seat, and withdrew an envelope.

She expected him to slip it into his jacket and leave, so she ducked behind a planter. When he didn't emerge, she looked around the corner again. He was standing with the envelope in his right hand, a scowl on his face, as if he wrestled with a decision. Lifting the passenger's seat, he replaced the envelope, then took it out again and put it into his pocket. He repeated this gesture once more, before returning the envelope to its hiding spot and rushing from the building.

Sitting in the dark behind a large planter filled with frangipani, she tried to figure out why the count did not take the letter with him. It didn't take long to come up with the answer.

"Rene!" he shouted from the stables. "Rene, I need my cart to be readied!"

The carriage house lanterns were still lit, but Lisette slipped inside to grab the letter and escape. Her body was wracked with pain but she ignored it. She kept the dead guard's sword with her, although she wished she'd exchanged it for his lighter dagger. Creeping to the cart, she slid her hand under the seat where she had seen the count hide the paper. She found it easily and stuffed it down her dress.

"Think you've found something?" The count stood at the doorway, holding a slender rapier. He offered her his other hand. "Give it to me."

Lisette stood, ignoring her own weakness, and pointed the broadsword toward him. "I think not."

He smiled, pointed his blade to the ceiling, and at her. "Then die."

She smiled back and gripped hers in both hands. "As I said. I think not."

They leapt toward one another, blades swinging in controlled arcs, circling and clashing. The count maintained a textbook fencing form. He was a more schooled fighter than she was used to and held to the methods he'd been taught. It was obvious he had never been in the kind of life-or-death brawls she'd experienced, but that did not make him a weaker fighter.

Had she felt better, Lisette would have enjoyed their match. As it was, she merely wanted to end it and get some rest. She returned his advances furiously and slashed with abandon. He smiled at her, no doubt believing that she was angry and that angry fighters lose their heads.

Instead, she pushed forward, moving the broadsword as quickly as she could, cutting off his parries and savagely backing him into a corner. He was wedged between the wall and the cabriolet, still attempting to fight his way out. She saw no hope for his escape.

"M'lord, you can still leave this place with your life and your family," she said, swinging her blade.

He lifted his sword to block her. "But not without my treasure."

She stepped away from his thrust. "Whatever is in your coffers, you may leave with that as well."

"Not my gold." He pointed to her bodice. "Without that letter, I have no more income."

"What does this letter contain?"

He shook his head, smiled, and pushed away from the cart. Lisette swung her sword again, backing away to find another place to corner him. As they both passed the doorway, another wave of burning pain rolled through her and she stooped over with a groan.

"Now, I shall have that letter," the count said and raised his rapier.

Lisette looked up at the descending blade and said a prayer for her daughter. The count's arm stopped in midair as he assumed an expression of surprise and horror. He flopped onto the ground, his sword falling to the stone before it rolled away.

Willem appeared where the count had just stood. He held a stiletto and reached down to wipe the blade on the count's body.

"You have to know just where to slice," he said, offering his hand to Lisette. "Otherwise, you merely wound them instead of killing them instantly."

She allowed him to help her stand, although she did not straighten immediately, putting a hand at her stomach and rubbing at the pain.

"M'lady, are you injured?" He appeared worried.

"No," she said between deep, steady breaths. "I seem to have an internal problem, but my help is needed to finish this task."

"Did you find the letter?"

"The count led me to it." She nodded. "Help me to that bench, where I may sit and let this pass."

She offered him her hand to grasp, but he picked her up in his arms and carried her, placing her carefully on the wooden seat before sitting next to her. Withdrawing the envelope from her bodice, she took out the letter and read.

"I, King Felipe of Spain, House of Hapsburg, do officially decree that the islands in the chain known as Los Peces Pequeños shall revert to island rule upon my death. These orders shall be carried out by my trusted servant and ambassador, the Count Fausto de Mendoza."

She looked at Willem and frowned. "What does this mean?"

"It means that Fausto had El Rey in the palm of his hand. King Felipe died last year. I've no doubt the successor was made aware of this document and has been paying the count ever since to keep it secret."

"But why not just destroy it?"

"If I know the count—my apologies—if I knew the count." Willem glanced at the body. "He escaped with the letter, to these very islands. What better place to blackmail the king?"

Lisette grinned. "I admit, it is clever." She put the letter back in her bodice. "But now we must find the countess and your ex-fiancée. What do you think they'll do once they find the count is dead?"

Willem was silent for some time. "I do not believe they know of the letter. The countess was always begging to go back to Spain to update her wardrobe, and I know that Renata was scheming for both of us to move back and begin our married life closer to the royal palace."

"So, if you delivered a message to them, that the count was sending them on to Spain and he would join them later—"

"They would believe me." Willem nodded. Sadness crossed his face. "After all, I still believe that they want us to be married."

"I'm sorry, Willem." Lisette frowned. A feeling of pity and sorrow rose up in her as she remembered her own betrothal to Eric. Her eyes spilled with tears, and she could not stop her sobs. "I'm sorry for everything. Sorry about your brother, most of all I'm sorry I can't stop crying like this."

Willem put her head to his shoulder and patted her back. "Now, now. I will survive being thrown away, so to speak, for a better offer. And my brother was not the best or brightest of this world. I'm also sorry that he's dead, but choices have consequences, and he chose unwisely. Let us dry our tears, now, and find mother and daughter."

"Yes." She took a few deep breaths and dried her eyes on her skirt. "We need to hide the count's body and tell Rene to bring the cart to the front. That way it will appear that nothing is wrong."

Willem nodded and got up to move the body behind a large chest. Lisette watched him go next door and heard the rumblings of voices. She stood, gingerly, and felt the pain was not as sharp, so she walked to the door. With the count dead, she felt Willem could handle the women. She needed to get this letter to…someone. Who?

62

Rocco stayed well above the battle until he saw Lisette put out the rest of the torches. The courtyard and surrounding jungle were now darkened to normal eyes, although the confused shouts and heavy-footed trampling told him of the chaos Lisette had wrought. His dragon eyes allowed better vision, so that he found Chunk and his crew easily. Setting down well away from them, he transformed back before approaching.

"Cap'n, we was awaitin' yer orders," Chunk said. "We found them archers you yelled about—as many gone as we could catch. And I can't find Poussin nowheres."

"You can say our little chick saved our lives," Rocco told him. "They revealed themselves when they killed him."

"Ah, no, now that is a shame." A mist passed over Chunk's eyes, followed by a scowl. "We'll leave none of 'em standin', jes fer our Poussin."

A birdcall made the group fall silent and take cover. Rocco surveyed the darkness and returned a low, chattering sound. The call repeated, and Begum stepped out of the shadows, staying low and scurrying to the men.

"It is good you are here," she said. "My crew has taken out the guards on the back wall and are ready to work their way down the west side."

"We shall then start on the east and meet you in the front gate." Rocco nodded. "Perhaps also a contingent in the courtyard to begin the sweep of the grounds?"

"Yes, a good idea now that we have the forces. The guards are more trained than the ones at the Medina castle, but they were no match for us as long as we use stealth. They thrive either by ambush or by attacking en masse."

"What about the walls? Are there archers?"

"There were, but no more," a strange voice said in the darkness.

Rocco, Begum, and their crews turned toward the voice, swords drawn, and bodies coiled to fight. Two silhouettes made their way forward, one substantially larger than the other.

Rocco and Luis recognized the Duke de Martinmas at once, along with one of his guards.

"Sire," Rocco said, "What are you doing here?"

"I am not a traitorous man, but the Mendozas do no favors to El Rey," the duke told him. "I cannot let pirates solve royal problems. I have brought ten of my guard."

"And you, Sire?" Rocco asked. "Why are you here?"

"I am hoping to discuss a peaceful abandonment of this property with the Count de Mendoza. If he resists, then the sword." The duke put his hand to the hilt of his blade. "Little known fact—I did my share of fighting in my youth."

Rocco turned to Begum, his eyes wide. "We shall

have to tell Lisette, her uncle is doing more than staying out of our way."

She smiled. "If the archers have been taken care of, then let us continue on our mission."

Rocco gestured toward the castle wall. "Lisette is inside, whether woman or dragon, I do not know. She extinguished all the torches, and now finds her way to the count and his family."

"It is difficult to wish for them to either leave or be killed," Begum said. "But Lizzie will choose wisely."

Rocco nodded and gave her a firm pat on the shoulder. "We shall meet at the front gate, then."

Begum smiled and slipped quietly back across the clearing.

"Gather, men." Rocco looked at his group of men. Even in the darkness, he could recognize each one. "Chunk, I need you to lead half the men to the eastern wall. You will kill the guards on that side—there are five or six to be dispatched. The quieter you can get the job done, the better. There are more guards around the front gate, plus the courtyard. Taking them out one by one is preferable to a full battle."

"Aye." Chunk's voice was unnaturally soft as he went among the men, tapping shoulders and saying, "You. Come wit' me."

Rocco turned to the rest of the men, motioning for Luis to come forward. "We advance into the courtyard. Luis, I need you to lead this group. Again, stealth is our best hope of taking the castle and the family inside. Use the darkness."

"And where am I best used, Captain?" the duke asked.

"I think you're best staying with Luis, Sire." Rocco gestured to Luis' group. "Work your way through the courtyard and meet us in the castle. Ultimately, we need to find the count."

Rocco strode toward the wall, glanced up, and turned back.

"Sire." He gestured at the duke, who stepped forward. Rocco lowered his voice. "I do not doubt your courage or skill, but perhaps it is best if you wait at the back gate. One of your men can let you inside."

The duke regarded the wall and nodded. "I must agree with your suggestion."

Rocco motioned for LeFarge, who stepped forward with a rope. One strong toss and the men were scaling the wall, one at a time, slipping over the edge and moving along the top, keeping their bodies low and unseen. Luis was the first up—his job was to signal the all-clear and direct the men. Rocco awaited his cue.

After a few silent minutes, Luis' head popped over the edge and he gestured. Rocco climbed up and over, pulling the rope up after him. He dropped it in the northeast corner of the courtyard side, turned to the men and touched his finger to his lips, and repelled down.

As he made his way across the yard, he saw the guards stationed at the entrances to the castle, but nowhere else. They stood uneasy, venturing a few paces away to peer into the darkness, whisper a call to another guard, and return to their posts. *It was an odd tactical move to not try to stop us earlier.* Whoever was in charge was counting on the pirates being decimated by the archers.

They had obviously never fought pirates.

Rocco looked up at the castle. There were no lights within that he could see. Odd, when the outside had been lit like a bonfire. He made his way around the yard, taking care to remain unseen and studying the castle. On the western side of the building, he finally observed a dim light from one of the upper chambers and a dark figure on the balcony, looking below.

Much like his blood dragon curse, being a moon dragon enhanced his senses as a human. The night was inky, but he could see the person on the balcony. A young woman, Renata, peered into the darkness. He turned to see what had her interest.

A tall, thin lad was leading a horse from the stables, a sturdy chestnut strapped with a harness. He backed him to a two-wheeled cart and proceeded to buckle the tug to the shaft on either side. A familiar man stepped from the shadows, pointing, and speaking, although he could not discern any words other than "mistress and her mother."

Willem d'Auguste had somehow escaped the hold and found his way to the castle. Was he here to raise the alarm? Rocco moved toward the carriage house, still attempting to remain hidden. As he grew closer, the thin lad jumped in the cabriolet and clucked to the horse, leaving Willem behind, watching.

Rocco was but a few steps from grabbing him when someone in the still-lighted carriage house caught his attention. Willem turned and went inside, reappearing with them, his hand at their elbow as they walked slowly forward.

Lisette.

Drawing his sword, Rocco approached them from behind, putting the point of his sword against Willem's neck.

"How did you get off my ship?"

"It was not easy," Willem said. "But it was done."

"Rocco, Willem has been helping me." Lisette turned to Rocco and collapsed against him. "I am having problems since I transformed."

He frowned and held her close. "Still?"

She nodded. "The count is dead. We've hidden the body and sent the cart for Renata and Catalina. Willem is going to tell them the count is sending them ahead to the port to catch the first ship, and that he will join them very soon."

"I admit," Rocco said. "I find it difficult to accept that

you would throw in with us."

Willem chuckled. "As do I. But knowing that the count would sooner borrow against my freedom, then leave me to be cast overboard, has soured me on joining ranks with the Mendozas. To be honest, it felt exhilarating to plunge that blade into his heart."

Rocco looked at Lisette for concurrence. She grinned. "He saved my life."

"Very well. But I shall accompany you two on your visit."

"I'm not certain you will be well received," Willem said.

"I will not be received at all," Rocco told him. "I will be in the shadows."

"As will I," Lisette said.

"No, Lizzie." Rocco held her closely. "If you are unwell, you cannot be put into danger."

"I doubt if there is danger awaiting in the castle." She frowned and gestured. "And exactly where would you stash me that is safe here?"

"She might be safer with us," Willem suggested.

Rocco growled. "Come along, then. I shall protect you as much as I can."

"If I could but trade this," she lifted the broadsword, "for a dagger, I would be most grateful."

"Ah!" Willem trotted into the carriage house and returned with a smaller blade. "The count will not miss this."

The trio quietly made their way to the castle. As they neared, Rocco put his hand out to stop them. "There are guards at every door, unless they've been disposed of."

Willem pointed to a tall, full bush. "Then we shall not use the doors."

He led them behind the greenery to a place in the castle that looked like the exterior stone had been cracked.

Running his fingers down the crevice, he stopped at a place where it widened, and pushed. The castle's wall opened, revealing an entrance to a tunnel.

"Secret entrances, my, my," Lisette said.

"The good part of being the ignored brother is that you are left to your own devices." He lit a candle and closed the door. "Like finding secret passageways. I'm surprised your castle has none."

"I suppose my father didn't see the need." Lisette followed Willem's candle down the narrow passageway. It reminded her of the cave on Isla de la Ballena where she found Sandoval's gold. As they strode through the dank corridor, she felt the pain in her stomach subside, and disappear. She allowed herself to stand taller and walk a little faster.

"You are feeling better?" Rocco asked, walking behind her.

"Much." She turned her head toward him.

"Shh," Willem admonished as they arrived at another door. "We exit behind the great hall and make our way up the stairs to the left."

He handed the candle to Lisette and pushed the door a sliver. The room beyond was almost as dark as the tunnel, so he opened the door enough to slip out. Lisette cradled the air around the candle to keep the sudden gust of the room from extinguishing the flame. She peered inside, holding the candle down so the light did not interfere with her vision.

A warm cheek touched hers. Rocco was also interested in what was beyond. She leaned against him, and they stood together in the quiet dark.

"Why didn't you tell me about Begum before?" he whispered.

She shrugged into his shoulder. "There has not been much time for heart to hearts."

"I suppose. She also told me of Ruhee's curse, that

you be forever without child." He wrapped his arm around her waist and squeezed. "I told her I would love you with one child or a hundred."

She looked at him. "Please do not wish for a hundred children."

"Come with me." Willem's face appeared at the doorway. "You will stay behind in the shadows. I will convince Renata and Catalina to join me in the carriage."

Lisette looked at Rocco, who nodded. She glanced back at Willem and brought the candle toward her mouth. A single puff of wind from her lips plunged them into darkness, and they all exited the tunnel, staying close to the wall and stepping lightly up the stairs.

63

Lisette followed the two men this time, watching Willem's back as she found each step. She was still trying to determine how the count knew of the pirates' attack, and how Willem escaped from *L'Implacable*. Could he be leading them into a trap?

She was glad that her pain had disappeared, although that was one more riddle to solve. At the moment, she needed to be prepared for anything. She closed her fingers around the hilt of her dagger and listened for other footsteps, voices, even breathing.

From the landing, there was a dim light visible, coming from a door halfway down the hall. Willem turned to Lisette and Rocco, his finger over his lips and gave a single nod toward the door. They pressed themselves against the wall, while he strode toward the light, calling, "Renata? Where are you?"

Within four long strides, he was through the door. It took a burst of rapid shuffling, but Lisette soon caught up with him just as he entered. She hung back, listening. Rocco crossed to the opposite side of the hall and waited.

"Willem!" A young woman's voice, followed by the tip-tap of heels running across the stone floor, signaled Renata's response to his call. "Father said you were kidnapped!"

There was a moment's silence. Lisette pictured them meeting, kissing, then embracing. That was the way normal people greeted one another. She heard coughing, throat-clearing rumbles from the room. Carefully, she angled herself so that she could see into the chambers without being detected.

"Willemmmm." An older woman's voice registered happy surprise, wrapped in disappointment. "We thought we'd never see you again."

"Why not?" he asked. "The count paid my ransom."

"He did?" Renata looked at her mother, whose eyes widened along with her nostrils as she inhaled.

"Is it possible you did not know?" Willem grinned, glancing at the door where Lisette could see him wink. "I just spoke with him about it."

"Where?" Catalina asked.

"By the carriage house. He was directing the stable boy to hitch up the cart. I was directed to find the two of you and escort you to the dock. He will meet us there, to sail back to Spain."

"Spain?" The countess sputtered. "We can't go back to Sp—I mean, the count has told me many times, we were sent here as El Rey's emissaries, we have to stay."

"I have heard him say that many times, but perhaps his mind is changed, especially with the castle under attack." Willem pointed toward the balcony, where the sounds of blades crossing drifted up.

"Yes, those filthy pirates—" Catalina huffed.

"Under attack?" Renata asked and turned to her mother. "Is that why you are keeping me in this room with no lights? Why did you not tell me?"

"Your father and I didn't want to worry you, what with Willem being kidnapped and all." The countess sounded placating, but Lisette could hear the nervous tone in her voice.

"But Willem was rescued. Right, Willem?" Renata was holding his hand, looking up at him, pleadingly.

"I am here," he said, stroking her hair. "But now we must go. Your father is tying up some business, and your carriage awaits." He pointed toward the doorway, causing Lisette to lean back.

"I believe the count will be busy for a long time," a strange voice said, as a figure walked out of the shadows. "Come, come, Marquess d'Auguste, I thought you were more honest than that."

Lisette leaned forward to see Amoy Simone standing beside the countess. She fought back a cry, and wanted to gesture to Rocco, but there was no time. Amoy put her arm around Catalina's shoulders.

"The Mendozas and I have developed a close friendship," the tall woman said. "I helped the count plan for the pirates' arrival tonight, not that it did any good." She turned to the countess. "I'm sorry to inform you that the count is dead."

Catalina gasped and Renata screamed.

"How?" Catalina asked.

Amoy looked at Willem. "Would you like to tell them, or should I?"

"I should be the one," he said. "At least I'm *capable* of telling the truth."

The smile remained on Amoy's face, but Lisette could see the hatred in her eyes. She was quite used to the former housekeeper's anger. She also could not let Willem face this alone.

"Perhaps I can better tell the tale," Lisette said as she stepped into the room.

"Oh—you!" Catalina grasped at her chest and backed away.

"Yes, me, the heretical, the vulgar, the—what else am I?" Lisette asked. "The count was trying to kill me. I was attempting to stay alive. Willem came to my aid. That is how the count died."

Renata pushed away from him. "You killed my father?"

"With no malice intended," he told her. "But I would not let him kill Lisette. After all, she was supposed to be my sister-in-law. I was looking forward to her place in my family."

"You were?" Lisette asked.

He shrugged. "You were the only person who ever saw me in a room."

"Touching," Amoy sneered.

A high-pitched wail interrupted them. Catalina was holding a silk square to her eyes and working her way toward weeping. Renata rushed to her mother, putting her arms around her.

"Look what you've done," Renata spat at Willem.

"It was regrettable but necessary," he told her.

"So is this." Amoy leapt toward him, her right hand gripping a dagger.

Lisette rushed to intercept her blade, shoving her arm up and back, away from her victim. Willem backed away as Lisette swung her own dagger toward Amoy's ribs. Amoy stuck her left arm out to block and pushed Lisette backward. Blood ran down the big woman's arm from Lisette's blade.

The two women circled each other, at times jumping forward with a thrust of their dagger. Rocco had entered the room, his sword drawn, to help. Ordinarily, Lisette would have called him off—this was her battle. But she felt an urgency to get these women out of the castle and off the island.

From the corner of her eye, she saw the glimmer of more metal. The countess had taken one of the swords from its perch on the wall and was charging at Willem. The sword was probably more decorative than useful, but its dull edge would leave a nasty scar. And Willem was unarmed.

"Help Willem," she shouted at Rocco and leaped at Amoy again.

Amoy drove harder, as if wanting to end this quickly, but Lisette did not relent. She backed, sidestepped, and maneuvered until the two were on the balcony and her back was at the edge. Her strength felt complete and healthy to her—if she needed to transform, she could.

Still, it felt good to have this dagger in her hand and fight for her life. As much as she hated Amoy for trying to destroy her and Rocco, her moon dragon tendencies might stop her from driving the blade into the woman's heart unless she was threatened.

"You look awful thoughtful for a woman who's about to die," Amoy said, jumping forward toward Lisette's chest.

"I am a contemplative woman," Lisette knocked Amoy's arm sideways. "But I'm not about to die."

She leapt forward, thrusting her blade upward in an arc. Smiling, Amoy sidestepped before rushing Lisette's left, unarmed side. Lisette also sidestepped right, out of Amoy's reach, and around to her back, where she shoved her dagger deep in the big woman's ribcage, aiming it at her heart.

Amoy let out a half-squeal, half-moan as Lisette used her weight against her, pushing her over the balcony's rail and onto the stones below. Her body hit with a crack and thud.

Lisette turned to see what needed to be done in the chambers still. Rocco had the countess somewhat under control. He had a strong grip on her right wrist, having forced her to drop the sword, and pressed his own epee against her side. This did not stop her from wailing and crying and attempting to fall to the floor in a supposed faint, something Rocco's hold on her prevented her from achieving.

"I would stop struggling if I were you, Countess," Lisette said. "I've seen this man kill many, man and woman. You can stand on your own, or he can keep you standing by running you through. You would not look good on a spit."

Willem appeared to have his own problems, as his fiancée was throwing anything she could pick up at him. He had a cut on his cheek, no doubt from crockery, and was fending off the bowls and statues with his forearms.

"Need a blade to calm the marquise?" Lisette asked.

"It would be helpful, yes."

Lisette handed him her dagger as the young woman squealed.

"You wouldn't!"

He scowled. "You were willing to steal my ransom from the Duke de Martinmas, keep it for yourselves, and let me rot in Davy Jones' locker. Why shouldn't you both be run through?"

Renata stopped and looked at her mother. "Is this true?"

The countess stopped her wailing. "Of course not. Lies."

"Not lies," Lisette said. "I overheard you and the count."

"You couldn't have," Catalina told her. "We were the only ones in the—oh!"

Renata dropped the silver goblet she'd planned to throw next and strode to her mother, who was still being subdued by Rocco.

"My dear, we were only looking after your welfare," her mother said. "Why marry a marquess, one with shaky ties to Spain, when you could marry Count Barragan and be well established with El Rey?"

Renata glared at her mother for a moment before slapping her across the face. "You are a wicked, greedy woman, and Father was a wicked, greedy man." She turned to Willem. "My apologies for my parents. I did not know of their plans."

"Apologies accepted," Willem said.

"Renata, how could you?" Catalina burst into a new round of tears, but at least kept her feet. Rocco took his sword from her side and offered her a chair, one that she gladly sank into and launched into a new round of wailing.

"Oh, mother, stop." Renata sighed and looked at Willem. "I confess, I am not in love with you, but I was willing to marry you and be a good wife. I am still willing, although I believe it's better for both of us if we don't."

"Under the circumstances," he told her, "It's probably for the best."

"What will you do, Renata?" Lisette asked.

Renata shrugged. "Get away from this place. It has brought me nothing but misery. I believe I shall catch the next ship anywhere. Perhaps make my way back to Spain and find a place to live and a man to love me." She walked toward the door. "If you'll excuse me, I'd like to be alone."

Rocco pointed at Catalina. "What do we do with this one?"

Willem shook his head. "Renata? Any ideas?"

The young girl kept moving, her back to them. "Davy Jones' locker, for all I care."

"Renata!" screamed Catalina. "You don't mean that!"

Renata raised her hand as she left. "My apologies, Mother, but I need to pack."

The rattling of pans startled Ruhee awake. Kurta was stirring a pot vigorously while the baby laughed at the noise.

"My apologies, did I wake you?" Kurta asked.

The old woman's expression remained pleasant, but her tone told Ruhee that she had slept too long.

"Of course not," Ruhee said, sitting up and rubbing her eyes and forehead. The sun was well up into the sky, burning her with its brightness. "I do not know why I am so tired."

"You spent much time washing two little bowls." Kurta shot a quick glance at her.

Ruhee looked down, trying to keep her expression placid and feeling the blush crawl up her neck. "I…I became distracted in my thoughts. The night was so beautiful."

"Seems it was very dark."

"Yes, beautifully dark. Um…cozy, like being under covers. I spent more time at the lagoon than I intended."

"Building sandcastles?"

Ruhee struggled for words. "I am…not sure what you mean."

"I mean, this morning I went to the lagoon to fetch water. There was a small mound on the beach, moist and crusted."

She shrugged. "Perhaps I let myself play a little."

"With an impression—" Kurta let the rest of the sentence speak for itself.

"I have no idea what you speak of." Ruhee spat her words as she rose from her bed. She looked at the path to the lagoon. "I must wash before breakfast."

She strode down the trail, her face burning. *How dare that old woman talk to me about what I did last night! It is not her business that I am ridding myself of an enemy.* She slowed as she saw the water and her sculpture of the previous night. The impression of her ankh could be clearly seen atop the mound of sand.

Ruhee pushed the mound over, flattening and blending it into the beach. Now she could tell Kurta that she was imagining things—there was no mound of sand. She disrobed and walked into the lagoon, feeling its cool touch on her skin. Lisette would soon be out of the way, but how to rid herself of the baby, especially with Kurta watching her every step?

I may have to get rid of the old woman, too. But how?

She swam to one side and floated back, her thoughts revolving around Kurta and the baby. In a perfect world, she would see the perfect ship passing—waving the perfect flag and going in the perfect direction. She could run, excitedly, toward the cliff, pointing. When Kurta approached, one trip, one push would send her flying to the rocks below. If the brat was with her, good riddance. If she wasn't, well, there were ways to correct that.

The wind picked up, making small waves that propelled her through the water. They were gentle at first, lapping at her sides and pressing her in random directions. As the moments passed, they grew stronger, until the water splashed over her body and her face. She spluttered at the cool liquid that burst into her nose, righting herself and coughing.

Enough of this. Time to head to shore.

She reached out in a wide stroke, kicking her feet as she did. Each time she pressed forward, the waves pushed back, keeping her in the same spot.

Well, if I can't swim against this current, I shall let it carry me to the other side and walk back around.

She turned around and paddled for the far side, but the waves switched their course, now keeping her from the far shore. No matter where she attempted to swim, the waves kept her in the same place. Ruhee kicked and pulled, swimming below the surface as well as above. It was no use. The lagoon was determined to strand her in its middle.

Her legs and arms soon lost their strength to continue, and her breathing was labored as she still fought to remain above the water. She waved her arms, maintaining an upright position while she tried to catch her breath and figure out what to do.

Stupid girl. She wept. *This lagoon has tried to kill you once, given you nightmares, and yet you bathe in it again. Now you shall surely die.*

As before, the next wave shoved her to the sandy floor of the lagoon, where she struggled for air until she could no longer put up a fight. As she lost consciousness, a voice whispered to her, high and beautiful, like a temple bell.

Ruhee, I give you all of the right chances and you are

making the wrong choice each time. You cannot kill Kurta, and she will not allow you to kill the baby. You will not even kill Lisette. There are great forces at work, magical forces. You are a gnat in their grand plan. Do not force them to swat you away.

She awakened with a sick lurch, heaving, and spitting up water. The waves had at least deposited her on the sand this time, instead of placing her back on her bed with no memory beyond that terrifying dream. Ruhee stood up, still coughing, and put her clothes back on.

"As the gods may witness, I shall never step foot in this water again," she vowed. Once was a nightmare. Twice was her own fault.

She walked back to the camp, imagining what frivolous activity Kurta would engage her in today. The lagoon had warned her—twice now, to make better choices. She considered what she could do, instead of killing Kurta and the baby and Lisette and sailing off with Rocco.

Catch the next ship, no matter where it goes, and start a new life—perhaps even meeting a new love. She could leave the baby with Kurta. The old woman would return her to Lisette, of that Ruhee had no doubt. She'd have to find someone to remove her tattoo. Her sisterhood with the *Dişi Aslan* was at an end.

Her new love…she tried to picture someone to take Rocco's place. Tall, broad-shouldered, dark-haired, with eyes the color of the sky. It was no use. She could not picture anyone who did not look like Rocco, or even act like him. Strong, decisive, ruthless yet tender.

"There is no retreat for me," she told the heavens. "I shall follow this path to its end—even if it is my end as well."

65

Rocco, Lisette, and Willem stood in the middle of Catalina's chambers, Rocco still standing guard over the countess.

"I do feel sorry for having to kill Amoy," Lisette said. "She could have gone away, healed from her brother's death, and started a new, better life."

"Not all of us are cut out for changing our course." Willem smiled. "I admit, I am impressed that Renata is going to take your advice and begin again. Perhaps I could work my way back into her good graces."

"You wouldn't, you murderer!" Catalina screeched.

Lisette nodded toward the wardrobe. "Willem, perhaps you could take care of the countess' mouth until we decide what to do with her."

Willem strode to the carved armoire and opened a

drawer, removing a scarf. "Will this do?"

Rocco took it and wrapped it about the Catalina's mouth as she squealed in protest. "Save your voice, m'lady. It might mean the difference between life and the bottom of the sea."

Catalina's squeal turned to sobbing.

"I'd probably try not to cry, too," Lisette told her. "You will make your nose stuffy, and it will be hard to breathe." She walked over to the countess and raised a corner of the countess' skirt to her eyes, dabbing the tears. "I am sorry for your troubles. It is not easy to be a noblewoman. We are not in charge of what the men in our lives do, either through good or evil intent, but we are meant to support them no matter."

Catalina nodded and let out a sigh.

"If you are going to be reasonable, I can take the gag off," Rocco said. "But at the first harpy screech—"

She lowered her head and relaxed against him, so he untied the scarf.

"Thank you. What was your name?"

Rocco frowned at her. "Let us save names for when I know you won't sell me to El Rey."

The countess gasped, her eyes large. "Oh, no! Of course not."

"While we figure out what we should do with the countess," Lisette said, "we first need to decide how best to present the contents of this letter." She withdrew it from her bodice and gave it to Rocco to read.

His eyes swept over the words, widening at times. Finally, he looked up. "This would give all the islands in Los Peces Pequeños total control of their own lives."

Lisette prepared for the same fight they'd had about removing the Mendozas. "Yes, but there are already islands that are governing themselves."

"I know what you are waiting for me to say. I shall

only offer that I cannot pillage Spanish ships if there are no Spaniards here to need goods or services."

"Pillage?" Catalina asked, and immediately lowered her voice. "I mean, that is, I have no opinion."

"Good choice, almost mother-in-law," Willem said, and turned to Rocco. "It seems to me you have many choices as well. You can expand your territory to the islands still under Spanish rule. You can defend these islands against invaders—you know they will come. Once France and England discover these islands are unclaimed, they will attempt to move in. Spain might even become reinvested." He took a deep breath. "Or, like Lisette, you can change course. She is giving up her nobility for you. Is it not possible that you could give up killing Spaniards for her? Become an honest merchant in the region?"

Rocco scowled. "It was not my plan."

"And it was not my plan to be sold to a pirate, kill men trying to kill me, become a dragon, or fall in love with you," Lisette said. "Yet I would not continue on my old path, now that I've been on this new one."

"I, too, should be headed in a new direction," Willem said.

"We can always use a good man on *L'Implacable*," Rocco told him.

"Thank you, but I believe I shall allow myself a brief time to be, what is the phrase—at loose ends? I have the funds to travel. Renata may need a familiar face on her journey—"

"No, I—" Catalina argued before Willem shushed her.

"As a friend, Countess, not a possible husband. I admire her greatly at this moment, but I do not think we should make a good match. I did kill her father. She might carry a grudge about that."

"I wish you success on your journeys," Lisette said. "Now. What do we do with Catalina?"

"I am less inclined to toss her overboard as long as she retains her manners," Rocco offered. "But I don't know if we can simply turn her loose. She does seem the kind of woman to carry a grudge."

Lisette strolled to the balcony and gazed out at the landscape. "We have forgotten something. The Duke de Martinmas is still on this island. I think we should lay the problem of the countess at his feet."

"He will merely turn her loose," Rocco said.

"No, I don't believe so, for a number of reasons." Lisette looked at Willem. "Renata will no doubt need a carriage for her trip to the port. Perhaps they could drop the countess and me at my old castle?"

Willem nodded his assent and strode from the room.

Rocco scowled. "I do not believe this is a good plan."

"The duke has been kind to me, even helpful. I have trusted him on key occasions, and he has never betrayed me." She glanced at the countess, smiling. "He might even suggest tossing Catalina overboard."

The older woman and sputtered.

"I was but jesting," Lisette told her. "He has only asked me to kill one person."

Catalina moaned and sputtered again but this time, Lisette ignored her.

Soon, a whistle from below made Lisette look down from the balcony's edge. Willem stood next to Amoy's body.

"The carriage is out front," he said. "And I checked— she is quite dead."

"Thank you," Lisette called down to him.

She and Rocco aided the countess in walking down the wooden stairs. The steps were uneven, and the older woman was having a problem keeping her balance, especially with her hands tied.

"I always hold the rail," she whined.

"And now you will let me hold your arm to steer you," Lisette said. "Unless you'd like to do it yourself. I'm certain Rocco will not mind if you tumble."

"No, no. Please continue helping me."

They at last maneuvered her down the stairs and out to the front gate. A carriage for four stood by, pulled by a large, dark charcoal gray.

"I can drive," Lisette said. "That way, you two gentlemen can sit next to the ladies and discourage them from leaping from the wagon, or from slipping a dagger in your ribs."

Rocco smiled and offered his hand to Catalina's arm, to boost her into the carriage. She could not heft herself in, so Willem stepped in and aided Rocco, plopping her down on a seat.

Willem turned to Renata. "Shall I load your bags?"

"Please," she said in a cold tone.

With everyone loaded and ready, Lisette fanned the reins on the horse's back and clucked. "Walk on."

The horse took a step, pulling into his harness, and walked, slowing at the closed gate to await further commands. Lisette looked up at the guard post and shouted. A familiar face popped out of the narrow window.

"Oleta!" Lisette grinned. "We have a little errand to run."

The sound of running on wood was punctuated by a woman in breeches and a muslin shirt, striding toward the carriage. Lisette leaped out to embrace her friend.

"It looks like the battle went well," Lisette said. "Are my sisters good?"

"A few injuries, but they will all live to fight another day." Oleta glanced over at the occupants of the carriage, nodding to Rocco. "What have we here?"

"The Countess de Mendoza and her daughter the

marquise, along with the marquess d'Auguste."

Oleta raised her eyebrows. "D'Auguste?"

"Eric's younger brother, Willem." Lisette smiled. "He has been most helpful to me."

"Good morrow, m'lady." Willem tipped his cap.

"We are taking the countess to the duke, as we are undecided what is to be done with her."

"And the count?" Oleta asked.

"I'm afraid he did not survive the fight," Willem said. "Renata, the marquise, has decided to leave for distant lands and leave distasteful memories."

Renata glanced at her weeping mother, shrugged, and looked away.

"Godspeed then," Oleta said, and walked to the wooden doors.

She lifted the bar and pushed them open. Lisette climbed back in the driver's seat and encouraged her horse to walk through. He did so without complaint and soon they were on the road that would take them to the old castle de Lille.

Rocco was sitting with his back to Lisette. He twisted around to her.

"What do you intend to do with that letter?"

She kept her eyes on the road and shook her head. "I am not certain. To be enforced, we should have to let everyone in the islands know about it, and let El Rey know it was enacted. He will not be happy. Mendoza was keeping this letter as insurance, to keep the coin coming into his coffers."

"I suppose the king will be happy to stop paying five thousand gold ducats every month. But he will lose more in trade and tributes."

"I believe…" Lisette let her words out slowly. "We could take this to the duke, being careful of course, for him to not succumb to his own greed. He can write…" She counted her fingers. "Five letters that say basically what the king is saying. These letters go to the five islands."

"Not six? There is Île des Anciens." Willem said.

"Have you known any Spaniard try to rule that island?" Rocco asked.

Willem laughed. "No."

"In the meantime," she continued, "the duke writes a letter to El Rey, explaining that he found this decree and executed it, according to the king's wishes. Of course, we keep the original decree safe from falling into the wrong hands."

"Of course," Willem said. "The duke's part is entire innocent. How was he to know El Rey was trying to get out of honoring the promise?"

"Exactly—if we can convince the duke." She glanced over her shoulder. Rocco was deep in thought, and she knew he was trying to find the holes in her plan. He was silent for the rest of the trip to the village.

At the large crossroad that divided the port into the shopping half and the inn-and-merriment half, Willem instructed her to pull over.

"I do not see a ship in port," he said. "And we do not know when the next one arrives. I think if you let us depart here, I will help the marquise with her baggage." He stepped down from the carriage and turned to Renata, offering her his hand. "Fear not, m'lady. I book my own passage on the ship I choose. We need never meet again."

Renata accepted his help with a small grin and nod. "Thank you, Willem. Perhaps while we wait, you'd like to share a meal at the inn?"

Willem picked up her bags. "Lead on."

Catalina opened her mouth as if to protest, but Rocco put his hand on her shoulder. She winced under his firm grip.

"Let her go, mother," he said. "Let her go, and you may see her again."

The older woman reached for her silk square to cry into.

Lisette used the wide street to turn the carriage about and head toward the castle de Lille, and a meeting with the duke. Morning was at its midpoint, and she yawned. It was difficult to remember when she slept last at all. Most sleep came with dreams of Alara, and futile attempts to find her. In her imaginings, she would reach out to hold her baby, only to hold nothing.

"I've missed you." Rocco broke the silence.

"And I you," she replied. "I want our baby back."

"Lizzie…" he stopped, taking a breath. "These islands were granted to the people. I will not argue. We will convince the duke to do the right thing."

"I hope so." She fanned the reins on the horse's back and clucked again. The horse picked up, rising to a slow trot that was somewhat faster than his walk. Lisette wanted to get to the duke and receive his agreement as soon as possible. She could not shake the feeling that Alara was impatient to come home.

They were at the castle before noon. Rocco helped the countess from the carriage and turned to help Lisette, who had leapt from the driver's perch, handing the reins to one of the guards.

"If I stop being a pirate, will you start acting like a lady?" Rocco asked.

She shrugged. "I'm not certain that I ever acted that proper."

They escorted Catalina through the front door, Lisette leading and Rocco following. Pinar was the first one they saw, scurrying toward the stairs with a tray in her hands.

"Where is the duke?" Lisette asked.

"Lizzie! I am so glad to see you. The duke is in his chambers." She nodded toward the tray. "I'm afraid he's gravely injured."

66

"Injured?" Lisette asked.

"Did you not see him last night? He joined the fight against the Mendozas—I'm afraid he suffered a serious wound."

Lisette glanced at Rocco and ran up the stairs, Rocco following. The duke was in his overstuffed chair by the fire, covered in a blanket. The room was stifling hot, yet he shivered.

"M'lord, what has happened?" Lisette asked, rushing to his side. "Why are you not in bed?"

"A mere scratch," he managed between coughs. "I'm sure the sight of you shall cure me."

"I am here, Uncle Oscar." She took the bowl of broth and spoon from Pinar and ladled a bit, carefully holding it to his lips. "Here, this will warm and strengthen. Pinar, send for Oleta."

Pinar nodded and left.

"Ah, the elixir of life." The duke smiled as he accepted the broth. "But where's my rum?"

"M'lord," Lisette said. "Rum is not apt to help you—"

"Give the man his drink," Rocco interjected, pouring a mug. "He's earned it."

Lisette set the bowl on the table and took the mug from Rocco. "Here, I shall hold it for you," she said as she held it to his lips.

The duke put his hands around hers, attempting to wrench the mug from her. "I'm not a child you have to coddle."

"You don't appear that strong to me at the moment," she told him.

"How can you sass a sick man?"

"With ease." She felt a slight twinge of regret. "My apologies, m'lord. When Oleta comes, she will have herbs to pack into your wound and set you right."

The duke took another large swig of drink, made a face, and brought his hand to his side. Lisette could see the dots of blood staining his shirt.

"Tell me," he said, his voice raspy and low. "How went the battle?"

"The Count de Mendoza is dead, his daughter is catching the first ship away, and the countess—well, we brought the countess here as we don't know what to do with her." Lisette took the mug away and set it on the table.

"I fear I am not up to making decisions at the moment." The duke coughed. "You may have to take over for me."

Lisette wiped at a spill with a cotton square. "Only until you are healed. You must rest and get better. Rocco and I will be bringing Alara home very soon and she will want to meet you."

"You found her?" He smiled. "Why is she not here?"

"Rocco and I are going to fetch her but we had some business to finish first. The countess, you know."

"What am I supposed to do with her?" He scowled and coughed. She patted his back and offered him more broth. He sipped from the spoon, took a deep breath, and groaned.

"M'lord." Lisette waited for him to settle. "I do not wish to vex you, but I have something urgent to discuss."

"More urgent than where to put Countess de Mendoza?" He grinned.

"This might secure her fate," she said, and removed the letter from her bodice. "I discovered why El Rey was sending the count five thousand gold ducats every month."

"Child, I am in no mood to read," he moaned and pulled his blanket tighter. "Read it to me."

"Very well, but it hardly makes a good bedtime story." She opened the decree and read it aloud, glancing at his face between sentences.

"Give it to the islanders? Outrageous!" His voice cracked, too weak to shout.

"M'lord—it is not for you to question, is it?"

He sighed. "No. It is the wishes of El Rey…at least El Rey's papa." He chuckled, coughing slightly. "I always liked his padre better."

"You have been nothing but kind to the people you've ruled," Lisette said. "Perhaps you could continue to live here—or on Isla de Pimienta—without the worry of representing Spain."

"Hmm, it is a thought." He nodded. "The Mendoza castle is insufficient for my needs, but the updates to the Medina castle are nearing completion. I could live there happily ignored, apart from occasional shipments of delicacies from my homeland."

"Be honest with me—could you let commoners hand down law?"

"Commoners?" His body erupted in another coughing fit as Pinar entered.

"Oleta is on her way," she said.

"Perhaps I could take a look at your injury," Rocco offered. "I've seen many wounds and received my share."

The duke nodded, so Rocco sat down at his side and opened his shirt. Lisette could see the wound from her angle—it was jagged and inflamed, with a thin line of scarlet that ebbed and flowed with the duke's heartbeat. Lisette glanced up at Rocco. His expression was stony, but she could tell he did not like what he saw.

Rocco grabbed a clean cloth and pressed down on the wound. The duke roared at him, attempting escape.

"I must press on it," Rocco told him. "I'm afraid you've nicked something, and we need to stop the bleeding."

"If you must," the duke said. "By the way, Captain Rocco, why haven't you rescued my—Lisette's daughter?"

"It is next on my list," Rocco told him. "Or should I say, our list?"

Lisette nodded. "Yes. We go to her right now, to bring her home."

"This home?" the duke asked.

"Yes." Lisette smiled.

"Then I shall wait for her." He sat back in his chair and closed his eyes.

She put the cup down and adjusted his covers before turning to Pinar. "Has the doctor seen him?"

Pinar shook her head. "He is apparently not fond of them."

"Doctors killed my wife." He opened one eye, frowning. "No doctors."

"No, m'lord," Lisette told him. "No doctors."

She motioned for Rocco and Pinar to join her outside. Once his door was shut, she turned to Pinar.

"Rocco and I must gather our daughter. She is safe, but I confess I am anxious to have her with me." She glanced toward the duke's door. "How soon can Oleta be here to attend to the duke?"

Pinar frowned. "Within the hour, although I do not think even her expertise can help him."

Rocco wrapped his hand on Lisette's arm. "Let us be quick then."

Lisette moved with him to leave. "We shall return as soon as possible."

"What about the countess?" Pinar asked.

Lisette and Rocco looked at one another.

"Offer her a choice," Lisette said. "The dungeon or scrubbing pots in the kitchen. A little hard work might calm her down."

Pinar laughed. "She might prefer the noose."

"If that is her wish, we will not stop her," Rocco said. "The hanging can commence when we return."

He led Lisette down the stairs to the balcony off the great room. "I've instructed my crew to meet us at Île des Anciens. We can get there faster than the ship."

She smiled in agreement. It would be faster to fly.

The sun was setting, though it hardly mattered to Lisette. Someone spotting her in flight was the least of her problems. She completely trusted Lamya with Alara's safety, but she'd had a nagging feeling of danger ever since the intense bouts of pain she experienced. Even her blood dragon transformations did not cause that kind of intense burning in her guts, and the pain never lingered. She was certain that Lamya would know why.

Rocco flew a few meters from her, looking toward the horizon. Île des Anciens took two days under sail. Flying was faster, but it still took almost a day to reach the island. Lisette was grateful that the monsoons had tapered off and prayed that they would not encounter a stray one on their journey.

Her wings would be tired enough with good weather and a strong wind at their backs.

I am also hoping not to fight a storm, Rocco said, even though his eyes never left their scan of the sea.

Lisette chuffed. *I do not know if I shall get used to you reading my mind.*

Why aren't you reading mine? He asked.

She glanced at him—there was a low undercurrent of words washing across her mind, but she'd been tuning it out as noise. It was much too embarrassing to admit to her lover that his thoughts were unimportant, so she told him, *I suppose I haven't been paying attention.*

Now he chuffed. *Never lie to me. It's true, my thoughts are running rampant, from fearing for Alara to fearing for your safety to returning to my ship.*

Will your thoughts ever calm themselves? She wondered.

I doubt it. Even when we have our baby with us, I shall always be vigilant. And you do not back away from danger. What am I to do with my two favorite women?

A downdraft caught them both by surprise, pushing them lower. Lisette adjusted her course left until she no longer felt the pressure. She rose, lifting herself high and checking the wind to her right. When she had risen above the air current, she banked toward her destination and resumed her trip.

Rocco had been on her right side. She looked for him there, but he was gone. Glancing around while maintaining her direction, she wondered if the wind had pushed him into the sea. She opened her mind, concentrating on him.

Yes, I am below you, came his answer. *I went right to try to avoid the wind. I should have flown left. I'll be with you as soon as I get out of this.*

Lisette stopped her forward motion, suspending her body in midair while she looked down to see if she could spot Rocco. The clouds had greyed and knitted together with soft wisps, making it difficult to see very far. Rain would be blowing through, soon. Maybe not a monsoon, but water blowing down just the same.

What are you doing? Rocco asked. *I told you to keep going.*

Not without you. Lisette glanced behind her and turned her body down. *There's a squall coming,* she told him, *behind us. I'm coming down to join you.*

The first droplets hit as she spotted Rocco. She could see the red of his feathers through the mist as her paws touched the water's surface. The last time she'd been through this at sea, the storm had been particularly vicious, driving her below the water. Fortunately for her, she was close enough to Île des Anciens to swim to shore.

The island was not nearly close enough now.

She sat down in the waves and pulled her wings above her head. The droplets became steady sheets of water that pummeled her without end. Sitting back on her haunches, she fought the wind that tried to push her head under.

Damn this weather, Rocco said.

Time felt like it had stopped in an eternal moment of perpetual drenching. Lisette pulled her wings tighter as the drips invaded her eyes and nose. The wind was driving her from behind, waves breaking up over her back as the rain poured down. She kept her back legs paddling while her tail waved under the water, keeping her afloat.

I'm glad I learned something the last time I nearly drowned. I'd hate to think this knowledge was wasted. She glanced around. *Rocco? Where are you? Keep your wings high and tight and sit back on your tail.*

The squall lasted, bucket after bucket after sheets upon sheets of water, until Lisette believed it was impossible for anything to be left in the sky. After a while, she thought the clouds were sucking up the ocean water directly to deposit on her. She snorted angrily, emitting a puff of cloud.

I need to be with Alara. She watched the cloud puff expand, thin, and dissipate, noticing that while it was still in cloud form, it did not allow the rain to penetrate. Opening her mouth, she breathed a larger cloud. It rose and flattened, absorbing the squall, and re-routing it away.

She heard Rocco shouting, if one could shout in their head. *By the gods, will this never end?* Peering up through the wet, gray vista, she saw the flick of a red tail slap the waves and disappear.

The whoosh of the wind behind her brought a stronger round, so she tightened her wings over her head, inhaled as deeply as she could with wet nostrils, and let out an enormous roar, accompanied by a large cloud, lightning dashing through its billows.

Lifting herself forward, she paddled until she was underneath it. It provided the shelter it promised—she just had to find a way to move it with her. Looking up, she breathed again, exhaling more cloud to join the first.

She kept moving forward this way, traveling under her own breath, until she was within grasping of Rocco's tail. His head kept rising above the sea, gasping for a breath, before being washed over again. Lisette kept breathing, kept reaching, until she was able to grab him.

He whipped his tail vigorously as he growled, *let go of me whatever you are.*

It's me, stop fighting and paddle backward, she told him, *I've got cloud cover to protect us.* She yanked his tail. When he was next to her, she dove under the water and used her body to prop him above the waves, lifting her own neck above the surface. From the weight of him, she knew he was exhausted, although she doubted that he would admit it.

Why admit what you already know? He asked.

She looked behind her. *If we can stay here, I see clear sky behind us. The squall will soon pass.* She breathed protection into her cloud, feeling Rocco's warm breath on her neck. Leaning into him, she absorbed his warmth, lending her own back to him. They hovered in the waters here, rolling up with the crest of the waves and sliding down to the trough.

Lisette felt the sheets turning to drops and the drops to droplets. The waves quieted and her body relaxed. She looked left and watched the deluge move with the wind, toward Isla de la Soledad. If the wind didn't change direction, they would not encounter the storm again as they flew southwest, to Île des Anciens.

Shall we? Rocco asked, his wings fanning their wetness away.

She nodded, drying her own. *I want my baby.*

Rocco flapped vigorously. It took a little finesse, but he managed to raise his front paws from the water. A little faster motion and he lifted his haunches, continuing to aim skyward.

Lisette followed, propelling her body up like a sea bird taking flight. She joined Rocco in the sky.

You make it look so easy, he said. *I feel like an albatross, heavy and uncoordinated.*

I may have been a moon dragon longer. Plus, I have lived through a squall before in this body. Basically, you must think like a dragon and fly like a bird—but not an albatross.

He made a grunting noise that she interpreted as a laugh before heading further up past the clouds. She followed, and together they sped toward Île des Anciens. Her wings were weary, and body tired from their continuous fight against the wind and water, but she could not think of that at the moment. All she could do was look for air currents to take advantage of, winds that could carry her faster while giving her wings a little rest.

The merest shards of light peeked over the eastern horizon by the time they saw the small, familiar island. As they closed in, Lisette saw bright flowers on poles. No doubt, these were signal poles to attempt to get the attention of ships passing by.

Why did Lamya want to signal a ship?

Not Lamya, Rocco said, *Ruhee. She wanted to get to Isla del Lagarto.*

Lisette frowned. *What is in Isla del Lagarto for her?*

I do not know. She was determined to take our baby with her and somehow seduce me into leaving you to marry her.

She stretched her wings and dug into the morning air. *I shall assume you are unwilling to do this.*

If she could not make me love her when she gave me that forgetfulness potion, I do not know what plan she would concoct to change my mind now. He flew closer to her and nipped at her shoulder.

Lisette whipped around and snapped at his neck. *Let us land on the other side of the lagoon and transform,* she told him. *We will need our words for dealing with Ruhee.*

Rocco nodded and they continued on their path.

The sun was at midmorning before they crossed the coastline. Rocco flew toward the lagoon, but Lisette found herself looking down at the camp Lamya had made for Alara and Ruhee. A fire burned in the middle, surrounded by multi-colored fabrics that she recognized as bedding. Two figures moved deliberately, performing morning tasks. One of the figures moved with quick, fluid actions, while the other was slow. The slow person had a large lump on her back.

This had to be Lamya with Alara. Lisette wondered why Ruhee was not carrying the baby, since she claimed to have wanted it. She heard Rocco tell her to hurry, but she was still admiring Alara—even if it was from a great distance.

Soon, my baby. Soon I shall have you in my arms.

Alara looked up at the sky, at her, and put two chubby arms in the air. Lisette felt her heart melting and resisted the urge to fly down and take her immediately.

Lizzie! Rocco startled her and she glanced up. He was hovering over the grove that held the lagoon, waiting for her.

Tearing herself from her baby, she flew to him. *I'm sorry but she looked up at me.*

Together they descended, alighting on the sandy beach. Lisette transformed first, as easily as she was accustomed, with no more pain. She watched the red-tipped dragon close his eyes, exhale a hefty breath, and finally change into the handsome pirate she loved.

68

Rocco settled into the sand and watched Lisette turn human before he attempted it. His transformations had become easy, thanks to Lamya's training, but the squall still occupied his mind. He had nearly drowned, and probably would have without Lisette's help.

Being in the middle of a squall when he commanded a ship was easy. Most of the time, he felt a rush of adrenaline at taming the wind and water at the helm. But as a dragon, he felt vulnerable. His feathers were not as buoyant as he assumed, and the torrents pushed him under the water with incredible force.

Now human again, he strode to Lisette and took her in his arms. "I know you want her back, Lizzie," he whispered. "So do I. Let us claim our daughter—and what should we do with Ruhee?"

"It might depend upon her." Lisette shook her head.

"She must be willing to let her heart break and begin a new chapter. If she won't…"

"She will never stop hunting us."

Lisette leaned into his shoulder, reaching up to kiss his cheek. "If there's killing, you must take the lead. I don't have the stomach for it."

He squeezed her waist and kissed her forehead. "Don't worry. It's a thing pirates are good at."

Even while he and Lisette spoke about what to do with Ruhee, the storm lingered in the back of his mind. Nodding toward the path, he finally told her, "Let's go get our baby."

He kept his hand on her waist, anxious for the time when they would be married. Even if she could not bear more children, he would be happy to live with this strong, fierce woman. Hopefully she could teach him how to stay afloat in all of life's squalls.

They came down the path into the camp with no fanfare. Ruhee was sitting at the cliff, looking out to sea. Lamya stirred a pot over the fire, Alara on a silken bed beside her.

"Welcome," Lamya said, without looking up. "Your meal is almost ready."

Lisette laughed. "Of course, you knew when we would arrive."

"Hmm, did I know? Let us say I keep track of the time, and how long it takes for humans to accomplish things."

"We are here now," Lisette said as she knelt down to take Alara into her arms.

Rocco watched the tiny hands reach to Lisette, the arms wrapping, the two bodies almost melting together. Alara closed her eyes, her bow of a mouth opening and closing with happy noises that sounded like, "ma-ma-ma-ma-ma."

"Is she talking?" Rocco asked.

"Not quite, but she will be there soon," Lamya told him. "She loves making sounds—cooing, giggling, yummy sounds when she is eating. I'm sorry, Lizzie, but she says 'mama' to everything and everyone."

"Oh, I don't care." Lisette held her out a bit, putting her forehead on Alara's. "I should not doubt that she would not know her mother after all this time."

"We will have all the time in the world to get to know her now," Rocco said.

"What…what are you doing here?" Ruhee stood just outside the fire ring, her face pale.

"Collecting our child," Rocco said. "My ship will be here in two days to pick us up."

She stared at Lisette. "How are you…here?"

"I flew with Rocco." Lisette stood, holding Alara close.

"But I—you shouldn't have—it would be impossible—" Ruhee stammered.

"Ah, yes, your little curse." Lamya had risen from stirring the food and was gathering bowls. "The island is silent at night and voices carry. I could not block your entire curse, but I…hmm…flattened it to do no lasting harm."

Rocco's eyes narrowed. "So the pain that Lisette was having from her transformations…?"

Lamya nodded. "You may thank Ruhee. She was trying to make your transformation fatal. She did not succeed."

Ruhee shrank for a moment, before a look of determination set into her eyes. "Yes, I did that. You do not deserve Rocco. He deserves an obedient wife, willing to do as he asks, and one who can bear him many children."

"Let me be clear, Ruhee Vaishya." Rocco lowered his voice and glared at her. "I have been blessed to find love again with Lisette. I have never required an obedient wife, nor have I required many children. This is all in your imagination. You will be blessed if you do not die from your actions."

"You would not let Lisette kill me," Ruhee said.

"I would not have to." His voice was cold. "I would do it gladly."

Ruhee gasped, both hands over her mouth. She burst into sobbing, turned, and ran into the jungle. Rocco turned to Lisette.

"I love you, too," she said. "Come. Hold your daughter."

He walked to them, hesitant. His lack of confidence with babies had not changed. Holding his hands out, he waited for her to hand Alara to him.

"You are not receiving a bag of grain from a ship." Lisette laughed. "Come here, closer, and put your arm around me."

He did as she requested.

"Now, your other arm around Alara."

Rocco looked at the child, who stared at him with green-gold eyes, just like her mother. Wrapping his arm around her, he watched her arms leave Lisette and reach to him. He leaned in, allowing her to embrace him and feeling the tiny fingers on his neck. In small, slow degrees, Lisette pulled away and allowed him to keep Alara upright and safe in his arms.

He held his daughter close to him, the slight weight of her acting like an anchor, holding her to his heart. Two hands gripped the side of his face now as his daughter held his gaze. She gurgled, mouthing "ma-ma-ma" again.

"She has your eyes," he told Lisette, "and your wild hair."

"Maybe," Lisette said. "But that smile is all yours."

"Come." Lamya interrupted. "Eat. I am interested in hearing about your journeys. Lizzie, I will hold the baby while you are nourished."

She handed them bowls of food that was now familiar to them. Roasted yam, dried boar meat, malanga, in a rich broth that filled their bellies as well as their senses. Between bites, Rocco and Lisette told her of the document giving the islands to the natives, and the fight to make that come true. Lamya listened, nodding, while she rocked Alara, mashing small amounts of yam and mixing it with broth.

Lisette pointed to the bubby-pot. "You shall have to teach me about her, Lamya. I have been away from her so long my milk is dry. And she has grown old enough to give a little food."

"You have two days to learn her routine." Lamya smiled. "It will be enough—for both of you."

Rocco raised his eyebrows. "Me, too?"

"Are you not this child's father?"

"Yes, but, fathers do not take care of their children." He frowned.

69

Lamya stared at him. "What good are fathers then? I do not understand this thinking. If Lisette cannot take care of Alara, you cannot put her in a box and save her until Lisette can take over." She picked up the bubby-pot. "You will no doubt have goat's milk, which is better, but I have fed her coconut milk, mixed with a few herbs. Are you finished? Come, sit with me."

Rocco put down his empty bowl and shuffled over to Lamya, sitting beside her on silk blankets, their backs against a log. She handed him Alara, positioning the child in his arms before handing him the bubby-pot.

"She suckles on the cloth." Lamya pointed. "It is very important not to tip the pot too high so that the milk flows without control. You want to feed her, not drown her."

Rocco flashed back to his head under water, the waves breaking over the top of him, and Lisette underneath, lifting him to the surface.

"Yes, no one wants to drown." He tipped the pot gently, feeling the weight of the liquid shift.

Alara put both hands around the pot and sucked hungrily at the cloth. She drank remarkably fast, and he had to be on constant alert to give her more without giving her too much. When she had finished the pot, he looked to Lamya.

"It is empty. Now what?"

"Now you put the bubby-pot down, put her over your shoulder and pat her back."

Rocco frowned, but did as he was told, once again having his hands and the baby's body adjusted until Lamya was satisfied. After a moment of patting Alara's back, Rocco stopped.

"Why am I doing this?"

"Keep patting," Lamya ordered. "She has air in her stomach."

Rocco frowned and kept patting. "So what?"

"Just do it," Lisette said.

As Rocco opened his mouth to argue, he felt a large spasm in Alara's tiny body, accompanied by a burp in his ear. "Can the child not burp itself?"

"NO." Lisette and Lamya answered in unison.

"Very well, then," he said. "Is she finished?"

"A few more pats," Lamya told him. "Just in case."

Lisette laughed. "You are an excellent father."

When Alara was sufficiently patted and burped, Rocco held her against his chest. Her body grew heavy, and he could feel her warm breath against his neck.

"She is asleep?" he asked.

"Yes," Lamya said. "Babies with full tummies are quick to fall asleep." She walked back to him. "Here, I will lay her down in her bed."

"Now what?" Rocco asked, watching his daughter

sleep, her fist against her mouth.

"Now we clean the dishes from the meal, we gather more wood for the fire, and we enjoy the day." Lamya picked up the pot and the bowls Lisette had stacked together. "One of us must stay here to guard Alara."

"You stay," Rocco told Lisette. "I'll help Lamya."

He kissed her and joined Lamya on the path. They walked quietly together, Rocco checking the brush and listening intently for any sign that Ruhee might be around.

"She is not here," Lamya said.

"I know better than to ask you how you know. But I will ask if you know where she is."

"Where she always goes when she is angry and wants to plan harm." Lamya gestured to her left. "Down at the shore, by the boat we arrived on. She visits the boat, with angry thoughts of rowing away. Then she remembers it is a little boat for such a big ocean. Then she reasons that alone in a boat in the middle of the sea is better than time spent with me. Finally, she decides to come back, distrusting me, and awaits an opportunity to kill me and the baby."

"Kill Alara? I thought she wanted to raise Alara—that was the whole point of stealing her."

"It was the point, until she found that she could not win Alara's heart." Lamya looked at him and smiled. "Your daughter is very special. She has many talents, including knowing who she can trust. She has also been aware, even before birth, that you and Lisette are her parents."

Rocco nodded. "I have a feeling that raising this baby will be harder than any battle I've fought."

"Yes, or any squall you've sailed through."

He scowled. "Returning to Ruhee, how do we prevent her from taking her revenge? Lisette is loathe to kill her, but I don't see a way to reason with her."

"If you are looking to me for permission to take her

life, you know I cannot give it. Even as a blood dragon, it was your choice and your consequences. All I can tell you is to do what you can to keep your family safe."

"And then?"

"And then do what you must."

They reached the lagoon and proceeded to clean out the bowls and pots, along with Alara's bubby-pot. Rocco had never cleaned a dish before, so Lamya had to take him step by step.

"Here, you run your hand along the inside of the bowl. Do you feel food? Crustiness? Then it is not clean." She sighed. "You were never the cabin boy?"

"I was," he said. "But none of the crew was as picky as you about clean dishes. I wiped them with a rag and put them back in the bins."

Lamya shook her head. "It is a miracle that you all didn't die of bloody flux."

"I shall personally oversee my cabin boy's cleaning from now on." Rocco sighed, thinking of Poussin. "My best cabin boy grew up to be part of the crew. He died in battle on Île des Oiseaux."

"Yes, I know. He was a lovely young man, even if he feared magic." Lamya gathered the sack of dishes and handed them to Rocco. "Let us go. You will carry these to camp."

Rocco took the sack and stepped down the trail, reminiscing. "His real name was Willie, but we called him Poussin. 'The little chicken.' Perhaps if Lisette and I have a son, we can name him Willie."

"Do you not believe that Ruhee rendered Lisette barren with her spell and her ankh?"

He shrugged. "It is not a problem if she did, but I get the feeling that Lisette's will is stronger than any curse, and if she wants another child, she shall have it—maybe with a little help from a friend."

Lamya walked next to him on the path, choosing her

way to avoid any branches, roots, or stones. "It's possible I have this power. I would not know until I am presented with the request."

"We shall wait for Lisette to make it," he said. "I will not have her think my love turns on producing a male heir."

"I cannot see her ever thinking that."

As they walked into view of the camp, Rocco saw Lisette with Alara in her arms, rocking gently. The baby still slept. Rocco set the bag down slowly, to keep any clanging sounds from waking her.

"Did she wake?" he asked.

Lisette shook her head. "No. I have not held her in such a long time, I could not let her sleep in the bed."

"You will spoil her," Lamya warned.

"Then let me spoil her for a few days, Lamya." Lisette caressed the baby.

"A few days." Lamya went over to one of the bushes and pulled a piece of cloth from a branch. "When she wakes, I will teach you both to change her clout."

For two days, Rocco and Lisette learned how to take care of their daughter, from changing and washing clouts, to mixing up a fine paste of yams and broth to feed her. Rocco spent part of his days on the cliff, looking to see if any ships were passing. *L'Implacable* was to sound the horn when they arrived, but if the *Dişi Aslan* sailed by, they could catch a ride easily.

The longer they stayed, the more concerned he was about Ruhee and any possible scheme she might have. In the meantime, he learned whatever Lisette was taught about childcare, making a competition out of it to keep himself interested in what he deemed "woman's work."

The second day was drawing toward night when he finally heard the bell-clear horn of *L'Implacable*. He ran to the cliff and looked over. Luis was at the helm next to Chunk, looking up toward the island, along with one of the crew in the crow's nest. Rocco waved at them, pulling one of the signal poles from the ground to get their attention.

"Cap'n!" Chunk shouted. "We'll send a boat fer ya!"

"Aye, Chunk," he yelled back. "Me, Lisette, and the baby will meet you on the beach below."

Rocco turned away from the cliff and made his way back to camp.

As Alara stirred, Lisette enjoyed the moment. Baby stretches, baby mumblings, her baby awaking. She pulled Alara away from her chest and looked at her smiling face. *Yes, this was worth it.* The pirates and battles, the dragons and transformations were pittances if this was the reward.

"I never even thought about babies, Lamya," she said. "They just come with the role—you're a noblewoman, you marry a nobleman, you have noble children. It never occurred to me that I might enjoy those children."

Lamya grinned. "She is not just any child, please remember that. There will be some difficulties. Be sure to give her your constant love and guidance. Rocco will give her discipline. And know that there will be some parts you do not love as much."

"Like what?"

"Like changing that clout." Lamya gestured to Alara. "She requires it."

Lisette nodded. "Yes, these are not the pleasant parts of motherhood."

Lamya strolled about the camp, picking up bowls and equipment, while Lisette got a fresh clout and laid Alara down to change her.

"My goodness, how does one little baby make such a big mess," she said, wiping the baby down and adjusting a clean clout to fit her. Picking her up, she gave her a kiss on the cheek and propped her safely into her carryall.

She was going to take Alara with her to the lagoon to clean out the clout but decided against it. It would be a short trip and she still struggled getting the baby on her back and the straps tied in front of her. She could ask Lamya for help, but she knew she had to learn to do it herself. Looking at the straps, she sighed.

"Lamya, could I leave Alara here long enough to wash out her clout?"

Lamya was already chuckling. "The carrier is difficult, but you will learn to manage it. For now, yes, I will watch her."

"Thank you. I know you have been watching over her for a long time. I appreciate everything you've done."

"It is well. Your ship should arrive today and when you leave, I shall miss her greatly."

Lisette took a few steps on the path and turned. "Will there come a day when we have to send her to you for…training?"

"Hmm…perhaps. Who knows what the future calls for?"

She nodded and went back toward the lagoon. Lamya was, as usual, correct. The future was much too far away, and it would do no good trying to look for it. It had been over two years since she was preparing for the gala, in the gold brocade dress that lit up her eyes. Her future was to marry Eric, live in a castle, bear his children, throw galas of her own.

She had no way of knowing that wouldn't come to pass.

As she scrubbed the clout and rinsed it, she tried to imagine what signs she should have looked for. Eric was not a brilliant man, although Mercedes had enough brains for both of them. Still, he should have left signs, clues as to what they had planned. She'd never known him to be able to keep a secret.

It did not matter now, I am not as naïve as I was then. If Rocco ever deceived her, she would know. And he would pay.

She strode back to the camp, bucket and clout in hand, humming a little tune. It was silly to think of Rocco betraying her the way Eric did. They had fought too hard to deny their love before accepting what their hearts wanted.

When she got to the end of the path, she was puzzled by what she saw. Her mind refused to accept what her eyes were telling her. Ruhee was in camp, standing at the fire. Alara was in her arms. Ruhee had her baby.

When she finally realized the truth, she stopped moving and looked for Lamya, who stood to her right, holding her sack, with a look of curiosity on her face.

"Ruhee," Lisette said. "I've been wanting to talk to you. Why don't we sit down at the fire and Lamya can prepare us something to eat?"

Lamya gave Lisette a small shrug and took a few steps toward her.

"You will all stay where you are." Ruhee's voice was flat, expressionless. "Or I will throw the baby into the fire."

Lisette and Lamya stopped moving.

"There's no need for that," Lamya said. "We do not have to go anywhere."

"Lamya. Hmpf." Ruhee sneered. "So that's your real name."

"I told you, I go by many names. My name on this island is Lamya de Sang. The name I needed for my journey was Kurta Rici."

"Ruhee, I know you are angry and hurt," Lisette told her. "This baby has not done anything to you—"

"This baby has done everything to me!" Ruhee lifted Alara as if to dash her onto the ground, then lowered her arms. "This baby bonded you to Rocco. This baby ensured that no matter what, he will honor his commitment to you, whether he loves you or not."

"But I do love her, Ruhee." Rocco walked up behind her.

Ruhee turned to him, baby still in her arms. Lisette held her breath. If anyone could say the wrong thing at the wrong time, that was it.

"It's not his fault," Lisette said. "Nor yours. It's no one's fault—we love who we love."

"But he could have loved me!"

Rocco kept walking, each step slow as if hoping she wouldn't notice. His voice was low and even. He reminded Lisette of someone speaking to a wild horse—calm, easy, trying not to startle the animal.

"No, Ruhee. I knew you well before I knew Lisette. I remember you from the *Dişi Aslan* and saw you bring in the coffee and the dinners to Captain Derya's cabin." He kept approaching, angling to her right. "If it was not meant to be then, it is not meant to be now."

"I saw you, too." She was crying. "I used to take twice as many trips to serve the captain, just so I could be in the cabin with you twice as many times. There has never been another for me."

The way she said it gave Lisette a horrible feeling in the pit of her stomach. She sounded more than heartbroken—she sounded hopeless.

"Ruhee." Lisette nearly whispered her name. "We can fix this, somehow."

"NO." The girl whipped about, from Lisette to Lamya to Rocco and back again, her arms and hands still gripping Alara, who now was screaming with the rage of an angry infant. "It can't be fixed! I can't be fixed! It is broken, all broken!"

Rocco was almost next to her when he made a desperate attempt to grab her. Ruhee spun away and backed up. She kept backing, keeping her eyes on the trio.

"There has never been another for me," she said again, her voice breaking with new tears. Then she turned and ran straight for the cliff.

Rocco and Lisette rushed after her, but she'd gotten a wide start. The cliff was at the end of a slight hill, which slowed Ruhee a little. Rocco sped past Lisette and reached out for Ruhee's skirt, but she lifted her legs and scurried from him. Lisette pushed forward, her arms stretching toward her baby.

"Ruhee, stop, please!" she shouted. "There's nowhere to go!"

The girl didn't even glance over her shoulder—she ran as if she was an arrow aimed at a bullseye. Rocco was two strides from her. He darted left, pivoted, and sprinted toward Ruhee. She took an evasive lurch around him and kept running until there was no more ground under her feet and she was flying through the air, dropping to the beach below, Alara still in her arms. She screamed all the way down, declaring her love for Rocco until her body hit jagged rock. There was a single shriek and then silence.

As Ruhee fell, the cry that came from Lisette was not human, but something roaring in pain, something that an honorable person would put out of its misery. She rushed toward the cliff to follow Alara and save her. Rocco grabbed her at the last moment.

"Transform first!" he yelled.

They heard the sickening splat of flesh hitting sharp rocks. Ruhee's scream stopped. Lisette's did not. Rocco held her in his arms. She could feel the tightness in his muscles. He was not comforting her as much as he was containing her.

She held her head up to look at him. He was weeping. His grip relaxed and she enfolded his head in her hands. They held each other in their shock and grief.

Somewhere in the timelessness of grief, Lisette glanced up to see Lamya approaching.

Pushing away from Rocco, she snapped, "Why didn't you stop this? You have the magic! You could have saved her!"

Lamya tilted her head, shrugging. "Yes, Ruhee's choice was unfortunate. She could have recovered, could have been happy."

"Lamya, my baby!" Lisette wailed.

Lamya pointed to the sky. "Your baby is fine."

Lisette looked up to see a small dragon, her feathers blended in tones of lilac and lavender, her tiny wings silver-tipped. The dragon flew down to Lamya and settled in her arms before transforming back into a chubby wild-haired baby with green-gold eyes.

Lisette's knees buckled as she heard Rocco groan. Alara giggled and reached her arms out to her parents. Lamya walked to them.

"I told you she was special."

L'*Implacable's* departure from Île des Anciens was delayed by Ruhee's death. Lisette insisted that she be given a proper burial.

"She was not a horrible girl," she said. "She was driven mad."

Lamya nodded. "It is this way, sometimes. The heart is too big, the mind cannot hold it in."

Chunk and LeFarge helped to lift the body into a silken body sack, comprised of bedding that Lisette stitched together. Lamya directed the men where to place the body, how deeply to dig, and which soil to cover the grave. Lisette stood with Alara in her arms, watching Lamya give orders, and taking in the exactness of what the Ancient One was directing.

The resting place must be here, not there. New soil, not the old. Deeper. Dig deeper.

When all was finished according to Lamya's direction, they all gathered by the mound of packed-down dirt. Chunk and LeFarge removed their caps and leaned on their shovels. Lisette looked about for Rocco—he was standing away from the group. She went to him, held Alara out.

"It was my desire to do this," she said. "Why don't you hold the baby while I finish what I started?"

"I understand," he told her, taking Alara into his arms. "It is the right thing to do. But you did not start this."

She opened her mouth to ask what he meant and decided they could discuss it later. Stepping back to the group, she led a brief, if casual ceremony for the woman who had cursed her, tried to kill her, and tried to kill her baby. At last, she managed a small prayer.

"Father may Ruhee Vaishya find the peace she seeks in your kingdom."

Lamya stepped forward with a small plant in her hands, a small white flower with purple edging. She knelt at the grave and planted the roots at Ruhee's feet. Standing, she rubbed the dirt between her hands before brushing it into the air.

"The island will gladly accept Ruhee's sacrifice and will use it to strengthen the life here."

Lisette looked at Rocco to see if he had anything to add to their service. He had stepped nearer to the grave but stared straight ahead, to the horizon. His mouth showed no emotion, although Lisette could detect the unease that wrinkled his brow.

"Amen," he pronounced, and walked away.

Lisette turned to Lamya. "I am anxious to begin my life with Rocco and Alara, but I confess, I do not wish to leave you."

"Leave you must." Lamya's soft, purring voice soothed. "If you need me, go to Dragon's Breath. I shall always meet you there."

Rocco joined them, holding out a very fussy Alara. "I do not know why she goes on so."

Lisette took her into her arms. "Perhaps she is hungry, or her clout needs changing."

Alara crinkled her nose and cried, twisting in Lisette's arms and reaching for Lamya. The Ancient One held her arms toward the baby, so Lisette released her into Lamya's hands. Alara stopped crying and smiled, gazing at Lamya's face and gurgling.

"She will miss you, too," Lisette said.

"Yes, and I will miss her. But I feel you will return, at least for a visit. And soon her world will revolve around her mother and father, and I will be a memory." She put her forehead against Alara's, where they stayed as if exchanging thoughts for a few moments. Lamya smiled and returned the baby to Lisette. "You must go now. I assume you return to Île des Oiseaux to complete your task with the duke?"

"Yes, we discussed the plans but had no time to put them into action." She hugged Alara to her. "Rocco and I were anxious to have our baby again."

"As it should be." Lamya raised her hand, palm facing *L'Implacable*. "Fair weather and fast winds to you. Now, be off before my blessing ends."

The ride to the ship was bittersweet. Lisette kept looking back toward Lamya, who had assumed her usual position of sitting in the sand and drawing circles. She could almost hear the Ancient One humming to herself. As the dinghy's lines were dropped to secure it, she took one last look and saw Lamya looking at her and the baby.

She could not hear it on the air, but in her mind, she could feel Lamya's purring voice saying, "You can do great things, Lizzie."

"M'lady." LeFarge was on deck, holding his arms out. "May I take the little one?"

Lisette looked up at the large hands reaching to

Alara. She stood and gently laid her daughter across his arms, keeping her hands ready to catch Alara if he dropped her. To her surprise, he scooped the baby into his chest as if it was natural.

"Have my own little ones at home, m'lady," he said as she stepped from the boat onto the deck.

She smiled. "Please call me Lizzie."

"Aye, m'lady." He handed Alara back to her. "I s'pose you know where the cabin is."

"Yes, I do." She adjusted Alara in her arms and strolled aft.

She stopped just inside the captain's cabin and gazed. The room where she'd been taken after being imprisoned in the hold. The room where she'd met Rocco and she was so frightened she thought she might faint. The room where she found her courage—and her love.

"Ah, welcome back, Lizzie." Chunk walked in behind her. "We done what we could to make you and the little 'un at home." He gestured to a rough-hewn baby cradle at the side of the bed, and a chair in the corner with extra cushions and a small table with a tea set.

"Thank you, Chunk, it's delightful. I'm sure Alara will love her bed. She's been roughing it for a long time now."

Lisette set her bag on the bed and put Alara in her crib. "Let me get a few things out and stowed, and then I shall be on deck. My legs have missed the feel of a ship."

"Aye, if'n ya need anything, gimme a holler. I'll send the cabin boy."

She gazed at Chunk, remembering a slight lad with the croaking voice. "I'm so sorry about Poussin, Chunk. If I'd but known—"

"Now, don't beat yerself up." He waved his hands at her. "We knew we was going into battle. We jes' didn't know they was bringin' the battle to us." He lowered his head, hand on his chest. "But I miss him awful."

Lisette gave him a hug. "I do too."

He brushed at a solitary tear, nodded, and left. She turned back to her unpacking, a feeling of melancholy on her heart. Alara gurgled and Lisette went to her.

Picking up her daughter, she held her tight. "Oh, Alara, I know I should not be holding you so much. But I have not seen you in a long time, and there was a time I thought I'd never see you again. Promise me you won't be spoiled by my arms around you."

Alara cooed, her hands against Lisette's face. She leaned in, putting her wet baby lips against Lisette's cheek in a half-kiss, half-suckling motion. Lisette laughed.

"Ugh, you are slobbery." She mopped the baby goo from her face. "And you need a quick change before we go atop."

There was no bucket to rinse a used clout, so she took Alara's wetted clout with her and climbed the steps. A young, gangly boy with black curls and large dark eyes was running about, attempting to help anyone who asked him.

"Are you the cabin boy?" Lisette asked.

"Aye, mum. Name's Quentin, but the men all call me Cue. Can I helps ya?"

"Yes, if you could find me a bucket to scrub the baby's clouts, I would be most grateful." She smiled. "Cue, eh? I suppose the crew can't be bothered with a longer name."

He shrugged. "I s'pose. I'll git that bucket." He scurried off, winding his way through the rest of the bodies who were adjusting sheets.

Lisette watched them work, envying their duties. She could feel the scratching of the rope across her palm, the weight of the sail in her arms and shoulders. Looking up, she saw one of the crew climbing the rope to the crow's nest. *Ah, how I envy him.*

"Missing your life on the ship?" Rocco's voice came

from behind her.

She turned and saw him at the helm. He stood square to the wheel, his sleeves rolled up and strong hands steering the ship. His eyes were still intense as he looked down at her, grinning playfully. It occurred to her that he was never as handsome or alluring as when he was there. There was something about his confidence in his own skill that made him twice as desirable.

Cue ran up to her, a bucket in his hand. "I already put water in it. If'n ya put the clout in, I'll get it washed and returned t'ya."

"That would be most appreciated." She smiled. "Thank you, Cue."

As the young boy rushed off, she climbed the steps to the helm. The day was bright, and the ship was away, on a course to Île des Oiseaux. Lisette adjusted Alara so that she could see the ocean before them.

"Look," she told her daughter. "This will be our life now." Rocco shot her a glance, so she said, "At least part of the time."

"Lizzie, we need to discuss this." He never took his eyes from the horizon, making small adjustments at the wheel and shouting orders here and there to the crew. "Is it truly your wish to make *L'Implacable* our home?"

She also watched the horizon, silent for some moments before sighing. "No. I miss this, and there will come a time when Alara will be old enough to take part in crewing. But right now, she requires much that the ship cannot offer." She turned to him. "How often could you visit us on Île des Oiseaux?"

He smiled. "Would you not want me to abandon my life at sea?"

"No! This is your life. Even if you become more of a seafaring merchant than a pirate, I would never take you from this ship."

"Then I suppose my route would include stops at

home…say…every other month?"

"That is most agreeable." She moved closer to him, stroking his arm and stretching up to kiss his cheek. "And perhaps I could make some trips with you?"

"I hope Pinar can watch the baby." He turned his face to kiss her lips. "This will be our first trip together that we do not try to kill each other."

She laughed. "Hopefully not our last."

The two days' sail to the island proved how difficult having a baby shipboard could be. Cue was helpful, washing clothes and clouts, and helping Lisette find foods that could be mashed with coconut milk. Alara had turned amazingly fussy, until Lisette discovered a small tooth poking through her gums. LeFarge came to the rescue, offering green onions and jerky for the baby to chew on. Lisette was skeptical at first.

"Nah, m'lady, we used these on my young'uns. They can't choke on 'em, but it gives 'em sommit ta chew."

Alara gummed the jerky happily under Lisette's watchful eyes. By the time they dropped anchor at the pirates' cove, Lisette understood too well what women endured if they had no nurse to help them.

Perhaps wishing for a simple life in a small house was premature. She bounced Alara on her hip as she watched the dinghies drop to the shallows and the crew row them ashore.

"Ready to talk to the duke?" Rocco asked, strolling up and putting his arms around her.

"Yes. Would it bother you if we lived in my old castle?"

"As long as my enemies don't believe I'm softening."

She chuckled. "If they do, your sword can set them straight."

"Then let us live in luxury, a common pirate and his noble wife."

"Half noble." Lisette smiled. "Half pirate. And I hope you mean to make me your wife soon."

"As soon as possible."

Oleta greeted them at the front door. "Lizzie, I am so glad you are here. I have been doing what I can for the duke, but he appears to be worsening."

"Take me to him." Lisette handed Alara to Rocco and rushed after her friend.

The duke's chambers were dark and stuffy, closed off by heavy curtains. Lisette dabbed at the perspiration around her hairline as she entered the room. A tall, shadowed figure sat by the four-posted bed, lit by a single candle. Connie was patting his father's arm, speaking words of encouragement.

"Uncle Oscar," Lisette whispered, approaching. "I'm back."

"Lizzie, thank God you are here," Connie said. "Look, Father. Lisette is back."

The duke turned his head toward her, slowly. She could see the dark circles around his eyes, and he seemed to have shrunken.

"My Lizzie, come." His voice was weak. "Bring me the baby."

"Oh. Rocco is holding her." She rushed from the room and called for Rocco, who came at once. "The duke wants to see Alara."

Rocco attempted to hand her to Lisette, who shook her head.

"Just bring her in." She held the door for him to enter. "Yes, Uncle Oscar, Alara is here."

Rocco scowled at her but brought the baby over to the bed. The duke's eyes opened fully as he smiled. Lisette thought he suddenly looked less sick, more healthy.

"Prop my pillows," he ordered. "I want to hold the baby."

"Oh, m'lord, you are so weak," Lisette said. "I wouldn't want to burden you when you could be resting and getting better."

"I have waited for this baby to be born for months," he scolded before softening his voice. "I know she is not my granddaughter, but I feel I should know her all the same."

Lisette looked at Rocco and nodded. He went to the far side of the bed, where Connie and the servants were plumping pillows and raising the duke to a sitting position. Rocco leaned down to hand Alara to the duke. The baby reached to the duke but one of her hands was tangled in Rocco's necklace. Rocco pried her tiny fingers from the silken thread when a larger, heavier hand grabbed at the golden amulet hanging from it.

"Where did you get this?" the duke commanded.

Rocco pulled the charm from the duke's hand. "It was my mother's."

The duke had begun coughing again, but his voice

still grew louder. "Where are you from?"

"A small town on the eastern coast." Rocco frowned. "Xàbia."

"Where did your mother get it? What was her name?"

Rocco shrugged. "She had it for my entire life. I never saw her without it. She said it was a gift from my father. Her name was Eliana de Rocco né Balenciaga."

"And your father?"

"I do not know," Rocco snapped, and took a breath. "I realize you are ill, m'lord, but I tire of this examination. Why are you not enjoying the baby?"

The duke's face turned red, and he burst into coughing again. Rocco attempted to remove Alara, but he held her tightly. Oleta came forward with an herbal broth, ladling a couple of spoons of liquid to soothe his throat. He calmed, his face returning to its pale tones.

"My apologies, and to my dear Alara, I hope I did not frighten you." He looked back up at Rocco. "I ask these for a reason. Who was your father?"

"I do not know, m'lord. My mother did not say. From my childhood, I knew only that he was not from our village, and that he brought my mother shame."

The duke's eyes became glassy, and a single tear worked its way down until he swiftly wiped it away. "Your mother's only shame was what her family placed upon her. I wished to marry her and approached her father, who falsely agreed, then hid her from me while his friends made certain my ship sailed with me aboard."

Lisette looked from the duke to Connie to Rocco. There was a certain likeness to them—the nose and the jawline.

"Rocco is your son?" she asked, her eyes wide.

Connie scrutinized Rocco's features. "I do see it. Brother?"

"Tristan!" The duke grinned. "Welcome home!"

Rocco sat down, rubbing his forehead. Lisette went to him.

"It would seem we are both a little bit noble and a little bit commoner." She kissed him.

"I gave that amulet to the woman I loved," the duke told him. "Her name was Eliana Balenciaga and she was from Xàbia. Tell me, does she live?"

Rocco shook his head. "Sadly, she died when I was but thirteen. She had been my protector from the cruelty of her family. The day she was buried, I went to the port and found work aboard one of the ships."

"Such a pity," the duke said, and looked down at the baby in his arms. She giggled and reached her hands to his face. "But do you know what this means? I have a granddaughter."

Lisette exploded in laughter. "I stand corrected, Uncle Oscar. My baby is your heir."

Connie grinned. "And that gets me off the hook for providing one."

The duke chuckled, then put his hand on his chest, his fingers tightening. He gestured toward the baby, so Oleta rushed to him and took Alara. The servants helped ease him back to a more reclining position.

Connie took his hand. "Father—"

"Little known fact," the duke interrupted him. "I have never understood you, but I have always loved you. Forgive my stubbornness."

"There is nothing to forgive. I rather enjoyed our game of life." Connie spoke with lightness in his voice, but Lisette saw the tears in his eyes and the way he rubbed his father's hand.

"Lizzie." The duke was sounding more labored, more whispered. "Maybe a boy next time. Little known fact…"

His voice drifted off as he took one last, raspy breath.

"Oh, Uncle Oscar." Lisette put her head to his chest,

weeping.

She could feel someone rubbing her back and she looked up to see Connie, who was also crying. He stretched his arms to her, and she embraced him, and as they wept together, they enfolded Rocco, who stood as their rock, holding them both. After a few moments, they dried their tears and were able to release each other. Oleta met them with Alara.

"He did not know how sick he was," she told Lisette. "I did not have the means to help him. The blood fever was already too much."

"It is a hard thing," Lisette said. "To find so much joy in one day and not be able to revel in it."

"It solves my mystery." Rocco had the amulet in his fist. "I am a duke's bastard son. No wonder my mother's family hated us so—we could have gone to live with a duke and left them alone in the village. Still, it's a harsh thing, to find my father and lose him in the same day."

"At least you have a new sibling if you choose to accept him," Connie said. "Perhaps you could help me with the burial arrangements? I believe my father would want to be buried back in Isla de Pimienta, and after the funeral, I must travel to Spain with Count Barragan."

"Why?" Lisette asked.

"Father tasked me to take the decree to Spain and let El Rey know we are carrying out his father's wishes." Connie smiled. "Two nobles presenting the decree will hopefully provide some safety in numbers."

"By the way, what did our countess choose—death or scullery?" Rocco asked.

Oleta nodded toward the door. "You'll find her in the kitchen. Turns out, she's quite happy to make pastries and sweep the floor—especially when the alternative is to be tossed overboard."

"What's next for you two?" Connie gestured to Rocco and Lisette.

"Find someone who can marry us," Rocco said.

"And find out if we can live here, so long as we do not try to rule anything," Lisette added.

"It so happens you know an ordained justice," Oleta said. "Horace the innkeep. And as for living here, you can take your petition before the new governing board."

"Who is on the board?" Lisette asked.

"Five individuals of some distinction," Oleta said. "Ghreta, Luis, Pinar, Quince, and Horace."

Lisette nodded and looked at Rocco. "We might be able to stay here."

****

It was after the wedding, after the festivities, after the giddy merriment when Begum approached Lisette and Rocco as they strolled through the courtyard.

"I have a little wedding present for you," she said.

"Is it sleep?" Lisette asked. "That is what I want at the moment."

"It might be." She gestured west. "I am going to watch Alara for you, while you and Rocco take *L'Implacable* on a run."

"The two of us are not enough to crew my ship," Rocco said.

Begum shook her head. "No, you are not understanding. You and your crew are going to pick up supplies from Tortuga. Lizzie is going with you."

"But the baby—" Lisette said.

"Will be with me and well taken care of. That's what grandmothers are for." She tapped their shoulders. "Now, you will sleep. When tomorrow comes, you meet your crew at *L'Implacable*. Both of you."

"Begum that is wonderful," Lisette told her, then turned to Rocco, thinking he might not like this gift as much as she did. "Isn't it?"

He grinned. "Welcome aboard, Lisette de Rocco."

"I like the name Rocco," She said, kissing him, "but my full name is Lisette de Rocco y Martinmas."

THE END

Acknowledgments

Thank God it's finished.

ABOUT THE AUTHOR

G.S. Carline did not plan on writing a fantasy, but one morning in the shower it occurred to her that there weren't enough girl pirates in literature. She thought she would write a single story, perhaps a novella, about a young woman who has Important Life Goals and instead becomes the terror of the seas…and then the dragons came. The whole thing ended up as a trilogy and here we are.

At the time of this bio, G.S. is living happily with her husband and a Corgi. She also has a son and two horses, all of whom she thoroughly enjoys even if they don't live with her. You can find out more about her by visiting https://gaylecarline.com/

Did you enjoy the story?

In all honesty, authors are a needy group. We shout our stories into the world, then lean forward and wait for readers to say, "Wow, that was fun-sad-scary-all-the-feels!" When we don't get that, our response depends upon our mettle. If we are insecure and easily dissuaded, we give up on writing and learn to play the ukulele.

If we are stubborn as mules, we will return to our pen and paper, insecurity notwithstanding.

Being stubborn, I shall continue to tell stories whether I have an audience or not, but if you like the tales I weave, this is where I beg you to leave a review.

It does not have to be a big, blathering paragraph of goodness. All you need is a title and a sentence (and throw a few stars at it). For example:

> **★★★★★ Couldn't put it down**
> I love dragons and pirates and this book had both!

You may leave it on Amazon, or Goodreads, or wherever my books are sold.

Thank you so much. I appreciate you.

www.ingramcontent.com/pod-product-compliance
Lightning Source LLC
Chambersburg PA
CBHW050959180726
48291CB00006B/1898